CHOKE HOLD

BRITT REIGN

Cover Design by: Enchanting Romance Designs

Editing by: Overbooked Author Services

Proofreading & Line Editor by: Cynthia Schoettker

Formatting by: Cleo Moran, Devoted Pages Designs

Trigger Warnings:

Death of a parent/grandparent
Suicide
Alluding to Sexual Assault (fades to black)
Explicit Sex Scenes
Foul Language
MMA Fighting/Violence
Alcohol Use
Mention of drug use
Depression/Mental Health/Dementia
Kinks: Praise, Impact, Breath
NO ANIMALS DIE

Tropes:
Love Triangle
College friends to Lovers
MMA Fighter
Enemies to lovers
Grumpy Sunshine
Tortured Musician

Playlist

Sleep Token - Chokehold

Ekoh, Loveless - WAYSIDE

Dayseeker - Paper Heart

Spiritbox - Ultraviolet

Imminence - Alleviate

The Plot In You - REPAY

Falling In Reverse - Last Resort – Reimagined

Jared Benjamin - Flatline

Dayseeker - Already Numb

Sleep Token - Are You Really Okay?

LANDMVRKS - Lost in a Wave

Bad Omens - Miracle

Fit For A King - When Everything Means Nothing

Seether, Amy Lee - Broken

Motionless In White - Eternally Yours

Bad Omens - If I'm There (Unplugged)

Catch Your Breath - Deadly

Until I Wake - Fool's Paradise

Eminem - Lose Yourself

Bad Omens - THE DEATH OF PEACE OF MIND

Imminence - To the Light

Lana Del Rey - Radio

Sleep Token - Rain

For all of my lovely besties out there, who feel like train wrecks on your best days.

There are no trains run in this book, but ALL ABOARD!

Let's wreck this bitch.

<3

Blurb

Beck Scott

My best friend. My fierce protector.

A safe space to breathe. He always remained my one constant, never wavering.

For years, I've masked my love for him but it still had me in a chokehold. Anytime I pictured my future, it was with him.

That was until August...

August Wylder

The mysterious brooding musician with a bleeding heart stormed into my cafe and demanded my soul.

He saw me for who I truly am. His words illuminated the darkness and summoned my light. Pushed me to my full potential and helped me face my fears.

Now I'm torn between past and future.

Two men. A constant war between my soul and my heart.

Reader Note

I still can't even believe I finally published Chokehold. I honestly am still in shock I even wrote a book at all and have a second one in mind already. I want to thank you all from the bottom of my heart for reading and I hope you enjoy this beautifully, messy love story.

I poured sleepless nights and so many tears into this. Purged my entire soul. Set my own heart on fire.

Initially it started out as writing a short story. Trying to find another outlet. A new hobby that was recommended by my therapist to help with my depression. But then one night I had such a vivid dream about the characters and woke up and just started writing.

I had so much fun writing it and bringing all of these characters to life. Sometimes they felt so real to me. It's been so surreal. My wish for you, is that you all get yourself a bestie like Quinn.

If you take away anything from reading this. Please take away, that no matter where you are in your life, your age, your career, if you've ever even thought for a second to start writing a book, pick up that pencil or pen, put it to paper and start writing. Pull out a keyboard or a typewriter and start typing. If you've always wanted to read a story about something and just quite haven't found it; write THAT story.

We all have beautiful stories inside of us. We need to be brave. We need to be graceful with ourselves. We need to create magic. We need to stop fearing fear. Follow your intuition, lovelies. It's calling.

I love you all so much. I am so grateful for you and to you. Thank you for being on this journey with me.

I hope you'll stick around, to see what's in store for book two. It's in the works.

Prologue

Sutton

"**P**lease someone just send me a sign!" I yell out to the universe.

I slam my hands against the seat in the Uber.

"Sorry," I whisper, grimacing, making eye contact with the driver in the rearview mirror.

My heart is split in two.

I love them both, but for such different reasons.

Beck's soft blue eyes, that dirty blonde hair, the calluses on his knuckles from years of hitting heavy bags and opponents in the ring; so rough, yet so soft and affectionate, leaving sparks in their wake with just the simplest touch. A touch holding so much heat, it burns my skin.

Beck is the sun, and I am like Icarus, flying too close. Drawn to his warmth, the comfort of his arms, his solidity and stability soaking into my skin, always protecting me. I could bask in the glow.

He is always there. Never letting me down.

I have always loved Beck, but there is this voice inside of my head warning me not to get too close, because I might get burned, but my heart wants me to throw caution to the wind and risk it all.

Then my mind wanders to the other half of my heart, to August and those tattooed hands covered in thick metal rings. Finger tips rough from years of playing guitar, wrapped around my throat, taking my breath away. That long dark hair, eyes as black as the night, my every desire and temptation wrapped up in darkness with skin painted in a stunning sea of artwork.

August creates incredible music to drown out the demons in his head from all of the pain he has endured over the years.

His lyrics grip my soul, pulling me to him.

August's the moon luring me into the dark unknown, this beautiful source of tranquility, an ethereal stillness, but he sets my soul on fire.

My every thought is consumed by him. I love him.

I gasp, and stare at the screen in the car, listening to the lyrics to the song that August wrote for me, with me. *"I look at you and see everything in that beautiful mind. The vein in your neck pulses, and the heat in your stare is all I see, until I'm blinded."*

"Can you turn the volume up please?" I ask the driver, wildly.

He gives me a nod and thankfully blasts it.

I let it drown out every thought in my head.

August actually did it! After everything.

He made it! Really made it!

I knew that *From Troy* would go viral.

I knew that he would end up on the radio someday, but this is the first time that I've heard our song out for the world to hear. Tears streaming down my face, is this my sign, to choose him?

The song ends, and the radio broadcaster announces the big fight tonight between Beckett Scott and Kenzo King.

Really universe?

I let out the biggest sigh.

We keep driving. The tears keep coming. I can't breathe. This poor driver probably thinks I'm insane.

I need a minute to just take this in.

August is selling out venues with his band *From Troy.*

Beckett has held and earned his title as heavyweight champion.

They are both going to be in Vegas tonight.

I flew here with just my purse and a Hail Mary.

I take one more deep breath as a calmness settles over me, and then it's his face I see so clearly.

I ask the driver to turn around up here and let my heart lead the way.

When he pulls over to drop me off, I'm diving out of the car before he's even at a complete stop, apologizing profusely, throwing an extra couple twenties at him for my behavior.

I start walking to the building where my future lies, if he'll still have me.

I wipe the tears away.

Deep breath, shoulders back, and head up.

I made this choice.

He will always have a piece of my heart, but I can only be in love with one of them.

I keep walking and finally get to the entrance.

I open the door and walk through.

I lift my head up, and there he is, eyes blazing, grinning right at me, sending shivers down my spine. "*Mine*," he mouths.

"*Yours*," I breathe with a teary smile.

1

Sutton

Six Years Earlier

"If I make this one, you are getting drunk tonight," Quinn squeals at me, as she lines up the cue ball with the eight ball.

I start to sigh, because I really didn't want to drink tonight. I just came out with her so she'd get off my back. Quinn says I haven't been as fun lately. I haven't been. I know this. But I don't really enjoy drinking as much as she does. The thought of not being in control, just makes me feel too uncomfortable.

Quinn goes to hit the ball and completely misses because she is staring directly behind me with hearts in her eyes and a dropped jaw.

Slowly I turn my head to see who she's staring at.

Because I know it's a who and not a what with that feral look in her eyes.

"Who is that?" she whispers with awe in her voice.

"I have no idea. I've never seen him before," I say and

shrug.

I line up the cue ball with the eight ball and sink it in, while Quinn's distracted concocting a plan to get laid tonight.

"You never let me win," Quinn huffs but continues to stare over my shoulder with a small grin on her face.

"You can't win them all, bestie," I smirk at her. "Go get your man."

"Oh, I am going to make him mine all right," she grins and with a sway in her hips makes her way over to the deliciously tall man.

I lean against the pool table and watch their interaction like a voyeur from a short distance, wishing I had just an ounce of confidence Quinn does.

Before she reaches him, his eyes flick up to hers and a slow smirk starts on his face.

He really is beautiful. Broad shoulders that fill out that tight blue shirt so well and a pair of jeans, perfectly snug, leaving little to the imagination, and he has to be at least six feet tall, if not taller.

He never takes his eyes off of Quinn.

She's so animated talking to him. Giggling and lightly touching his arm as they talk. He gives her his undivided attention, and his friend with him smiles and listens just as intently, both hanging on her every word.

Of course, he'd be interested in someone like Quinn. So confident and sure of herself; that long Barbie blonde hair, doll like baby blue eyes, a petite figure, and an ass that would make any man salivate.

My best friend is a stunner. With a heart of gold to match.

Passing my pool stick off to a few of the frat guys we met up with, I finally make my way over to Quinn.

She senses me and grabs me by the hand, dragging me

over.

Stumbling into a hard figure, she introduces us. "Sut, this is Beckett, Beck for short. Beck, this is my best friend, Sutton. That's his friend Asher," she says pointing at the other equally gorgeous man standing next to him.

"Sutton, nice to meet you," Beckett, the name of the man, with the incredibly hard figure, currently steadying me says.

His voice so deep and chocolate rich, it feels like velvet on my skin.

His friend, Asher, gives me a curt nod, his eyes never leaving Quinn though. *Interesting*.

"Nice to meet you," I say softly, holding Beck's eyes, until I'm startled by hooting and hollering in the other room and immediately look away.

"Let's go play!" Quinn squeals, grabbing mine and Beck's hands pulling us to where the beer pong tables are set up.

Asher follows close behind us.

Eyes often tracking people in the room, but never leaving Quinn long.

"So, who are they and why have we never seen them before?" I ask while Beckett and Asher set up their cups and fill them with beer.

"Well, they're friends of Nate's, I guess. He, Beck and Asher train together. They are boxers, so they don't party much, that's why we've never seen them before. Beckett's freaking hot though, isn't he? I feel like he was sculpted by the Gods!" she pretends to swoon, eyeing Beck like she does a piece of red velvet cake.

"And boxing! That's so masculine. Boxers are up there with hockey players, being all bad ass and shit. I hope Beckett knows I'm going home with him tonight," she squeals, softly.

"Q, boxers? Really?" I ask, worried.

"Why are you always so quick to judge people?" she scolds me.

"I'm not judging anyone. We just don't know them. I have a hard time trusting people, especially men, and even more so when they look like that. You know this," I frown and wave my head over toward Beck and Asher.

"We're fine! Lighten up. Let's play!" Quinn says as she rolls her eyes and nudges me with her shoulder.

A few hours later, Quinn is slurring her words and clinging to Beckett for support to stay upright. She keeps wrapping her little hands around his very well sculpted biceps, her fingers not even touching. That's how well sculpted they are.

"Let's get you home babe," I say wrapping my arm around her waist and putting her other arm over my shoulders.

"We can walk you guys back," Beckett says, nodding to his friend Asher.

"Oh, that's okay, we're just a 10 minute walk from here," I say, voice shaky, as I try to get Quinn to walk with me.

She starts to lean the other way, and I try pulling her toward me again.

Beckett gently puts his hand on my shoulder, "Please let us walk with you. You can't protect yourselves if you're focusing on getting her back safely. We would just feel better knowing you got back safely."

"And who is going to protect us from you? We barely know you," I scoff.

Beckett puts his hand on my shoulder, eyes darkening as they meet mine, "Do you honestly think you are any safer walking in the dark alone with her hanging off of you? I know we told you we're training to become fighters, but we would never lay our hands on a woman."

"Unless of course they asked first," he says almost smugly

but then softens, "We would just feel more comfortable if you'd let us walk with you, instead of leaving you vulnerable," Beckett says genuinely.

When I look up at Beckett, our eyes lock, his bluer than the Caribbean Sea, and filled with so much determination like he won't take no for an answer.

Asher with a face of stone, stands next to him with pleading eyes that soften slightly with a silent plea.

"Okay," I whisper on a sigh, too tired to argue. "Thank you."

Beckett and Asher each take a side of Quinn, and we walk back to our dorm room in comfortable silence.

Beckett has me walk close to him, on the inside of the sidewalk, our hands brushing softly every so often.

Warmth radiates down my fingertips, sending a sensation unfamiliar to me, with each light brush of his hand. Usually, the thought of any guy touching me, makes my stomach turn.

"Can I have your phone really quick?" Beckett breaks the silence as we make it to the entrance of our dorm.

Handing him my phone before I even really think about it; he types his and Asher's number in it quickly and hands it back to me, "In case you need anything tonight, you have both of our numbers in there."

"Thank you, and thank you for walking us back," I put an arm around Quinn's waist and drape her arm around my shoulders.

She's passed out, snoring softly.

With a final glance over my shoulder, I catch two sets of eyes watching us intently.

Giving a curt nod, I drag my very drunk best friend— three doors down to our room without anyone seeing us.

*T*wo weeks later, we're back at the frat house for a highlighter party.

Quinn looks just like Barbie, dressed in a tight white dress, hot pink lipstick painting her full lips, with a hot pink highlighter stuffed in her cleavage.

She sashays into the party, kissing all the guys we're friends with on their cheeks leaving lip imprints in her wake, while signing their shirts with a big heart with a Q in the middle.

I just shake my head and laugh, as I give them each a quick hug hello.

"You ladies look gorgeous as ever!" our friend Nate says.

"Don't I know it!" Quinn grins, grabbing his face and planting a big kiss on each of his cheeks, leaving those hot pink lip imprints on each one.

Nate rolls his eyes at her, and I chuckle.

We walk onto the dance floor, and it's filled with people. Strobe lights flash to the beat of some EDM music. Sweaty bodies are pressed against each other.

A bottle of tequila is being passed around, and people are just shooting it back.

Not even questioning it.

Shaking my head when it eventually reaches me.

It boggles my mind how people so freely trust strangers like that.

Closing my eyes, getting lost in the music, swaying my hips, letting go of life's inhibitions, without a care in the world.

After what feels like hours, but was probably only about eight songs, Quinn grabs my hand and screams that she needs some air.

We make our way out through a side door to a patio. The breeze instantly cooling my skin.

It's late in the evening, tall buildings in the distance light up the night surrounding us.

Music from the dance floor leaks out as people walk in and out, but otherwise it's fairly quiet, minus the few smaller groups talking while playing beer bong and the few car horns in the distance.

My eyes wonder to the night sky. Always drawn to the moon and its soft glow illuminating my skin.

Quinn snaps me out of my small piece of tranquility, perking up when she spots Beck and yells his name.

I look up and see those ocean eyes staring at me, but no sooner do our eyes meet, his rove back on Quinn.

Asher throws the ball for the win, easily sinking it into the cup.

Quinn walks up and asks if we can play winner, kissing both guys on their cheeks, like she's known them forever.

Five minutes later, we step up to the table to take on Beck and Asher.

I look to the opposite end of the table and notice Beck staring at me, but it doesn't last more than a second before his eyes flick back to Quinn.

A jealously, like I've never known, rises up like bile at the way his eyes linger on her.

Why doesn't anyone ever look at me like that?

She's lost in a story she's telling them as she sets up our cups and fills them with water.

Grateful that she's carrying the conversation, until I realize, that Quinn has that bottle of tequila in her hands that was getting passed around.

"Quinn," I start to say.

She puts her hand up in my face, "You know I hate beer, Sut. I'll just take a shot for each cup, and you can drink your mixed drink. I won't even have to drink that much. We'll win."

Not even 10 minutes and several shots later, we are definitely not winning.

We are getting demolished.

Thankfully, Quinn didn't notice me pouring cranberry juice instead of alcohol into my cup. I was pretending to be just a little bit buzzed, while she got wasted.

We end up losing.

"I need to take a break. Sutton, do you want to partner up with Beck? Quinn and I will sit this round out," Asher asks, "And I'll get her some water too," he whispers as he walks past me.

I nod, "Thank you."

"You can stop pretending now. Quinn's probably too drunk to realize how sober you are," Beckett whispers to me when I make it to his side.

I growl at him, "Why do you even care?"

My skin breaks out in goosebumps from the heat of his breath on my skin when he edges closer to me. Dropping his deep voice an octave, "I don't. I'm just telling you. You can cut the act."

I take a step away, not entirely sure of this feeling. I shake it off and decide the goosebumps had to be from the wind.

That doesn't exist.

What the hell is wrong with me?

Quinn likes Beck.

Since we met them a couple weeks ago, she has talked incessantly about him, nonstop, *"Beckett is so hot. Did you see his biceps? My hands didn't even fit around them. And he's so tall. And those eyes. He has to have stamina if he boxes. I hope he doesn't have a girlfriend! I never even got to ask. Remind me to ask. It was so sweet of him to walk me back and get me back safely!"*

Blinking out of a haze, "It's not an act. So, mind your business."

"In that case, here, take a sip," Beck smirks.

"No. I'm good, thanks," I glare at him.

"What you think I roofied it or something?" Beck jokes.

"That's not even funny! And it wouldn't be the first time someone tried. So, like I said, I'm good." I growl and take a step away from him, shaking off the discomfort of having this conversation.

"Shit, Sutton, I'm sorry. I would never," Beck rushes to say, sobering immediately.

"Let's just play," I sigh.

"If you're sure?" Beck responds, with a questioning look in his eye.

"I'm sure," I say, letting my guard down slightly.

Staying sober isn't an issue with Beck as my beer pong partner.

Continuously sinking cup after cup.

Losing must not be in his vocabulary, because he's just as competitive as I am, if not more so.

"So, boxing?" I ask while the other team takes their shot.

"Who told you that? I told you we were training to be fighters," Beckett smirks.

"Quinn; but isn't that the same thing?" I shrug.

"Not quite. Right now, I fight in a few underground fights for some extra money and experience, but mostly I'm just training to become a fighter. The end goal is to win an MMA Heavyweight Championship," Beckett says.

We get the balls back and sink in the last two. Winning again.

After five games, we decide to call it a night.

"I should probably go find Quinn and make sure she's okay," I grimace.

"Asher is probably still with her. He would never leave a woman at risk like that, so I'll go with you," Beckett says and leads the way into the party.

His large frame is enough for people to move out of his way without him having to ask.

The skin of my wrist tingles where his fingers tenderly grip it, as he gently leads me through the crowd to our friends. *What the hell?*

We find Asher sitting on a futon in one of the guys' rooms with Quinn asleep on his shoulder.

He smiles softly at me, "She's been asleep for probably a half hour."

"Gods, I'm so sorry," I sigh, "I'm so embarrassed."

"Don't be. We'll help you get her back. Don't worry," Beckett responds.

2

Sutton

Weeks soon turned into months, time flashing by in a blur.

It seemed like at first we ended up at the same parties, always running into each other, as if by chance. Partnering up and kicking everyone's ass in beer pong or cornhole.

The more I learned about Beck, the more I found myself constantly gravitating toward him. Getting more and more comfortable being around him.

Sometimes I would catch myself leaning into the warmth of his body, because it felt so good against mine, sitting in the stands at the Pitt football games. Telling myself if he ever questioned it, that I would use the fact that it was cold outside as an excuse to cuddle up closer to him.

Beck never questioned it though.

I'm not sure if it was just my imagination, but I swear I thought I felt him push just a little closer each time.

Eventually we found ourselves having movie nights, mini golfing, hitting the batting cages, and going to haunted houses and escape rooms together to let loose after a long week, but always the four of us as a group.

Quinn noticed that I was letting my guard down with Beck before I even did.

And I noticed that his eyes didn't quite linger on Quinn as long anymore, which made me a bit more comfortable to quietly explore whatever these feelings are he's been igniting in me.

Quinn still privately makes jokes to me that she wants to hook up with Beck, but every time we're all together she ends up too drunk and rests her head on Asher by the end of the night.

Both Asher and Beck are proving to be great, protective, incredibly observant and attentive guys. Always lingering until we get into our dorm safely. Making sure they walk on the sidewalk closest to the road.

And I can't help but swoon a little when Beck turns his attention to me. Serving me cocktails from sealed bottles, instead of previously opened ones. Giving me his sweatshirt if the temperature seems to drop at night. Having our favorite snacks at his apartment.

But it's not just what I see, it's what I feel; having his full undivided attention; it's like my skin has been kissed by the sun, and I can't help but bask in the glow.

Quinn though can't see past his killer physique.

*B*efore we knew it, we found ourselves front row, cheering for Beck at his underground fights. I was really hesitant about it at first.

A total ball of nerves.

Nervous for Beck. Nervous for our safety.

These places are freakin scary. And so are the fighters.

By the look of some of these men, they've had to have done time.

Had to have.

Thinking back on our first time here, I chuckle to myself.

"Are you sure we're safe here?" I asked Quinn nervously.

"Yes! Of course, we are! Plus, Asher will be here any minute," she said, and then immediately yelled "Kick his ass!" at the top of her lungs.

But once I saw Beck in action though, something lit up inside me.

Excitement? Fear? Maybe both.

I know firsthand what a violent man looks like, and while the way Beck slams his fist into his opponent's face makes him look like a feral animal, Beck doesn't do this for fun. He doesn't enjoy making his opponent feel small or beneath him.

At least not in the way the men in my past did.

My father used to be violent.

He never used his fists on my mother or me, but his words hit harder than any fist could land.

Words cut like knives on my skin. Scars so deep, but none anyone could see.

Showing love in his warped, twisted way, wielding words like weapons, always keeping them locked and loaded, ready for the next blow, to make sure we feared him.

To make sure we stayed small.

The day my parents died in that car accident, here then gone in a blink; was both a blessing and a curse.

The loss of my mother was a soul wrenching pain I wouldn't wish on my worst enemy!

It was a blow to the solar plexus. Not just grieving her physical loss, but the loss of what a relationship could have been between us, if it weren't for my father and the way he tainted our relationship.

Leaving me to always pick up her broken pieces, holding her while she cried.

But no one was ever there to pick up mine in the aftermath; when the house was finally quiet, him finally storming out, and her tears no longer flowing.

The relief that came with losing him, and then the guilt that ate away at my core at feeling relief, for hating him, but wishing things could've been different made grieving my parents incredibly messy and ugly.

Yet, old habits die hard and as much as I tried to avoid men who reminded me of my father, my ex, Jax, turned out to be his carbon copy.

Blinded by his pretty words and promises until it was too late.

Finally understanding how my mother must have felt.

In over my head, in too deep, with no one to ask for help.

Inflicting fear, was how he got off too.

Punching walls instead of my head, but always just a near miss.

Using my body however it benefited him. Not asking for consent, because I was "His."

Gutting me with his cruel words, leaving me hollow inside.

Those words are always on a never-ending loop in my head.

Breaking me over and over again.

"Baby, I'm sorry."

"You just really upset me when you don't believe me."

"Why are you nagging me? I said I'd never hurt you."

"I would never cheat on you, baby. That's crazy! That girl was lying." Jax defended himself.

"You don't trust me? But expect me to trust you?"

"My phone died. Why are you so fuckin crazy?"

"Did you really need that second piece of pizza?" my ex accused.

"Why aren't you wearing makeup today?"

"Why are you wearing so much make up? Do you want people to think you're a whore?"

Funny thing is, I thought that was love. Because that was the only kind of love I'd ever known.

Instead, I ended up a butterfly, trapped in a spider's web, slowly wilting away until there wasn't a single piece of me remaining.

Showing me off, when it was convenient and beneficial for him, but tying me up and leaving me with nothing when it wasn't. Just leaving me hanging for days on end.

Right before he devoured what was left of me, a more beautiful butterfly came along and stole his attention away.

Allowing me to escape, but barely. Barely hanging on by a single thread.

Fighting a war, soaked in pain and sadness took herculean effort to come back from.

Refusing to allow myself to ever sink that low for a man

again. I worked too damn hard trying to glue shattered pieces back together, and while Quinn fit her pieces in with my shattered ones and refused to let me push her away, no matter how hard I tried, trusting people just didn't come easily for me.

So, when Quinn told me Beck was a boxer, alarm bells were blaring loud in my head.

The thought of violence immediately conjured visions of me in a chokehold.

That hollow feeling creeping back in, tearing open those deep-seated wounds that lie within me.

Thankfully though, Beck was proof that not all violence was the same.

Proof, that not all men were the same.

*I*t's Halloween, my favorite time of the year. Slipping into someone else's skin, into a different version of myself for the night, where I can be whoever I want to be, without the judgement of others. It's so freeing.

Even though our friendship has blossomed over the last ten months, Beck and Asher still vetoed our idea of a group costume. Saying it made us appear as if we were trying too hard.

Dressed in blue boxing gloves, tight white compression shorts, a blue silky robe with the hood up and nothing but that rock hard stomach underneath, Beck holds my eyes. He never glances below my chest, but I watch his Adams apple bob before he holds his arm out to escort me into the party, eyeing my sexy little referee costume and thigh-high boots so quickly I almost missed it.

"You look..." Beck clears his throat.

"You're not so bad yourself, Scrap," I bump my shoulder against his, trying to break the awkward tension.

Whether it's the costume, the crowd, or the lack of Asher and Quinn tonight, Beck seems more territorial than usual.

Looking almost unhinged and ready to crawl out of his own skin.

Beck's eyes are constantly scanning the room. Like he's looking for a fight or threat.

Glaring at any guy whose eyes linger too long on me.

"Why so broody?" I question, making him close the gap between us, his arm brushing mine and sending electric jolts everywhere our skin touches.

He shakes his head, like he isn't sure he should answer. "The way you look tonight, Sut," he croaks, "Every man is pining after you."

"Well, I guess you'll just have to fight them off for me," I wink and giggle.

"That's not funny, Sutton," he growls, so close to my ear, the hair on the back of my neck stands at attention from the heat of his breath so close.

"We should dance!" I smirk at him with mischief in my eyes, lacing my fingers through his and pulling him toward the dance floor.

Our bodies lightly brush as we move to the beat. Beck keeps a firm grip on my hip, but never moves it as I dance directly in front of him. My entire body is buzzing; I'm not sure if it's the alcohol flowing through my veins or how close

Beck is to me but it's euphoric.

"Hey, I need to pee. Do you want to go get us drinks?" I yell in Beck's ear, stepping away from him to get some much-needed air.

Looking at my phone making my way to the bathroom, I smirk to myself. It's been nearly an hour since we've been dancing. It felt like no time at all; pressed up against Beck, smelling his woodsy scent, getting lost in the music and the heat of his skin so close to mine.

"**B**eck, what the hell?" I squeak out, startled by the commotion behind me, as I wait in line.

"No one fucking touches what's mine," Beck growls at the guy behind me.

"Who's yours?" I grilled exasperated, "Me? Who said I was yours?"

Before I know it, the other guy throws a punch, knocking Beck back.

"Big mistake," Beck says, chuckling darkly.

"Beck, No!" I yell, going to grab for him.

It takes two guys to pry Beck off of the poor guy, his face a bright red from lack of oxygen.

Beck's face is filled with rage and something else I can't quite put my finger on.

Finally looking at me, he sort of snaps out of it and rushes over to me, "Sut, are you okay? Please tell me you're okay!" his rage instantly morphed from worry to regret in an instant.

Confused and irritated, I all but snap out. "I'm fine, Beck."

"Gods, Sut. I'm sorry! I just saw his fuckin hand on your ass and reacted," anguish in his voice.

"Come on Beck, let's just go, it's fine," I whispered, turning around and walking toward the door, immediately curling in on myself.

Static fills my ears, as Beck grabs my arm lightly, whirling me around, "It's not fine, Sut," he growls out. "He put his fuckin hands on you. Without your fuckin consent!"

Noticing I'm starting to shut down on him, he shakes his head, like he knows he fucked up with a pleading look in his eyes.

Taking my hand gently in his, we walk outside together.

My heartbeat drumming in my ears and the tears pricking the back of my eyes are the two things I focus on to try to center myself.

"What the hell were you thinking in there, Beck? Just because you are a boxer, and you dressed like one tonight, doesn't mean you get to act like one all the fucking time," I snap.

Tears start to fall. Suppressing a sob, I turn away from him.

"Seriously, Sutton?" hands fisting his hair. "Do you really not expect me to do anything if someone puts their hands on you? I watched him..." he croaks out, anguish in his voice.

Giving him a halfhearted laugh, "I never felt his hands..."

"I saw him! I saw his hands! He touched you, Sut!" desperation in his voice.

Facing him, there's nothing but agony in his eyes. My heart freezes.

"Okay, maybe he touched me. That still doesn't give you," I point at him, "The right to choke him! To put your hands on him!" I huff out.

"Let's just go," I say defeated, walking toward the car.

Neither one of us says a word on the drive back.

The silence is deafening.

For the first time since I've known Beck, fear prickles up my spine.

"I'm sorry! I promise it won't happen again," he mumbles when he pulls up to my dorm.

Taking a minute to collect my thoughts.

I let out a soft exhale and shake off the fear, "You can't promise that. Knowing you were fighters, it made me so nervous, what with my past. These last few months, Beck, you've become a sort of safe space for me. Even the nights of your fights, I've never been afraid of you. Not like.." not finishing my sentence, shaking off that fear from my past that's always ready to creep in.

I take another deep breath.

Unable to meet his eyes, because I can't bear the agony that I might see on his face. I open the car door and start to get out, "But tonight, I was. I was afraid of you, Beck." I whisper, voice cracking.

"Sut," he says with such agony in his voice.

Not letting him finish, I close the car door.

Tears immediately started falling.

Making sure I never chance a look back.

I walk into my dorm as fast as my legs will carry me and crawl into bed.

Crying myself to sleep.

Like I always used to.

Tiny arms drape over my waist, startling me awake in the middle of the night, from the nightmare that always plays on repeat.

Night after agonizing night.

"I got you," she murmurs in my ear.

Allowing Quinn's soft cupcake smell to comfort me.

I lull back into a dreamless sleep.

3

Sutton

$\mathcal{B}$eck takes those sexy-as-fuck glasses off, rubs his eyes and shuts his computer. He rests his head back on the couch for a minute with his eyes closed. I take advantage of the moment and just stare lost in him, while he's not paying me any attention.

He is an Adonis; his tight shirt stretches over his broad chest, displaying his muscles that are droolworthy when they're covered in sweat during his fights. Those bicep and forearm muscles so defined from boxing and the hours a day he spends in the gym. Gray joggers that leave nothing to the imagination. Dirty blonde hair just long enough on top for a handful with the sides buzzed. It's like he was sculpted by Michelangelo himself.

When those black rimmed glasses are on and he's lost in his coding, it's game over. Beyond distracting. My core clenches just looking at him.

I'm not sure when it happened, but we fell into this comfortable friendship. Beck is like coming home and slipping into a warm bubble bath. Several days a week, we find ourselves working side by side on our assignments and ending the night curled up on the couch watching Jeopardy.

Quinn finally lost interest in Beck, friend zoning him and Asher, making me feel less awkward about spending time with him outside of all of our group outings.

We're in our last year of undergrad, thankfully.

I'm a business major. Sometimes it sucks the soul out of me, but if my business plan turns into reality, it will all be worth it in the end.

My dream of opening a bookstore, that's also a café, with a stage for live music performances on the weekends is so close I can taste it.

All that's left is turning in this final project and then it's smooth sailing to my dreams! Books, music and iced coffee in that order every day. How could it get more perfect than that?

Beck on the other hand is smart as hell. He's studying computer science and is exceptional at coding. His professor thinks he could be a hacker, but he would rather be a heavyweight MMA fighter. His education is for when he retires from fighting, he claims.

Hopefully he doesn't take too many hits to the head in the meantime.

Watching Beck fight is an art form.

The man is hot as sin, covered in a sheen of sweat with his muscles flexing. It makes me wild just watching him. The desire to lick every drop of sweat off that tight stomach. And that V, cut so sharp, dipping down into those tight compression shorts he wears, crosses my mind way more than it should.

Being overcome with the desire to nip the peak of his bicep with my teeth, and then scolding myself for objectifying my friend.

And that's all he is still, my friend.

After getting over all the nerves that came with attending his fights, a rollercoaster of emotions waved through me while watching him in action. It's both stressful and exhilarating. A privilege and a curse. No one should look that good covered in sweat, knocking someone's lights out. Violence shouldn't be so beautiful. But he makes it look effortless.

Beck lets out a deep breath, and I blink out of my haze and realize he still has his eyes shut.

"Hey, you okay," I inquire with concern in my voice.

"Just tired. I swear they're trying to squeeze as much last-minute information into us as they can before we graduate. And that on top of my training schedule. I'm just beat!" he says on a sigh, eyes still closed.

"Come here, put your head in my lap," I whisper.

He opens his eyes and they look weary when they meet mine.

Hesitating, before he gets off the couch.

He puts my laptop and papers on his end table, before finally lying down and resting his head in my lap.

"Close your eyes," I say, smiling softly at him.

"Okay...," he whispers.

Remaining tense, he closes his eyes.

Watching as they flutter softly but remain closed.

I start to massage his scalp, running my fingers through his hair and digging my nails in, giving the ends a little tug.

Making my way down his neck and shoulders, really digging in deep, to those extremely defined shoulders and traps. Focused on rubbing out each knot.

His skin is so soft and warm under my fingers.

He lets out a deep groan, making me blush slightly.

"That feels incredible Sut, thank you," Beck croaks out.

Looking up at me with warring emotions, an appreciative softness, but also a fire in his eyes, like he isn't sure how he should feel about this.

"Anything for you, Scrap."

Melting into my touch, I feel his muscles start to relax.

With his warm body so close to mine, I can feel his chest rumble.

Leaning forward, I ran my thumbs deep into the muscles of his forearms.

His nose grazes my nipple, causing me to gasp, so softly.

Just under my flimsy shirt; my nipples pebble with the heat of his mouth so close.

It has my mind spiraling with need.

If he just leaned forward the slightest bit, he could suck it into his mouth.

And it's like he heard my thoughts or something because he lets out a delicious groan. *Fuck.*

Pulling back like I've been burned, our lips almost brush too.

My heart is ready to explode out of my chest. It's beating so rapidly; it's a whooshing sound in my ears.

Never in my life have I wanted a man's lips on mine as much as I do his.

Fuck, now my panties are damp.

I should not be thinking this way.

We're just friends.

But I'm not sure we are just friends.

This plan might have backfired.

Tapping his shoulder and breaking the tension, "Now get up and go get the popcorn. Jeopardy is about to start."

"Ahhh, this was you buttering me up to get the popcorn going," Beck teases with crinkled eyes and a chuckle. "I see how you are."

I gasp dramatically, hand over my heart in a saccharine sweet tone, "I would never!"

Winking at me, as he gets up off the floor, I notice him adjust himself slightly, right before he heads to the kitchen.

Lying back on the couch to process whatever the hell that just was.

Calming my racing heart, I catalog everything I love about his apartment.

Keeping the city vibes, with the old brick and industrial fixtures, the remaining walls of his small one-bedroom apartment are painted a soft grey, making it actually quite cozy and nothing like the bachelor pad I initially envisioned.

Off of the kitchen there's a small balcony where a bistro table sits.

A fire blazes in the fireplace, lighting the room in a soft amber glow.

In the living room a picturesque view of the city glitters through the beautiful bay window. One of the bridges is off in the distance.

Dropping down next to me with the popcorn in hand, he always leaves just enough space between us. Inching just the slightest bit closer, I sink my toes under his legs for warmth.

Our fingers graze as we both reach in for a piece of popcorn at the same time. It's like a lightning strike to my heart. Every atom in my body on high alert after that massage.

But he remains stoic, not even a flicker of a reaction.

Nights like these, where we're cuddled up on the couch, doing things like couples might, I allow myself to fantasize about what a future could look like with Beck as my partner, not just my friend.

A fantasy, that's all it will ever be.

Fighting has always been Beck's number one priority. With his strict fitness schedule, and it only getting stricter when he graduates, he always says he has no time for relationships. It wouldn't be fair to his partner that they'd come second.

Fighting in Vegas, it's his sole focus.

Even after the fight on Halloween, Beck's the first man I've grown to trust in a long time. He groveled for months after that. Never breaking his promise, only ever fighting at his underground fights since that night. It probably helped that his coach was pissed at him for stepping out of line too.

There have definitely been nights like tonight, where I've thought about what his lips would feel like on mine or how good the weight of his body would feel pinning me into his mattress. Being friends with Beck has allowed me to focus on my own life and healing myself within the safety of his friendship.

What's that saying? *You have to love yourself first, before you can love someone else.*

Helping me build trust in men, while also allowing me grace in learning to trust myself and who I choose to have in my life.

"Shit, I didn't realize it was going to snow so much," I gasp when I look outside and see snow blanketing the city, sparkling under the streetlights, where not a lick of pavement can be seen. The roads completely covered.

We were so lost yelling out answers to Alex Trebek during

Jeopardy, we never even noticed the steady snowfall through the window.

"You can stay here Sut, it's no big deal. I'll just sleep on the couch," Beck offers in his gravelly voice.

"I can sleep on the couch. It's your place. Thank you though, Scrap!" I give him a hug and kiss on the cheek.

"You and that nickname!" he groans, hugging me back tightly.

Beck gives the best hugs. I think to myself, burrowing into his warm embrace.

"What?" I wink. "It's cute, you and your little brawls you get into, you're a Scrappie," I smirk mischievously.

"Go to bed. I'm sleeping on the couch," he states firmly, like it's end of discussion.

Before I even take a step, he's scooping me up and throwing me over his shoulder, running to his room and tossing me on his bed.

I let out an *oomph* when I hit the mattress and then burst out in a fit of giggles!

"Your bed is big enough you know. You sure you don't just want to share it? Promise I don't snore," I grin up at him with sleepy eyes, while making snow angels on his bed sheets.

"It's okay Sut," he chokes out, his eyes wandering down to the skin exposed at my hips.

"Okay, night Scrap. Thank you," I spoke softly, meeting his eyes.

"Night baby," I swear I hear him whisper.

"What?"

Already headed down the hall, he doesn't answer.

Getting out of bed and heading to his bathroom, I rinse my face and use my toothbrush that he keeps for me under the sink.

Wasting no time, I dive back into his fragrant bed, that smells just like his woodsy sandalwood body wash. Shoving my nose into his pillow and inhaling deep, I bury myself deeper under the comforter and immediately fall asleep, without Beck.

"Mmmm, I smell coffee," I groan and roll over.

Staring at me with the smallest grin on his lips, Beck leans in the doorway, in black joggers and a hoody, looking like a whole snack.

I could get high off the look in his eyes, like catnip for the soul.

Heat flickers in his eyes, just as quickly it disappears.

Still half asleep, I probably just imagined it.

"It looks like they've plowed the roads. There's a to go cup of coffee and a protein shake for you on the counter, so you don't have to stop before class. I'm heading to the gym."

Beck walks over and kisses my forehead. Pulling back and looking in my eyes, an emotion crosses over his face that I can't quite put my finger on.

"Ugh, thank you! You're the best." I respond. While yawning and stretching out, my shirt raises to just under my breasts and my little under-boob tattoos poke out.

I swear I catch him staring. Heat prickles my skin where his eyes linger, but as soon as I think that, he's walking out the door yelling, "Lock the door on your way out."

"Yes, sir!" I yell back, as I hear the front door slam shut harder than seems necessary.

Rolling out of bed. I throw my sweatpants back on from yesterday and steal one of his hoodies. Breathing a deep inhale, relaxing in the comfort of the smell of Beck's sweatshirt wrapped around me.

Taking a sip of the protein shake, and instantly spitting it out in the sink. Dumping that down the drain, and taking a large gulp of coffee that burns going down, but tastes so much better than that toxic waste he calls a protein shake. I immediately text him.

Sutton: OMG ARE YOU TRYING TO POISON ME? 🤢

Sutton: This coffee is your only saving grace. 🥴

Scrappie: Drink the shake Sut. You need the vitamins and protein. Coffee isn't breakfast.

Sutton: Not a chance. That's straight sewage.

Scrappie: Add protein shakes to your business plan then.

Sutton: Ooh.. I think you're on to something.

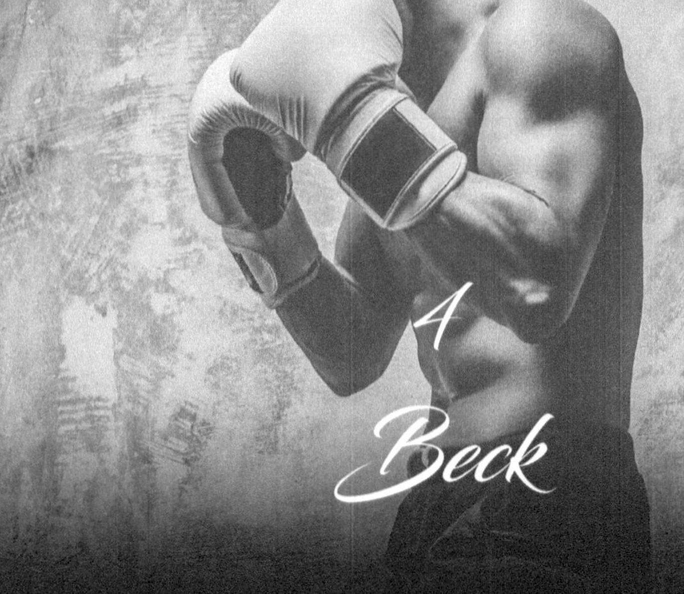

Beck

$\mathcal{I}$ wipe the sweat off my face. No matter how many miles I run, I can't outrun the vision that was Sutton in my bed this morning; in just her panties and band tee riding up to just under her tits. Those fucking tattoos poking out just under them asking to be licked, tattoos covering those thick thighs, and that plump ass with that little peach tattoo just asking to be bit into.

My wildly beautiful, jade eyed, violet haired girl in my bed this morning, without me, hair tousled, make up free, and that bare leg just peeking out of the sheets.

I groan and have to adjust myself.

She even suggested it last night, but there was no way I could sleep next to her and keep my hands off her. I would've wanted to wrap myself around her like a koala bear.

"Shit, what the hell man?" I berate myself.

"Bro, snap out of it! You completely went off to la la land. Daydreaming about smashing Sut again?" Ash razzes with a devious grin.

I throw a few hard punches at him.

"Keep her name out of your mouth!" I growl and then throw another.

"Okay, Scrap," he winks.

This fucker winks.

I love sparring with Asher. He's just as competitive as I am and never goes easy on me.

He knows I've been pining after Sut for almost a year, so he gives me nothing but shit about it.

Sut has no idea though.

Realizing quickly, I knew that she was going to keep her distance because of her best friend and whatever those ghosts are I see behind her eyes, that haunt her from time to time.

Sut's loyal to a fault and puts other people's happiness before her own.

The second our eyes met though, she stole my breath. I didn't stand a chance!

But neither did she. I've seen her reaction. Her cheeks always flush a gorgeous shade of pink when I get close. I've even caught her biting her lip subconsciously at times.

Where Quinn is gorgeous in an always perfectly done up way, Sut is just stunning in that naturally beautiful way. Curves in all the right places, devilish little grin and mischievous twinkle in those gorgeous as fuck green eyes.

A hurricane, that's what she was, barreling her way into my life.

I half expected her to be cold and distant the way she always let Quinn take the limelight and hides in her shadow.

That couldn't be further from the truth of who she is though.

The woman has no filter and is competitive as hell, which is such a turn on, but she's also an incredible listener, genuine, with the softest heart.

And I've fallen hard for her over the last year!

But I know I can't act on it. I've kept those feelings at bay because as much as I care about her, I can't put her first like she deserves. Fighting will always come first.

Every so often, those feelings try to make an appearance, like when Sut's tangled in my sheets without me, half naked, or gives me the best massage of my life.

"Fuck." I rub my jaw, blinking out of the daydream.

Ash got me good that time.

"Sut has you lovesick my friend. You need to either tell her how you feel or get over this obsession you have with her. This isn't healthy," Ash levels with me.

"You know I don't do relationships. There's no time with all this training. Who wants to date someone constantly on a diet? No one!" I grumble, rubbing my jaw from that earlier hit he gave me.

"You sure that's really it? Because as far as I see it, you make time for Sutton regularly, at least weekly, and do "Couple-y" things. You're basically dating without the sex," Ash retorts, leveling with me.

"Look, there isn't a time in my life that I can remember my parents ever being happy together. If they weren't fighting, my dad was away for work, and my mom was essentially a single mom. My mom never had anything nice to say about him. Resented him. Who wants to end up in a relationship with someone they rarely see? Completely miserable? Sut and I have a really good thing goin', I can't fuck that up. Especially when she may not even reciprocate those feelings," I sigh, running my hands through my hair still bouncing on my toes.

"Man, you're crazy. I've seen her look at you. You're the

only guy she spends any time with," Ash winks.

"You have?" I drop my stance, my heart rate spiking at the thought of Sutton wanting me.

Asher isn't a guy to just say shit, so I know if he's saying Sutton's got eyes for me, then it's true.

"See, this is what I mean! She has you wrapped around her finger. I could've just laid you out, no problem," Ash snaps and shoves me back.

"Get it together! You need to talk to her. Just have a conversation. You aren't your parents. Just because their relationship failed, doesn't mean yours will. You being at the gym or away for a few fights, isn't always being gone. You could make it work," Ash genuinely encourages.

"It's not that simple," I shake my head, shaking off the thought of Sutton not feeling the same and ruining our friendship.

Getting back into a fighting stance, while Ash continues to run his mouth.

"Come on. You don't want to lose the next fight! The girls are coming to watch. Quinn said she took off at the restaurant, and Sut said she's free, so we'll all be there cheering you on," Ash says wiggling his eyebrows.

I swear every time Sutton shows up for one of my fights, I have one of the greatest fights of my life. It's like she brings out the best in me without even trying. Just her showing up for me, motivates me to fight harder, smarter. To win the match, just to impress her. Knowing she could be anywhere else, but she chooses to show up for me. Just the thought is a shot of adrenaline rushing through my veins.

"All right! Now let's get your head back in the game!" Ash punches me lightly in the shoulder. "You feelin' ready for the fight this weekend?" Ash asks, bouncing on his toes, getting amped up.

"I got this in the bag!" I smirk and throw a punch at him, that he blocks perfectly.

We continue to spar for another half hour. Throwing punch after punch after punch, until both of our arms feel like jelly.

Taking Ash down to the ground in a headlock, when he lets his guard down. Just to be an asshole! He finally taps out.

"See, I got this," I chuckle.

"Dick," Ash chuckles back, while shoving me.

We get up and head into the locker room to change, then head to meet with the trainers and nutritionist before we need to head to class.

We meet weekly to make sure I'm staying in tip top shape. I work with a personal trainer for cardio and weight training, a jiu jitsu specialist, Ash for sparring, and the wrestling coach here also offered to train me a few times a month, as long as I keep my grades up and avoid fighting outside of training and the underground.

He thankfully forgave me for choking that guy out at the Halloween party, if I promised not to lose control again. He definitely didn't have a problem with it when I told him it was because I was defending Sutton against the asshat of a guy. Which I haven't, since I made that promise to Sutton too.

Asher sits in with me and the nutritionist when he can, since he's about to graduate with a degree in nutrition. The plan is that he will eventually take over managing my nutrition plan, when I go pro.

My diet is pretty restricted. I'm not much of a drinker or a partier, but sometimes I celebrate a win with a few beers.

But I'd much rather be celebrating with a jade eyed vixen sitting on my face, but beggars can't be choosers.

5
Beck

When I was a senior in high school, the wrestling coach caught me in another fist fight in the school parking lot. One more strike, and I was out, was what I was told after my last fight.

I knew for sure I was finally getting expelled.

Coach surprised the hell out of me though that day, by taking me to his office instead of the principal's office.

After sitting me down and letting me sweat for a little bit, he offered me one final chance before expulsion.

After school, he would train with me, to give me an outlet for my aggression, as long as I kept my hands to myself and continued to keep my grades up.

Coach was the first person to see me and give me a real chance.

Twice a week we'd meet after school, and he would teach me everything he knew. Training me in groundwork and fine-tuning my punches. Giving me structure, a routine, and the control that I craved. It was a safe space to let go of all the rage I held inside toward my parents.

My parents divorced when I was fourteen. Leaving me with a bitter mother, who always played the victim and expected me to step up and be the man of the house, and an absent father, who moved out of state and never returned.

We haven't spoken since I moved out after graduating high school.

Pure rage was all I ever felt when I thought of my parents. So much so, it consumed me.

They never even noticed the damage they had done.

But thankfully Coach did. Seeing me, and what I needed.

Forever grateful to him for giving me an outlet, a second chance, and an in with the wrestling coach at Pitt, since he had wrestled there and remained friends with their coach over the years.

As soon as I finished orientation my freshman year, the Pitt wrestling coach, Bill, and I met and essentially made the same deal. Keep my hands clean, and he'll continue to help me train.

What I hadn't known though, was that he was going to give me even more experience by showing me the underground world. Another escape that I didn't even know I needed.

The first time he took me to one of these fights I was frothing at the mouth to get in the ring.

It was fuckin torture, only being allowed to watch the first few times.

The energy in the room was insane! It was like static electricity. People were either holding their breath or chanting someone's name.

The rules were simple: no eye gouging, biting or crotch shots.

That didn't stop these fights from being brutal. Some men left covered in blood. Others were missing teeth with eyes swollen shut. Some on a gurney, immobile.

It's incredible how much damage can be done to the human body in less than ten minutes.

The place smelled like blood and sweat. Dank and moldy. Fear. Exhilaration.

I think Coach Bill wanted me scared.

But I wasn't. At all.

Why would I be with nothing to lose?

My phone chimes from an unknown number with an address, start time and password, while I'm sitting in my living room running through a few yoga poses, doing deep breathing exercises to get my mind focused, getting ready for tonight's fight.

Sending a quick text to the group to give them the password so they can get in tonight too.

The location isn't far from my apartment.

Double checking that I have my lucky gloves. A present from Sut last year for my birthday. I haven't lost a round since she gave them to me.

I grab my keys, throw on my hoody and head out the door.

Giving the bouncer the password. He checks my ID and lets me through the entrance.

Stepping into the empty basement of this old vacant building, surrounded by cinder blocks and a few overhead fluorescent lights, the buzzing starts under my skin, adrenaline building.

Insulation is falling out of the ceiling.

A makeshift boxing ring sits in the center of the room.

There's a smaller crowd of maybe a hundred people surrounding the ring, gazing intently at the two fighters currently beating the hell out of each other. One referee and an EMT waiting on the edge of the ring in case there's foul play.

Covering my mouth to hide the smirk on my face when I think back on Sut wearing that referee costume last year. *Gods damn!*

Some of these fighters are savages. Out for blood. Some are here to work through their shit in a more controlled environment to try keep their asses out of jail.

When I first started fighting years ago, it was to feed my inner beast. Tamp him down. But now, it's for the adrenaline rush. We're all here fighting some demon or another.

Being in the ring is like nothing I've ever felt before. It's just me and my competitor. Someone of equal size and height. Usually a real challenge.

Just living in the moment, releasing all the stress and tension from my life.

Winning in that ring makes all the hours on hours of grueling workouts and dieting worth it.

The respect and praise you earn from strangers is like nothing I've ever experienced outside of these walls.

Pulling up my hood, popping my headphones in, blasting Eminem's *Till I Collapse* to amp myself up, I stand off to the side and wait for my turn. Drowning out the crowd.

A tingling sensation, like I'm being watched, has my eyes popping open.

That's when I notice the girl of my dreams and our friends are here.

Our eyes meet.

I nod and Sutton gives me the most blinding smile, and mouths, "You got this, Scrap."

My inner beast growls.

Watching, as heads turn from several men and women captivated by her, as she walks past them.

Absolutely stunning in tight ripped black jeans, an off the shoulder blood red sweater and her black combat boots. Her gorgeous violet locks in waves around her face.

She has no idea how fuckin beautiful she is! It's hard to take my eyes off her, but I have to focus.

6
Sutton

Quinn, Asher, and I are standing around waiting for Beck's fight. There were six other fights, and we were a little late getting here, but thankfully we made it before Beck was up. But he's next.

Anxiety is high as we wait for our friend to hopefully knock out his competition.

Wringing my hands and trying not to chew my fingernails.

We impatiently wait for this fight to start and hopefully end, quickly.

In Beck's favor.

It never gets less nerve wracking.

"Ladies," the announcer dramatically alerts the crowd, "And gentlemen...,"

The crowd goes wild, especially the women.

"At six foot three, two hundred and fifty-two pounds... Cain Knuxx!" the announcer continues.

People are stomping their feet and hollering as a giant of

a man, wearing a red robe with the hood up, walks into the ring.

Taking off his robe, he smirks and winks at the crowd, and the women go wild again.

The sound is deafening.

"Oh fuck!" I gasp, my eyes go wide.

"He's got this Sut, quit worrying. He's ready," Ash tries to calm me, squeezing my shoulders.

"But that dude is huge! I thought Beck was big, but that guy is like a brick shithouse Ash," I whimper. Covering my eyes and then spreading my fingers to see through them.

Quinn squeezes my hand and eases my anxiety. "He trains for this every day Sut and you watch him every fight. He's got this. Breathe!"

"Up next," the announcer pauses, "Coming out at six foot four, two hundred and fifty-six pounds...Beckett Scott!"

We scream our heads off, "Kick his ass B!" Quinn yells, as Beck walks out in his black hoody and silky blue shorts.

Beck's attention never leaving his opponent, as he sizes him up.

Ash stands behind me, continuing to squeeze both of my shoulders, bouncing on his toes with anticipation.

Beck takes his hoody off and it takes everything in me to keep my jaw off the ground. My best friend-- and every toned inch of his edible body is standing in the middle of the ring.

I'm ogling my best friend.

Friends don't ogle their friends. I internally scold myself.

My belly fills with nervous energy for my best friend. If anything happens to him...

I can't think like that.

Asher is right, Beck's got this.

But Cain doesn't look nervous at all. He's bouncing on his toes, taunting Beck.

I can't hear what Cain's saying, but I watch as his mouth moves. Then he's baring his teeth like a rabid animal.

Beck restrains his movements, staring intently at Cain like he's his prey.

Never taking the bait.

They bump their large fists together, Cain grinning smugly. Beck expressionless.

"Let's keep it legal boys," the referee instructs, looking at each of them, "Fight!"

With my heart in my throat, death gripping Asher's hand on my shoulder, I flinch as Cain throws the first punch almost instantly. He grazes Beck's eyebrow and I gasp.

Beck looks back and makes eye contact with me for the briefest moment, almost like he heard me, but there is no way he did. He wipes his brow off, a trickle of blood on his fingertips, the most devious smirk on his lips.

Quinn yells, "Fuck him up Beck!" over the deafening sound of the crowd chanting Cain's name.

Then in a blur, Beck looks like he's about to throw a punch, but fakes him out and immediately takes Cain's knees out from underneath him.

Landing on top of him, Beck throws a brutal punch that immediately knocks Cain out.

It was over before my brain even caught up with the fact that Beck just won.

"He won!" I gasp, eyes wide.

The crowd is silent.

Asher is yelling, "Hell yeah!"

Quinn starts cheering.

But all I hear is static. White noise.

Because Beck spins around and pins me with a stare so heated. I don't even think. I just run.

Next thing I know I'm leaping into my best friend's arms.

Wrapping my legs around his waist.

Thankfully he has quick reflexes and catches me like I weigh nothing.

Before I know what I'm doing, I'm slamming my lips down on his.

And he kisses me back. *Beck's kissing me back!*

Time stands still for a second.

I melt into his warm, smooth lips that taste just the slightest bit metallic from the blood that has dripped from his forehead to his mouth.

But I couldn't care less because this kiss is magic.

In the blink of an eye, it's over though.

With my body still warm from how searing that was, we're interrupted by the emcee as he calls Beck over to claim his winnings.

I sense him hesitate to leave my side.

But he sets me down by his corner of the ring, throws on his hoody and walks over to the center of the ring.

Once Beck's back, he holds my stare a few seconds longer, like he can't believe that just happened either, and he throws his arm over my shoulder. Pulling me close to his side we walk over to the exit to meet our friends.

He pushes the door open.

The cool night air hits us, "Do you want to..." Beck starts to say, but is cut off when he notices the cop cars swarming the street. "Shit, we gotta run!"

"Oh my gosh, are they here because of the fight?" I whisper, while running.

"It doesn't look like it, but I'm not sure and I'd rather not find out. This isn't the best side of town, but they also could've gotten word of the fight," Beck whisper back. "Keep running, Sut."

"Ugh, I hate running! You know I've always said I'd just lay down and play dead in any situation where I should run, but that sounds like the dumbest idea right now because we'd just get caught," I gasp, trying to take in air.

We all make it far enough down the road and pop into a 24-hour pharmacy. We hide out for 10 minutes before calling a cab to pick us up.

The cab driver allows the four of us to cram in.

Beck pulls me onto his lap, like I belong there.

The drive is silent.

We pull up to Beck's apartment first. I get out first, so he can get out.

He pulls me into a hug and kisses my forehead.

He acts like he wants to ask me something.

When I think he's about to, the cab driver hollers out, "I don't have all night."

"Night Sut, thanks for coming," he kisses my forehead again and holds his lips there a little longer.

I sigh and look down at the ground. "Night, Beck."

Hopping back into the cab, I stare out the window.

His eyes hold mine until we're far enough down the road that I can't see him anymore.

Quinn squeezes my hand, like she knows I need a little support.

Asher gets dropped off next, "Night ladies" he says as he

taps the roof of the cab.

As soon as we get in the door of our place, Quinn spins to face me.

I know I'm not going anywhere until I spill all the details.

"Are we going to talk about that inferno of a kiss, bestie?" Quinn squeals at me.

"It was just the adrenaline, a lapse in judgement," I say shrugging.

"You keep telling yourself that, but I know you Sut," she squeezes me.

"He doesn't feel the same and you know it," I respond dejectedly.

She frowns at me and squeezes my hand.

"That kiss didn't look like he didn't feel the same to me. He kissed you back babe!" Quinn gives me a hug. I hug her back tighter.

"Good night!" we both say, and we each head into our own rooms, never speaking of that kiss again.

*E*ven years later, Beck and I never spoke of that kiss.

It was almost like it was a dream.

Almost like it never happened to him.

But for me, it's something that keeps me up.

Night after night.

7

Sutton

Groaning, I roll over to shut off my alarm.

Rolling back over, pulling Khaos close to snuggle him for a few more blissful minutes.

After giving him a few kisses on his big fluffy, golden block head, I hop out of bed to get ready for the day.

After deciding my hair isn't worth taming, I throw it in a messy bun on my head. I decide on my favorite ripped jeans, crop band tee and purple converses and head to my little slice of heaven.

WaggingWithWords, my pipe dream that I turned into reality.

The best part, my loft apartment is upstairs, so I get to just roll out of bed and come to work.

Is it really even work if you love what you do? This place has been a dream come true.

A book store and coffee shop in one, but it's so much more than that.

Carrying mostly thrillers and romance novels because those are my favorite.

Local coffee beans that taste out of this world.

And my favorite part, live music and dog adoption days!

Khaos my golden retriever, and Mayhem, Beck's German Shepherd are rescues and are the best dogs, so we felt we needed to help their furry friends find homes too!

When Quinn and I decided to open our little haven together, we made sure to keep our friend group in mind.

Quinn created the menu, making sure to create healthy options for Beck and Ash.

And delicious treats and coffee for ourselves.

We sell smoothies and protein shakes, wraps, soups, and salads, as well as the best coffee in town.

Plus, our macarons are to die for!

We wanted to attract various groups of people. Wanting it to be both cozy enough that customers would want to sit and read, while sipping coffee or enjoy an afternoon treat.

But also, darker, and industrial enough that it would attract musicians to play here on weekends.

The open area out back has bistro tables set up and a beautiful garden filled with various shades of white and purple, peonies and roses.

Making it a great place to soak up some sun, while reading a book with a furry friend.

Bands set up their sets at seven and perform until roughly midnight.

Typically, two to four bands perform full sets on a given night.

If for some reason we don't have a band booked, we just take the night off.

With us being a smaller venue, we haven't had any big names perform here, but there have been some really great bands who have so much potential.

Quinn comes barging through the door demanding her usual toffee crunch iced latte.

At this point, I don't think coffee even gives us a boost of energy anymore. We just can't make it through the day without it. It's our biggest vice in life.

"I can't wait to see what puppies are up for adoption today!" she squeals. "No offense, but I think Saturdays are my favorite days here."

Did I mention my best friend works with me?

Quinn went to culinary school, and while working here is probably below her expertise, everything she creates here is orgasmic.

When she suggested we mesh our dreams together, hers of opening a café, mine of a café bookstore; it was really a no brainer for us.

Saturdays are my favorite days here too if I'm being honest.

Today is Saturday, and I get to spend the whole day with puppies. Lots and lots of puppies. And that makes my heart happy.

Not long after we turned our open sign on, the volunteers from the local humane society walked in with five adoptable dogs. They are all beautiful, freshly groomed, in the cutest bandanas waiting for their forever homes.

We set up out back and make sure the dogs have water and a few toys to chew on while they wait to see who shows up.

We put a sign out front for Adoption Day, and we offer a

coupon for a free coffee and book on the house for anyone who adopts a dog today.

Khaos always greets the adoptable newcomers with excitement, but then heads back to his favorite spot in the shop.

A bean bag closer to the bookshelves, directly under the air conditioning.

His fluffy tail wags anytime someone walks past him to browse for a book.

Beck walks in next with Mayhem in tow, gray shirt clinging to those muscular shoulders and biceps. Requesting his post work out protein shake that Quinn did in fact recreate to taste delicious.

Delicious enough that I actually drink this one.

Mayhem walks over and hops on the bean bag with Khaos.

They immediately snuggle up together.

Watching them cuddle never gets old, especially because we rescued them on the same day.

Poor Mayhem had some separation anxiety at first. Although he's adjusted because Beck is the best doggy dad out there—you can tell Mayhem loves spending time with his buddy, Khaos.

Honestly, the dogs are together more than they aren't. We take them everywhere with us, since Beck and I are always together.

Mayhem stays with me when Beck has a fight out of town.

Khaos always stays down here with me except for Saturday nights when we have live music. Then he's at Beck's.

It's only about five minutes from here.

It's the same cozy apartment he's lived in since we met which means, he stops in most days to grab a shake and say hello. It's also on his way to the gym where he trains.

"Think anyone will get adopted today?" he asks, smiling at the five dogs lying near the garden out back.

"I sure hope so! They are so cute, if I had the time and space, I would adopt all of them!" I squeal, hearts in my eyes looking at their sweet faces.

"We know you would, but you cannot do that Sut," he chastises me.

I roll my eyes at him.

He grumbles under his breath.

"Hopefully though! It's a beautiful day. They all seem really well behaved, and the last couple weeks has really gotten the humane society's attention, especially with us posting on social media too," I respond hopefully.

"That's great, Sut. You girls are really making a difference here!" he says with a small smile.

"That's all Quinn! Her social media skills are top tier. Probably from all those years of taking selfies in college," I chuckle.

"Morning Quinn, thanks for the shake!" he yells back into the kitchen.

"Mornin'. Of course, got to keep those muscles pristine," Quinn yells back.

We both laugh.

"Want me to take Khaos for the day?" Beck asks, staring over at the dogs.

"Yeah, that would be great! I think it's going to be a hectic day, so may be better for him to get some fresh air," I smile and grab his leash for Beck.

"Thank you, Scrap!"

He gives me a quick peck on the cheek and grabs the dogs'

leashes.

"Always, Sut," he affirms as he walks out.

*P*eople have been in and out of here all day. There's been so much commotion. I'm grateful Beck took Khaos.

I'm dead on my feet, but have to push through because it's about time to get ready for the show tonight.

It's really one of the only drawbacks of living in the loft above the shop.

Overall, it's been a great day, even if we haven't had a breather.

We ran out of all our pastries, sold some really great romance novels, and all of the dogs are pending adoption, as long as the background checks go through.

*T*hankfully we only have two bands performing tonight, so we should get to close a little earlier. The first band, *Night Terror*, is setting up downstairs already. They got here right as we were locking the doors, and *From Troy* is setting up directly after.

From Troy is a new band playing here tonight. Their drummer stopped in here the other day and asked if they could perform.

I had never heard of them before.

Quinn and I headed upstairs to take a quick shower and get ready to reopen. She leaves half of her wardrobe at my place because this is a common Saturday night out for us, but she has her own apartment not too far from here.

Quinn comes out of my bathroom looking smoking hot in a bright red mini skirt, wedge heels and a tank top slashed down the front, with her long blonde locks hanging in waves down her back.

Whistling at my bestie, "You look smokin!"

Ready to head downstairs in my black leather pants, cropped ripped band tee, and thigh high black boots. My lips are painted crimson red, cat eye drawn sharp enough to kill a man, and space buns thrown in just messy enough, with the rest of my hair flowing down my back.

"Hopefully one of these musicians is looking for a groupie tonight," Quinn says slyly grinning at me and doing a little shimmy.

"You are wild, but I love it! I hope for your sake there is, and he knows how to take care of his groupie's needs too," I laugh.

Snapping a selfie and sending it to the guys in our group text, we head downstairs to get ready for the show to start.

"Khaos is panting over this," Beck texts back.

"LOL! Have fun sexy ladies," comes from Ash.

We giggle. Our boys, always hyping us up.

8

August

Walking through the doors of WaggingWithWords, I'm completely thrown off by what I see in front of me.

After the venue we were supposed to play at cancelled last minute, we were kind of desperate for a new place to perform at.

When Ty mentioned this was a bookstore, I scoffed at him.

Figured he was fuckin with me.

A little odd that a bookstore would also have live music.

Even the name of the store is unusual. But from what I hear though, the owner just loves music and books and wanted to mesh the two together. And there were great reviews for other live bands on Saturday nights, so we figured it was worth a shot.

Ty mentioned he stopped in here for a coffee a couple weeks ago, and it wasn't a huge place, but there was a big enough area for us to set up.

Standing here now I can see what he meant. The open floor plan and the back door opens to another smaller area

It looks like it would fit a decent amount of people.

Dark wood floors. Deep graphite gray painted walls. The café counter is dark wood with industrial accent pieces. Mason jars filled with lights hang from the ceiling, dimly lighting the room.

One side of the room opens to a wall covered in books on built in shelves, with a metal ladder that looks like it could be slid to grab books from the top shelves. There are black floral arrangements in gold vases. Gold accented skull and snake pieces perfectly placed on the shelves. Dark gray bean bags in each corner for people to sit in while reading.

The other side of the open area looks like it would hold tables to sit and enjoy a meal. Tonight, they are stacked up against the wall to allow for more floor place.

Further back in the area there is a built in mini stage that is elevated about a foot off the ground, just big enough to fit our four band members.

There is a door that opens to a backyard that is fenced in, right next to the stage. Several bistro tables sit out there with twinkling lights wrapped all the way around the fencing, a small garden with solar lights adding a soft ambient glow, making the area almost cozy.

The whole place has this dark, industrial vibe with a feminine touch.

Almost like gothic meets folklore.

It seems like the owner put a lot of thought into putting everything she loved into one place without overdoing it. It's quite unique and kind of awe-inspiring!

*O*ur guitars, drum set, and sound system are placed against the back wall away from the band currently set up.

Performing after other bands has been a hit or miss for us. Sometimes it brings us new listeners, other times their fans leave when they do, leaving us with a smaller crowd than we'd like.

Almost every weekend we play at smaller venues, just trying to get our name out there.

We hardly make any money, and I'm fuckin broke, but music is all I know. It's all I'm good at.

Writing lyrics is usually the only time I play guitar; being self-taught I'm decent, but nowhere near as good as Ty.

Ty is our guitarist. Beau is our drummer, and Knox is our bassist. We've been friends for years. They're the only family I've got. They love music just as much as the next person, but it isn't their life.

They have nine to five jobs they go to during the week to pay their bills.

College wasn't for me, like it was for Beau and Ty. I bartend a couple weeknights per week to pay the rent of my shitty studio apartment, but I don't have much left over. Bartenders make more money on the weekends, but I would rather be playing music than serving people.

I live and breathe music. It soothes my soul. Quiet my demons. I need it like I need oxygen.

Loud giggling takes me out of my head.

Coming down the stairs behind the café counter is a pretty, petite blonde in a little mini skirt, she says something that I can't quite hear. I go to turn my head, and the air is sucked from my lungs.

All I see is violet hair, the color of a velvet sky, and skintight black pants over the finest ass I have ever laid eyes on.

There's that giggle again.

It's like a tinkling of music notes.

I catch her smile and Gods it's fuckin blinding, soft plump lips painted in a blood red surrounding that heart stopping smile! I can't stop staring at her.

She sucks in a breath when her eyes meet mine.

I flash her my signature cocky smirk at her.

Never breaking eye contact, she continues to walk down the stairs straight to me.

Blondie is smirking and ogling me from head to toe, but purple hair looks hesitant.

The violet haired vixen tucks her hair behind her ear and reaches her hand out to me, "Hi, I'm Sutton Raven and this is Quinn Wren. We're the owners."

I look at her hand, but don't reach for it.

Instead, I stare at those lips, which she runs her little pink tongue over and purses.

I have to fight back a groan. *Why was that so hot?*

Sutton draws her hand back to her side, and then our eyes clash again and hers burn a hole straight fuckin through me.

"August Wylder. This is Ty, Knox, and Beau. We're *From Troy*," I explain, still smirking at her.

Knox and Ty both offer up a "*Hey.*" Beau nods at her.

"Hadn't really heard of you guys until your bandmate asked if you all could perform here. Looking forward to hearing what you've got!" Sutton says with a little bit of attitude.

"Oh, don't worry, we'll perform for you all right," I confidently remark and walk back toward our equipment with the guys, but not before noticing her cheeks flushing a gorgeous shade of pink.

I feel her eyes burning into my back.

Looking up at the guys, they're shaking their heads like they're disappointed in me.

"You're a real dick!" Ty grumbles.

"For someone who wants to perform for a living, you probably shouldn't burn bridges before you build them," Knox grunts.

Beau just shakes his head at me.

"I need a groupie like I need a hole in the head. You know I don't have time for a woman. Don't need them getting in my head," I scoff at them.

"She's literally the owner. She was being friendly. Not hitting on you, asshat," Knox says, smacking me in the back of the head.

Beau and Knox love to try and snag groupies when they can after shows.

Even though we're basically unknown, some women still can't pass up a chance with a musician; and with Beau being the silent one, it's like they flock to him.

Ty already has a fiancé, Rachel. She supports us as much as she can and tries to come to shows when she's free. She's a nurse, working different shifts weekly so it makes it hard for her to show up as often as she'd like.

My life just isn't conducive to relationships—staying up late writing songs into the early morning, living in a shitty apartment, being broke. I'm not exactly boyfriend material, and casual sex is a disaster waiting to happen. So, I just avoid women.

It's fuckin lonely though. Every night I feel like I'm suffocating, drowning in the loneliness.

Hopefully one of these days we'll finally have a song that

makes this misery and everything we worked for worth it.

As Sutton and Quinn head to the front door to unlock it, the other band stops to talk with her and her friend.

"Looking hot as sin as always ladies!" one of the other band members yells.

She and her friend both just shake their heads and laugh.

I roll my eyes.

Watching her as she walks outside, I notice she bends to write the featured bands on a chalkboard near the door. Damn, even her handwriting is pretty.

"Fuck!" I huff under my breath and run my hand down my face.

A line of people wait outside to enter, giving me some semblance of hope.

After Sutton situates the sign, I watch her and her friend take cash and stamp hands of hopefully future fans. They are both so animated chatting with customers and welcoming them inside.

I can't take my eyes off Sutton! Immediately I wish I had a pen and paper. There should be songs written about her!

It looks like she and her friend are quietly arguing with each other, but I can't hear them from this far away.

Trying to avoid staring at her, I continue to take in the place. The fact that she closes the café portion of her venue for the shows speaks volumes to how much she actually enjoys the music.

The outdoor area glows, really setting the ambience for the evening.

The space fills up with people in the blink of an eye.

Sutton must truly do this for her own personal enjoyment. That almost makes me smile.

Almost.

9

Sutton

"What a prick," I whisper yell to Quinn.

"A hot prick, and probably with a big one," she winks at me.

"Gross!" I say exasperated.

"They say tall, skinny emo boys have big dicks, Sut. It's just a fact," she says cackling.

"Well, I don't plan on finding out whether that fact is true or not. He's a total asshole," I huff.

"You're just saying that because he wouldn't shake your hand and you are used to people gushing over you," she says rolling her eyes.

"That's false. People don't gush over me. I expect to be respected. We are letting him play here tonight. For free. They should make money. He can be respectful," I whisper yell as we're taking cash and stamping hands at the door.

"That Knox guy is hot as fuck too!" Quinn wolf whistles, bumping her shoulder with mine.

I just laugh and shake my head at her.

We don't check IDs because we don't serve alcohol.

Music is my outlet. Everyone should have the opportunity to enjoy it without us having an age limit here. We obviously expect younger teens to come with an adult, but otherwise all ages should be able to enjoy live music. It gives them something to do that keeps them out of trouble.

"You aren't denying that he's hot though, all tall, dark, and broody, like a storm cloud. The complete opposite of your sunshine boy," Quinn smirks.

I roll my eyes at her, but I don't deny it.

"Beck isn't mine. You know that!" I grumble.

"Ha, that's all you got from that," she chuckles. "Still aren't denying he's a hottie."

"Okay, yes, he is hot. So is Knox. They all are, but I'm not interested Q," I gripe.

August is deliciously tall. He may even be taller than Beck and Beck's well over six feet.

The line picks up and I forget all about him while we collect money and stamp hands.

The show starts at seven, and Beck or Ash usually come around seven thirty to release us of our duties so we can enjoy the show. They also help keep the crowd from getting too rowdy.

If they can't make it, they usually send one of their other friends from the gym.

*N*ight Terror is already halfway through their set by

the time we make it through the crowd over near the stage. They're pretty good. They've played here once a month for the last several months and seem to bring in a good-sized crowd.

Completely submerging myself in a song, getting lost in the lyrics, letting the guitar and drums completely drown out my thoughts, feeling the vibrations from the sound move through my body, it's a balm to my soul.

When a voice can be so tender and yet so rough and gravelly, I am a complete goner.

And watching the guitarists strum so quickly puts me in a trance.

Sometimes I feel a song so deeply, it gives me goosebumps, and makes my eyes water instantly.

This band hasn't done that for me yet. They have talent, no doubt, but I just don't feel a connection.

Night Terror's set finishes. They thank everyone for coming out, letting their fans know they'll happily take pictures with them out back after the show.

We give them a few bottles of water and they give us each a sweaty hug and thank us for letting them play and then they take their equipment out to their van.

From Troy is setting up now.

I take a minute to go check the front door and make sure everything is running smoothly before grabbing Quinn's hand and pulling her as close to the stage as we can get. In hopes of adding a little pressure on the asshole.

The guys are doing sound checks. They've even brought in some of their own lighting.

August is completely ignoring my existence.

After about twenty minutes, their stage goes black.

Getting ready to go check and see if they blew a fuse, I'm stopped dead in my tracks by the most angelically sounding voice I have ever heard.

Goosebumps instantly breaking out on my skin.

A halfhearted laugh escapes me, "Of course."

Of course, it comes out of the asshole himself. And completely silences the audience.

A small bluish hued spotlight is on him now and he has transformed into a fucking vision in front of my eyes.

He's dressed in all black from head to toe, looking like *Lucifer* himself.

Long straight black hair falls down his back; untied combat boots on his feet and big tattooed hands with chunky metal rings on his fingers gripping a microphone; he's sin incarnate.

Completely frozen in my spot. Air trapped in my lungs.

I need that tattooed hand gripping my throat. *What the fuck is wrong with me?*

He's larger than life up there, hitting a note while harmonizing, sending chills down my spine.

This beautiful melody pours out of his soul to the crowd.

And then the lights go out again and his drummer immediately starts playing.

Their lights flick back on, illuminating the stage red and blue.

Then their guitarist and bassist join in, as he continues to sing about his journey of how music is his solace in this dark world. His only escape. The only thing keeping him afloat.

How he's embraced the night and its darkness.

Pouring his emotions into every sound and lyric.

"Heaviness is all I feel. My chest is aching, the pain is hard to conceal. Grief in waves, I feel like I'm drowning. Intrusive thoughts, in a loop, so confounding. So tired, just want to sleep. But the words keep cutting, cutting so deep..."

He is filled with overflowing sadness and it's tearing him into pieces.

This song is tearing me into pieces.

Trying to use his words and sound, to create a masterpiece in a world devoid of color to him.

Breathy and whispery with so much desperation, he sounds like an angel as he continues to sing.

And I just stare, completely lost in him. Transfixed.

And, Gods, I feel every ounce of pain he pours into this song, deep in my bones.

Quinn squeezes my hand and snaps me out of the spell he put me under.

And it's then I realize my cheeks are wet. I hadn't even realized I was crying.

I wipe my cheeks and smile a small smile at her.

"He's really good," she mouths to me.

The song ends, "We are *From Troy*. Thank you for coming out tonight. We hope you enjoy the show," he says in the microphone, immediately diving into another song.

It's almost a softer metal, mixed in with more metalcore. I have never heard anything like it. They perform for the full hour, and perform they do.

Just like he said they would.

The entire show my eyes never leave him. Sometimes my eyes drift to the guitarist but not for long. Watching their fingers move over the strings is hypnotic for me, but August's voice is spellbinding.

I am at a loss for words. I don't think I have ever felt so many emotions at once in my life.

They are definitely going somewhere one day. I can feel it in my soul.

10
August

No one has ever watched me as intently as she has. It's almost like she sees straight through, into the deep dark abyss of my absent soul. Her eyes were glittering with unshed tears for our first song, and I caught her wiping her cheeks at the end.

It's taking everything in me to avoid making eye contact with her.

Seeing tears in her eyes almost made me feel something.

Almost.

You can't feel much when your soul is pitch black.

There was a larger crowd than I was expecting tonight, and they cheered louder than any crowd ever has for us. I can see why so many bands have signed up to play here now.

It seems like a lot of people really love this place and adore her and her friend too.

The atmosphere is buzzing with good energy.

While she thinks I'm not watching, I've caught her

talking to so many different people throughout the night.

But I am watching, it's hard not to pay attention to her though. She's absolutely radiant.

She gives people her full attention when they're talking to her, treating them like they're the only person in the room and giving them that blinding smile.

I'm craving her smiles. Wanting them solely focused on me, but all I've gotten are scowls and pursed lips.

I guess I brought that on myself not taking her hand. But I hate being touched.

Maybe I should've seemed more grateful for this chance, but if I'm honest I didn't expect this kind of turnout at a bookstore.

When Ty suggested this place, I legit thought he was fucking with me.

We've made maybe a hundred bucks at other bars, or we've played for nothing, just to try to get our name out there.

All our equipment is packed up in the van and we're ready to head out when I notice her walking towards me.

She slams a stack of cash into my hand, "Here's your half, have a good night," she says and goes to walk away.

Grabbing her wrist lightly to stop her, my skin instantly feels like it's being seared.

She turns toward me but pulls her arm away.

"Yes?" she says gritting her teeth.

"I just wanted to, uh, say thank you, uh, what are the chances you'd let us play next weekend again?" I ask while looking sheepish and rubbing the back of my neck.

Her eyes immediately catch on my hand, and as fast as I catch her, she looks away.

She huffs out a low husky laugh that goes straight to my dick and shakes her head.

"You have a lot of nerve," she grumbles.

She precedes to nibble on her lower lip, as she glares daggers at me.

But I immediately zoned in on that lip. Want to take it between my teeth.

What the fuck. Why am I reacting like this?

"Please, Sutton?" I ask in a low raspy voice.

She stops nibbling on her lip, her eyes catch mine and flare with the slightest bit of heat.

"No, you can't play here next weekend," she says so matter of fact.

Squeezing the back of my neck, I nod and go to walk away, "Thanks for the chance tonight at least."

She stops me with a hand on my forearm. I flinch.

She notices and immediately pulls her hand away.

But then she surprises me and says "You can play the next two weekends after though if you want. We just already have three bands next weekend."

I catch her eyes and look straight into those pools of green. I've never seen eyes this color before. They remind me of pieces of sea glass.

I give her the smallest smile, "Thank you, we will be here."

She nods and softly smiles at me.

And then, me and the boys head toward the exit.

By the time I get to the door, I still feel her touch coursing through my veins. Chancing one more glance over my shoulder, and sure enough those green eyes are burning a hole straight through me.

11

Beck

Beck: *photo of Khaos* Khaos wants to know if his mum will take him for a run at the park?

Sutton: LOL, Remind Khaos that he and his mum only enjoy horizontal running. How about frisbee and a picnic instead?

Beck: His ears perked up at frisbee. Want to meet at Schenley at eleven?

Sutton: See you then, I'll bring the picnic basket. 

I jogged with the dogs to tire them out a little bit so I can enjoy some time with my girl.

Sutton parks her car and starts to climb out.

Jogging over to her car, Khaos starts whining and barking, the second he spots his mom.

At the sound of him, Sutton turns around and beams at us.

"Who's mommas good boy?" she coos at him.

Immediately kneeling down as he reaches her; she

starts giving him kisses and pets.

"Hi sweet boy," Sutton whispers, gently petting Mayhem and giving him a kiss on his nose.

If only I was one of these dogs right now.

"Thanks for taking care of my baby, Scrap," she smiles at me.

I pull her into my side, giving her a hug and quick kiss on her temple.

"Anything for you, Sut." I smile back, reaching into her car to grab the picnic basket.

She leans across the front seat, grabbing two iced coffees and the picnic blanket.

My eyes instantly are glued to her ass in those tight black leggings. And her shoulder, as her long sleeve shirt hangs off on the one side, just enough, that her flower tattoo pokes out.

We make our way to a spot under a tree with our dogs in tow.

Laying the blanket down for us, Sutton pulls two pop up dog bowls out for the dogs and fills them with water.

After they empty their bowls, they plop down next to her on the blanket and immediately fall asleep.

She hands me a chicken salad, a peach, an iced coffee, and a bottle of water. Taking the same out for herself.

"How was the show last night?" I ask, while taking a sip of my coffee.

She makes the best iced coffee.

"It was good! The first band I'm pretty sure you've heard play there before. The new band was also pretty good. The singer is kind of an asshole, but his voice isn't bad," she says almost lost in thought.

"Were the boys good for you?" she questions.

I don't like how quickly she changes the subject. Usually she's so animated when she talks about the musicians.

I laugh. "You make it sound like we share custody of them when you ask that way, but yes, they were good. Attached at the hip as always."

Sutton laughs," I guess it does kind of seem like we do share custody sometimes, and they are better together than apart."

Like us. I think to myself.

Rolling over on her stomach, grabbing her peach and biting into it, Sutton lets out the tiniest moan. I'm not sure if she even heard it but it goes straight to my dick.

The juice dribbles down her chin.

She flips over giggling and swipes her tongue out to catch it.

Transfixed by her tongue, those pouty lips, and that little sound she made.

Without thinking, I'm climbing on top of her, licking up her chin and taking her lip between my teeth.

She gasps, green eyes wide.

Taking a chance, I slide my tongue between her parted lips, sucking the peach juice from her tongue.

Groaning at the same time, she melts into the kiss, tongues twirling, she tastes so fuckin good, sweet and tart.

Deepening the kiss, diving my hands into her hair, while she scrapes her nails down my scalp.

Laughing nearby startles us both.

We're both panting as we break apart, realizing we're in public.

"How is training going?" Sutton asks shyly, looking

down at the picnic blanket, cheeks flushed a gorgeous shade of pink.

"It's been good. Since Ash has taken over managing my macros and meal prepping, this is the most cut I've ever been. We've been focusing more on my boxing skills and jiu jitsu. He thinks it will allow me to be more versatile and dynamic during my bouts," I say clearing my throat, and adjusting myself.

"I didn't notice," she deadpans.

"I'm hurt!" I grab my chest and pout. Then I tackle her and start tickling her.

"Beck! Stop!" She gasps while giggling.

"Beck! I'm kidding!"

"You look just like Thor! I didn't mean it," she cackles loudly.

"Too late, Sut," I keep tickling her and she writhes against me, squealing.

Gods she's so soft and warm, pliable in my hands, and fuck, I realize I'm starting to get hard again and immediately back off, like I've been struck by lightning.

"Thanks boys," she pretends to be appalled that our vicious beasts didn't even wake up to save her and she chuckles.

As she tries to catch her breath.

She looks so flushed and disheveled, smiling so brightly, so beautiful it hurts to look at her. I wonder if this is what she would look like after being thoroughly fucked.

I need to stop thinking with my dick when it comes to her.

We lay side by side next to the dogs in comfortable silence. It's always like this for us. We can talk, but we can also just be. The warmth from her arm seeps into mine. Every inch of our arms is touching. It would be so easy to tangle my fingers with hers. To pull her to me and just kiss her again, but I feel like the moment has passed.

I go to reach out my pinky to touch it with hers and then she jolts up and starts giggling.

Khaos sneak attacks her with kisses.

Then he sprawls out on her lap like *Superman* and licks her face as she continues to giggle.

I love the sound of her giggle.

Mayhem perks up and walks over to me.

Jumping up, she grabs the frisbee and tosses it; they both tear off after it. They both come running back with half of it in each of their mouths. Grabbing it from them, I toss it again.

She smiles a small smile at me and just lets out the smallest sigh.

"What?" I ask.

"This is just nice. Thank you for suggesting it," she responds softly and leans her head against my shoulder.

As I go to kiss her hair, I take in the moment. Yeah, this is nice, but it always is with her.

And then the boys are back with the frisbee, stealing the quiet moment.

12

Sutton

Sutton: Sooo Beck and I might've accidentally kissed at the park today...

Quinn: Ooh did you just accidentally trip and fall on his face? Like in one of your romance novels?

Sutton: HA! No, I'm not even sure how it started... but I swore... nevermind

Quinn: DONT LEAVE A GIRL HANGIN!

Sutton: I swore he was hard, Q. One second, I'm biting into a peach, he's staring in my eyes smirking, and then all of a sudden, he's devouring me, and then poof, like it never happened. Like the fight.... It's like whiplash...

Quinn: ...I'm telling you; he wants you. He wants more. I see the way he looks at you sometimes.

Sutton: and how's that?

Quinn: like you hung the moon babe... like you hung the moon.

Monday morning rolls around and I still keep

thinking about Beck and that kiss.

His warm lips on mine, that groan that left his chest and the warmth of his body against mine.

The perfect place where he let me rest my head on his shoulder when we were throwing the frisbee yesterday, until it started pouring and we had to make a run for it to the car.

When he tickled me... I know I didn't make it up.

I felt him.

I felt all of him.

Every hard muscle under his shirt that I wanted to dig my nails into and him, hard against me.

As if I dreamed him up into existence, the bell on the door chimes and in walks Beck in his tight blue t-shirt that he fills out so perfectly and gray joggers.

What is it about him in the gray joggers?

Quinn elbows me and I blink out of my haze.

"Mornin ladies," he greets us with a smug grin.

"Hey, want your usual?" Quinn asks.

"That'd be great, thanks," he says.

Quinn disappears into the kitchen and winks at me.

Just as we make eye contact the bell chimes again.

Beck steps aside and in walks August, shoulders hunched, dressed head to toe in black.

"Mornin, how can I help you?" I ask nonchalantly.

He looks over at Beck and back to me.

Beck waves his hand, letting August know he can go.

"Uh, I think I forgot my mic here Saturday. I dropped by yesterday, but you were closed," August mumbles.

Sticking his hands in his pockets, like he's uncomfortable

even being here.

"Let me go check in the back," I say.

He nods.

"August is here. Beck is here. What the actual hell?" I whisper yell, barging into the kitchen to have a freak out with Quinn.

"Why are we freaking out?" she whisper yells back.

"Umm.. because why are they both here the day after Beck and I shared that incredible kiss?" I say exasperated.

"Again, why are we freaking out? I thought we didn't even like Tall, Dark and Broody," Quinn grins smugly.

"Stop calling him that! And we don't!" I growl.

"Hmm... I think you're lying, but whatever helps you sleep at night, babe. Did he say why he's here?" Quinn asks.

"He said he forgot his mic here, he thinks," I respond.

"Ah, he did. I put one back in the office when we closed Saturday. I didn't know who it belonged to," she says.

I sigh. "Why am I reacting like this? August is an asshole. Beck is my friend. Ugh!"

"Maybe because you've always harbored more than friends' feelings for Beck, and you finally kissed, again, after years. And maybe because August doesn't bat an eye at you, but you really loved his music, and we know how you are about music, and that bothers you too," Quinn explains shrugging.

"Quit psychoanalyzing me," I huff.

She squeezes my shoulder.

Stomping back to my office, just throwing a small tantrum, and sure enough, there is a microphone sitting on my desk.

"It's going to be fine," Quinn encourages as I walk past her.

Peeking through the window of the kitchen to my front counter, I stare at both of them for a second.

Beck is watching August like a hawk, but August surprisingly is kneeling down petting Khaos and oblivious to Beck glaring at him.

My heart flutters at the sight of Khaos and August.

Ugh stupid heart.

Why is Beck glaring though?

Taking a deep breath and blowing it out, I walk back out to the counter.

"Is this it?" I ask, holding the mic out.

He stands up and looks at me, sighing with relief.

"Yeah, thanks," he mumbles, taking it from my hand.

August pets Khaos on the head a couple more times, then he turns away to head toward the door.

He noticeably flinches and half turns toward me, when I call out "Hey, wait."

"Since you had to wait for your mic. On the house. Sorry about that," I say trying to hand him a fresh chocolate chip muffin and a cup of my favorite iced coffee.

He hesitates, looks in my eyes and back at the coffee and muffin.

"Just take it, or she's going to be upset all day," Beck almost growls.

August makes eye contact with Beck, nods, puts the mic in his hoody pocket, and grabs the coffee and muffin.

"Thanks," he mumbles and walks out the door.

"I imagine he was from the band Saturday," Beck

grumbles.

"Yeah, *From Troy*, he was the singer," I say.

"Looks the type," Beck grumbles.

"What's that supposed to mean?" I ask giving him side eye.

"Nothing, dude just looks like a moody, unpleasant fucker," he huffs.

I scoff, "You don't even know him."

"Neither do you. So why are you defending him?" he asks almost hurt.

Quinn comes out with Beck's food to go. Eyeing both of us, she puts his food on the counter and runs back into the kitchen.

We make eye contact, and he blows out a breath and then shakes his head.

"Do you care if I leave Mayhem here while I go to the gym?" Beck asks while staring at Mayhem laying with Khaos on the bean bag.

"Nope, that's fine. See you later," I say tight lipped.

He looks at me with a hint of sadness in his eyes, "Sut."

Thankfully the bell rings and a few customers step in and break the tension.

Beck just nods and walks out.

I just catch him watching me for a second through the glass before he turns to keep walking, and then he stops.

Following his line of sight across the street, where sitting on a bench eating a chocolate muffin and sipping a coffee is August.

Beck's head starts to swivel in my direction again, but I hurriedly turn my head to my customer.

"Welcome to WaggingWithWords, what can I get for you?" I say with a smile.

But I can feel Beck's eyes burning into me through the glass, before I see him finally walk away, out of the corner of my eye.

Completely forgetting I have a customer; my eyes track back to August. He sticks out like a sore thumb with his black *Deftones* band tee, tight black jeans that sit on his hips just right, and slick black combat boots, left untied.

I watch as each person that walks past him turns their noses away, just like Beck did, brushing him off.

From this far away it's hard to make out, but it almost looks like he's enjoying the muffin and coffee.

Throwing his trash away in the garbage, he glances back at the café with the smallest smile on his lips.

My heart melts a little at the sight.

"I'll take a hazelnut latte please with almond milk," from my customer, breaks me out of my trance.

13

August

 was such an asshole to her.

Purposely a complete dick on Saturday, and she was still kind enough to feed me the best thing I've ever put in my mouth.

That muffin and coffee were out of this world! I groaned the second it hit my tongue.

I freaked out when I couldn't find my mic. Stressed all day Sunday.

Those aren't cheap and I can't exactly afford a new one right now.

But she kept it safe, locked away in her office.

I wonder if she knew it was mine.

No one's been that kind to me since Ty.

People tend to treat me like I'm a criminal; always keeping a close eye on me or turning their noses down at me.

Just like that guy did who was standing talking to her

when I walked in.

But not her.

She seems to just see people and treat them each as a human. Never any judgment on her face.

Who even is this girl?

Lying on the dingey mattress on the floor, in our studio apartment asleep, I hear something shatter and immediately jump up, heart pounding so hard, I can hear it drumming in my ears. Turning to wake up my mom, but she isn't lying next to me anymore.

"Mom?" I whisper.

No answer.

We don't live in the safest neighborhood, so I'm always on guard for a break in.

Keeping a baseball bat behind the mattress underneath the living room window.

Going to get up off the mattress, quietly, reaching for the bat.

My heart drops when I look up.

My mother stands in front of me.

Holding what looks like a broken piece of glass clenched tightly in her hand.

But there's so much blood. So much!

Closing my eyes, feeling all the blood rush from my face,

and shaking my head.

Shaking it so violently because this must be a dream. Begging myself to just wake up. This can't be real. This isn't real!

Finally opening my eyes, frozen in place, from the ghostly look on my mom's face, tears streaming down her cheeks.

The color crimson dripping down her hands onto the carpet from the open wounds running from wrist to elbow.

I can barely make out what she's saying over the loud drumming in my ears, "I'm sorry August! I'm so sorry! I..." her pleading words turning into a sob before she can finish what she's saying and collapses to the floor, knees hitting the ground.

Running to grab towels, blankets, anything to make it stop.

Rushing back to see her slumped on the floor.

Throwing everything on the ground, pulling her lifeless body into my arms, "Mom!" I shriek barely above a whisper.

"Why mom? Why? Why would you do this? Why would you leave me?" I cry out, holding her so tightly to me.

She's so cold. I feel paralyzed, frozen. We're both covered in her blood.

"Mom!" I croak on my final plea. Knowing she's already gone.

"Police, open up," is yelled, a loud pounding on the door.

I immediately sit up, gasping for air. I'm drenched in a cold sweat, hair stuck to my face.

"Fuck," I run my hand down my face.

It was just a nightmare. A nightmare, that was my reality.

When the police finally showed up, after my neighbor

heard my screams, they removed my mother's lifeless body that had been in my arms for what felt like hours.

I hadn't even realized I was screaming.

As a twenty-nine-year-old single mom, addicted to heroin—at least until my dad overdosed and died—I honestly expected drugs to take her life. Not suicide.

Seeing her lifeless body in my arms still has me feeling nauseous, still haunts my dreams at night.

She was a shit mom most days, but she was always trying to get better. Always showing up when I needed her the most, working all hours of the night to keep a roof over our heads and food on the table.

But in the end, it just wasn't enough. I wasn't enough. I'm never enough for anyone to stay.

To this day, I've refused to even touch a single drug. Drugs have taken too much from me already.

After my mom died, I went to live with my grandmother.

She didn't really have the means to care for me either, but being able to sleep on her couch kept me out of the foster system. She was never warm or affectionate, like some would expect grandmothers to be, but she was never unkind either. More apathetic. She was all I had in this world until she died too three years later.

It's amusing that my only interaction with the police was the night my mother died, but the world still views me as a criminal, solely by my appearance.

Getting tossed in the foster system was my biggest fear, so I always made sure to just lay low. Taking the bus to school in the morning and a different bus after to the local diner to work as their bus boy. They offered me one free meal a shift, and whatever tips and wages I earned, was saved.

One night after I got home from a late shift, I found my grandma lying on the kitchen floor, cold and rigid, just like my mother had been in my arms.

Just one month shy of eighteen years old, watching the EMT's carry the gurney out of the apartment with my last living relative lying on it. I don't remember shedding a single tear.

As I was getting ready to close the door, the landlord grimaced as he told me my grandmother had been two months late on rent, and I would need to be out within the month.

I remember just nodding my head at him. Completely numb.

Two weeks later, while I was packing up my grandmother's things to donate, I found a small shoe box under her bed with a thousand dollars cash and a photo of her, looking down at me as a baby in my mother's arms. I squeezed it to my chest. A rush of utter relief filling my body.

That in addition to the money I had saved at my job kept me from being homeless, and I had never been more grateful.

Now I live in a dump in the city. It's a small studio apartment, with an air mattress, a floor lamp, and my guitar; a couple books and the same stack of all black clothes and old combat boots I've had to my name since high school.

Finally getting up and heading to the shower to rinse off that nightmare.

Of course, the water's fucking freezing. It almost never gets warm here. It's a fucking shithole but I can't afford much else and I'm honestly not used to anything better.

Making my way to Ty's for a quick run through practice before tonight's show.

My voice is fucked after that nightmare. It still has me shaken. The guys are on it today though so hopefully they can mask it.

"You good, August?" Ty asks after we go through our third song that we usually perform.

"Yeah, yeah, just feel like I'm getting a cold or something," I say, shrugging him off.

"I'll be good. Let's do one more song and then we can break til the show tonight."

He just looks at me like he knows I'm lying but nods anyway.

Ty knows more about my past than the rest of the guys.

Some nights after school, if I didn't have a shift at the diner, we'd screw around making music at his parents' house. Jamming out on our guitars while I screamed or sang.

When Ty met Beau and Knox in college, they decided after a few months to get a house together. We quickly discovered that Beau was actually an incredible drummer and Knox a pretty good bassist.

They welcomed me into their group, and we became fast friends, with our love for music.

Those fuckers are the only family I've got.

Many long nights were spent in their basement; writing lyrics, strumming guitar strings, and snapping drumsticks until we fine-tuned our sound, and now here we are, *From Troy*.

My whole life has been a battle, so I thought it was fitting.

Thankfully, the guys liked it too.

*S*utton is giving us a second chance and I hope that if we perform well, she may consider keeping us on as regulars.

It's the best paid gig we've had and the largest crowd by far.

I sing without the guys at a bar downtown sometimes, but I don't get paid. I'm just hoping somehow, someday someone important is going to stumble upon us.

We walk into WaggingWithWords around seven, scheduled to go on stage around eight.

Sutton was putting the sign outside for the show when

we got here.

All that long violet hair, those curves in those tight leather pants, she's so stunning, it's disarming. Just looking at her has my heart hammering.

I've never been this viscerally effected by a woman.

She said, "Hi!" to us when we walked in but didn't make much small talk.

The sound of her giggle has me turning to look toward the entrance; that big blonde guy from the other day is here, scooping her up into a hug and kissing her forehead.

She hugs him back and smiles up at him, with a comfort I've never felt with anyone, lighting up like a Christmas tree; her smile is breathtaking.

I want that smile to be for me, but being an asshole like I am doesn't get you smiles, it just gets you a cold shoulder and scowls.

Are they together? I wonder to myself. They seem so comfortable together, familiar.

I guess it's none of my business. She would never want someone like me. A dark cloud.

Honestly, she deserves better. She deserves someone to look at her like he does, deserves to have someone who can take care of her. I can barely take care of myself.

The ache in my chest at the sight of them has me unconsciously rubbing over my heart, like somehow massaging it will make the pain of seeing her with him better.

Ty shouting at me, has me tearing my eyes away from Sutton and the blonde guy, as the first band finishes up.

"You ready man?" Ty asks me pointedly. Hopping on Knox's shoulders, getting amped up.

He knows not to touch me.

"Fuck yeah, let's do this," I growl.

During the first band, I watched as Sutton stayed toward the back with the bouncer watching the show and carrying on quiet conversation.

Selfishly, I hope she doesn't check in with him during our performance.

I want her full attention. On me.

14

Sutton

$\mathcal{B}$eck is here tonight to keep things under control.

I always trust his friends from the gym to bounce for us, but I always prefer when it's Beck.

I've just been a little uneasy since Monday, when things got awkward between Beck and me, because he was completely out of line about August.

He acted like he always does when he sees me, so hopefully that means we're okay.

He stopped in with Mayhem and grabbed his breakfast every day this week, but I still felt the tiniest bit of distance between us. And I hated it!

Beck was pulling the doors closed when I last checked in with him, and now as I glance over my shoulder, he's just leaning against the back window, watching me intently.

I'm standing a lot closer to the stage to watch *From Troy* than I was for the previous band. There's a questioning look in Beck's eyes, but I pretend not to notice from this distance.

Instead of starting with that haunting song he sang a few weeks ago, the band starts playing first.

The drums start out low, then get louder.

In a blink, August is center stage letting out this deep guttural sound that I'm pretty sure came straight from the depths of hell; bending almost completely in half backwards as he projects his voice through his microphone.

Feeling each deep growl in my chest from the vibrations of the speakers on stage.

The sound of his voice and the way our eyes lock has my core clenching, each growl sending electric shocks straight to my soul.

People cheer. Loud.

He smirks and bows his head to thank them.

The crowd quiets down immediately.

They're puppets and he's controlling the strings.

He has their full undivided attention.

Mine too.

Commanding everyone's eyes to the stage, stealing the show.

But something's off.

He's singing that haunting song he sang a couple weeks ago that took my breath away, except even though he still sounds incredible, it's lacking the emotion I felt before.

Almost like he's disconnected himself from the lyrics, from the pain.

I continue to watch him intently as he sings and screams a few more songs, while his band plays incredibly.

Then he is thanking everyone for coming out and supporting them and asks them to follow them on Instagram.

As I turn around to head toward Beck, I notice a man is yelling at him.

Beck looks tense, rigid, making me feel uneasy as I approach him.

Making my way over, I hear the guy demanding a refund.

"Excuse me, I'm the owner, what's the problem?" I ask as nicely as I can.

"Those dudes sucked! Screaming isn't music. I want my money back!" he demands.

"I'm sorry you didn't enjoy the show, but the entry fee is nonrefundable," I say apologetically.

He gets in my face, "I want my money back! The show sucked! You should make people aware of what they're getting into," he crowds my space further.

Beck steps up, "You better step at least a foot away from her right now, before I personally throw you outside. You heard what she said!" Beck growls at him.

I can feel the heat radiating off him from the rage coursing through his body.

"If the bitch would just give me my money back, I'd be on my way!" he snarls back at Beck.

"Watch your fuckin mouth!" Beck sneers and goes to crowd him.

And then, that's when I feel another warm body come up behind me and see Beck look up. But I don't look. The smell of leather with a hint of tobacco clues me in that it's August.

"Listen here asshole, you came into my store to listen to live music. You stayed for the entire show. You could've left already if it wasn't for you. You could've looked the band up. They're listed on the website. The bands that perform here are bands trying to get their names out there. They're talented bands, but they aren't bands playing at Heinz Field, at least not yet. This is a stepping stone for them. A safe space to get their names out there. To be heard and have a good time. They aren't going to be everyone's cup of tea, but they're really wonderful and unique. You clearly have poor taste!" I bark at him.

I can't help myself. Who does this guy think he is? I can't contain my rage.

"Do you also ask for refunds after you've eaten your meal if it wasn't a 10/10 for you? Do you return a book after you've read the entire thing front to back? No, you don't and if you do, you're an even bigger asshole than I thought. Now get the fuck out of my venue and don't come back! Your entry was nonrefundable," I snarl in his face.

I hear someone clear their voice, "Um.. Sutton, it's okay... you can give him..." August starts to whisper to me.

I hold up my hand in his face to get him to keep his mouth shut.

The customer is eyeing August with a little bit of hope in his eyes.

"I said GET OUT!" I yell.

"Whatever, this place sucks anyways! Just let the trash give me my money back and I'll go," the customer grumbles, but looks at August hopefully over my shoulder.

"He doesn't know what he's saying. If he gives you your money back, anyone could ask for their money back, and this is my store and my business and I'm telling you, you don't get a fucking refund! Now leave and don't fuckin come back!" I growl.

"I'll write a bad review about your store," he says grinning like a *Cheshire* cat.

"Cool, go for it, you Twatwaffle. I don't give a flying fuck. Now leave!" I yell.

The crowd starts to wolf whistle and cheer.

The guy walks away flipping everyone off.

"Booooooo!" the crowd yells after him.

Beck has a shit eating grin on his face and then he winks at me.

August looks sort of forlorn, but those eyes tell me everything he can't, and they are blazing with heat.

"Hey, it's okay," I whisper to August while looking into his eyes.

"He can hurt your business, because...," August whispers.

"August, he's just another asshole in a world full of them," I shrug it off. Like it isn't a big deal.

"I know, but today I wasn't on my game, and because of that you had to deal with that asshole," he sighs, looking so broken up about it.

"I could tell you were off, but that guy wouldn't have known," I reply softly, lightly squeezing his hand.

August's eyes burn into mine, "How would you have known that?"

"Because I see you, August," I whisper back and squeeze his hand again.

He looks down at our hands connected and then pulls his hand away.

"You don't even know me Sutton, so don't act like you see me," he snarls and turns away, but I see the sadness in his eyes.

"Wait," I say softly.

He barely turns toward me.

"Here," I hand him his half of the earnings.

He stares at the pile of cash. His eyes seem to go just a little wider.

"And I do. See you, August," I tap the money in his hand.

"You wouldn't like the real me if you did, Sutton. So, you can't possibly. Everyone sees what they want to see," he growls and goes to walk away but stops, "Thank you, for this," he waves the handful of cash.

Warm arms wrap around me, as I stare off at the broody man walking away from me.

Beck puts his head on my shoulder, and I inhale his woodsy smell.

Letting it calm my racing heart.

"You good?" he asks softly in my ear.

I sag into the hug, "Yeah, I'm good."

"Who needs fists, when they have your feisty little mouth to put someone in their place?" He chuckles in my ear.

"Twatwaffle?" he snorts.

I elbow him in the stomach.

He pretends to groan and buckle over like I nearly killed him.

Chuckling in that deep, delicious voice of his.

I turn around into his warm embrace and steal a real hug from him.

"Thanks for helping out tonight and being there for back up, Scrap."

"Anything for you, Sut," Beck says kissing my forehead.

*W*e stand outside with the door open, letting the rest of the crowd out to leave.

Some stop to take quick selfies with the guys.

From Troy is the last to leave.

"Thanks for a great show," I smile and wave them goodbye.

"Can we come back? Perform again?" Ty the guitarist asks, bouncing on his toes.

My eyes land on August, who's just watching me

lean against Beck, with an expression I can't quite read.

"Do you guys want to come every weekend or every other weekend for the next couple months and see how it goes?" I offer with a shoulder shrug.

"Every weekend? Really?" August asks with the tiniest bit of surprise in his voice.

"Yeah, I mean you guys had a pretty decent crowd these two times. I have a few bands scheduled for the next several weeks, but not entire nights booked. So, if you want to, you can, until you find somewhere else to play that you prefer..." I'm saying.

And then I'm being scooped up and spun around by Knox; "Hell yeah!" he whoops.

Beck growls behind me.

I just giggle.

"Put me down you oaf. As I was saying, we can say every weekend for the next two months, then reconvene," I say smiling.

August just stares at me. Eyes drilling into me, like he's looking for some hidden agenda.

Ty hits August's shoulder for a second before pulling his hand back, but he has the biggest grin on his face, "You good with that man?" Ty asks August.

"Yeah, yeah we'll take it, thanks!" August says, looking completely shocked and in awe.

"Tell Blondie I'm coming for her," Knox gently squeezes my shoulder and winks at me.

I snort, "Good luck with that!"

The guys let out a whoop, except for August. He looks at Beck's arm around my shoulder and then in my eyes.

His look almost pained.

He hesitates and then nods. Turning and walking away with the guys to their vehicle.

August's eyes are boring into me through the

window of the back seat as they drive away. Holding my stare until I can't see his face anymore.

Beck gives me another tight hug, his lips lingering on my forehead, "Night, Sut."

"Night, Scrap," I smile up at him.

His eyes holding mine slightly longer than normal.

Then he nods and walks backwards to his car.

Locking the door and shutting out the lights once I get back in the building.

I wave to him from the front door when he gets into his car.

He pulls away and I head upstairs to my bed.

Fuck.

What was that? What did I just get myself into?

This should be fun.

Two months of August tearing into my soul with his music, with Beck here to witness it no less.

Sutton: I'm a dumb bitch.

Quinn: What the hell did you do now?

Sutton: I may have offered From Troy to play EVERY weekend for the next two months and I think Beck is covering over half of those for me. ☺

Quinn: You ARE quite the dumb bitch...

Sutton: HEY!

Quinn: But, you're MY dumb bitch.

Quinn: Maybe lover boy will finally confess his feelings to you if he senses you falling for someone else.

Sutton: Um.. I'm not falling for anyone.

Quinn: Sure. Okay. Keep telling yourself that. Just like you aren't in love with your best friend.

Sutton: ...UGH

Sutton: Knox asked where Blondie was tonight! 😉

Quinn: I hate that nickname... but he is fiiiine 😉

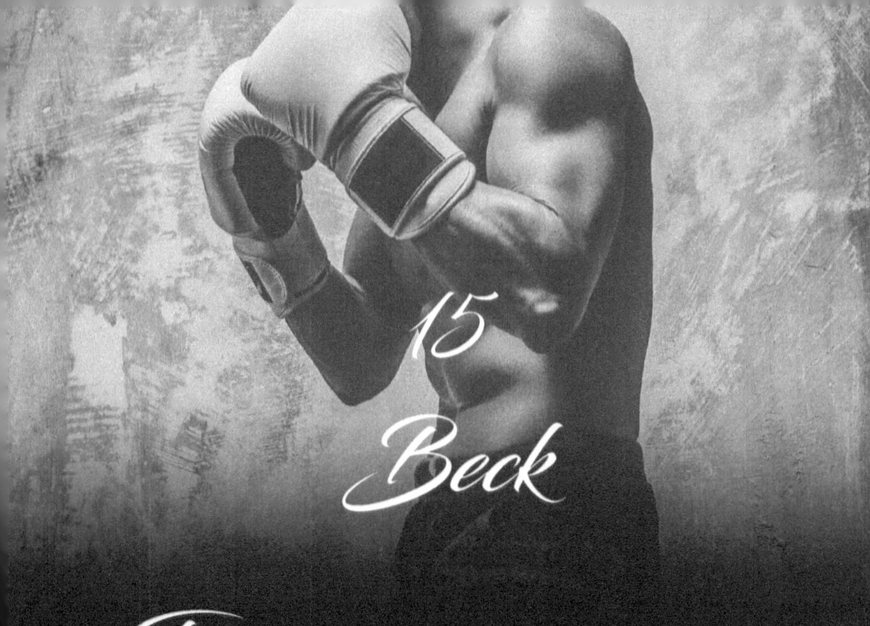

15
Beck

That girl is 24/7 music; it's like there's a juke box always playing, inside of her pretty head.

If she isn't blasting it, she's humming a tune to herself.

Always swaying those sexy hips to a beat only she can hear.

The only time she ever seemed comfortable when we were at parties in college was on the dance floor, dancing with Quinn, eyes closed, head thrown back, guard down for just a few minutes before realizing where she was and shutting down again.

I know Sut loves music. It drowns out her thoughts apparently, but the way she watches August sing so intently, makes me want to throw her over my shoulder and carry her out of there.

The way her face transforms while he sings, I've never seen some of the expressions on her face before.

She's usually a vault when it comes to her emotions.

But the emotions painting her face as he sings or screams, her eyes never leaving his, it's like she's lost in him, like she feels everything he does, every word from his mouth.

So, I know it's not just the fuckin music that she's into.

Occasionally they wander over to his guitarist, watching his fingers strum the strings, but it's the singer that she watches more, not the guitar strings.

She doesn't watch other bands like this.

Usually during other band performances, she checks in to make sure things are running smoothly, but not for him. Her eyes don't leave him until the entire performance is over.

Defending him to that asshole customer, defending him to me.

Usually, I'd love to see my girl defend herself, but I don't like her defending him.

The thought of her, with him, stirs something inside me that I don't fucking like.

I've had her all to myself these last six years.

Fuck this broody motherfucker! He doesn't get to just waltz in here and steal what's mine. And Sutton is mine!

I growl, punching my steering wheel.

16
August

$\mathcal{S}$eeing her with bouncer boy, how comfortable and affectionate they were together, looking at each other like maybe they weren't "Just friends".

They are the spitting image of a perfect couple after all; well matched, well dressed, everyone around them seems to gravitate toward them like the sun.

Now though, after what happened earlier, they are in fact "Just friends".

Even though I know at least one of them, if not both of them, wants to be more.

The couple of times I've bumped into him around her, Beck puts his arm around her like he's staking his claim, lingering just a little too long. Making sure he always meets my eyes, like he's letting me know she's his.

Kissing her forehead but never those pouty lips, even though his eyes are always on those lips too long.

Sutton never seems to mind, but Gods what I wouldn't give to have those supple lips wrapped around my cock.

They probably taste divine too.

Just the way she kept looking at me tonight and then defending me, fuck, it had my dick hard.

I heard everything that asshole said when he was demanding his money back.

And her defending me? Hot as fuck!

But her knowing I was off tonight though scares the hell out of me! What was that? It's like she is already in my head.

That nightmare really fucked with my head and it's like she could sense it.

It's fuckin unsettling.

I don't deserve her, not in the fuckin least. I'm way too fucked up and flawed.

Don't have a fuckin clue how to physically love someone.

I would literally poison all of that goodness within her.

No, she needs someone to give her that fairytale ending.

Someone like the bouncer.

But fuck, I'd love to find a way to make her mine.

To fuckin sing straight into that heart of gold and bring her down to hell with me.

My darkness could use a little light.

17

Sutton

*F*uck.

I didn't think this through.

Every Saturday August puts on a performance with his whole fuckin soul.

Every Saturday Beck just so happens to be available to keep an eye on the door for me.

A whole month of torture, but fuck do I love it!

Two beautiful fuckin men, that couldn't be more opposite, pulling my heart in completely opposite directions.

And neither of them wants me. At least not in the way that I want them.

Beck has seemed a little more affectionate with me, especially when August is around.

I notice August loves to smirk at Beck too, like he's in on some secret I'm unaware of.

I've always known where I stand with Beck. He's my

best friend.

That hasn't stopped me from daydreaming about what a life with him could look like though.

A beautiful log cabin in the woods, with a gorgeous wrap around porch, surrounded by acres of forestry filled with wildlife; a fenced in area where the dogs could run and play, and maybe a few other fur babies too. Flying to Vegas together for his fights. Quinn and I still running WaggingWithWords.

August on the other hand hasn't been a complete prick lately.

Though I still don't trust my heart around him, so I've kept somewhat of a distance.

While Beck and Ash have helped me heal some of my trust issues towards men, it's my own heart I don't quite trust around August.

A part of me feels like it would be so easy to give my heart to him and that scares the hell out of me.

Afraid of what would happen if I did.

Because Gods does his music break my heart already.

*T*his Saturday, August stood up on stage looking like a dark, sinful angel.

"We're going to play a new song tonight that we've been working on," August croons into the microphone, right before the guitar strings strum a haunting melody. Then he starts singing in his tender, husky voice.

Gods, he writes the most earth-shattering lyrics, making me get utterly lost in the heartbreaking words he's singing.

Tears prickle behind my eyes. Everything he's singing hits way too close to home.

"I am so deeply lost in the depths of my own soul; how could I expect her to understand me?" August croons in this tenderly soft, desperate way.

Can you fall in love with someone because of a song?

The song's over; the crowd is cheering, but everything is muffled; like I'm sitting at the bottom of a swimming pool as our eyes hold each other for what feels like hours, but is only seconds, before the band picks up the tune of another song, and he snaps his eyes from mine and begins singing.

The crowd has grown every week, and it's a full house tonight.

Not one more body would fit in this room. People are bleeding out into the outdoor area, packed like sardines all to watch *From Troy* perform.

I feel August's eyes on me but feel Beck's eyes biting into my skin too.

Slowly turning my head, Beck is leaning against the back wall, eyes pinned to me, with an unreadable expression on his handsome face.

I blink at him and realize my eyes are blurry from the unshed tears.

Turning back around when I hear August's voice say, "Thank you so much, everyone! We are *From Troy*, and we will be back next weekend."

The most genuine smile I've ever seen is on August's face right now, as the crowd wolf whistles and cheers for them.

Ty slaps August on the back.

Our eyes meet and he winks at me and turns back around to start tearing down their set.

The sensation of hands on my waist steals me from the sensation of butterflies fluttering in my belly from that one tiny wink.

"Hey, I have to head out early. I have an early training session tomorrow. Be safe locking up," Beck says in a somber tone in my ear.

Turning around to hug Beck goodbye, I feel his hands leave my waist, and he's already starting to walk away.

Frowning, as I watch him leave.

"Thank you again for letting us play this month. I couldn't have dreamed up a turnout like this!" I hear August's husky voice exclaim in my ear.

Turning toward him, he's smiling the softest smile at me.

It's so beautiful on his haunting face!

The softest kiss of a moon lit glow; I just want to bask in it.

My fingers are reaching up to touch the soft smile on his lips, before realizing and yanking my hand away and offering him an awkward hand shake.

"You earned it. That was incredible!" I say smiling softly, cheeks flushed.

As I go to pull my hand away, August shocks the hell out of me and pulls me into a quick hug but lets me go just as quickly.

"You're incredible, beautiful!" I think I hear him whisper in my ear.

And then he's gone; but the butterflies in my belly are back, and a hint of leather and tobacco linger on my clothes.

I'm so screwed!

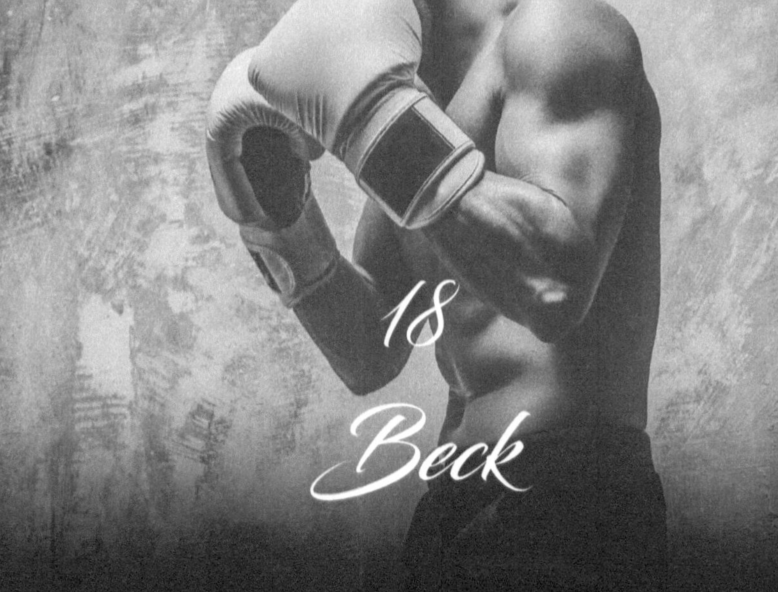

18

Beck

*D*eciding an early training session is necessary on my rest day, I shoot Ash a text to see if he would come in and spar with me to let off some steam.

I never lie to Sutton, but if I had to stand there and watch her eye fuck that musician for another second, I was going to lose it.

Last night is on replay in my mind, the way their eyes locked on one another.

Making my chest ache with jealousy.

She's mine!

I'm throwing heavy punches into the punching bag, trying to punch this ache out of my chest, when I hear a small squeak and some shuffling.

Turning around, seeing someone in gray hoody and sweatpants, who's maybe five feet tall, walks quickly to the front door.

"Hey stop!" I yell.

They go to make a run for it, but I catch up to them and block the door with my hand.

The person noticeably flinches.

"What the hell are you doing? I snap.

Jet black hair spills out of the front of the hood when she turns her head.

"I'm sorry! I thought you were open. I saw a sign for self-defense classes. I didn't realize you were closed today. I guess I didn't even realize what day it was," she rambles so softly without ever making eye contact with me.

Lightening my tense expression, I gently respond, "Stay there for one second and I can get you the self-defense schedule. We hold the class two nights a week. We have a beginner class and a more advanced class. My friend, Asher, and I teach them. It's free for women."

She nods at me, but is acting like a cornered animal, wringing her hands, looking everywhere but directly at my face, so I try not to make any fast movements to spook her.

Then the front door opens and Asher walks in, "Hey man, uhh who's this?"

Before I can even give her the pamphlet, she's jumping up and sprinting out the door.

"Whoa!" Asher looks at me eyes wide.

"I'm not sure who that was. She came in here when I was hitting the bag and asked about the self-defense class. She seems pretty spooked," I frown, glancing at the door she ran out.

Ash looks back outside but she's nowhere to be found. He just shrugs his shoulders.

"Tape the pamphlet on the door. Maybe she'll come back for it. But anyways, why are we sparring on your rest day?"

I sigh, massaging the ache in my chest, "I think Sutton

wants the musician."

"What musician?" Asher asks puzzled.

"There is a new band that's been performing most Saturdays now, and the way they watch each other, it's almost like there's this tension between them, and it's killing me to see her look at him the way she does. I don't know what to do," I grumble, throwing my gloves at Asher.

"Have you asked her about him?" Asher questions.

"Ha! No. But she defends him every chance she gets," I sigh.

"So, ask her. Ask her how she feels. Or better yet, tell her how you feel!" he throws a jab at me.

"I don't think I can risk our friendship. We've kissed a couple times, but it's almost like we never did, because we never bring it up again. Plus, you know I need control in ways she might not be okay with," I smile a mischievous grin.

"This has been a long time coming. You can't pine after someone for five years and expect them to just wait for you. Have the long overdue conversation. You won't know anything until you do," Asher shakes his head.

Finally getting to a point where I'm out of my own head, shelfing this battle of my feelings for Sut. Ash and I leave the gym.

"Nice work today! Think about what I said though about Sut," Ash says giving me a wave goodbye.

On my walk back to my apartment, I realize Ash is right. Sut and I really need to have a conversation before it's too late.

"Let's go out dancing tonight. I need to let loose, it's been a long ass week," I say to Quinn, hopping up onto the counter she just wiped down, after I locked up the café.

"You don't have to ask me twice," she says with a shit eating grin and a little shimmy.

We shut off the lights and head upstairs to get ready.

"Want to pre-game power hour to save some money," I say holding up a bottle of whiskey.

"Ah, duh," she says grabbing the bottle and taking a swig.

Blasting early 2000's hip hop because it's the best hip hop, taking shots and dancing around the room while we get ready.

Looking fine as hell in our black skinny jeans, thigh high boots and off the shoulder sweaters, mine a deep magenta, Quinn's a blush pink.

We call a cab when we're well and clearly buzzed to take us to the South Side of Pittsburgh where all of the bars and clubs are.

When we pull up to our favorite night club, Belvs, our favorite bouncer, Josh, is working, so he lets us cut the line.

The dance floor is already full so we shove our way to the center, find a spot and get lost in the music and warm bodies surrounding us.

Quinn and I are dancing and shaking our asses.

Our favorite throwback song, *Lollipop* by Lil Wayne, comes on and we both squeal and start grinding on each other, yelling the lyrics to the song, heads thrown back, sweat glistening on our skin, hair a mess, just feeling the music.

When the song ends, we head outside for some air, both giggling from how much fun we're having.

Once we're outside we decide to walk further down the street, when we hear what sounds like a band playing.

Following the sound of the music, we eventually stumble upon a few guys playing in a little dive bar.

Heading straight to the bar to grab a whiskey ginger ale, my skin starts to tingle.

Instantly feeling the sensation that I'm being watched.

Looking around, I don't see anyone, but tingles still race down my spine.

Squinting my eyes through the darkness, I spot August leaning against a wall not far from me, staring right at me.

We hold eye contact, neither of us blinking, until Quinn grabs my arm, distracting me by handing me my drink, my eyes leaving August just for a beat.

I turn back around, still feeling his presence, but he's gone.

After standing and listening to the band for a while, I

let Quinn know I'm heading to the bathroom.

It's a little busy in here, so she stays to hold our spots.

On my way, I feel those same tingles again, and there August is sitting over in the dark corner.

Hair pulled back in a low man bun, black Nirvana tee shirt with his signature fitted black jeans, blending in, like a shadow in the night.

As if he senses me too, he immediately looks up, eyes locking with mine.

Whiskey buzzing through my veins, I decide to march right up to him, "Why are you sitting in the corner alone being all mysterious and edible?" waving my hand around in the direction of him, I ask curiously.

He smirks at me, "Did you just say edible?"

"Of course, that's all you heard," I huff, rolling my eyes.

"Why did you come over here Sutton?" he asks with a hint of rasp when he says my name.

"Why are you such an asshole?" I ask exasperated.

"Maybe because I don't like to be bothered, Sutton," he says on a shrug.

"Well sorry for bothering you, August," I huff, rolling my eyes and go to leave.

Grabbing my wrist and immediately releasing it like I burned him, "Why, Sutton?" I can barely hear him, but I read his lips.

Looking at my wrist, tracing my finger where he touched me and then looking back at him, "You have the voice of a fuckin angel, and a demon, and it completely incinerates me, turns me inside out" I rasp and his eyes soften the slightest, "And it just has to come out of that stupidly gorgeous face of yours!" I practically yelled at him.

I swore he frowned then, but my big unfiltered, drunk mouth keeps rambling on. "I think I need to fuck you out of my system or something."

He continues to frown, then he blinks and just stares at me.

Like he's trying to make me feel uncomfortable.

Then taking me by surprise, he leans forward, eyes lighting with the smallest amount of heat.

My body instantly betrays me and leans closer to him, and then that stupid, smug ass smirk is back on his face, "Let me make one thing clear Sutton, you would not be fucking me. I would be fucking you. I would fuckin wreck you. And I won't be doing that, not right now while you're drunk, and not ever, so go back to your friend and back to doing whatever it was you were doing before you saw me!" he says with a snarl.

"Gods. You are SUCH an asshole, August! I hate you!" I yell in frustration, sending daggers at him with my eyes.

Turning and heading straight to the bar, middle finger pointed directly at him over my head. Quinn hands me two shots and I throw them back in quick succession.

After we watch the band for a bit longer, we make our way down the strip of bars until we see a sign for karaoke.

Squealing while ripping the door open, Quinn and I walk in.

Heading straight up to the DJ, I sign up to sing *Man I Feel Like a Woman* by Shania Twain.

After about six people sing, my name is called.

Quinn wolf whistles for me, and I start giggling.

The bartender just shrugs her shoulders, when I ask if I

can get up on the bar to sing.

The DJ hands me the microphone, and I climb up onto the bar and nod to the DJ.

People immediately start cheering for me.

Winking at them, I start singing, *"I'm going out tonight I'm feeling all right..."* I get the crowd into it, walking the length of the bar, singing and dancing, shimmying my shoulders, whipping my hair around, really giving it my all.

Cat calls and whistles ring out and someone even yells "Shake it girl."

I'm getting lost to the music and eating up the attention, drowning out my thoughts, finally letting loose, and just as the song is almost over, I slip on a spilled drink.

Bracing for the fall off of the bar with my eyes squeezed tight, because there's literally no other option.

I'm caught before hitting the ground, as I yell the last line, *"I feel like a woman."*

Everyone is cheering for me.

Someone even yells "Encore", and I giggle as I slowly peel my eyes open after realizing I did not in fact slam into the hard ground, but a hard body instead.

Eyes as dark as midnight are shooting daggers at me.

He literally looks like he's in physical pain with me in his arms, and he is ready to murder me.

"You can put me down now, thanks," I say with a huff and the biggest fake smile I can muster.

No sooner do my feet hit the ground, I feel his strong hand squeezing my throat.

The cold of the metal from his rings feels delicious against my burning skin.

Loving the feeling, I push hard into his hand, crazed smile on my face, making him realize that he's touching me.

Jumping back, raking his hands through his hair, a blazing fury in his eyes, he growls, "What the fuck, Sutton? This isn't fucking funny. You could've been hurt. What the hell were you thinking singing on the bar?"

"Well, August, I was thinking that I needed to let off some steam since I was rejected. I was thinking I fuckin love karaoke, so I fuckin sang karaoke," I yell back getting in his face.

"On top of the bar!? You couldn't sing on the ground like a normal fucking person? Christ, woman, why are you so infuriating?" his voice growing darker.

"Don't you dare woman me!" I stomp, shoving my finger into his chest.

"Says the girl who literally just sang *Man I feel Like a Woman!*" he growls.

"You know, even though that whole display was a disaster, you actually held your own up there," he smiles smugly.

Making my insides melt.

After a beat, realizing what he just said, "OH MY GODS! Did Mr. Tall Dark, Tall and Broody just give me a compliment? Is the world burning down?" I ask sarcastically.

"So dramatic. Come on, grab Quinn and I'll call you a cab," he says rolling his eyes.

"What are you going to do?" I ask, stopping, softening towards him slightly.

"I just walked here, so I'll walk home after you girls are safely in the cab," he replies with a shrug.

"Hmm..." I hum and grin.

"What are you hmming about?" he says side eyeing me and moving the slightest bit closer.

In a drunken haze, I try to softly inhale his scent without him noticing.

"Oh, nothing! Just that you might actually have a little bit of a heart in there after all," I say smiling softly at him, giving his chest a little tap over his heart.

"Night, Auggie. Thanks for catching my bestie," Quinn squeals diving into the cab.

"Yeah, thanks Auggieeeee!" I giggle, exaggerating the nickname Quinn gave him.

Reaching out his hand hesitantly, I grab it and feel that electric current run through our fingertips again.

He looks down at his hand, almost like he felt it too and then looks back up at me. August shakes his head, like he's shaking the feeling off, "...Goodnight Sutton. Quinn," he says in that raspy voice and taps the roof of the cab.

From the backseat of the cab, I blow him a kiss.

The cab is taking off, but I think I see the faintest smile on his face.

20

August

It's been two months since she literally slipped and fell into my arms at that bar, and I can still feel Sutton's warm skin pressed against my arms and chest.

That vanilla scent is permanently etched into my veins. The way her dainty neck fit into my grip so perfectly, and shit I swear she leaned into the hold for more.

And somehow, she can fuckin sing too. How did I not know this?

We've continued to play at her venue every Saturday as part of the line-up, but it's like she's trying to avoid me.

Every time I talk to Sutton, she's short and won't hardly look at me.

She's friendly to the rest of the guys. Always laughing at Ty's stupid jokes, flirting back with Knox right in front of me, she even gets Beau to smile sometimes, but all I get is the cold shoulder.

My mind is spinning, because the other day on Instagram there was the coolest action shot of us performing on stage with our lyrics as the caption.

We just couldn't believe she started promoting us on her personal and business pages!

The photo was so killer! We had no idea they were even taking photos of us.

The signs outside every weekend have gotten bigger.

A few posters of us around the city have even been spotted; fans tagging us on their Instagrams.

We would've never known because she's never mentioned anything.

Quietly, selflessly, without asking for anything in return, Sutton has gone above and beyond for us, promoting us every way she can, trying to make accommodations for more people to watch our shows without getting code violations, as our fans grow.

This girl has done everything to make sure we're successful.

Sutton is everything! Fuckin magnificent!

And she hates me!

What she's doing right now is driving me crazy.

I'm not sure she'll ever know how grateful I am to her, and I have no idea how I'll ever repay her.

Every emotion flickers through her eyes during our performances, viscerally affecting her every weekend, and then immediately she puts her mask back on as soon as the show ends.

I've been trying to make it seem like I don't notice her while I perform, but she is all I see. My eyes always tracking right back to her.

Every word I sing, I sing for her.

At the end of the night, she hands me our money, and

says goodbye to the guys, but just side eyes me.

I can't take it anymore. I'm gonna lose my damn mind!

I'm not sure if she's upset that I rejected her at the bar, or if it's something else.

She was clearly drunk and fuck if I'm going to take advantage of a drunk girl.

I guess I didn't have to be as gruff about it. She can't keep holding this grudge though.

When I walked into that bar and saw her shaking her ass on that stage, a rage I've never felt before instantly coursed through me.

But damn the way she sang her heart out! Putting on a show, that sparkle in her eye, had me captivated and wanting.

Wanting something I've never considered for myself.

Everything stopped, the second I saw her slip though.

I couldn't fucking breathe, but then she slammed into my arms with that soft, warm body of hers.

The way she felt in my arms; I haven't been able to stop thinking about it.

The way her gaze held so much heat and passion in it, until I opened my mouth and ruined it.

Fuck, she was so Gods damn beautiful!

It took everything I had in me not to take her home and demand she be mine.

Not to crash my lips against hers and claim her in the middle of that bar.

I caught a cab here today in hopes of catching her right before she closes for the night.

Watching from across the street as Sutton tidies up her store.

I love to watch her.

The way she dances around the tables as she's cleaning.

Hair pulled up, that sexy as hell back tattoo noticeable.

I can't get enough of her! I'm completely enamored by her, and I hardly know her, but I feel her everywhere.

I feel so drawn to her, and I can't quite pinpoint what it is that I'm drawn to.

It's like my darkness is seeking out her light. Like our broken souls yearn for each other.

It's completely out of our control.

I wish I could erase the flicker of pain I see behind her eyes. She thinks she's hiding it behind that smile she puts on, but I see it in the way she's deeply moved by our music.

She lets her guard down without even realizing it when we play, and I get this private glimpse of her.

Music has this way of drowning out your thoughts and lyrics have a way of finding the person who needs them the most.

Helping them feel less alone.

She feels our lyrics and music so deeply. She doesn't ever react in the same way with the other bands.

Blinking out of my haze, I notice she's done wiping everything down and is just patiently waiting for her final customer to leave.

Fifteen minutes ago, I watched her disappear with her dog through a door behind the counter, but he didn't come back with her.

From here she looks tired, like she's carrying the weight of the world on her shoulders, but she's still so fucking captivating.

Shutting out the light and locking the door, she waves

her final customer off.

Making my way over, I knock on the door, making her jump back as she whips around.

She looks startled but then sees its just me.

"What do you need August? I'm closed for the night," she says wearily through the door.

"Let me in, Sutton, please. I just want to talk," I almost beg her.

"What is there to talk about? Kind of hard for a girl to want to talk to a guy who's always surly and constantly rejecting her," she mumbles.

"Please Sut," I run my hand down my face.

"Don't shorten my name! We aren't friends!" she says with so much heat in her voice, throwing daggers at me with her eyes.

"What if I want to be your friend?" I ask staring back at her.

Hands squeezing the back of my neck. "What if I do want to be around you? Want to talk to you? Be someone that you want as a friend?" I continue to implore softly.

Her eyes soften the slightest bit, and then she looks at my hand gripping my neck and then back to my eyes. I must look as pathetic as I feel, because Sutton unlocks the door and opens it, holding her hand out for me to enter.

"I don't need another friend, August, but you can come up if you want, I guess. I'm not sitting down here. I'm tired," she says on an exhale.

As she heads through the swinging doors behind the counter, I see a set of stairs.

Following her up the stairs, we reach the top step where a dark wood door sits.

As we walk through the door, I'm met with Khaos jumping up to greet me, two paws on my stomach, "Ah! Hey there to you too!" I pet his head.

"Khaos, down!" Sutton commands him. "Good boy! Sit."

Khaos immediately sits perfectly right next to my feet and rests his head against my shins.

Her eyes soften the slightest bit more at her dog's reaction to me.

Looking around her place, it's a really cool loft style apartment, and it couldn't be more her vibe if Sutton tried.

It's warm, open and inviting with a soft vanilla smell.

The walls are painted a soft gray. There are light wood floors throughout and a white built-in bookshelf against the back wall in the living room with books tastefully placed in a rainbow pattern.

It's almost the opposite of how she's designed her store downstairs. This is softer, more feminine, where downstairs has an edgier appeal to it.

A small charcoal gray sofa sits in the middle of the room with added hints of lilac from throw pillows and a shag rug that sits perfectly center beneath it.

The kitchen cabinets and island are white with two industrial bar stools set against the island.

A set of spiral stairs look like they lead up to a room with a king size bed.

It's a breath of fresh air, serene even, just like her.

"I had no idea this was up here," I say almost in awe, but catch her looking away from me, "Sutton..." my voice barely a whisper. I look at her with pleading eyes.

"Do you want a drink or anything..." she asks, barely

any emotion in her voice.

"I'm good, thanks;" I attempt to smile but it probably looks like a grimace.

"I'm going to change really quick. Make yourself at home," she says with a weary look in her eye.

Khaos is curled up, hogging most of her sofa, but I squeeze into a small space next to him.

He doesn't even open an eye and acknowledge me, but I softly pet his head.

He lets out a little contented sigh, so I take that as a good sign and continue to run my hand through his fur.

Hearing Sutton's feet pad down the stairs, I turn and suck in a breath the second my eyes land on her. She's absolutely fucking breathtaking, face free of makeup, hair thrown up on her head, black leggings, an off the shoulder lavender shirt.

"Gods, you're beautiful!" I softly groan.

"Why are you here August? I'm tired of these games!" she spits, words like venom.

"I'm not playing any games, Sutton. I don't do girlfriends. I've never had one. Never had the means to take one on a date. Never had a nice place to take one back to. Figured I'd save myself the time and embarrassment. Haven't even been with a woman physically in a couple years. So, forgive me if I'm not really sure how to act around you. I don't deserve someone as good as you. My full focus has been on my music, but I can't stop thinking about you," I rasp.

"I love your music, August, but I can't do another "Friend". I've spent the last five years in love with my best friend, who has never given me a second glance..." she says, voice cracking and unshed tears glittering in her eyes.

We're both silent. She's staring straight ahead at nothing, and I can't take my eyes off her.

"Have you ever been surrounded by people but still feel so deeply lonely? Like bone deep weary? Because I have three of the best friends a girl could ask for, but I'm still so fucking lonely. WaggingWithWords has been a dream come true and I'm surrounded by people every day but I still feel so lonely. I ache inside, desperately wanting someone to just see me, to hold me, to choose me, to allow me to be the one who falls apart instead of putting things back together. I don't just want to be "The friend". I'm always just the friend. I don't have the time or energy for that anymore. I want to be someone's everything," she whispers, her voice shakes and she sounds so defeated, tears breaking free down her face.

"It always makes me feel like I'm not good enough. Why am I not good enough to be more?"

Feeling the heartbreak and vulnerability in her voice.

I stare right at her, making sure I have her full attention, "Eyes on me."

Staring into those pools of green, I say fiercely and with as much desperation as I can muster, "You are good enough, Sutton. You are so good! Too good, that I don't deserve anyone close to as good as you are. I don't know how to do this. I haven't cared about anyone but myself for a long time. I've only had myself to look out for. I know I'm going to fuck this up. But I also know that I feel drawn to you like a moth to a flame, and I don't care anymore if I get burned. I've been trying to fight it, but you ignited something inside of me, and there is no dousing it out anymore."

Just staring at her and the expression on her face inspires me to write a new song. Making my fingertips itch to put pen to paper.

It's looking into those beautiful eyes made of sea glass, I know with certainty that I could write a thousand songs for her, about her, and that still wouldn't be enough.

Vowing in this very moment, to do just that.

"How poetic," Sutton whispers voice cracking, finally breaking the silence.

She goes to turn away, but not before wrapping her arms around herself, lip trembling.

"Don't do that!" immediately turning her face toward me and catching the one lone tear that escapes with my thumb and putting it in my mouth.

Her eyes go wide.

"Don't hide from me, Sunshine," I say fiercely, grabbing her by the neck, pulling her to me and crashing my mouth down on hers.

She gasps and I use that reaction to deepen the kiss. She whimpers when my tongue teases with hers. I feel her melt into me and I pour everything into this kiss.

Devouring all of her little sounds. This kiss is searing, all consuming.

It takes the air straight from my lungs. There will never be another kiss that feels like this. It's only Sutton and I that exist in this moment.

"Bedroom, please," she whimpers, digging her nails into my scalp.

Breaking the kiss, Sutton grabs my hand and pulls me off the couch and leads me up the stairs to her bed.

"Are you sure?" I question, slowing us down, kissing her forehead, her nose, and her lips again as we enter her room.

"Yes, please!" Sutton gives me the softest, most mischievous smile.

Pulling her back to me, walking her backwards until the back of her knees hit her mattress.

Pressing her down into the sheets; with one hand on her throat and one woven in her hair, kissing her like my life depends on it. Because it does.

I tilt her head back more with the grip I have in her hair.

We're a mix of mewls, whimpers and groans. Her lips taste like honey and vanilla, so soft and warm, and I can't get enough.

I think I could kiss her forever!

Whoa, the thought pops in my head and disappears just as fast, her hands clawing at my shirt, a perfect distraction.

Pulling my shirt off with one arm without breaking the kiss, she moans.

Sucking one of her pink nipples into my mouth, taking it in my teeth through her shirt and tweaking the other one with my fingers, Sutton gasps and writhes under me.

"More please, August," she pleads.

Pulling her shirt over her head and pulling her leggings off, "Fuck, Sunshine," I growl, when I see she's bare for me.

Something primal takes over. I have never felt this ravenous for another human being.

Fumbling fingers unbutton my jeans, as she helps me push them down with my boxers until I can kick them off the rest of the way; my hard cock springing straight up, she lets out the sexiest little gasp, her eyes hooded and lust filled.

Sitting back on my feet, taking her in, as she's sprawled out on the bed.

"Come here," Sutton whispers, reaching for me.

"Just let me look at you for a second first," I smirk at her.

Violet hair tangled, cheeks flushed, eyes hooded, all of her soft curves, "You're breathtaking, Sunshine!" I gasp, grabbing her by the throat and pulling her face to me, kissing her deeply again.

I can't get enough of her! It's too much and not enough all at once.

It gets frenzied, she's pulling my hair and digging her nails into my back.

My teeth making little love bites up and down her neck.

Running my tongue from her collarbone to just under her ear.

Pulling on her earlobe with my teeth and then blowing gently against it as I release it from my teeth.

Goosebumps pepper her skin, and Sutton sighs into me.

"Lay back, Beautiful," I whisper.

She lays back, and I slide one finger inside of her as I bite her neck.

She groans and clenches around my finger.

Flicking my tongue over the bite to soothe it, "So wet for me," I growl in her ear.

Sutton whimpers, "Yes, August, please! I need you!"

"Be a good girl and let me in," I growl and give my cock one hard tug before lining it up with her entrance, as her legs fall open for me.

Immediately slamming into her, we both sigh in our moans. She feels fuckin incredible, so warm, wet and tight, squeezing my cock! She digs her heels into my ass and tilts her pelvis up, driving me deeper inside her; we both moan.

"I'm going to take your breath away, like you always take away mine. Tap me twice if it's too much," I growl as I squeeze her throat.

I keep applying more pressure as I watch her face in awe as I continue to pound in and out of her.

Her face turns a beautiful reddish-purple hue, making me pulse inside of her, but it's her eyes that almost have me losing control.

Not only are they glassy, filled with lust, but there's a little bit of trust there too.

When her eyes start to roll back into her head, I feel her start to clench around me.

Feeling her getting close, I reach down with my other hand and rub her clit hard with my thumb, "Be a good girl and cum for me," I growl.

Immediately detonating for me, "Good Girl!" I growl; before releasing her throat and slamming my mouth back down on hers, sucking her tongue into my mouth, our teeth hitting. This kiss is desperate and messy but it's perfect.

"August," she moans as she takes a deep breath.

Thrusting into her three more times before reaching my climax, cumming deep inside her with a loud groan.

I collapse forward and rest my head on her shoulder.

The smell of vanilla, sex and *her* engulfs us. Comforted by her hands running through my hair in this incredibly soothing way. She starts to trace my tattoos from my shoulders down to my fingers so softly, lulling me into this safe, sated space.

Sutton touches me like no one else ever has.

And it doesn't hurt.

"You're beautiful when you cum," I whisper in her ear, leaving a trail of kisses down her neck to her shoulder.

When I pull back, she's blushing. So adorable, I can't stop leaving a trail of kisses all over her; kissing her on her forehead, the tip of her nose and her lips one more time.

I go to pull out to remove the condom, "Oh fuck! Fuck!" I growl.

"What's wrong?" Sutton asks eyes wide and glassy from her orgasm.

She reaches for me and I shove her hand away.

"I forgot a fucking condom! I never fuck without a condom! Fuck! I can't believe we did that. You're so fucking distracting!" I yell.

She sits up so fast, pulling the sheets up to cover herself.

"Wow, first off, fuck you. Second off, I'm on birth control and haven't been with anyone in a while. Don't you worry your pretty little head! I have zero plans of trapping someone like you!" Sutton yells with pain in her voice.

"Shit, I'm already screwing this up, I'm..." I say reaching for her.

She shoves my hand away, "Get the fuck out of my apartment!" she says in the calmest fiercest voice I've ever heard, while literally shoving me off the bed.

Getting up, grabbing her t-shirt and leggings, throwing them on quickly; she shoves me almost down the stairs.

"Fuck, Sutton! I'm sorry! I just freaked out. I didn't mean it." I plead.

"Leave, August. This was a mistake!" she says while opening the door and forcing me down the stairs to the front of the store.

She's furious, but I also see the anguish she's trying to hold back.

"Don't say that. It wasn't a mistake. I'm sorry, Sut, please don't be upset! I'm sorry, I didn't mean it." I plead with her, trying to pull her into my arms.

Shaking her head and pulling away, refusing to look me in the eye, her lip begins to quiver.

Sutton unlocks the front door and opens it, shoving me out.

Immediately locking the door and walking back to the door that leads to her apartment, without ever looking back.

"Fuck!" I yell and punch the brick wall outside.

Chancing a look through the window, just a voyeur to her sadness, watching as her shoulders shake, before she disappears through her apartment door.

Taking my bleeding heart with her.

21

Sutton

Sutton: How much do you love me? 😊

Quinn: What do you need dear bestie?

Sutton: ugh, rude.

Sutton: But I do have a favor or two to ask?

Quinn: Is this a cuddle your adorable dog for the night or get rid of a dead body on a pig farm kind of favor?

Sutton: Goodness, lay off the true crime.

Sutton: But the former, plus one maybe?

Quinn: umm Beck hasn't asked me to watch Mayhem...

Quinn: OH SHIT!!

Quinn: Are you about to do what I think you're about to do?!?!?

Sutton: ......

"*G*irl, Spill!" Quinn comes barging into the store the next morning.

"There's nothing to spill, Q," I say with a grimace.

She looks me up and down, walking closer to me and pulls me into a hug. "What happened babe?"

"I'm so stupid! August stopped by last night after we closed. Just showed up and asked if we could talk. One minute we're talking and the next we're sprinting up the stairs to my bed. Everything that comes out of his mouth is so fuckin poetic, my brain just turns to mush. I barely even know him and it's like I want to bury myself inside him, every time I see him. In seconds, he had me spilling my guts to him, just letting my guard down. Then I started crying, and there he was wiping away my tears. Then he just gave me this look, and then bam, he's kissing the hell out of me and then you know, one thing led to another..." I ramble and blow out a breath.

"So, you and Mr. Dark and Broody finally got groovy?" Quinn teases and covers her mouth with a laugh.

"You did not just say that!" I chuckle and shake my head.

"Made you laugh, didn't it? Was it good at least?" She grins but frowns at me.

"Ugh, that's the worst part..." I start to say.

"No fuckin way! That man has to be good in bed! There can't be a worst part!" she yells back.

"If you'd let me finish... the worst part is that it was incredible! Our chemistry! I can't even describe it. It all just happened so fast; it was like an out of body experience. We were just drawn to each other and then there were flames and sparks and then just complete ash, when he lost his shit and I shoved him out. Literally shoved him Q," I grimace and wipe tears from my face.

"Oh babe... why?" she hugs me again.

"It was just so all-consuming. We forgot to use a condom, and August immediately freaked out and acted like an asshole. He made me feel like it was my fault, so I kicked him out as he was apologizing to me, but I couldn't even look at him. I sat in the scalding hot shower and cried after that. Khaos came in and bumped his nose on the glass door, and I finally blinked out of it and got out. I didn't even notice how cold the water had gotten," I sigh and wipe my cheeks again, feeling defeated.

"This is huge for you, Sut! You never let anyone in, let alone drop down that guard of yours. The fact that you confided in him and then also jumped in bed so quickly and forgot a condom, that has to mean something, right? That heart of yours is Fort Knox," Quinn says.

"It means I was stupid, that's what it means! But it's like my brain shuts off when he's around and I'm not second guessing and questioning everything. It makes no sense," I sigh.

"You aren't stupid, Sut, but what was that text about?" Quinn asks, hopping on the counter.

"Do you need me to watch the dogs? Beck hasn't texted me, but I know he has a fight in Vegas this weekend..." Quinn pauses, giving me an all-knowing glare. "Wait, are you going to ask if you can go with him? Is that a good idea?"

"It's probably not a good idea, but I can't be here this weekend. I can't see August right now, and I definitely cannot listen to that man's music. It guts me on a good day," I respond, nibbling on my lip.

The bell chimes and I wipe my face. Quinn gives me another hug, and I walk out to the counter.

Speak of the devil.

"Hey Sut, you okay?" Beck says really looking at me.

"Yeah, I'm good, just didn't sleep great last night," I lie.

"Are you able to watch Mayhem this weekend for my fight?" he asks smiling softly at me.

"About that, actually..." I bite my lower lip.

Quinn bursts through the kitchen door, "I was hoping I could watch those two handsome boys this weekend, if that's okay?" she says grinning, mischief in her eyes when she looks at me.

"Um... why wouldn't Sut be able to do it?" Beck asks Quinn, while looking at me.

"Because Sut needs a vacation. She's been working too hard and we can't both go away, so I thought maybe she could come with you to Vegas?" She chirps with a wide grin, "And I will watch my two favorite angel babies."

"Isn't there a show this weekend? Are you able to get away?" Beck asks me with a little surprise in his eyes.

"There is, but it's only one band, and Quinn said she'll just stay here, and the boys can stay upstairs. That way she doesn't have to worry about coming and going during the show. She can just run up and down to check on them." I say, while wiping down the counter.

"We're sitting together on the plane," he says, while shaking his head with a little surprise, "If you want," giving me a sexy smile.

"I'd like that!" I smile back. Feeling some of the heaviness from last night instantly leave my chest.

"Want to just ride with me to the airport too?" Beck asks with a big smile.

"That'll be perfect! You can just drop Mayhem off then," I suggest, looking up at him through my lashes.

"Here's your shake," Quinn breaks the tension with the biggest grin on her face.

"Thanks! Later Sut, Q," he smirks walking out the door with a little extra pep in his step.

Before the door fully closes, Quinn screams.

"What?!" I yell, jumping back, hand over my chest.

"You two are totally fucking this weekend," Quinn screeches under her breath, eyes twinkling with mischief.

"We are definitely NOT!" I glare at her.

"Maybe, it's finally time! See what happens," she says on a shrug.

"Q, no. That'll ruin everything. Absolutely not!" I yell.

"Listen Sut, I love you. I do. But that man has feelings for you. You either need to act on them, or you need to stop pining after him. I'm sorry," she kisses my cheek and heads back to the kitchen.

Following behind her, "I cannot fuck two different men in the same week, Q!" I say exasperated.

"You can and you should. Babe, you're single. With the exception of last night, it's been years, Sut. Years, since you've let a man touch you! You can do whatever you need to do to make a decision," she says.

"A decision about what?" I ask almost whispering.

"About who you actually want to be with," she shrugs.

"I can't be with either one of them!" I say throwing my hands in the air exasperated.

"Yes, you can, Sut. They both clearly like you. You have a choice here. Make one!" Quinn demands.

"Fuck!" I lean my head against the counter.

22
Beck

*S*till in shock that I'm sitting next to a passed out Sutton on the plane to Vegas, I take in her soft features as she sleeps peacefully next to me, her vanilla scent cocooning around us.

Sutton hasn't flown out to any of my bigger fights. I'm pretty sure she hasn't seen me fight since my underground fights in college.

Occasionally she and Q will stop by the gym and watch Ash and me spar, but they've been so busy at the café that they just don't have time to travel much.

It's sort of sad because she always had big dreams of traveling the world, but she chose to stay back home in Pittsburgh to be closer to her grandmother. But I'm damn proud of her. She's grown her business from the ground up.

Of all weekends for her to come here though, this one is perfect. This was the only weekend this year Ash couldn't make it, because there was a huge event at the gym that he couldn't miss.

Otherwise, Ash is always in my corner, keeping me in the zone, chirping tips in my ear about the competition that he's noticing from the outside during each round.

My personal trainer, Brody, is going to be there in his place, but he won't be here until the day of the fight and is staying in a different hotel than we are.

The pilot announces that we will be landing soon.

Gently running my fingers through Sut's hair and rubbing her cheek, I try to rouse her awake.

Her eyes blink open, "Hi Scrap!" She smiles softly at me.

"Hi!" I smile back softly.

She nuzzles her head on my shoulder as we descend, reaching for my hand and squeezing it tightly as the wheels touch down.

"I hate this part!" she squeezes her eyes tight.

"I got you, Sut," I squeeze back.

"I know," I think I hear her whisper.

Moments later, waiting for our luggage at baggage claim, I ask, "Do you want to grab dinner after we get settled in our rooms?"

Sutton goes pale. "Oh my Gods!" she looks up at me with wide eyes.

"What's wrong? Are you okay?" I ask, cupping her face.

"Scrap..." she closes her eyes and blows out a breath, "I have been so out of it this week. You booked the flight. I literally didn't even think to book a room. Oh my Gods! I am so stupid! Shit!" Tears start to roll down her cheeks.

"Hey, hey.. it's okay.. we can see if they have any rooms here, and if they don't you can just stay with me. It isn't a big deal. It'll be like college—when you would accidentally fall asleep on my couch. Don't cry!" I wipe her cheeks and kiss her forehead.

She lets out the biggest sigh and says so softly, "Okay."

"**S**orry sir, we are completely booked because of the fight this weekend," the hotel receptionist says.

Looking me up and down she asks, "Hey aren't you one of the fighters? Beckett... Beckett Scott!" eyes wide, flashing with heat.

"Yes ma'am. Nice to meet you. My friend came to watch me fight but completely forgot to book a room because it was so last minute. Are you sure you don't have anything?" I ask leaning closer toward her, flashing her my best grin.

She blushes, "I'm so sorry sir, but we really are completely booked. Not a single room is available."

Sut looks so defeated. I just want to pull her in my arms and protect her.

"Okay, thank you ma'am. Have a good night," I say with a nod.

Sut and I head back towards the main entrance.

"Ugh, Beck, I am so sorry. I can't believe I forgot to do this," she looks so disheartened.

"Sut, It's fine. Really. I'm sure there are two queen or full beds or whatever they put in hotel rooms. It's not a big deal," I say nudging her.

"What seriously! I thought for sure you'd get the penthouse suite," she says faking exasperation and winks at me.

"Har Har, you know I don't like all that luxury bullshit. I just come here to fight. Win. Then go home. I don't need a penthouse to just sleep in," I say shaking my head at her.

"But what if there's someone you want to bring back to the hotel? I'm sure all the girls are dying to get with Beckett Scott, and I am totally going to be cockblocking you," she says with a touch of jealousy in her voice.

"Sut. Enough. You're staying with me. End of story. I don't care about other women," I growl at her.

Her eyes go wide, "Yes, Sir!"

Fighting back a groan hearing those two words come out of that perfect pink pouty mouth, I grab her bag and we head to the elevators.

We stand on opposite sides of the elevator just staring at each other. The bell dings for our floor and I swear she jumps, but she moves to walk out.

We get to the door and I scan the key and push the door open. I watch as her eyes go wide at the one king size bed in the room.

She's completely frozen in the doorway.

"Get in the room," I grind out through my teeth.

She nods and walks over to the window, almost trying to avoid looking at the elephant in the room.

"It's a beautiful view," she sighs out.

"Yes, it is," I mutter standing behind her, looking at her, and not through the window.

"Beck..." she whispers.

I pull away. "Do you want to change or freshen up

before dinner, or are you ready to go?"

"Let me just, um, brush my teeth and change my outfit quick and then we can head out. Give me like ten," she stutters.

"You take the bathroom. I'll change out here," I say on a smirk.

"Yup. Okay. Thanks," she grabs her suitcase and quickly escapes to the bathroom.

It's cute how flustered she gets.

I'd like to think it's because of me and my presence.

I hurry changing out of my sweats that I wore on the flight and throw on some navy chinos and a light blue button down.

I run my hand through my hair a couple times, leaving it a little messy on top.

Grabbing my phone and wallet, I head downstairs.

It seems like Sut needs a little bit of space to have her freak out.

Fate seems to be giving us a little nudge out of the friend zone, after five long years.

I had no idea she didn't book a room this weekend, but I'm not mad about it one bit.

I shoot her a text, telling her to meet me at the bar near the lobby when she's ready.

Fifteen minutes later, I hear the bell chime at the elevator.

When I look up, my jaw drops.

Sutton is looking like a goddess in a tight off the shoulder emerald green dress. Hugging her curves in all of the right places, stopping just above the knee.

Black leather heeled booties to extenuate her perfect

legs.

Getting just a few feet from me, she does a little twirl, and my heart stops briefly.

Her long violet hair is in curls down her back, lips painted a gorgeous purple color that almost matches her hair. I instantly have the urge to bite them. Want to see that color smudged on my cock. Want to devour her. Need to devour her!

When she's directly in front of me she looks up at me through her lashes, almost looking shy, "Is this too much? Should I go change?"

"It is perfect. You are perfect," I whisper and get up and kiss her forehead.

Relaxing into me as Sutton smiles up at me. I stare into her eyes and Gods I want to kiss her, want to see what she'd look like on her knees for me, looking up at me, just like she is right now.

"Would your lady like a drink?" the bartender breaks our stare off.

"Do you want a drink, or do you want to head to dinner?" I ask her.

"I haven't eaten much today so I probably shouldn't drink yet," she responds, looking embarrassed.

"Sut, you need to eat more often. I hate that you just skip meals because you "Forget," I grumble at her while making quotes with my fingers.

"Yes sir," she says rolling her eyes and giving me a little salute like a smart ass.

"Don't roll your eyes at me or I'll take you over my knee."

Her eyes go wide, "Excuse me?"

I grab her hand. "Let's go."

We're both quiet on the cab ride to the restaurant, Sutton against one window and me against the other.

We get to the restaurant and the hostess seats us toward the back. This was the best she could do to try to keep us out of the public eye. I'm not insanely famous, but people come to see me fight in Vegas, so when I'm in Vegas I get noticed more than I do anywhere else.

"Omg, are you Beckett Scott?" I hear a woman's voice and feel a hand touch my arm.

I shrug her hand off and smirk at her, "I am."

"OMG! I loved watching you fight and demolish Ryan Jensen! You literally knocked him out in the first round. So freakin impressive!" she squeals, leaning close to me.

"Thank you, hey, not trying to be rude, but we're trying to have dinner. Did you want an autograph or something?" I try to ask as nicely as I can.

"OMG! I'm so sorry. I'm just such a fan. I would love an autograph, thank you!" she hands me a napkin and a pen, pushing her tits too close to my face.

I sign the napkin and hand it back to her as quickly as possible. "Have a nice night. It was good to meet you," I say and nod my head to hopefully give her a clue to leave.

"Gah, thank you. Would you mind taking a picture with me too?" she squeals.

"Sure," I grimace but get up for the photo.

She leans in too close to me to take a selfie. Giving my biceps a squeeze, she gushes "Thank you" and then walks away.

Sut bursts out laughing, "Seriously. I think she would've humped your leg if you let her. Does this happen all the time when you're out here?"

"It happens more here than back home. People respect me from back home because they know me there. Here it's like I'm more of a celebrity. I don't mind it, but I don't love it either," I shrug.

We finish eating our dinner and I notice Sut's a little buzzed, giggling more and more and being a little more touchy feely than she normally is. I don't see her drunk very often because I don't drink during training season, and she usually doesn't drink in general.

I think she might be stress drinking a little bit, after seeing that we'll be sharing a bed this weekend.

After dinner we decide to walk back to the hotel. It's a nice, warm night out. The sidewalk is busy, so many people carrying on conversations, drunken stumbling, and music blaring from clubs into the street.

Sutton loops her arm through mine and rests her head on my shoulder, as we weave in and out of people.

"I've always wanted to see the Music Fountain of Wynn," she sighs softly.

"Okay, so let's go," I twist us back around the other direction.

"Wait, are you sure? Don't you have to get up early?" she asks with the biggest grin on her face.

"Yes, baby girl, but it's not too late yet, let's go," I continue to nudge her in the direction of the fountain.

Her eyes light up at me and she smiles a wistful smile. I love this softer side of her. Sutton rarely lets her guard down enough for anyone to see it.

We get to the Music Fountain and she squeals.

"Be Our Guest" from Beauty and The Beast is playing, and the fountain moves with the melody, lights flickering through the water.

Grabbing Sutton, twirling her around, I tug her close to me and dance with her, wrapping one arm around her waist, keeping our hands locked in the other, holding her close to me, every inch of her warm skin kisses mine, lighting it on fire.

I spin her out again and then pull her back to me and dip her backwards.

"This is so perfect! I'm like Belle, since I love to read, and you're the Beast, since you love to fight," she smiles so wide.

Sutton lets out the most beautiful giggle, cheeks warm and glowing from the night air and the alcohol running through her bloodstream.

Gods she's radiant.

"You're so fuckin beautiful, Sut," I exclaim on a rasp.

Her eyes go wide, skin flushing a deeper shade of pink.

"You aren't so bad yourself, Scrap," she beams up at me.

Throwing caution to the wind.

"Fuck it," I growl and with my hand behind her head, I pull her up to me and kiss her softly at first.

Sutton tenses for just a second before she kisses me back.

Everything around me stops.

There is only Sutton and me. Kissing outside in the

middle of Vegas.

The rest of the world is a complete blur. There are no lights. There is no music. There are no other people dancing or mingling around us. Only the feel of her soft lips on mine.

She lets out the most delicious groan when I tug her lower lip between my teeth and bite down.

Letting me in, pushing my tongue through her lips and twirling it with hers, deepening this kiss.

She mewls in my mouth, and I kiss her even harder.

Showing Sutton every feeling I've held back from her with this kiss. That I want more. That I need more. That I don't just want to be friends anymore. That I own her. That she's mine. And I'm hers. That it's always been her.

Someone wolf whistles in the background.

We pull apart and just stare in awe at each other. Her cheeks are beautifully flushed, eyes glazed over.

She's mine now. I just hope she's ready.

We walk back to our hotel, hand in hand.

She keeps taking small glances at me, and her cheeks turn the faintest hue of pink every time I catch her doing it. She nibbles her bottom lip.

"Keep my lip out of your mouth before I bite it myself," I growl at her.

"Yes sir," she giggles, but stops chewing on her lips.

I groan. She fuckin obeyed me.

Her eyes go wide, "You... you like that? Don't you?" she stutters.

"Like what, Sut?" I grin.

"You..um.." she pushes her hair behind her ear, "You, um, like to be called Sir?"

"Was that a question or a statement?" I ask grinning at her again.

"Both?" she chirps.

"I do," I say matter of fact.

*W*e're the only two on the elevator as we head up to our room. The air is thick with whatever just happened back there. I stare at Sutton, willing to her to meet my eyes. But she continues to stare at the ground.

But I can smell her arousal from here. I know she felt it too. And I know she wants me as bad as I want her.

I take a deep inhale and her eyes shoot up to me.

She nibbles on her bottom lip again.

"What did I say about that lip?" I growl.

"So—sorry..." she stutters.

"Sorry what?" I growl and smirk.

Eyes wide, she looks in both of my eyes, "Sorry, Sir," she squeaks out.

"Good girl," I growl.

Her eyes are saucers, her cheeks flush instantly, her breaths coming more rapidly.

"You like that?" I smirk.

"I..um..think so..Sir.." she whispers and I notice her rubbing her thighs together.

The elevator door opens with a ding, and Sutton jumps.

I grab her hand and pull her toward the door.

Scanning the key, I pull her into the room.

The second the door is closed I'm pushing her up against it.

She lets out a little whimper.

"Here's the thing baby girl. I have wanted you for years. I want to make you mine. Want to take my time with you. Want to devour every inch of that porcelain skin. Mark it as mine. Want to trace every single one of those tattoos with my tongue. Want to taste every inch of you. But you were drinking tonight, and I need to know you want this as much as I do. I need complete control and consent when I fuck what's mine."

Sutton lets out another whimper, eyes staring directly into mine, pupils blown with heat.

"So, you are going to be a good girl and listen to me tonight. I want you to take off this delectable dress, get into your pajamas, drink a glass of water, and take an aspirin. Then you are going to get into that bed and let me hold you tonight and kiss you some more, and then we are going to go to sleep."

She groans but then nods her head.

"I need your words, baby," I growl.

"Yes sir," she smiles softly at me.

"Tomorrow, you are going to stay sober. After my fight, you and this gorgeous body are going to be what I earn for my winning victory!" I growl.

"Yes sir," she smirks at me and pulls me down to kiss her.

I deepen the kiss with my hand in her hair, tugging

slightly for a better angle.

The moans that escape from her throat! "Okay baby girl, I need a minute," I groan and pull away, adjusting myself.

When she turns to rush to the bathroom, I give her ass a little swat.

She lets out the cutest squeak.

*I'*m sitting up in bed with the lamp on. There's a soft glow in the room. The covers are pulled up to my waist, but my chest is bare. Sutton comes out of the bathroom, hair in a bun, fresh faced in the tiniest little shorts and tank top.

I groan, while she lets out a little "O" sound.

"I'm sorry. I thought I'd have my own room. This is what I normally sleep in," she says blushing, looking down at the ground.

"Get over here Sut. Stop apologizing. You're perfect!" I rasp.

She hops in the bed, literally hops, and climbs under the sheets.

Pulling her down to lie flat, she lets out a giggle before I'm on her, kissing her and licking her bottom lip.

Sutton moans and grinds herself against me.

I grab her hip hard to stop her, "Not tonight Sut."

She pouts, and I bite her bottom lip and suck it into my

mouth.

I roll back over and shut out the light.

"Come here," I growl and pull her to me.

Sutton nestles into my side and puts her head on my chest and her arm across my stomach. I tilt my head into her hair, so I can smell her signature vanilla and coconut scent. I inhale softly and kiss her forehead.

She traces her fingertips in circles over my stomach.

I stop her hand, intertwining my fingers with hers.

She lets out a little contented sigh and melts deeper into my side.

Her breaths come softly now, and sleep pulls me under not long after.

"No, please stop, no..." Sutton whimpers in her sleep, as she tosses and turns.

I jump up, "Sut..Babe... wake up..." I try to shake her gently, running my fingers over her cheeks.

She continues to toss and turn whimpering next to me. She must be having a bad nightmare.

I turn the light on, "Sutton, baby girl, wake up!"

She gasps and sits up. She's trembling, skin ashen, eyes wide.

"Hey, come here, you're okay; it was just a bad dream," I pull her toward me and rub small circles on her back.

"Are you okay?" I whisper to her and kiss her forehead.

"Yeah..." she whispers and burrows deeper into my side.

"Do you want to talk about it?" I ask softly, holding her close to me.

"No, it's okay, you have to get up early, let's just go back to sleep," she whispers and buries her face in my chest.

I reach over and shut out the light; running my fingers through her hair until her breathing steadies again and then I fall into a restless sleep, wondering what has my girl so rattled in her sleep.

23

August

It's six thirty on Saturday. The door of WaggingWithWords is locked, the lights are dimmed and there isn't a soul anywhere to be found.

Knocking on the door, there's no answer.

Taking a seat on the ground, going over what I rehearsed in my head to grovel to Sutton for fucking up so bad.

I hoped to be able to clear the air before the show but guess not.

I've been in my head all week about how much of a dick I was. She was so angry and had every right to be. There was no worse way to react than how I did, blaming her, when it was my fault for being so fuckin consumed by her.

Quinn finally appears, opening the doors at seven on the dot, but Sutton is nowhere to be found.

"Where's Sutton?" I inquire desperately, leaping up from the ground.

"Not here. Where's the rest of your band?" she asks

coldly.

"They should be on the way. I came early, hoping to talk to her. Please let me talk to her! I know I fucked up. I want to make it right. I don't know how to do this. But I want to try for her," I answer pulling at my hair.

Quinn looks away from me, giving me the cold shoulder, "It might be too late."

"What the fuck do you mean?" I growl.

Taking a step closer towards her.

"First off, don't you dare get loud with me! I will snap you in half. Second, she's in Vegas," Quinn responds giving me a smug smile, like there's more she's just not telling me.

"With who?"

"A friend." Quinn looks guilty and I'm trying to figure out why.

"A friend?" Then it dawns on me. And I know exactly which friend she is talking about.

"No... Fuck... She's with him, isn't she? That bouncer guy? Her *friend*!" Agony laces my voice, my blood running cold.

I can literally feel my heart shattering.

Fuck. I really fucked up this time.

"What are they doing in Vegas?" I barely croak out.

"Beck's kind of a big deal," Quinn simpers and shrugs. "He's an MMA fighter. He just does the bouncer thing on the side to help us out."

I'm frozen. An MMA fighter? I have no chance.

Quinn continues to scold me, getting me out of my head, "Listen August, you really fucked up. You made her feel like it was all her fault, when you," she points at me, "Forgot the condom. So, take my advice and give her some space," Quinn advises spinning around and walking further into the café to set up for the show.

"Space for what? For her to run into his arms? Fuck. That," I growl, following after her.

Quinn stops and I almost walk right into her.

Spinning around facing me, she glares daggers at me, "August, honey, I'm gonna be real with you for a minute. Are you listening?" she almost sneers.

When I nod my head yes, she goes on, forcing me to keep eye contact with her.

Shit. For being so tiny, she's fuckin scary.

"Sut has feelings for you. Loves your music and what it portrays, which is obviously a huge part of you. So, I don't want to say you don't have a chance. Your music has brought out a different side of her that I've never seen before. She's more open than she's ever been in all the years I've known her," Quinn softens slightly.

Getting fierce again, "But that girl has had some shit happen to her, trusting people and letting them in is so difficult for her. And you fucked up when you freaked out. You made her feel like every other guy in her past has."

I go to tell her how sorry I am, but she holds her finger up to my mouth to silence me.

"I've also watched her love our best friend for years. And Ash and I are pretty sure Beck is in love with her too. They've always just been too chicken shit to do anything about it. Neither of them wanted to ruin their friendship. But if you become competition, he may not be afraid anymore because if you steal his best friend, he ultimately loses her anyways, and let's be honest, Beck loves a good competition and he hates losing," she grins smugly.

"So, what, they just went to Vegas together?" I ask so quietly I'm not even sure if she hears me.

"Yeah August. They went together. Alone," Quinn replies, but with a little less bite.

"I'm not saying this to be a bitch, August. I see the way you look at her, and honestly, I'd be happy for her if she ended up with either of you. She deserves to be so happy. But you need to do better. If you're serious about her, you need to try harder. Sutton may appear to be tough on the outside, but she has the heart of a hopeless romantic, and she deserves that kind of love, because she has that kind of love to give," Quinn says with so much conviction.

I appreciate her honesty and how fiercely protective she is of Sutton.

After staring at her for a beat, I just nod my head.

Lost in my head at the thought that Sutton's with Beck. In Vegas. Alone.

As Quinn goes to walk away, done with our conversation, "I do. Care about her, you know. I just. I don't know how to do this right," I say defeated, raking my hands through my hair again.

She turns back toward me, eyes softening, "None of us do. But you have to try, if she really means something to you. She's worth it. Sut would burn the world down for the people she loves."

"I'd burn, if it meant she'd ever love me," I whisper.

Quinn's eyes go a little wide and she gives me a soft smile as she walks away

*W*hen the guys show up, we immediately set up the stage.

Quinn was a little less cold after our conversation and made sure we were all set for the show.

We're the only band performing tonight, so we play a few extra songs.

The crowd cheers and asks for an encore.

"This is something I put together this week for an incredibly special girl. Let me know what you think," I tell the crowd before starting to sing the song that I wrote the second I got home, after I left Sutton's place the other day.

Ty strums on the guitar, as I sing about begging for forgiveness and doing everything I can to make up for my mistakes.

Beau and Knox just sit on the edge of the stage, having people wave their arms in the air. It's mainly just an acoustic version right now. We haven't added in the drums or bass yet because it isn't quite finished.

With the smallest grin on her face, Quinn stands off to the side watching me.

I wink at her, and she nods her head, like maybe I have her approval.

*Q*uinn walks up to us when we're packing up our equipment and hands over the biggest stack of cash that we've ever gotten.

"Um... this seems like too much," I side eye her.

It's just you guys tonight. I'm tired and don't feel like doing math. I'm closing up early, so you can just keep it all. Sut won't care," she smiles at me.

"Thank you!" I smile back.

Knox walks up to Quinn and throws his arm around her shoulders. "You want company tonight, Blondie?" I hear him ask.

She chuckles, "By company do you mean someone to veg on the couch and watch true crime with or a groupie lay?"

Knox pulls her closer to him and winks at me, "As long as you don't plot my murder, while watching true crime, I'm in on the true crime, unless you are up for a lay," he wiggles his brows at her.

She slugs him in the chest, "I am not up for your shit tonight, Knox, but if you can behave like a decent human being, I'll let you in on the true crime fun. Let me text Sut and make sure she doesn't care that you stay at her place."

The mention of her name already has me reeling. I need to talk to her, but I'm not even sure she'd hear me out right now.

A moment later Quinn bursts out laughing reading a text from Sutton. "She says it's fine as long as we stay out of her bed."

"So, the kitchen counter it is then. You'll have three beasts for company tonight baby," Knox whispers not so quietly in Quinn's ear.

She huffs a laugh, shaking her head at his outrageousness.

"She responded quick. She must not be having a good

time," I smirk.

"She worries about her baby. She makes sure her phone is always on when she's away from him. She would lose her mind if something happened to Khaos. Don't get your hopes up lover boy," she says side eyeing me.

"Can you let her know I want to talk to her, please?" I pout at Quinn before walking to the door.

"No, August. She needs to figure out what she wants and what she needs. This might be their only chance to figure it out. You can try to talk to her when she gets back, but make sure you know what you're doing," she sighs.

Quinn walks me and the guys to the door.

When we get outside, there is a man in a blazer and dark jeans right outside the door standing off to the side. When he notices me, he hands me an invitation.

"What's this?" I ask him curiously.

The guys hover over my shoulder as I open it.

"It's an invitation to perform at The Wicked Tour in a couple months. I've been scouting out places, trying to find a few unlabeled bands to give them a shot. You need a 30-45 minute set. It seems like that shouldn't be a problem, after seeing you perform tonight. What do you say?" the man asks.

Silence.

And then loud whoops.

Grinning so hard, "Fuck yeah!" We scream in unison.

"Look forward to seeing your set," the man responds, shaking my hand.

"Thank you so much!" We all say.

Quinn squeals and jumps on Knox's back.

My mind immediately goes to Sutton. I wish she was

here!

"Can you let me tell Sutton, please?" I beg Quinn before heading out.

"Sure, I'm happy for you guys!" she smiles.

Knox stays back with Quinn hanging on his back, arms wrapped around his neck and her head resting on top of his.

He's like a whole foot taller than her, so it's funny to see her so high off the ground. She pretends to choke him out and cackles loudly.

"Why are you so abusive, Blondie?" he groans.

"Quit calling me that," she tugs his hair and he shuts the door.

Knox helps Quinn lock up for the night and she lifts her hand to wave. I watch her shut the lights out, and I hop in the car with the guys.

Before we pull away, I watch as Knox starts to climb up the stairs, flipping Quinn over his shoulder like a caveman. She slaps him on the ass, and I watch her face as she laughs hysterically.

All I can think is that should be me climbing up those stairs with my Sunshine, as we pull away from the curb.

24

Sutton

Quinn: So, August was here before the show. I told him I wouldn't tell you so he could figure out how to grovel properly.

Sutton: I don't care.

Quinn: Yes, you do. I think he cares about you in his own way.

Sutton: What if that's not enough? What if I'm just a muse?

Quinn: I can't answer that, but I don't think you're just a muse, Sut.

Sutton: Me and Beck kissed last night… more than once…

Quinn: UMM WHATTT?! Did you bang?

Sutton: Do people still say bang?

Quinn: Frolic in the sheets?

Quinn: Shag?

Sutton: LOL. No. I had been drinking. He said he didn't want me drinking for our first time.

Quinn: ......

*W*aking up the next morning, my eyes flutter open, rolling over to an empty bed and cool sheets.

My chest aches with disappointment. Was I dreaming? Did Beck actually kiss me?

Ugh, I definitely had a nightmare about that horrible night. How embarrassing!

Rolling over to check my phone, there are a few texts from Quinn about her night with Knox, where they thankfully did not christen my counter, but did fall asleep cuddled up together on the couch.

Heading to the bathroom to take a much-needed long shower.

On the mirror is a note taped that says:

I had to get up early for training this morning. I'll be at the gym most of the day. There is a ticket for you at the main entrance and someone will let you in backstage after so I can see you. Be a good girl and eat and drink this.

And be ready for me tonight! XO, Beck.

Be ready for him tonight?

I've been ready. I can only hope he means having hot, mind-blowing sex with him. Kissing him wasn't enough. Gods those five words have heat burning low in my belly.

Looking down at the counter there is a bottle of water, an ibuprofen, toast, and fruit.

Smirking to myself, but obeying his demands, I eat and drink what he left me.

Then taking the note off the mirror, smiling softly at it,

I place it in my favorite book I packed to read on the plane.

Since there is some time to kill and I've never been to Vegas, a shopping excursion seems like a no brainer.

There's a lingerie shop up the road, and since I didn't pack much for this trip with it being so last minute, I decide to try and find something nice to wear for Beck tonight.

Walking back to the hotel, a storefront window that is filled with leather and lace catches my attention. Walking through the door, I'm immediately hit with the smell of leather infiltrating my senses.

Looking around taking everything in, I am literally obsessed! With everything!

Spending way too much time trying on outfit after outfit. Loving the feel of the leather mixed with the delicate lace on my skin. My body is on fire, heating with need, with each piece that caresses my skin. Imagining his eyes taking in every inch of me. Each piece edgy, but sexy.

Taking my stack of clothes up to the store clerk. I realize I probably won't be able to fit all of this in my suitcase, but it's completely worth the risk.

After grabbing a small bite to eat, I head back to the hotel to freshen up and change for Beck's fight.

*A*rriving at the arena an hour later, I grab my ticket from will call. I head directly to the suite where I'm supposed to be sitting.

Feeling a bit out of my comfort zone, it's incredibly loud in here and packed with people. There are strobe lights flickering around the room, with the octagon in the dead center.

A jumbotron sits directly above the ring, ever changing with the fighters and their rankings listed.

The energy in the room is electric, palpable. Buzzing with excitement.

Sitting in my seat, anxiously chewing on my nails.

I'm not sure if I'm more nervous about Beck's fight or what comes after.

Quinn and I have talked in depth about finally taking the leap and seeing if the chemistry between Beck and I is really there. The tension certainly is. That kiss last night was scorching!

It was like he was demanding me to give myself over to him without directly asking.

I never thought I'd like something like that, giving up control, but with him, it felt right.

My biggest worry though is we can't go back.

If things don't work out, we can't hit rewind.

Our friendship could be over.

The announcers' voice draws me out of my head, "Ladies and gentlemen...Fighting in our Heavyweight Division tonight is reigning champion, Beckett Scott, facing Atlas Gorgiev in a hard-hitting affair.

A video starts playing on the jumbotron, Gorgiev is walking through a hallway and *Get Low* by Lil Jon & The East Side Boyz is playing.

Flashbacks of Beck's underground fights run through

my head as this massive, terrifying looking man enters the octagon. Reminding me of the last guy I watched him fight, all those years ago. Ready to crawl out of my skin with anxiety, envisioning him coming after my best friend.

Hoping that tonight may finally be our moment. An almost rewrite of that night has my mind wandering to how that fight ended, with one of the best kisses of my life, a promise for more, quickly snuffed out by the cops showing up.

People are yelling and whistling, making the room feel like a live wire around me; breaking me out of my memories of the past, when a video starts up of Beck walking through a hallway with Eminem's *Lose Yourself* playing.

The announcer starts talking about how Beck's been the champion for a couple years and is here to hold his title.

People are screaming, clapping, and whistling so loud, but my heart is beating wildly in my chest at my best friend looking fine as hell in his video, wearing the hell out of a navy pin stripe suit tailored perfectly to his body with sunglasses on his gorgeous face.

My heart completely stops when Beck enters the octagon in tight little blue shorts and no shirt. Drooling over every inch of defined, exposed muscle on his delectable body; envisioning running my tongue through the ridges later.

My mind is made up. I'm ready for it! I'm going to cross that line with my best friend.

When Beck reaches his corner, his camp immediately starts taking care of wrapping his hands up.

"Ladies and Gentlemen, this is the main event of the evening," says the announcer.

The referee comes to the center and explains the rules.

He confirms that they understand, both nodding. The fighters return to their respective corners.

The ref asks if they are ready, looking at each opponent for confirmation.

Both fighters take their fighting stance. They touch gloves.

I notice Gorg, whatever his name is, growls at Beck, but Beck remains expressionless.

Beck still demands the attention of the room, even in his stoicism. Just like he always did during his underground fights.

"Let's go!" he yells and steps out of the center of the ring.

They bounce around each other a bit, sizing each other up.

Atlas throws a punch and Beck dodges it.

I'm on the edge of my seat, adrenaline coursing through my veins, my knee bouncing with anticipation, so focused on every move Beck makes.

My eyes never leave him. My heart pounding so hard I feel it in my ears.

Beck kicks Atlas in the shin and Atlas jumps back.

Atlas goes to throw a punch and I duck and squeak.

Flinching at every punch Atlas tries to land.

Beck quickly dodges and counter strikes with a left hook that lands perfectly on Atlas's jaw and knocks him to the ground.

Immediately on my feet, standing. Holding my breath. Fist to my mouth. Watching the sheen of sweat coating Beck's skin.

Beck quickly goes to finish the job with two punches to

the face before the referee comes over and breaks up the fight and calls the knock out.

Winner Beckett Scott!

The crowd goes insane! My jaw is dropped. Eyes wide. It takes a minute to register that it's over already.

And then I am screaming my head off! Tears running down my cheeks.

Looking down to the ring, when I feel eyes on me, and Beck is staring straight at me with the biggest smile on his face.

He is incredible! A beast! My beast! I smile back, just as big.

Before I can blink, I'm up and running to get backstage.

The second I spot Beck, walking in from the octagon, I'm launching myself at him. Catching me in the air, as if I weigh nothing; I wrap my legs around him, grab his face, and kiss him with every ounce of adrenaline coursing through my body.

"You were fucking amazing!" I squeal, pulling back with his cheeks still between my hands.

"This seems like déjà vu," he smiles softly at me.

I let out a soft breath, "You did remember."

"I never forgot, baby girl," he groans, nuzzling into my neck.

"That knock out seemed way faster than your college days," I giggle.

"What can I say, I was motivated," he smirks.

"Oh yeah?" I smirk back.

"Yeah, I wanted as much time with my girl as I could get. I have to do a quick interview and then we can head out. You look fuckin amazing by the way! I want to peel every inch of that leather off your body later," he kisses my forehead and puts me down.

Making me instantly blush at his comment.

The announcer comes in "That was incredible! Scott, how does it feel?"

"It felt amazing! I felt motivated as soon as I stepped into the ring," he replies never losing eye contact with me.

"Ah, I see," the announcer looks at me and then back to Beck and smirks, then he pats him on the back, "You go enjoy that victory, man!"

Scooping up my girl, her legs naturally wrap around my waist, so I can carry her outside.

There is a car waiting for us when we step out; there was no way in hell I was wasting a single second tonight.

From now until we leave for the airport, I don't expect to leave our bed.

Placing Sutton into the backseat of the car, I immediately climb in next to her and pull her to straddle my lap, where she fits fuckin perfectly.

Running my hands through her hair, pulling her to me, I slam my lips down on hers, claiming her mouth. Claiming her little noises. Claiming her.

"Mine!" I claim.

I feel her smile against my lips, while she grinds on my hard cock that's straining against the tight fabric of my compression shorts.

Tracing the flower petals in her tattoo with my tongue, as her shirt slips off her shoulder.

Sutton gasps and groans.

"You like that baby girl?" I tease.

"I like your hands and mouth on me, Scrap," she rasps.

I groan. I can't keep my hands or mouth off her. She feels so fuckin good.

The second we pull up to the hotel, I'm hauling her over my shoulder and running to the elevator.

She's giggling so hard, out of breath, flushed and so fuckin beautiful.

The elevator door opens and thank fuck it's empty.

Hitting the button to our floor, the second the doors close I'm on Sutton. Prowling toward her, scooping her up under those thick thighs. She wraps them around my waist, rubbing her warm core against my straining hard on.

Slamming her against the wall, Sutton grinds against me as I lick the seam of her lips. She opens for me, and I twirl my tongue with hers. Her hands are in my hair, tugging at the ends. My hands are up her shirt, digging my fingers into her soft skin. Pulling away from her lips, I leave open mouthed kisses down her neck to her collarbone.

Both of us are panting. The temperature in the elevator feels like it's 100 degrees.

When I nip her just under her ear, Sutton yelps at the same time the elevator door opens.

Carrying her to our door, I'm not sure who's heart is racing harder, hers or mine.

Pulling the key out of my pocket, Sutton scans it without ever getting down.

Walking into the room, never putting her down, I kick the door shut, and then I'm pushing her back against the door with her legs still wrapped around me. I can't get enough of her.

Kissing down her neck, pulling her shirt over her head while holding her up against the door with my pelvis. I continue down her sternum tattoo and flick my tongue over the tattoos under her tits. Something I've been dying to do for years.

"Beck, wait," she stutters catching her breath.

"I have waited! Five. Fucking. Years. Sut," I moan with my forehead pressed against hers.

I go to kiss her again. "Please just give me a minute," she whimpers.

I set her down. "This is about him, isn't it?" I growl.

"Who? What are you talking about?" Sutton asks completely caught off guard.

"The musician that you can't keep your fucking eyes off of," I snarl.

"Wait. What? What does he have to do with anything?" She asks confused.

"Ha. You're stopping me because of August. Because you want him. But I want you!" I respond with so much conviction.

Sutton puts her small hand on my chest. "Beck, I have always wanted you. Since the night I got snowed in at your apartment. Since I kissed you at your fight. But you haven't wanted me until now! You pretended like that kiss never happened. So, why? Why now? I just need to know before we ruin everything," she says with tears in her eyes.

"Because you're mine. You've always been mine. He can't have you!" I protest.

"So, this is a pissing contest? You're trying to claim me because you're threatened? Are you fucking kidding me?" Sutton yells, shoving me and going to grab her suitcase.

"Sut. No. Please stop! I'm fucking this up. Please let me

explain!" I beg her.

"Forget it! I'm catching a red eye back. I'm so happy for you, that you won," she angrily says and goes to grab the doorknob pulling her suitcase behind her.

I stop her from opening the door with my hand against it.

"Quit fucking running, Sutton," I growl.

She growls back, staring straight at the door, not wanting me to see the tears that are about to start crashing down, "I'm not running, I just won't be treated like a piece of property."

"Sut, look at me. It's been you. It's always been you. I just didn't want to ruin our friendship. You are too precious to me. You haven't been with anyone since I've known you. I've always thought... always hoped... well I don't know what I thought," I sigh defeated.

"You thought I was just what? Ha, waiting for you? For years?" she responds exasperated, with hurt in her eyes.

"Sut... no... I just maybe hoped that you were," I say sheepishly.

"Hoped, that I was? But you took this long to decide to choose me? Seriously?" she pulls at her hair.

Something like rage fills her eyes, "Someone fucking hurt me, Beck. Not long before I met you. Someone disrespected me. Took from me what wasn't theirs to take. Ripped my fucking soul out of my body and just left me there to pick up all of the broken fuckin pieces. I met you at a time when I wasn't ready to be with anyone. When I was still trying to heal myself. I figured you and Quinn would be together, and we would just be friends, but then time went on and you guys just stayed friends too. The more time I spent with you, the safer I felt. I started to trust you, and I don't trust people. You became someone I could rely on. Someone I didn't think would destroy me. I couldn't stand the thought of someone even touching me until that day I thought you were hurt in your fight and my instincts had me charging you to kiss you. That was the first day in years I felt like maybe there was a light at the end of my darkness. Like maybe I could just be again. But then the cops were there, and we never talked about it again, so I just let it go. Figured you didn't feel the same, and I wasn't going to ruin our friendship over a kiss. But while I have loved you from a distance, I have still been guarding my heart. So, if you really have been hoping that I've just been waiting for you for five years, do you really even know me at all? You haven't ever said anything, but you decided all of a sudden you want more? How am I supposed to trust that this is even real?" she rambles, tears running down her face now.

"It is real for me, Sut. It's always been real. I promise! I would rather have each of my fingernails ripped off one by one, than ever lose you. I wasn't sure how to move forward. Wasn't sure if you felt the same," I declare, running my thumb over her cheek to wipe her tears away.

"That's a disturbing image. Thanks for that," she chuckles, shaking her head.

Holding her hands in mine, staring into those beautiful green eyes, heart on my sleeve, "I don't ever want to lose you, Sut. But the more I've thought about it, that more I realized it could happen eventually though. Either because it's too late and you've fallen for someone else, and I was too chicken shit to admit that I've been in love with you, or because I would tell you I had feelings for you, and you wouldn't reciprocate them. Either way our friendship wouldn't be the same. It may seem like it's out of jealousy; and maybe it took seeing you look at someone else to realize it, but I want you, Sut, so I just had to tell you before it's too late, in case choosing me is an option."

"You've never been just an option, Beck. You've always been the only choice," she confirms, putting her bag down.

"Yeah?" I growl, "You mean it?"

"I mean it," she whispers before I pull her face to mine and slam my lips down over hers.

Sutton's lips are so soft and warm. She moans into the kiss, and I deepen it. Licking her bottom lip; she opens up for me, letting me dive my tongue in and swirl it with hers.

When she pulls away, I kiss down her neck.

She bites my ear lobe and I growl.

"Are you ready to be my good girl?" I ask with a smirk.

Sutton pauses for a second, but then smirks back, "Yes sir."

"I want to take this slow, Sut. As much as I want you, as you can probably already tell, I need to be in full control. I will never do anything you aren't okay with. I don't want to move too fast or push you. I don't want to hurt you or scare you. Just know that everything is for your pleasure, but I will be controlling every second of it," I explain, rubbing her cheek.

"Okay," she breathes out.

"One more thing, Sut," I murmur, grabbing her chin and tilting her head up so that our eyes meet, "If anything gets to be too much, just say, "Jade" and everything stops. No questions asked. Everything stops. Okay, baby?" I detail for her.

She blushes, "Jade, got it... Sir...."

"Now, strip for me," I demand.

"There's no music," Sut complains.

"I said strip, Sut. Don't make me ask twice," I growl.

Pupils blown wide, "Yes sir," she obeys.

Never breaking eye contact with me, biting her lower lip, Sutton kicks her shoes off first, then tucks her thumbs in the waist band of her skintight leather pants, and achingly slowly shimmies them down her hips, over those thick thighs.

Shaking my head grinning at her, biting my own lip at how fuckin gorgeous she is.

Porcelain skin wrapped in the sexiest little red lace bra and panty set; little studs on it just between her tits and just above her pussy. It's so perfectly her and so fuckin hot!

Biting down on my knuckles, I groan, "You are a Goddess, baby girl! Do a little twirl for me."

With the shyest smile on those sweet lips, Sutton turns around, seductively moving her hips side to side like she's swaying to a melody in her head.

She turns back toward me and meets my eyes. Waiting for my next command. *Good girl.*

Grinning at her, as if challenging her, "Now crawl to me."

She hesitates, cheeks turning red from my command. She stands staring at me for what feels like forever. Pupils blown, her beautiful face flashes with so many emotions, at war over that one statement. I can't tell if she's turned on, or if I'm already pushing her too far. But then she shocks the hell out of me and drops to her knees.

And damn does she look fuckin beautiful crawling toward me.

Sitting on the edge of the bed with my legs wide, waiting for her. My eyes follow every sway of her delectable hips, the arch in her back, tits tipping out beautifully over that bra. Chin held high; she never breaks eye contact with me.

Panting, with desire in her eyes by the time she reaches me and sits on her knees between my legs.

"Good girl," I stroke her cheek with my thumb. She leans into my touch and lets out a little whimper.

"Now lay over my lap, with that perfect ass in the air," I order.

Getting up off her knees, she lays across my lap. Turning to look over her shoulder at me, I nudge her, to push her head back down.

"Stay still or I'll make it hurt worse," I grind out.

"Yes sir," she whispers.

Running my hand down her spine, grabbing her ass cheek firmly, squeezing and kneading it, I give her one slap.

She gasps out but doesn't move.

"Good girl, not moving like I asked," rubbing her ass where I just slapped it, soothing the sting.

Using one hand to stroke her back, as my other hand goes to her other ass cheek. Groping it, massaging it and taking a fuckin bite out of that little peach tattoo. Smacking that cheek, she flinches slightly, but lets out a groan.

"I've been wanting to bite that little peach since I saw it poking out from under my bed sheets that night you got snowed in at my place," I growl.

I notice she's subtly moving her thighs together, "Is my girl wet for me?"

Her back arches when I smack her ass cheek again.

That perfect ass is turning the prettiest shade of pink though.

After rubbing smoothing circles on her ass, my fingers make their way to her damp panties. The second I feel her slick heat, I groan, "You are wet for me, baby girl."

She moans but tries to hold still like the good girl she is.

Pulling her panties down her legs and tossing them aside, I run a finger through her slick folds. "Gods, you're soaked," I groan.

"Please, sir. Please touch me," she begs.

"Fuck, baby girl, do you know what that does to me? To hear you say that?" I tap her back, "Get up, baby."

Taking off my shoes, shirt, and shorts; leaving just my boxer briefs on, I lie back on the bed.

"Bra off, baby," I rasp.

Unhooking her bra and tossing it aside; those beautiful eyes are tracing heat over every inch of my body. When they reach my cock, her tongue darts out and she bites her lip, seeing just how hard I am for her through my briefs.

"Now come sit on my face so I can make you cum," I demand.

She startles, "I'm sorry, you want me to what?"

"What did I say about having to ask twice?" I growl again.

Pushing her hair behind her ear, she looks down at the ground, "Umm... what if... I don't want... I'm heavy... I don't want to suffocate you...Sir..."

"Sutton, if you don't get that sweet ass over here in three seconds and sit on my fuckin face, I am going to punish you by not allowing you to orgasm at all tonight. If I die by suffocation from that pussy, I will die the happiest man. Now. Sit. On. My. Fuckin. Face." I order.

"Yes sir," she squeaks out, crawling up the bed and hovering over my mouth.

"I said sit," snarling, pulling her down closer to me.

Fuckin finally that precious pussy is on my lips and fuckkkk does she taste divine.

"You taste like fuckin heaven, baby" I rasp in between flicking my tongue over her clit and diving deep into her folds with my tongue, spearing her.

She's dripping down my face and making the most beautiful sounds.

"Yes. Sir, please. Don't stop," Sutton moans, writhing on my face.

"I could never," I groan as I continue to devour her sweet pussy.

Sliding one finger, then two into her, rubbing her g-spot as I continue to suck her clit into my mouth.

"Cum for me," I demand, as I graze my teeth over it, she clenches hard as her orgasm barrels through her and she cums all over my face.

"Oh, Gods," she cries out, legs trembling as she falls forward toward the headboard panting.

"You good baby girl?" I ask, sliding her down my body.

"Perfect, sir," she whispers, as she grinds her hot center against my thick length, feeling the heat of her through my briefs.

Pulling her face to me, kissing her deeply as she comes down from her orgasm.

Gripping her hip hard, halting her movements. "I'm gonna need you to stop that baby girl or I'm going to cum in my briefs," I groan.

Sutton giggles, and I smack her ass. She groans and deepens our kiss.

"Do you like when I spank you?" I smirk at her.

"Yes... Sir..." she blushes.

"You're beautiful, Sut," I whisper and kiss her again.

Her small fingers reach for the waistband of my briefs to pull them down; grabbing her hand and stopping her, "Are you sure, Sut? I promised we could go slow."

She nods at me.

"I need your words, baby girl," I say firmly.

"Yes, Scrap. I'm sure," she whispers, glassy eyes staring at me.

"Be a good girl and get up on all fours for me," I order.

"Mmm my girl got her cum all over me" I groan, standing up and pushing my briefs down.

Watching me over her shoulder with so much heat in her eyes.

"Like what you see?" I question.

Grabbing a condom from my bag, I stroke myself a couple times.

"Mmhm," Sutton licks her lips and moans.

Her eyes never leave mine, watching me so intently, as I put the condom on and step behind her.

"Are you ready for me?" I rasp.

"Yes sir," she answers me.

Slowly pushing into her an inch at a time until I'm seated in as deep as I can go.

We both let out a deep moan, when I start thrusting in and out of her, slow at first.

"Harder, please Sir," Sutton moans.

Wrapping her hair in my fist, tugging her up toward me; I thrust in deeper and harder. Kissing down her neck with her hair fisted in my hand. Running my tongue over the flower at the nape of her neck, trailing my tongue down to her shoulder, tracing every tattoo I can reach. Gods she tastes and smells divine!

"Touch yourself baby girl," I rasp in her ear, biting her lobe.

Running one hand down her chest, tweaking her nipples and then down her soft belly until she gets to her clit and starts rubbing that little nub. Her other arm comes back and wraps around the back of my neck, her fingers running through the hair at my nape.

"Yes, just like that," I whisper, panting in her ear. Watching as goosebumps pebble down her neck.

Every so often I feel her soft finger tips that are rubbing her clit graze my cock while I thrust in and out of her. It feels incredible.

As I feel her start to clench around me, "That's it baby, be a good girl and cum on my cock," I moan, sucking on her neck hard and tugging her hair back harder.

"Oh my Gods!" she screams, orgasm slamming through her, core clenching so hard, as she cums on my cock, causing my orgasm to come barreling through me.

Releasing her hair, peppering kisses down her neck and shoulder, I slowly pull out of her. Pulling the condom off, tying it off, and tossing it in the garbage.

Scooping up her limp body into my arms, she gives me the sweetest blissed out smile.

I carry her into the bathroom and place her on the counter, turning the hot water on in the shower. Pulling her face to me, kissing her deeply. She mewls into my mouth and puts her arms around my neck.

Pulling back, I press a kiss to her forehead and just breathe her in.

Carrying her into the shower, holding her under the

spray, kissing her again.

I can't get enough of her!

"I love these lips," I whisper.

I feel her smile through the kiss.

Grabbing her shampoo, I squeeze some into my hand.

"What are you doing?" Sutton asks with glassy eyes.

"Let me take care of you," I whisper back.

Her eyes are soft, trusting, when she nods her head and closes her eyes.

Running my fingers through her hair, massaging her scalp. She melts into me.

"That feels so good," she mumbles.

"Tilt your head back, baby girl," I run my hands through her hair under the water and get all of the suds out.

Repeating the same thing with her conditioner. Squirting her body wash in my hand and gently running my fingers over her skin from shoulders to toes, gently massaging her skin as I go and leaving a trail of kisses too.

Sutton's so quiet, just watching me intently as I show her how much I adore her.

After a few minutes, she grabs my body wash and puts some in her hands and slowly, so softly, rubs my tight muscles with her fingertips.

"That feels incredible!" I manage to croak out.

Humming softly to herself, Sutton puts me in a trance. All I smell is her. All I feel is her. I want to drown myself in her.

We both rinse off and shut the water off.

Getting out first, wrapping her in a towel, pulling her to me and kissing her softly.

I dry myself off next and toss the towel on the hook on the door.

Scooping Sutton up under her legs, she nuzzles in close to me.

Carrying her to the bed and gently setting her down, pulling one of my tee shirts over her head and pulling on a pair of boxers myself.

She looks so vulnerable and beautiful, totally sated, smiling softly at me.

Pulling back the covers, I pull her close to me, kissing her on the forehead and shutting off the light.

"A girl could get used to this kind of treatment," Sutton whispers in the dark.

In seconds she's sound asleep next to me. Her soft breaths on my chest lulling me to sleep not too far after, loving the feeling of her wrapped around me.

26

Sutton

Monday arrives faster than I expected. I still haven't wrapped my head around the last week of my life. It feels like it was all just a dream. What are the odds that the man I have loved for years finally tells me he loves me back during the same week that the man whose music turns me inside out decides to act on the sexual tension that's been brewing between us.

At this point, I'm not really even sure where I stand with either of them.

Beck woke me up this morning with his face buried between my legs and the delicious smell of sugar and maple syrup from the pancakes he had waiting for us from room service.

Our flight back was quiet but comfortable. He held my hand, never letting it go, while I slept with my head on his shoulder. Dreaming about his rough callused hands and how they felt on my skin. The hard grip he had on my hips left small bruises while he thrust in and out of me. His warm hard body pressed so deliciously up against all my soft curves, cocooning me, making me feel safe. How easily he picked me up and maneuvered me around, making me feel so small in his arms. His tenderness with me afterwards. My lips still tingle from his kiss.

Beck and I arrived back in Pittsburgh about an hour ago.

We walk into the café hand in hand. Krysta, one of our part-time employees, is working the register.

"Hey guys," Krysta says looking directly at our hands. "Let me go grab, Quinn."

As Krysta disappears into the kitchen, my ears perk up at the sound of a guitar strumming and a soft tender voice singing.

I can't quite make out the song but it's beautiful.

Completely oblivious when we walked in, I didn't even notice the music or the fact that the café is full. People just silently staring at the stage in awe.

When my eyes finally land on the stage, there sitting on the edge, strumming his guitar, singing softly into a microphone, with Khaos on one side of him and Mayhem on the other, is August. Long black hair draped forward almost covering his face and so fucking mesmerizing!

My eyes wander, taking in all the customers, their eyes never leaving him. Everyone in the café is under his spell.

Enjoying their lunches on a beautiful spring day.

The back patio is open and full, with people leaning in watching him.

One song after the next, never looking up, August just keeps on playing. He's hypnotic.

My traitor of a dog never even leaves his side when I walk in.

A hard squeeze of my hand takes me out of my trance.

I look down at my hand clasped with Beck's and look up at him.

His eyes look somber and a little bit angry.

I squeeze his hand back and give him a little smile. Just then Quinn pops her head out of the kitchen and breaks the tension.

Pulling me into a hug, Quinn whispers in my ear "He's been sitting there playing for a couple hours. Everyone seems to love it. We haven't been this busy during the day in weeks. The dogs even love him. August said he needed to talk to you."

She lets me go and our eyes meet and hold, a silent exchange between us about how screwed I am.

Squeezing my shoulder, Quinn turns to Beck and gives him a hug.

"You better have taken good care of our girl," she chirps.

"Oh, I did," he winks at her.

I grimace. *Ugh. Why do I grimace? We had such a nice weekend!*

The thoughts racing through my head come to a halt, immediately noticing that the music has stopped.

When I turn around, August isn't looking at me. He's glaring at Beck. Who looks smug when I turn back to face him.

August lays his guitar down and walks over to us. The dogs, of course, follow him.

"Hey Sutton, once you get settled, could we...um...talk please?" he asks almost shyly, stuffing his hands in his pockets.

"Maybe another day. I still have a lot of unpacking and

catching up to do," I say barely able to meet his eyes.

Beck pulls me to him and kisses my forehead, "I'm going to take your bag upstairs and then I'll run and get us take out, okay baby girl?"

Beck whistles for the dogs to follow him, still smirking smugly at August.

The dogs oddly don't leave August's side. Perfectly sitting content on either side of him. It's like a stare off between August and the dogs; and Beck and me.

"Um..yeah..tha.." I start to mumble uncomfortably.

"Are you fucking kidding me?" August says exasperated, running his hand through his hair.

My eyes go wide.

"Watch your tone with her," Beck snarls at him.

"August, not right now. Please!" I beg.

"Ha, you said I'm a piece of work! That I'm an asshole!" August jams his finger at his chest.

"What? You fuck me and then a week later run off to Vegas with him? Instead of staying here and having an adult conversation with me? Seriously Sutton? Are you two a couple now or something?" August yells.

Now catching the attention of several customers.

"Keep your voice down!" I hiss.

"You fucked him?" Beck yells and pokes August in the chest.

"All of you. Outside. Now!" Quinn whisper yells.

As I walk outside with Beck and August, Quinn's eyes meet mine, wide and sad. I'm not even sure who the sadness is toward. I fucked up! Royally. This situation is fucked up and it's my fault.

August rushes towards me once we get outside.

"Sutton, I know I freaked out and I'm so sorry. I tried to apologize. I regretted every word that came out of my mouth as soon as I said them. I told you I didn't know how to be in a relationship, but I fuckin like you. I want to be with you. I wanted to try. For you," August says sounding so defeated.

My heart shatters. Completely splitting in two.

"I can't believe you fucked him! Then what, used me as a rebound?" Beck says getting in my face.

"Whoa, back up!" August says, putting his hand in front of Beck.

Beck slaps his hand away and goes to shove him back.

Stepping in front of Beck, putting my hand on his chest. Willing him to look at me.

"No! Beck, what? You weren't just a rebound. I j-uu-sst..." I start to stutter, tears rolling down my face.

"Ha, really? This girl loved you for five years and you never once made a move? A girl like her. How did it take you five years to see what was right in front of you? How does that make you her rebound?" August retorts, shaking his head.

"How the fuck would you know that?" Beck growls.

"Did you feel threatened? So, you figure might as well shoot your shot? Do you even care about her, or are you just upset that she may finally be done pining after you?" August sneers, getting up in Beck's face, but getting Beck out of my face.

"Get the fuck out of my face! Sutton is mine! She has always been mine. Until you started fucking coming around! Don't think I didn't notice the way you watch her. You aren't worthy of her! What can a guy singing a couple songs on the weekend offer her?" Beck almost roars at

August and shoves him back.

"ENOUGH! BOTH OF YOU!" I scream. "I don't belong to either of you!"

Pointing at Beck, I enlighten, feeling my heart break, "Beck, I have loved you for years, and this weekend with you was perfect, but I'm not a piece of fucking property! I told you this already. If you only want me because you're afraid you're going to lose me... then... then fuck you!" I say, chin held high, tears rolling down my face.

And you, I point at August, my soul screaming, "I don't even know what this is between us. We've barely spent any time together, but I just feel this connection to you or to your music. I'm not sure. I'm not even sure how to describe it. But I can't just sit here and let you hurt me, because you don't know how to care about anyone but yourself. You starting this argument was selfish!" I say pointing to August, "But you goading him was just as bad," I say pointing at Beck.

"Both of you, get the fuck out!" I demand. Screaming, in hopes it'll relieve this ache.

"I need space. I need to figure out what my heart needs. If it's even either of you. If either of you truly care about me, you will respect that I need time. You will have to prove what I mean to you. Earn it! Neither of you are a rebound. I care about both of you for different reasons and in completely different ways, but I need time to figure my own heart out." I let out my breath and wipe my face.

"But baby girl, you're mine, you've always been mine. This weekend was perfect! You're perfect for me," Beck says with pure anguish on his face, gripping my hand.

"But have I? Always been yours? Really?" I press Beck.

"He wants to own you, Sunshine. I just want to get to know you, spend time with you, watch you flourish, and bask in your light," August coaxes turning my face toward him, wiping the tears from my cheeks. "I see you. Truly see you!" he declares, holding my stare.

"I care about you both, but I just... I can't do this right now," I hiccup on a sob and walk back into the café, straight into Quinn's waiting arms.

"I got you babe. I got you," she murmurs in my ear, as I release years of built-up anguish, sobbing into her.

27

Sutton

Quinn walked me upstairs before too many prying eyes noticed my breakdown.

After sobbing into her arms for what felt like an eternity, she quietly made me a warm bath and lit some lavender candles before heading back downstairs to lock up for the night.

Slipping under the water, I hold my breath and settle into the darkness. With my eyes closed and the sound of nothingness consuming me, my mind paints a picture of long fingers strumming a guitar and then those same callused fingers tracing my skin. The image is so vivid, I can almost hear the soft croon of August's voice playing in my head, allowing me to sink deeper into the darkness and letting it drown out the never-ending thoughts racing through my head.

Khaos barking has me pulling my head above the water and inhaling deeply.

He whimpers and nudges his head against me.

"I'm sorry, angel, I didn't mean to worry you," I say softly, kissing his head.

After draining the tub, I wrap myself in my favorite warm fuzzy robe.

The second I climb into bed, Khaos lays in front of me. At this moment he's my lifeline. The only thing that's soothing the pain from earlier. The pain from my past.

Snuggling into his fur, instantly beginning to sob again.

I wish I could talk to my grandma about this whole thing! Instantly crying harder.

How the fuck did I get myself in this situation? Better yet, why the fuck did I get myself into this situation? Never in a million years would I wish this on someone.

I thought I wanted love, but is this what it is?

Would Beck have slept with me or told me how he felt if he wasn't threatened by August? Has he actually loved me all of this time?

Could August even figure out a way to be with me without sabotaging us? Could I with my past haunting me almost every night? What happens if he finds a record label? We would end before we could even begin.

Tiny arms reach around me and envelop me in the smell of sugar. Quinn snuggles up behind me.

Sighing into her, I squeeze her hand to let her know I'm awake. I must have cried myself to sleep.

"What time is it?" I barely rasp out.

"It's only nine. You've been asleep for a few hours. I didn't want to wake you. I imagine you need to talk though," she encourages.

"Q, what am I going to do?" I ask rolling to face her. "I do like August. I know it sounds insane, because we haven't spent much time with each other, but I feel like I know him. I feel like he gets me." I pause, waiting for a voice of reason to kick in.

"I think he likes you too, and I think he could be good for you. If he could get over himself. He definitely is carrying a lot of heaviness though. Are you willing to take that on?" Quinn asks, concern shining in her eyes.

"I think I could. I don't think he wants someone to carry his weight for him. I think he just needs someone to see it and still choose him anyway. To keep him from allowing the darkness to take him under. He needs someone to shine some light on him," I sigh.

"How did this weekend go?" Quinn asks.

"Krysta said you two were holding hands when you walked in. I don't want to assume but, spill!" she teases with a wink.

"It was perfect, like we were on a weekend getaway together! We had dinner, then danced by the music fountain. He was incredible in his fight! The sex was insane! Nothing like I've ever experienced before. He kept telling me I was his and I had always been his," I frown.

"Why does that bother you? Girl! For five years, you've looked like you've wanted to climb him like a tree and bang him like a screen door during a hurricane! What are you so afraid of? Isn't that what you've always wanted?" Quinn says almost exasperated.

Giving her a small chuckle and wiping my nose on my sleeve, "It was. It is. I just don't like how it makes me feel like I'm a piece of property to him. I obviously have wanted to be his for years and wanted him to choose me, but when he says I've always been his, when I've always felt like he was just out of reach, it doesn't feel right. What took him so long to speak up then?" I sigh feeling defeated.

"They each make me feel so different. My heart is literally split. Beck makes me feel safe, like he would protect me from anything. The way he worshipped my body, he was so controlled but so soft and tender; I felt cherished, beautiful even. I think if he was truly ready to be together, we would be happy and comfortable. It's easy with him, like our friendship would just remain but become more intimate. But is that enough?" I ramble.

"On the other hand, August makes me feel alive. His music makes me feel so many different emotions. It's like being on a rollercoaster blindfolded; you have no idea when the dips and loops are coming, but they are and they're exhilarating and terrifying all at the same time. If August is in a room, it's like I feel him somehow; my eyes are immediately drawn to him. Just like today, I heard his voice, and it was like my body just took over and found him sitting on the stage. I'm holding one man's hand, while my eyes are drawn to another man's. August makes me want to throw my inhibitions out the door and just live in the moment. Would August be reliable though? I have no idea. He doesn't even know if he can be, which makes me uneasy," I shake my head feeling the anxiety creep its way up around my neck like a noose.

"Fuck, what are you going to do? Cause I'm pretty sure both of them are ready to choose you," Quinn mutters.

"Fuck. How is this happening? I went from zero love interests to two totally opposite, yet incredible, ones," I say on a sigh.

28
August

Throwing my fist into the wall, I scream, "FUCK!"

Over and over again, I keep fucking up! I don't want to hurt her.

I start pacing the floor.

Fuck! Why do I keep hurting her?

Subconsciously, I think it's so she doesn't have a chance to hurt me first.

The pull I feel toward her is relentless, but I am so undeserving of her.

I have to try to prove to her that I can be dependable. That I'm going to show up and stop putting distance between us and allowing her to do the same.

That's the only way I'm going to have a chance with her.

She said we haven't spent enough time together, and she isn't wrong, but her soul whispered to mine, and it's been revived since.

I was dead inside before her; there is no way in hell I'm

giving her up!

I decide to walk to the café to see if I can play an acoustic set and reach her with my music.

If she won't spend time with me, at least I can be near her this way.

Every time I try to talk to her, I manage to fuck it up, but my music, it always steals her attention.

The bell chimes above my head. Quinn is at the register. She looks up and grimaces before she smiles softly at me, "Hey August, what can I get you?"

"Is Sutton not here today?" I question, my eyes wandering the room for her.

She hesitates. Looking up the stairs, "Sutton is, but she texted me saying she was going to be late. She hasn't left the apartment though."

"Can I set up and play like yesterday? I know Sutton said she needs space. I want her to know I'm willing to give her that, but I also want her to know that I am here. I am choosing her," I rasp.

"Yeah, sure," she nods. "Everyone seemed to enjoy it yesterday."

"Thank you," I smile softly at her.

Turning to make my way up to the stage, I sit on the edge and start singing quietly while strumming my guitar.

Just like yesterday people pull their chairs closer to the stage and sip on their drinks, while listening to me play.

With the back patio open, people lean in watching and listening intently.

Tuning them out as I let go and just feel the music. Song after song bleeding one into the next.

A soft brush against my leg has my eyes fluttering open

to a golden fluff ball at my feet. Khaos really seems to enjoy my music or my company, I'm not sure which, but I enjoy his too.

"I am a disaster, the worst of its kind. You are a wildfire burning every thought other than of you in my mind. Your touch is madness with a mix of reckless abandon, and my soul refuses to sleep since yours left it undone." I croon into the microphone while softly strumming my guitar.

Khaos nudges his snout against my knee, making me look up.

Sutton sits on the counter, legs crossed, the saddest green eyes pinned to me with tears running down her cheeks. Violet hair in two braids runs down each of her shoulders, her t-shirt is hanging off her one shoulder with her flower tattoos exposed.

The visceral need to pull her into my arms, press my lips to her soft skin and inhale her sweet vanilla scent has me laying my guitar down and walking straight toward her.

People clap softly as I walk past them. I wave awkwardly to thank them, but my heart is set on getting as close to Sutton as possible.

"Hey," I say softly, wiping the tears from her cheeks with my thumbs and putting each of my thumbs in my mouth to lick off her tears.

"Why do you do that?" she whimpers with her head tilted to the side.

"Tears are how our heart speaks when we can't find the words. I want to taste your unspoken words," I barely rasp out.

"How poetic," she responds sarcastically looking toward the stage, eyes glittering with unshed tears.

"Your dog must really like music. He's hung out with me the last two days," I quip trying to make her smile.

"He actually hates the live music on Saturdays. What you're playing is softer though, so maybe it's that... maybe he just likes you..." Sutton shrugs, smiling softly at Khaos.

"Doubtful, most things don't like me," I frown.

"Don't say that! I like you. Khaos likes you. Sometimes dogs have a way of finding people who need them, you know. Khaos chose me. He's filled an emptiness I hadn't even realized I was carrying," she says softly.

"I'm happy you have him, and he has you," I say rubbing her cheek softly.

Sutton flinches at first, but then leans into my touch, before realizing she let her guard down, then pulls away just as quickly.

"I know you asked for space, but I got some really great news and wanted to share it with you," I grin.

"Oh yeah, what's up?" she smiles back.

"Well, Saturday night a guy came in and invited us to play at The Wicked Tour in July," I start to say, but Sutton leaps off the counter squealing and pulls me into the biggest hug.

"Oh my gosh, August! That's amazing! I'm so happy for you!"

Wrapping an arm around her, I say into her hair, "He said he had been looking for a couple unlabeled bands to play on one of their smaller stages. I know it's not the main stage but it's something. Maybe we can find a label or find a more mainstream band that will let us open for them. We're really excited! I couldn't wait to tell you! It's all because of you, Sutton. Letting us perform here so often. Giving us a chance. I really owe you," I say sheepishly.

Sutton squeezes me even tighter to her. I stiffen for just a second before melting into her. Her vanilla scent calming my racing heart. Squeezing her back tighter and sinking into her warm embrace.

"Oh, please. That was all you! You don't owe me anything," she swats at me.

Gods, I want to kiss her so fucking much! The feel of her body against mine makes me want to pick her up and carry her upstairs. But I know I can't. I have to respect her space.

"Hey, if you can, but it's okay if you can't, but I'd really love it if you did, could you maybe sort of come to The Wicked Tour to support us?" I try to plaster on a smile through my grimace at how fuckin awkward I'm being.

"Ah, stop. Quinn and I will so be there! I'll just close the café that weekend. I'll put a sign on the door. Tell my customers to go to The Wicked Tour instead," she says chuckling.

Pulling her back into a tight hug, "Thank you, Sutton. For real!"

Kissing my cheek, she steps out of the hug, "I have to get back to the customers. Feel free to keep playing if you want. It's really... nice. Calming."

Heading back to the stage with Khaos in tow, I play softly the rest of the day with a smile on my face.

The fact that Sutton let me stay is huge, after everything I've put her through.

The sandwich and iced coffee she brought me around lunch time tastes like heaven.

But what makes it even better is that it tastes subtly like how she did the first time I kissed her. Making me wonder if this is her favorite and warming my heart that she's sharing it with me.

Standing up, swinging my guitar over my shoulder, I walk toward Sutton when I notice she's locking up.

"Soooo, I know you said I barely know you, but I'd like to get to know you. Can we just sit outside and talk for a bit please?" I invite while squeezing the back of my neck.

"Sorry, I can't," she says giving a small shrug and turning to grab for the leash.

"Khaos and I have plans," clipping the leash to his collar and taking him through the door.

I try to smile and shove my hand in my pockets, following behind her.

Looking down the street, I turn back and give Sutton an awkward wave, "Well I guess I'll see you…" but before I can finish, she cuts me off.

"Do you want to come with us?"

I can't quite read her expression.

"Um…Yeah…Sure. I'd… I'd like that. Is that okay? Can I?" I ask fidgeting with the guitar strap over my shoulder.

She takes my hand, placing the leash in it.

"Let's go," she says walking down the sidewalk.

For about twenty minutes we walk in comfortable silence until coming to a stop in front of a red brick building. *Briar Nursing Home* is written on a sign above the two front doors.

Giving her a sideways glance, Sutton pulls out a badge and scans it, opening the door for me and Khaos to walk through.

"Good evening, Ms. Sutton," the security guard, who reminds me too much of Santa with his jolliness, plump belly, and white beard, says to Sutton at the check in desk.

"Hi Charlie, how are you this evening?" she beams at him.

"I'm doing well. I see you brought an extra friend today," he smiles at me.

"This is my friend, August. August, this is Charlie," Sutton says, almost shyly.

Charlie and I shake hands. "Well, I'll let you get to it. Ya'll have a good evening," he says, smiling softly at Sutton.

As we walk down the hallway to a recreation room, Sutton stops and says, "I'll be just a minute. Could you hang on to Khaos for a second please?"

"Sure thing," I respond standing with Khaos sitting perfectly still next to me.

Watching Sutton closely, as she walks over to a woman in scrubs and has a short conversation with her. Noticing her shoulders drooping slightly as they talk.

Sutton makes her way back to me, stopping just in front of me, looking away quickly, but not before I see the sadness in her eyes, "She said we can go sit at that table and she'll be back in a couple minutes. You're more than welcome to play your guitar if you want, but you don't have to. Some of the guests may enjoy it though," she squeezes my hand. Almost like she needs it to ground her.

A couple minutes later, the nurse assists an elderly woman, walking slowly with a walker over to our table. She is probably in her early eighties with white blonde hair and a frail stature.

Just before she gets there, Sutton gets up to help her sit at the table with us and gives her a hug.

"Hello, Ms. Margaret. I'm Sutton and this is August. We came to sit with you and play some music if that's okay. This is our friend, Khaos. He's really gentle, if you want to pet him," Sutton speaks softly and kindly to the woman, while gently rubbing Khaos' head.

"Hello..." the elderly woman mutters looking at each of us with confusion on her face.

Khaos bumps her leg with his snout, and she reaches down to pet him.

"He's very soft," she says with a tiny chuckle.

Ms. Margaret looks up at me blankly. I ask quietly, "Would it be okay if I played a song for you ma'am?"

She nods with a smile, "I'd quite like that."

I'm singing softly, strumming the guitar, when a moment later a haunting, soft breathy melody joins in.

Next to me, Sutton is singing softly along with me. Her eyes are closed, tears stream down her cheeks, and she holds the woman's hand gently. Her voice is so beautiful, soft, and tender, almost childlike.

The elderly woman just sort of stares off into space. Occasionally there's the tiniest flicker of maybe a small smile on her lips.

Several other people have gravitated towards us, their eyes never leaving Sutton.

Sutton blows my mind, as she sings quietly next to me, to every single song I play.

Getting lost in the music and in her. My chest aches as she sings. Her pain bleeding out in the desperation in her voice will haunt my dreams at night.

This girl is going to bring me to my knees!

Tears continue to stream down her face, as she sings, never letting go of this woman's hand. This woman, who doesn't seem to know Sutton at all.

The nurse returns. An hour has come and gone. "Ms.

Margaret, it's time for bed. Visitation is over," she says squeezing Sutton's shoulder.

Sutton gives Ms. Margaret a gentle hug and kisses her cheek.

"Rest easy, Ms. Margaret," I hear her whisper before she nods to the nurse that she's ready.

Standing there watching Sutton stand beside this woman completely guts me for some reason. This woman looks so small and frail in comparison to her. Even though Sutton can't be more than a few inches taller than her.

As we get ready to leave, people thank us for coming and ask us to come back again next week.

Swinging my guitar over my shoulder, I grab Khaos' leash with one hand and take Sutton's hand in the other.

When she looks down at our joined hands, I give it a squeeze. Her sad eyes meet mine and she squeezes my hand tighter, like she needs me to anchor her, like it's a lifeline.

Signing the checkout form for us, we head out the doors.

Walking back toward her place, Sutton's extremely quiet. I look over to her and she has tears silently crawling down her face.

Stopping, I turn her towards me.

"Hey, come here," I say as I wipe her tears with my thumb before putting it in my mouth.

Her eyes follow my thumb, and she gives me a soft smile, shaking her head.

Pulling her close to me for a hug, "I feel like that was a really important person to you. You don't have to talk about it, but thank you for bringing me. Your voice is beautiful, Sunshine. You should really be singing on your own stage," I pull back and kiss her hair. Breathing in my favorite vanilla scent.

Sutton remains quiet, burying her face into my chest, and then so softly, I have to bend down to hear her, she says, "That was my grandmother. She has dementia. I'm just waiting for the day that her body goes too. She's left me in several little deaths over the last two years. The first time was when she forgot my name," she sniffs softly.

"The second was when she forgot who I was but knew once I told her. The third was when she forgot who I was but didn't know, even when I told her. She just stared at me like I was a stranger. Kept asking where I lived, like it might jog her memory, but it never did," she pauses, trying to fight through the lump in her throat.

Gently running my fingers through her hair and down her spine, trying to soothe her.

She shivers as she melts into me. Pulling my shirt into her hands and sighing softly.

"She was all I had left after my parents passed away in a car accident during my sophomore year of college. Prior to that, she was still one of my most favorite people. My love for reading is because of her. She used to buy me books when I got good grades in school. We used to spend the weekends together. Shopping and laughing, going to the movies, getting brunch together. We even went to the beach together once. She used to be so full of life! Now she's just a shell of who she used to be. I think her soul has already left her body; at least I hope so. Her body is just waiting to catch up. Her final death will be when her body finally shuts down. So, I visit her and sit with her sometimes, but it takes a piece of me every time. It just hurts so much," she says with a sob.

"Her spirit heard your beautiful voice, Sunshine, and

I'm sure it brings her peace. That's all you can do. You're doing everything you can," I comfort her, pulling her tightly into me, fusing us together, resting my chin on her head.

Khaos shoves his snout into both of our legs, offering his own support.

Holding each other in silence, while people pass by us for a few minutes. I've never felt this comfortable, this close to someone.

"Will you come back and sit with me for a little while, please? We don't have to talk. I just don't want to be alone right now," she whispers, breaking the silence surrounding us.

"Of course," I kiss the crown of her head and take her hand in mine.

We make our way back to her apartment.

"Thank you," she says on a broken whisper.

"Would you like any tea or anything? I'm going to make myself a cup," I ask August while he sits on one of the barstools at my island.

I like him sitting in my kitchen. He has this quiet strength about him that puts me at ease.

"Tea? I don't think I've ever had tea," he frowns.

"What in the bloody hell do you mean you've never had tea before now, good sir?" I say exasperated in my faux British accent.

"Was that supposed to be a British accent?" August asks with a chuckle and a raised eyebrow.

"Hush, you," I say as I whip around scowling at him.

"Bloody brilliant, that one," he teases back with a much better faux accent, winking at me.

I chuckle, "So tea or something else?"

"I'll try the tea. However you have yours is fine. The coffee you've given me has been the best coffee I've ever tasted," August compliments with the softest smile on his face.

"Oh yeah?" I hop on the counter and grin like a *Cheshire* cat at him.

"Hush, you," he chuckles, giving me the same scowl that I gave him, as he walks around the island.

I stare at him and hold my breath as he makes his way over to me.

"August, I can't. Not yet," I say turning away from him.

Grabbing my chin, so that I have to look at him, he stares into my eyes. "Hey, no. I want to take this slow."

Releasing my chin, August pushes the hair off my face, tucking it behind my ear. "I respect your boundaries and your space. I told you I just want to get to know you better. You had a really vulnerable evening. I just want to be here for you. Whatever that looks like for you. Can I just hold you?"

Closing my eyes, letting out the breath I was holding, "Yeah, I'd like that, thank you."

Hopping off the counter, I add a lemon slice and some honey to our tea.

We make our way over to the couch and sit facing each other with our legs crossed.

Handing him his tea, he takes a long sip.

Looking up from his cup, August places his hand on his chest, "My lady, this is quite good."

Smacking his arm, I burst out laughing, "Why thank you, good sir."

"Do you want to watch a movie?" I ask tenderly, placing my tea down on the coffee table.

"If you'd like, but I wouldn't mind just listening to music and talking to you instead, if that's okay," he says smiling at me.

Resting my head on August's shoulder to hide the fact that my cheeks are flushed, "Do you ever get tired of listening to music?"

Lifting his arm so I can burrow into his chest, "Come here."

"Music is my life. It keeps me sane. Quiets my mind. Makes me feel alive! I don't think I could ever get tired of it."

"I love that! I would rather listen to music than watch a movie too, but I'm really comfortable now and don't feel like moving," I chuckle, burrowing further into his chest.

"Silence isn't so bad either," he mumbles into my hair, squeezing me a little tighter to him.

"Thank you, for coming with me today. For being there. For playing music, even though you played all day. It means more than you could ever imagine!" I whisper.

Falling into a comfortable silence, listening to his heartbeat and his steady breathing, as it calms the storm inside me.

I feel my eyes start to drift closed when he asks, "Why don't you ever sing on Saturdays? You sang karaoke downtown and then today at the nursing home so beautifully. People would love your voice if you performed here."

"I can't write music or play any instruments. I just enjoy singing songs I know the lyrics to. I wouldn't be very original. It would be all covers, and people don't want covers," I shrug.

"If we wrote a song together, and the guys were on board, would you sing a song with me one day?" August probes, in his velvety voice.

Glancing up at him, his expression is so open and honest. He's serious! I'm completely taken aback.

This man who came into my venue all smirks and arrogance, giving me essentially the cold shoulder, who knows he's an incredible musician, wants me to sing with him?

"You can't be serious, August!" I huff out an exasperated laugh, shocked, eyes wide. "Your voice is out of this world and so unique! How on earth do you think my voice could even compare to yours? That it would sound good harmonizing with yours? You'll end up with more than one asshole demanding a refund, and it would be valid this time."

Grabbing my face, he stares into my eyes with so much fierceness, "Were you not listening to us, harmonizing, at the nursing home? Did you not notice how many people were watching us? They weren't just watching me, Sutton. They were watching both of us. They were watching the beautiful girl with tears streaming down her cheeks, eyes closed, singing with her whole fuckin soul, in such a haunting way. They could feel every emotion you portrayed into each song. We could create a masterpiece! The two of us. All I ask for is one song. You and me. I think the guys will be for it, but I can check to confirm."

Looking into August's eyes, they are shining with so much sincerity.

I have to look anywhere but at him, so I look down at my lap, where I'm wringing my hands.

Looking back up into his eyes, I chew my inner cheek, chewing over this crazy idea.

Blowing out a breath, I agree, "Okay. One song."

"Gods, I could kiss you!" August pulls my forehead to his.

"So, kiss me," I rasp out.

Wasting no time, he crashes his lips down to mine, pulling me over to him to straddle his lap.

Instantly, his hands are in my hair and mine are in his. Gripping and tugging.

Our souls merge. Time stops. I don't know where either of us begins or ends.

We're hot breaths mingling, warm insatiable kisses, gasping and moaning into each other's mouths. He tastes like honey. I can't get enough! I want to devour him whole!

Deepening the kiss, August bites down on my bottom lip.

I groan and nip his bottom lip, feeling his chest rumble with a growl.

This kiss is soul shattering and all consuming. I feel him everywhere, but it's like everywhere isn't enough. Feeling this deep need to just claw my way into him.

Gods, he feels amazing and smells so fuckin good, like tobacco and leather!

All I want to do is wrap myself in every inch of him.

Before it can go any further, August's pulling back, leaning his forehead against mine, with his hands still buried in my hair.

"I promised I'd take this slow, so as much as it physically pains me to stop kissing you, we have to stop," he grinds out, adjusting himself.

"Okay," I manage to croak out. Eyes closed, forehead still touching his.

"I should go," he whispers.

"Not yet, please! I promise I won't ask you to kiss me again," I plead with my eyes, not ready for him to go.

"Okay," he mumbles, pressing his lips to my forehead.

Climbing off his lap, August lifts his arm so I can tuck myself back into where I was prior to that soul searing kiss.

Kissing the crown of my head, he says so softly, "Thank you for sharing that part of yourself with me today. That couldn't have been easy."

"It was a little easier with you there. Distracting me with your music. I didn't feel as alone," I whisper.

With his warm chest, gentle fingers caressing up and down my hair, soft breathing, and steady heartbeat at my ear, I'm soon lulled to sleep.

I'm slightly stirred awake by the feel of a soft blanket being placed over me, but I burrow deeper into the warmth and fall back to sleep immediately.

A peaceful, dreamless sleep.

*T*he sound of soft snoring rouses me from sleep in the morning. With this kink in my neck, I expect to see Khaos curled up in a ball under my arm, but instead it's this beautiful man.

Tracing my eyes over every inch of August, taking him in while he's still sleeping peacefully.

This is the first time I've ever seen him without frown lines or a scowl.

All that porcelain skin with his long, incredibly soft

inky black hair.

August's big tattooed hand is covering my small one over his chest.

Itching to trace the lines of his artwork, but I don't want to wake him.

On the top of his left hand is a beautiful, intricate detailed piece. A pirate ship with octopus tentacles coming off each finger, diving up from the depths of the ocean ready to swallow the ship whole.

Under my palm, I feel the steady thump of August's heartbeat. Watching the steady rise and fall of his chest. *He could be mine.*

This gorgeous, tortured man held me all night and covered us with a blanket. I'm pretty sure physical touch pains him, but he didn't leave. Never let me go.

August shoved his demons aside and held me when I needed it most. He saw me. Saw some of the jagged edges and didn't leave.

My chest aches at the thought of it.

He rasps in his gravelly voice into my hair, pulling me from my thoughts, "Mornin, Sunshine."

"Mornin," I respond with a wide smile.

"I love this tattoo! What does it mean?" I ask tracing the tentacles on his hand.

"The octopus symbolizes the ability to overcome difficult situations with creativity. To disguise themselves so that the enemy can't see who they really are. Folklore says that the sea monster was called the devilfish, and something about that really resonated with me," August says, never taking his gentle touch from my cheek.

"I like that. Like good and evil. Dark and light. It suits you," I smile tenderly looking up at August from under my lashes.

His eyes hold mine for a second. They're the softest I've ever seen them.

Then the softness is gone in a blink and he's pulling me to him to kiss my forehead, "I should probably get going. I imagine you have to work, and I could use a shower."

"If you want to shower here and come down for a coffee and muffin on your way out, feel free," I kiss his jaw and then his cheek and go to get up.

His eyes light up, "Really? That would be great, thank you!"

August stands up, pulling me to him. He kisses my forehead, my nose and then my lips gently. "I'm sorry I spent the night. I promised I'd give you space and then didn't at all. But you fell asleep and looked so peaceful that I didn't want to move and wake you, and then I accidentally fell asleep too. That's actually the best night's sleep I've had in a while," he chuckles and looks away.

"It was nice to wake up to you. My best night's sleep in a while too! You were so warm and cozy, so don't apologize," I nudge him and wink. "I'm going to go change quickly and then head downstairs. The shower is down the hallway on the right. There are fresh towels in the cupboard in there. Use whatever you need. I'll see you in a bit."

"Thank you," August kisses my forehead one last time and heads down the hall.

When I hear the bathroom door click, I find myself tip toeing down the hall, pressing my ear to the door.

I know I shouldn't eavesdrop, but that hot as sin man getting naked in my bathroom has my heart fluttering.

A few seconds later, the water starts running, and then I hear August groaning.

My eyes go wide. There's no way he's…

He just got in there.

Another low groan has my skin flushing.

Pushing my ear closer to the door because I just can't help myself.

I realize this is totally crossing so many boundaries, but I won't open the door.

"Gods this feels so good! I don't know what I did to deserve this but thank you. I haven't had a hot shower in years," I hear August contently exclaim.

Guilt and embarrassment wash over me.

He's groaning because the water is hot! Not because he was doing what my dirty ass mind thought he was doing!

Scolding myself internally for invading his privacy, I run up the stairs to my room and realize I don't have much time, so I change as fast as I can, throwing my hair in a bun, grabbing Khaos and heading downstairs.

I don't know a lot about us right now, but I do know I need to figure out how to get that man to take more hot showers here. Not just for August, but so I can listen to him groan like that more often.

30
Sutton

When I get downstairs, the smell of cinnamon and browned butter hits my nose, making me salivate. My stomach immediately grumbles.

Quinn must be in the kitchen, already prepping today's baked goods.

Hopping on the counter, snatching a fresh cinnamon roll, "Mmm...it smells like heaven in here!"

"Someone's in a much better mood today. Have an epiphany?" She quirks her brow.

"Ha Ha! Not yet. August accidentally stayed over last night. He's upstairs showering," I say stuffing the last of the cinnamon roll in my mouth to hide my cheesy grin.

"Umm... how does that accidentally happen? Actually, scratch that. I guess Knox did the same thing while you were gone," she counters hand on her hip, but staring at me like she needs more details.

"Nothing happened. Well, we kissed but that was it. We were up late just talking and ended up falling asleep.

No nightmares. And he came to see Gram with me," I mention, twisting my hair between my fingers, trying not to make eye contact.

Quinn gasps and sets the macarons down, so she doesn't drop them from shock, "Wow, no nightmares... Wait, you what?"

I shove a macaron in my mouth to stall answering her question.

"You let him come along with you? You NEVER let anyone go with you!" she exclaims completely shocked, disappointment lacing her tone.

Quinn's shock isn't misplaced though. She's only met Gram once, at our graduation.

My gram is so special to me! Even though I lost my parents in college and was old enough to technically be on my own, my gram made sure I never felt alone.

Every winter and summer break were spent with her. Hot chocolate and a book by the fireplace. Hallmark Christmas movies always on in the background.

Planting flowers and sipping lemonade in the summer. Long walks at the local park.

Anonymous care packages always showed up to my dorm conveniently after I would call Gram after having a breakdown about missing my parents or being worried about an exam or project I had coming up. When I failed to believe in myself, she always believed in me. My biggest cheerleader.

After her diagnosis of dementia, I moved in with her to help her with things around the house. She had a few small falls here and there that she bounced back from quickly. But there was one specific day where, she had fallen outside after getting the mail. Thankfully, a neighbor was around and saw her. They were able to call an ambulance, but after that we had to have Gram placed in a memory care home. I had to work, and she couldn't be left alone.

Her decline since then has been steady. Her memory used to come in waves, but now Gram's just a shell of herself. A body with eyes so empty, it's as if the lights are shut off behind them.

The pity on the faces of the nurses at the facility and the way Charlie treats me like a granddaughter is hard enough to handle. I don't think I could handle the pity from my friends too, so I've never allowed them to go see her with me.

Giving Quinn a guilty shrug. Quinn rolls her eyes and turns around to put a batch of muffins in the oven. "I don't know, it just kind of happened. August was here playing until I was ready to lock up, and he asked if we could talk, but I told him I had somewhere to be. He looked sort of forlorn, so I asked him to come and bring his guitar. Everyone there really loved the soft acoustic music. Gram barely blinked but it was just nice, you know."

Coming up to me, Quinn gives me a squeeze, "That's huge for you, Sut. You're letting him in bit by bit without even realizing it."

A tap on the kitchen door has us both turning around. August waves in the small window.

Quinn gives me a wink and gets back to baking.

Hopping off the counter, pointing towards the door, "I'm going to grab him a coffee for the road."

"Here, give him a few muffins too. It's the least you could do, since he had to sleep with you last night!" Quinn cackles.

"SHHH! Will you shhh? He can probably hear you," I hush her with a light laugh, swatting at her.

I turn and grab a couple of muffins and bag them before heading out the door.

"Hey, thanks again. I left the towel hanging over the shower curtain. I hope that's okay. I also sort of used your hair dryer. I hope that's okay too," August says sheepishly stuffing his hands in his front pockets.

"Of course, it's okay. Anytime. Here, Quinn said they're super fresh, so I'd dive in. They are divine straight out of the oven," I exclaim.

August quirks a sexy smile.

"Not as divine as that sound that just came out of your pretty little mouth," he flatters while brushing my hair behind my ear. Making me shiver from the heat of his hand and the chill of his metal rings brushing my skin.

"What the fuck? I thought you needed space, Sut!" Beck barks from behind the counter.

Jumping back from August, I meet Beck's eyes, that are filled with rage.

"I could've sworn I saw him walking down the stairs from your loft through the window. Correct me if I'm wrong," Beck growls.

Beck makes his way over to us, but August stops him, putting his body, like a shield, between mine and Beck's body.

It catches me completely off guard for a second. Beck has always been my protector. I never really thought I'd need to be protected from him, but this is the second time August has put himself between us, when Beck has gotten loud. Like he's seeing something in Beck that I'm blind to. And I am trusting August to see it.

"It's okay, August," I put my hand on his forearm and look into his eyes, letting him know that I can handle this.

"You're protecting her? From me? Seriously? What the actual fuck, Sutton?" Beck belts out, grabbing my arm and walking us back toward the kitchen door.

Yanking my arm from his grasp, "What the hell do you think you're doing? You literally walked in here and got loud with me. He doesn't know you. He doesn't know that you won't hurt me. Please lower your voice before customers come in and witness this! We don't need another blow up like Monday," I harshly whisper.

Turning around, I make my way back toward August. There's something about standing next to him and his quiet strength. It makes me feel more confident.

"So what? You chose him?" Beck queries pointing at August with so much anguish and disgust on his face.

"I didn't choose anyone, Beck. August and I are friends getting to know one another. I just need to figure out if you only want me because of August, or if there is actually something between us. You've been in my life for six years, Beck, and now, just out of the blue, you want something? It's confusing," I respond giving him a pleading look.

"I also need a chance to get to know August. I have feelings for him too, and I need to see if what I feel for him could be something," I say squeezing August's forearm.

"If you think you're safe, I'm going to head out, so you two can talk. I don't want to make this worse for you. Text me if you need anything," August whispers in my ear and kisses the side of my head.

"Thank you," I whisper back, leaning into him.

"You hurt Sutton, and I swear to the Gods," August threatens, giving Beck a glare that could kill right now.

Turning, August gives me a wink and heads out the door.

"Ha, that's cute. What's he going to do? I fight for a living and probably have 50 pounds on him," Beck rebukes with a patronizing laugh.

Shaking his head, Beck starts to turn around when I grab his arm, "Are you serious right now? What has gotten into you? This isn't the same guy who I've called my best friend and have loved for years."

"Sutton, that guy doesn't deserve you! Have you seen August? He doesn't wear an ounce of color. He's always frowning. He walks everywhere. Does he even have a car? A driver's license? He doesn't work. All he does is play around on his guitar and sing here on Saturdays. What can he even offer you?" Beck ridicules with so much earnestness in his voice.

"Oh my Gods! Seriously? Jealousy isn't a good look on you, Beck. It's disgusting that you are basing August's value on what he can offer me in the superficial sense. I have my own business. I don't need a man for anything other than a partner and companionship. Someone who listens to me. Who sees me! Who wants to spend time with me! Who respects me and is faithful. Who makes me smile by being kind to my dog and other human beings. That guitar he plays creates magic from his soul! He is going somewhere; he just hasn't gotten there yet. I can't believe you right now!" I shake my head so disappointed in my best friend.

"Sut, look, I'm sorry, okay. You have been my best friend for years. I want to move forward with you. I can't do that if you're sitting here fantasizing about that guy."

"Beck, if you want to move forward with me so bad, you need to show me that. Being unkind to someone when you don't even know him isn't a great way to win me over. Are you jealous because you actually love me, or is it because he could take your best friend away? Either way, you're better than that Beck," I say wrapping my arms around myself, shaking my head, not meeting his eyes.

"So let me take you out. Let me plan a date and take you somewhere. Just the two of us. I won't even bring him up," Beck offers with a plea.

I stare at him, making him sweat out my answer.

"Please, Sut. Please!"

I give Beck a half smile, "On one condition."

"Anything," he says, nearly dropping to his knees at my feet.

"It better not involve physical activity or sweating. If so, I'm out on both accounts!"

"Done! I'll pick you up on Friday at lunchtime. Think Quinn or Krysta can cover the afternoon?" he smiles.

Quinn pokes her head out of the kitchen, "Quinn can cover it!"

Turning around, giving Quinn wide eyes at her eavesdropping, I chuckle before looking back at Beck.

He picks me up and gives me a bear hug.

"Okay, okay. I think you've squeezed all the air out of me!" I swat at his back to put me down.

Beck loosens his grip and kisses me on the forehead. Putting me down, I take a deep breath in, when I nearly jump out of my skin.

"Order up!" Quinn announces through the kitchen doors.

She hands Beck his smoothie for the day and quietly makes her way back toward the kitchen doors.

"Thanks, Q," Beck shouts at Quinn.

"No problem-o," she says with a wave in the air.

Beck turns his attention back to me, "So I'll see you Friday afternoon then?"

"Yeah," I reply with a soft smile.

I'll see you Friday at noon, Sut," Beck winks and heads out the door.

Quinn's arms circle around my waist, the smell of sugar filling my nose. Her chin resting on my shoulder, she teases, "What the hell are you going to do now babe?"

Letting out a huffing laugh, I squeeze her arms that are wrapped around me, "I have no fucking idea! How is this even my life?"

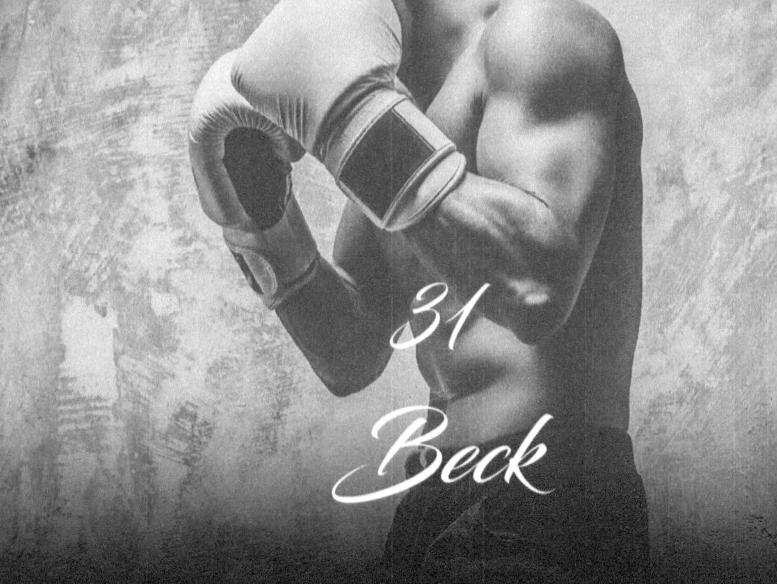

31
Beck

Sutton: Where are we going for our date?

Beck: It's a surprise.

Sutton: Can you give a girl more than that?

Beck: Nope.

Sutton: Scrap, come on. I need to know what to wear.

Beck: Just make sure you wear your converse and not any heels or boots.

Sutton: Scrap, I said NO sweating or exercise.

Beck: ;) see you soon, baby girl.

Stepping up to Sutton's door, I give it a classic knock.

Two seconds later, she's opening the door, looking like a fuckin knock out!

"Punctual. I like it," she responds giving me her back and walking back into the kitchen.

Closing the door and following close behind her. Trying

not to look at how amazing her ass looks in her jumpsuit.

"When am I ever late for anything baby girl?" I smirk back.

"Touché," she answers rummaging through the fridge.

"Let me make us some iced coffees for the road and then we can head out."

Pulling out iced coffee, half and half creamer, and that disgusting caramel syrup Sutton loves so much. I almost laugh.

"I don't think it qualifies as coffee if you put all of that in there."

Giving me an annoyed glare back, "Only a serial killer would say that!"

"Well, if the shoe fits. No flavoring for me please. Just the coffee, black."

Rolling her eyes, "Like I said, serial killer."

"Har Har," I roll my eyes back at her.

"I imagine we aren't bringing the dogs unless Mayhem is in the car?" she asks.

"No dogs today. I left him back at my place."

"Okay. Let me get Khaos downstairs and bring him up here really quick, so Quinn doesn't have to worry about him," Sutton says putting the coffee tumblers down.

"I got it. You finish up those coffees."

Whistling for Khaos, he comes prancing over, tail wagging. "Hey boy, let's head upstairs so your momma and I can go on a real date."

Khaos follows me up the stairs at my heels and darts toward the couch the second we walk into Sutton's apartment, instantly curling up in a ball.

I refill his water bowl and make sure he has everything

he needs.

Walking out of her apartment, I lock the door behind me.

When I get downstairs, Sutton's leaning against the counter holding both of our coffees looking like a fuckin knock out.

I grab my coffee and kiss her cheek. "You look beautiful baby girl."

Wearing a lavender jumpsuit, cut low enough to show off her rose tattoo between her tits. Sutton's flower tattoo on her shoulder is peeking out just under the sleeve on the left side. She has her black high-top converses on. Hair pulled back in a high ponytail with curls hanging down her back. Minimal make up, looking fuckin stunning!

I have half a thought to just throw her over my shoulder and run back up to her apartment to have my way with her. Then I realize I have to do this right or I'm going to lose her.

"Thank you," her cheeks flush a beautiful shade of pink.

Sutton threads her arm through mine. "Let's go!"

We head to my car, and I open the door for her. When she's situated, I shut the door and head over to my side.

"How chivalrous of you!" she quips.

Getting into my side, I turn the car on and *The Great Escape* by Boys Like Girls is playing.

"Ahh, this is so nostalgic," Sutton says, humming the song and dancing in her seat.

Resting my hand on her thigh, I pull out of my parking spot. Heading away from the city, across the bridge, further out toward more farmland.

"Where on earth are we going?" she asks staring out of the window.

"I'm doing a favor for someone, but I figured you'd want to come along," I squeeze her thigh.

We pull up to a barn when a bearlike man comes walking out. His big barrel chest and long scraggly beard really accentuate his faded jeans and black suspenders.

Looking over at Sutton, she looks back with so much confusion on her face.

"Did you bring me here to kill me and let the pigs have their way with me?" she asks eyes wide.

I burst out laughing, "You and Q really need to stop watching so much true crime, Sut. Come on, let's go."

Walking up to the man, I reach out my hand for a shake. "Hey, my name is Beck, and this is Sutton. We're here for the puppies. We're helping with the transport for The Foster Farm."

Taking my hand, he gives it a good squeeze before speaking, "Name's Ben."

Seconds later, Sutton lets out the shrillest squeal, nearly breaking my eardrums.

"PUPPIES!?"

Ben crosses his arms over his chest, giving me a questioning look, "If you're here with transport, why doesn't she know about it?"

"Sorry sir. I am here with transport. I can show you the email for the pick-up location. I brought my friend here with me to help out, since there are so many. She loves dogs more than anything in this world! They are in good hands," I swear to him.

Ben nods his head, "This way then."

We head into the barn where we hear little yips and woofs.

Sutton looks like she's about to burst at the seams with excitement, but she is trying so hard to contain it.

I just give her a shit-eating grin. She may sweat a little, but I don't think she'll mind much.

Ben opens the barn doors, and sitting in the middle of the room with chicken wire surrounding them are six Australian Shepard puppies. They are the cutest little balls of white, tan, gray and black spotted fluff with little pink noses and baby blue eyes.

"OH MY GODS BECK! Am I dead? Are we in heaven? Look at these babies!" Sutton gushes.

Rushing over to them, she picks one up and brings it to her face and gives it a kiss on the nose.

"Look at you, you little angel! Aren't you the cutest thing I've ever seen? Don't tell Khaos I said that. Oh my goodness! I could just eat you. You're so freakin' adorable! EEEP!" She rambles on, cooing at the puppies.

I shake my head, chuckling.

When I look over toward the bearded man who has been frowning since we got here, Ben has the smallest twitch at the sides of his lips, like he might want to try and smile at my beautiful girl.

"Beck, don't you want to hold one? Come on! This is like a surge of serotonin and dopamine. You will immediately feel amazing!"

"We have to get all of them into my car in one-piece Sut," I say still laughing at her excitement.

"Okay. Well, what are we waiting for? I want to hold each and every one of them for at least five minutes. So, like they know they're loved, you know? You know what?

I'm going to sit in the back with them. Is that okay?" her smile couldn't get brighter.

"Ha ha! Okay Sut," I squeeze her shoulder.

"How should we do this? I brought a hamper and set it in the backseat with that side of the seats pushed down. Do you think they all will fit in it?" I ask Ben.

"I think they should fit just fine. They've mostly stayed in this pen since birth, so they're used to smaller spaces," Ben grunts.

Pulling my car up a little closer to the barn door, I open the backseat and get the hamper ready to go.

Sutton comes walking over with two puppies in her arms, alternating kissing each of their noses and heads.

It's probably one of the cutest things I've ever seen.

I hurry up and snap a quick picture of her.

This is probably the happiest I've seen Sutton in months.

So gingerly, she sets them down into the hamper.

Walking with Sutton to get another puppy, she puts her hand up to halt me, "You stay here and watch those angels. I can bring over two at a time so that I can snuggle them all."

She's almost skipping to the barn door, when I notice Ben is smirking and just shaking his head at me.

With a puppy in each arm, Sutton makes her way back to the car, simultaneously telling them how precious they are and how much she loves them.

This girl's heart knows no bounds. She gently places them in the hamper and heads back for the last two.

With Ben standing next to me, I pull out the form for him to sign to surrender the puppies to the rescue.

Ben signs it and shakes my hand. His eyes wander

toward Sutton, softening at the edges, the faintest smile on his lips, "Looks like you got a good one there. Hang on to that one."

I nod. "Thank you for surrendering them. They will be well cared for."

$\mathcal{S}$utton is sitting in the backseat, buckled in, holding one puppy in her lap, while petting the other puppies in the hamper sitting next to her.

Snapping one more candid picture of her while she's whispering in the soft hairs of the puppy in her arms.

Sutton looks up at me and beams, "Best date ever!"

We head back toward the city to The Foster Farm Rescue to drop the puppies off. I help with transport when I'm in town and have time. I also make sure a portion of my winnings from my fights are donated to their rescue to help with the animals that they are caring for. They are solely donation based, so everything counts. They don't always get healthy puppies that are easy to adopt out. Unfortunately, they have found injured dogs on the side of the road, or dogs with special needs that require more medical attention, which ends up costing them a lot more money over their budget.

Pulling up to the rescue, Sutton hops out of the car and grabs two puppies.

I grab the hamper with the other four puppies, and we

carry them in alongside each other.

Walking up to the door, I see a couple of friendly faces.

Abby and Mare welcome us in.

Abby reaches for a puppy and starts cooing at it.

"I'm going to get their room ready," Mare says, making her way down the hall.

Moments later, we follow Abby down the hallway. When we come to a spacious room, there is a small pen set up with a few plush dog beds. That is where the puppies will stay for now. A few dog crates line the back wall. A table with a scale and medical supplies sits in the opposite corner. A bin of toys and treats sits directly next to the table.

Leaving Sutton with Mare and the puppies, I follow Abby to her office to give her the paperwork from the farmer who surrendered the puppies.

"Hey, can I talk to you for a second?" I go to ask.

Cutting me off, "Hey Beck, thanks so much for helping today. We were so busy, I wasn't going to be able to get out there, and the farmer wanted them gone today, or else," Abby frowns.

"He seemed alright. They were in the barn, and they didn't seem mistreated from what I could tell. Hopefully you don't find anything," I grimace.

"I appreciate it. So, what's up?" Abby asks.

"I promised that girl in there the best date of her life today. This was part of it because dogs are her favorite thing on the planet. I was wondering if there was anyway, we could take Kingston and Queenie out for the day. I'd love to take them to the park and maybe for a cheeseburger and an ice cream. Would it be okay to sign them out for a few hours and give them a fun day? I'll have them back by curfew," I grin, putting on the charm.

Abby chuckles, "That would be great, Beck. No one has taken those two out much in the past few weeks. We've been swamped here. I think they'd love that!"

"Perfect. Thank you so much. I'll have them back by say six this evening?"

"Sounds great. See you then. I'm sure I'll still be here working on those guys," Abby points toward the door, where I hear Sut still talking to the puppies and loving on them.

Abby goes down the hallway and I hear her open one kennel and shake the leash, "Hey King, who's a good boy? Who wants to go for a walk?" I hear him woof out.

Abby walks over to me and hands me his leash.

Heading back down the hall, "Hey Queenie girl, does my pretty girl want to go for a walk?" Abby coos.

I watch her leash Queenie, then brings her to me too.

Poking my head in the room. Sutton is laying on the floor letting all of the puppies crawl all over her as she giggles loudly.

Mare looks up at me, pointing at Sutton and mouths, "I love her."

"Me too!" I mouth back to her, smiling softly.

Gods, Sutton's breathtaking. "Hey baby girl, you ready to head out? I have another treat for you."

"What could be better than this? This is heaven Beck!" she sighs into the puppies as they lick her face.

"Okay. Okay. Unfortunately, I have to leave you sweet angels. I love you so much! I hope you find the bestest homes ever. You deserve it." She kisses each of their little heads and gets up off the floor.

Sutton comes out into the hallway and stops, "And who do we have here?" she kneels down and puts her hands out for Queenie to sniff, "Aren't you so pretty?" she coos.

"This is Queenie. She's unfortunately been here for a year. Someone adopted her for a brief period and brought her back because she's a bit of an escape artist. She's the sweetest girl. We are taking her on an adventure today with her boyfriend," I pull Kingston forward so he can sniff Sutton's outstretched hand. "Kingston."

"Ooh... aren't you handsome?" Sutton coos at him. He sniffs her hand and then nudges his block head into her hand.

She scratches his head and scratches Queenie's, "What's his story?"

"Kingston's also been here a little over a year. Sadly, no one has even put in an application for him. He's a silver Pitbull. He does excellent with other dogs, cats, and older children, but because of the bad rep they get, people turn a blind eye to him," he frowns.

"That breaks my heart. He's so handsome too. That gorgeous silver fur and big muscly body, just like you," Sutton nudges me and winks.

"I see your interest in Queenie," she pats Kingston on the head.

"Not only do your names fit you perfectly, but all that silver fur and the blue eyes. Match made in heaven," she coos at them.

I chuckle, "Queenie is a bit high energy, being a husky. Being an escape artist has made it difficult too. The families who don't have a fence can't adopt her and those who do, she thinks she's a track star and tries to hurdle them."

Sutton laughs, "So what are we going to do with these two then?"

"Well Abby and Mare let people who volunteer here sign out the dogs and take them on day adventures sometimes. So, we are taking them on an adventure. They just have to be back by six," I smile.

"Awe, Beck. I love that so much! Let's go give these babies the best day!" she squeals and grabs Queenie's leash from me as we head toward the car.

I put the seat back up and help Kingston into the car. Queenie jumps up with no issues and off we go.

We take them to Schenley Park.

I pull a few tennis balls and a frisbee out of my trunk, plus a bottle of water and bowl. We take the dogs for a short walk around the park and then play fetch and frisbee with them until they're tired out.

"This is perfect, Beck! Thank you," Sutton smiles and leans her head on my shoulder.

"Anything for you, Sut," I kiss the top of her head.

"Look how happy they are. I wish we could adopt them too," she sighs.

"I know Sut, me too, but neither of us have a yard."

"What if we get The Foster Farm on board with adoption day on Saturdays? I wonder if we could get these two and some of the puppies adopted too, if we host them one weekend instead of the other rescue," she suggests eyes lighting up.

"I could certainly ask Abby. I know they post pictures of them with an application on Facebook, but if people saw them out in the real world, acting like this, it could give them a better chance," I smile at her.

"Let's take pictures and a couple videos of them playing. I can post them on my Instagram and tag the rescue. That can give them an extra chance too," Sutton's grinning so wide. "Dang it. I should've taken a couple of the puppies too!"

"I actually took some really great candid photos of you with them. I wanted to keep them for myself, but if it'll help the puppies and you're comfortable with posting them, I can send them for you to post on Instagram," I smile.

Sutton swipes through the pictures of her and the puppies. Her eyes are so soft, the sweetest smile on her lips.

"Beck, I love these! They're so precious. Thank you for taking them," she says kissing my cheek.

Kissing her forehead, I stand up and throw the ball, as Sutton films Queenie and Kingston tearing after the ball. They both come back together, with Queenie being the clear winner. Then I throw the frisbee and Kingston catches it easily, and Sutton gets a great shot of him catching it. Her eyes are lit up and she's smiling so big at the pictures. "These are perfect! Hopefully it gets these babies a home."

"Ready to head out and get these guys a cheeseburger and ice cream?" I grab her hand that isn't holding the leash, and we head toward the car.

"Oooh, did you hear that, guys? Cheeseburgers AND ice cream!" Sutton squeals, both dogs' ears perking up at her high-pitched tone.

Queenie howls.

Sutton throws her head back laughing. So fuckin radiant!

$\mathcal{B}$oth dogs have their heads out the windows, tongues dangling in the wind. They look happy and free. Sutton's watching Queenie out of her side mirror, smiling sweetly at her.

I squeeze her thigh, and when she turns to me, a tear runs down her face.

"Hey, what's wrong?" I ask softly.

"I'm just really happy, but also really sad that we have to take them back. I wish I could save them all," she frowns, then smiles softly.

"I know, Sut, me too. At least with your help we have a fighting chance to get these two love birds adopted," I wink and give her thigh a reassuring squeeze.

She rests her hand over my hand and squeezes it back.

We pull up to my favorite burger joint that has outdoor seating and allows leashed dogs. We hop out and grab the dogs and head to a picnic table. Both dogs lay under the table in the shade. The server brings them a giant bowl of water.

"Thank you so much," Sutton smiles at the server.

He smiles back at her.

"What can I get for you guys?" the server asks.

"Can we get two burgers, just the burgers with cheese on top for the dogs. I'll take the black and bleu burger with a side salad," I order and then point at Sutton. "I'll take the buffalo chicken sandwich and fries, please."

"I'll have that right up," he says and walks away.

I look under the table and the dogs are perfectly content and well behaved.

I reach across the table and grab Sutton's hands.

She meets my eyes and smiles softly. Then her eyes widen a bit because I think she knows I have something to tell her.

"Sutton, I need to say something. And know it's the honest truth. You light up a room any time you walk into it. There could be a thousand people surrounding me, and I would still seek you out. You blew into my life like a hurricane six years ago and have been a constant in my life since. I can't even remember a single day before you anymore, and I can't imagine a life without you. I was so afraid I would ruin our friendship if I told you that I had feelings for you. I didn't want to shake the friend group if you didn't feel the same way. I wish I would've held on to you longer when you kissed me in the ring. I wish I would've gone home with you afterwards, instead of letting the cab take you home. We deserved each other's love long before now. I chose you in college for cornhole and beer pong so I could be closer to you and to keep you safe. I sat next to you at football games because I loved when you leaned into me for warmth. I loved seeing your eyes solely glued on me during my fights. I should've known all this time, but I was blinded by my own fear. You are so effortlessly yourself that it's awe inspiring and beautiful. Your love is so pure. The way that you handled those puppies and these dogs today, you give love so freely. I want to give my love freely to you in return. My heart is yours. It's been yours." I state fiercely, staring into those gorgeous green eyes that are glittering with unshed tears.

"Beck, I..."

She swallows, "Beck, wow, I'm...I was not expecting you to say that. I..."

"It's okay, Sut. You don't have to say anything. Let's just enjoy the dogs for a little longer. Just think about what I said when you get home tonight," I clear my throat and try to say so she's not so anxious.

Even though it's killing me that she's not sure how to respond. My girl always has a response. She's a spitfire through and through.

"Here yinz go, chicken for the lady, burger for the gent, and two burger patties for those adorable dogs," the waiter sets our food down.

I place one burger in front of each dog under the table.

Sutton blinks her lashes a few times and turns her head and wipes her cheek and clears her voice, "Thank you so much. These cuties are up for adoption, so if you know anyone who is interested. We're just on a day date," she informs the waiter.

"Oh. How cool! Where is the rescue information? I am happy to pass it along," he inquires beaming at Sutton.

"The Foster Farm Rescue," I chime in, not liking how he's ogling my girl.

"Great, thank you! I will check them out. Enjoy your meal. Let me know if you need anything else," his eyes never leaving Sutton until he walks away.

Sutton is just staring at her food, not touching it, and nibbling on her lower lip.

She's being so quiet and won't meet my eyes. Tension radiates from her. The silence is deafening.

The dogs are under the table devouring their burgers.

Of course, she tried to find them homes, and now it seems that she's at a loss for words.

"Sut... Please eat your food," I encourage.

A few minutes pass, which feels like an eternity, when Sutton finally looks up at me, blinks, and then bites into her sandwich and chews slowly.

We finish our meals in heavy silence.

I notice Sutton's only eaten about half of her meal. She gives the dogs a few of her French fries, and then the waiter comes back over. "Can I get yinz anything else?"

"Can we get two bowls of vanilla ice cream for the dogs please? Sut would you like anything?" I ask her.

"I'll take an Oreo Milkshake please," she perks up.

"Coming right up!" the waiter promises and walks away.

Reaching my hand over to hers, trying to rub soothing circles over her palm.

Sutton's quiet and lost in her head.

"Sut, you can talk to me. It doesn't have to be a response to earlier. We can just talk like we normally do."

"I know we can. I'm just sort of enjoying the quiet. The feel of the dogs leaning on my legs. The sun on my face," she replies.

"Here you all go. I brought the check as well. I can take it whenever you're ready," the waiter instructs.

"Thank you," I hand him my card, and he walks over to the register to settle the bill.

Sut puts a bowl of ice cream under the table for Queenie, and I hold the other bowl for Kingston. They devour the ice cream. Sutton and I both have sticky fingers.

She's giggling while Queenie licks her face. "Girlfriend you are so sticky," she giggles even louder.

The waiter brings my card back and thankfully hands us a washcloth and a to go cup for Sutton's milkshake.

We put the bowls on the table and wipe our hands. We grab the leashes and I reach for Sutton's hand and her milkshake. We walk toward my car and get the dogs back in. They both climb in and lay down and are immediately snoozing in seconds.

Sutton takes a few sips of her milkshake, and a tiny moan escapes her throat. I hold in a groan at the sound. This woman and her little sounds are going to put me in an early grave.

"I think that was a success. Their bellies are full, and Kingston and Queenie seem at peace," she sums up, taking another sip of her shake.

"I think so too. Now let's hope we can get them adopted," I rest my hand on her thigh.

We pull into The Foster Farm Rescue parking lot. I knock on the door, and Mare lets us in. "How did everything go?"

"They are wonderful. I absolutely love them! I wish I had a yard so I could keep them," Sutton gushes, then sighs.

"I know. I wish I could keep some of them too," Abby seconds, walking up and leaning against the wall next to Mare.

"Sutton and I wanted to run something by the both of you. You can totally say no, but we wanted to see what you'd think," I say.

"Shoot," Abby says.

"I own a café bookstore in the city. Every Saturday one of the local rescues brings three to five animals to us, and we hold an adoption day. I have a fenced in back bistro area where the dogs are usually set up. There are tables back there with some shade. I put a sign out front and post about it on my Instagram. For extra incentive, I also do a café promo for people who do adopt. So far we've had a lot of success getting dogs and cats adopted. I was wondering if you'd want to bring these guys there and maybe even some of the puppies, or whoever you think, on any Saturday so that we can try to find homes for these angels?" Sutton offers hopefully.

"That would be incredible!" Abby and Mare both chime in at the same time.

"If one of us couldn't bring them, I'm sure we could get a volunteer from here to help out, or even if you could help out, Beck, you could hang out with a couple dogs and just have applications with you," Abby responds beaming.

"Perfect!" Sutton squeals. "Let's pick a date. I will get everything set up. I will post on my social media and have a sign ready to go. Let's find Queenie and Kingston a home!"

We excitedly say our goodbyes to Abby and Mare.

We head back to the car. Once we get seated in the car. Sutton finally speaks, "Beck, about earlier. I'm not good with words. I know I read a lot of romance novels, but I never really thought romance was in the cards for me. You make me feel so safe and protected. You planned this perfect date, that I'm pretty sure can never be topped. I wish I could explain how wonderful you are and how much you mean to me. You're like soaking in a warm bubble bath after a long day. We slipped into this affectionate, tender friendship that helped slowly heal me from my past, and then I started wanting more from you, but I wasn't sure how to move forward after so much rejection in my past. You are so special to me! I am just at a loss for words."

I lean over and kiss her cheek and take her hand. "I told you to think about it, baby girl. You are special to me too, and I don't want to rush you into anything."

I pull up to the café and park outside, putting my hazard lights on, "I want to kiss you good night, but I'm not coming up. I want to take this slow with you and respect your boundaries. I want to prove to you that you are it for me, Sut."

I get out of the car and open her door. Sutton takes my hand and I help her get out. I shut the door and walk her to the café door. She unlocks it and turns back toward me.

"Thank you for the best day of my life, Scrap, truly!"

"Anything for you baby girl," I push the strands of hair that have fallen from her ponytail behind her ears and slowly bring her face to mine.

I kiss Sutton softly and pull her closer to me with my hands still on her face. Her hands are gripping my shirt tightly and she tries to deepen the kiss. I give in and dip my tongue into her mouth to swirl my tongue with hers. She groans. I pull away and place a tender kiss on those soft lips. My hands are still on her cheeks. "Goodnight, Sutton," I rasp.

Cheeks tinted pink, eyes sparkling in the moonlight, "Goodnight, Scrap."

I watch Sutton walk in and lock the door. I get in my car and get ready to pull away. I turn to give her one last glance, and she's tucking her hair behind her ear, smiling gently, as she waves to me.

My heart beats only for this girl.

32

Sutton

*L*ying on what feels like a soft mattress, my eyes are open, I think.

I'm blinking, waiting for them to adjust, but the room remains so dark.

Where am I? How did I get here?

My eyelids feel so heavy. I can barely keep them open.

Dozing in and out of consciousness.

So cold. Teeth chattering. My skin feels like it's wrapped in a sweatshirt, but goosebumps cover my skin.

I go to reach out for anything, but my arm won't move.

Staring at where I think my hand is, willing my fingers to move.

Nothing.

Panic starts to set in. Breaths become rapid.

Why isn't my arm moving? Am I paralyzed?

Trying to sit up, but my body feels so heavy.

Why does my body feel like it's weighed down by lead?

Why can't I move?

Where is everybody?

Why isn't anyone looking for me?

Tears prickle my eyes. My heart begins to race so fast, ears are ringing, the little vision I have is closing in at the edges. Thumping in my ears is all I hear.

Panting, I hear panting.

Trying to look around the room for anybody. It's so dark. My head won't move.

After a few seconds, it's me, I realize, who's panting.

From fear.

Suffocating fear. Throat constricting.

Need to claw at my throat for air, but I can't move my hands.

Trying to take calming breaths. In through the nose, out through the mouth.

Trying to focus on something else. Anything else.

My therapist told me to find three things, when in a panic, to distract yourself.

A smell, a sound, something I can see, to center me.

In through the nose, hold, count to four, exhale for four.

I can hear the soft whirring of a fan. I think it might be above me, but I still can't see.

That must be where the cool draft is coming from.

Shivering again. I picture what the goosebumps painting my skin look like.

Can feel the hair standing up, like static on my arms.

Can feel the wet tears streaming down my face.

Can taste the saltiness of my tears.

Are my eyes even open? They feel so heavy.

I can't hear anything else. Silence, the sound.

Where is everybody?

Why am I alone?

How did I get here?

Where even is here?

The whirring is ramping up my panic again.

Trying to yell for help, but I can barely speak. The tiniest whisper and rasp leave my mouth, "Hel—help."

No one is going to be able to hear me.

Trying to roll over, I can barely move.

Trying to will my fingers to move again, but they barely twitch.

Where I think my toes are, I can feel the end of the mattress.

Using everything in me, I try to roll again.

Thud.

Glass shatters.

Hopefully someone will hear that.

I think I hit the floor, and something else fell with me.

My head hit something pointy, maybe a nightstand, before hitting the hard ground, knocking the air from my lungs.

My fingers graze what feels like broken glass.

Trying to reach for my head, but it's no use. My arm is so heavy. I still can't lift it up.

I'm lying face down on what feels like hardwood floors.

Trying to push up to crawl, but I can't.

Why do my limbs feel so heavy? What happened?

*A*ll I remember is sitting out by the fire with a few of Jax's friends.

Noticing Frank's eyes boring into me.

Jax pulled me onto his lap and handed me a drink.

Watching as he and his friends passed a joint around the fire.

Turning it down once it made it to me.

"Such a prude," Jax snubbed me under his breath.

Squeezing my hip hard, he whispered with an edge, "Drink up, princess."

Looking around at Jax's friends, my stomach in knots, I took a few sips. It was fruity and tasted good, bubbles tickling my nose every time I took a sip.

Frank watches my every move, while I sit on Jax. It's making me uncomfortable.

I set the drink back down. I hadn't eaten much today and didn't want to get too drunk and embarrass him.

Jax rarely invites me to parties with him and his friends, so I always make sure to look my best, not "Too slutty" and not "Too frumpy," as he says.

Barely eating, so I won't be bloated in my outfits, he chooses clothing for me to wear.

Trying to look perfect, to avoid him making comments about my body in front of his friends.

Ensuring I'm on my best behavior, not flirting with his friends, avoiding making eye contact with them, but also not being too rude and ignoring them.

Being with Jax is like walking on eggshells every second of every day. Always on guard. Never sure what mood he is going to be in. Never knowing what might upset him that day.

He kept handing my drink back to me. I never thought anything of it, but maybe I should have.

Shivering, I excused myself from the group and walk back toward the house to get a sweatshirt.

After that, everything goes black.

My eyes must be open, because I notice a trace of light, from what I think is the bottom of a door.

Trying to army crawl my way to it, I think I'm moving, just at a snail's pace.

I'm not even sure if I'm moving. It's like crawling through sludge.

I might've fallen back to sleep on the way. My body just feels so tired.

Is this what dying feels like?

The door creaks open, and I try to open my eyes.

All I see are muddy boots.

I can't move my head to look up.

But they're men's boots.

"Well, well, well, someone's finally awake," Jax says in a snarl.

"Jax..." I try to croak out.

Cigarette smoke and stale beer permeates my nose, as Jax picks me up from the ground and throws me on the bed.

The room instantly begins to spin.

I feel like I'm going to be sick.

Trying to breathe through my nose, so I don't vomit.

"Gods, you're a fuckin embarrassment!" Jax sneers, disdain lacing his voice.

"Wha—what's wrong with me?" I barely croak out.

"What's wrong with me?" Jax mocks me in a high-pitched voice.

"Well, since you've been a little bitch and withholding that virginity of yours, walking around like a little tease in front of me and my friends all of the time, I figured it was time I took what was mine. I owe Frank some money too, and he's willing to take that virgin pussy as payment. It seemed the only way to do that was by giving you a little something to help you relax. And how easy that was you stupid, stupid girl! You shouldn't take drinks from men, Sutton. Did no one ever teach you that? Oh wait, who would? No one cares about you!" Jax snarks with so much cruelty in his voice, yanking my pants down.

"No...no..." I whimper out, tears pouring down my face.

Jax climbs on top of me, pinning me down with his weight. Suffocating me.

"Don't worry, baby. We'll make it hurt," Jax growls.

"*Is she ready for us?*" another male voice grinds out.

It must be Frank. I never even heard him come in over the ringing in my ears.

"*Please…stop!*" I cry out, trying to fight, but unable to move.

"*You'll take what we give you, whore!*" Frank growls.

Just then I feel a hard slap across my face.

The room goes black.

33
Sutton

"*Please...stop!*" *I cry out, trying to fight, but unable to move.*

"*You'll take what we give you, whore,*" *Frank growls.*

Shooting up in bed, Khaos is licking my face and whining next to me.

He sits on my lap and nudges his head to mine.

My face is wet, skin covered in a cold sweat. Khaos licks my tears away.

Wrapping my arms around him, I take a deep breath. In for four. Hold it for four. Out for four. Using those same techniques from years ago, I try to settle my breathing after a night terror.

Except it wasn't just a night terror. It's a horror movie that haunts my dreams at night when I least expect it. Their cruel words still cut like knives on my skin. *To suck it up, that I begged for it. Deserved it.*

Sometimes when I look in the mirror the bruises that marred my skin appear like ghosts, taking me back to the morning after that horrible night. How they tossed me aside like trash! Gashes from the broken glass, bruises from their rough hands, matted hair, bloody sheets, mascara-streaked cheeks. Filth caked skin, haunted eyes, a broken soul is all I see staring back at me.

After I let Khaos console me for a few minutes, I get up and take a hot shower.

I need to scrub this nightmare off my skin. It always makes me feel dirty. Used. Disgusted.

I've been in therapy. I learned how to calm myself down when I have a panic attack, but never learned how to let myself heal from that night. I'm not sure if I ever will.

I haven't told anyone except my therapist and Quinn about that night. Quinn found out soon after we started living together. I woke her up screaming in my sleep during our second night as roommates. I had eluded to Beck years ago at a party that someone had once slipped something in my drink before which was why I didn't drink much at parties, but he doesn't know the whole story.

I'm afraid of reliving it, but also of what people might say. I wonder if they'll say I asked for it because of the types of clothes I wore. That it's a lie because he was my boyfriend. The looks they'll give me. Like pity, or worse, disgust, and I just can't bear it.

My therapist isn't sure if the nightmares are because I have lapses in time from that night. The drugs may have blocked out certain things, and it's making it hard for me to move on from it subconsciously.

It's been impossible for me to trust people since that incident. How can I trust myself, judging other people's character and intentions? If my own boyfriend could do that to me, and his friends wouldn't stop it, how on earth can anyone be trusted? They just turned a blind eye. Didn't care about the type of scars that would leave on a person.

And the scar is a hole they imprinted on my soul, so deep that it got too big to fill. I've hardly had a drink since, unless I've made it myself or I'm around people I think I can trust.

Other than being affectionate with Beck over the years, I hadn't been truly intimate with anyone until I was with August.

It was years ago. It shouldn't still haunt me this way.

Khaos helps the most though. He always seems to wake me up right before the worst part. As if he senses my distress. He chose me, and sometimes I think it was so he could heal me.

*H*eading downstairs to make an iced coffee, I grab a romance novel off my shelf. I snuggle up with Khaos on the couch and start reading. A good romcom always seems to lift my mood.

Fifteen chapters in and my phone chimes. Putting my book down, I reach for it. Butterflies explode in my belly from the name on the screen.

August: Hey Sunshine, got any plans today?

Sutton: ooh we have pet names now? Just reading a

book, snuggling with Khaos. What about you Auggie? ;)

August: How original. Want company? Maybe work on our song?

Sutton: You were serious about that?

August: Dead. Your voice needs to be heard and I think we can make something special.

Sutton: Okay, be here at noon. I'll make lunch. I am not changing out of my pjs though.

August: Fine by me. As long as you share your coffee.

Ten minutes later, I hear my phone chime again.

August: Here.

Not even a minute passes and I hear August knock on my door.

Trying to calm my racing heart, I open the door.

August is leaning in the doorway, guitar slung over his shoulder looking dark and divine.

I know Beck comments on August's lack of color in his wardrobe, but I love it.

Black is my second favorite color after all.

He pulls me into his arms and kisses me on the top of my head, "You feelin okay? You look great, but you look a little pale."

"Um yeah, I'm okay. Didn't sleep great last night," I mumble into his chest.

"Me either, but I rarely do. The curse of the musician," August mumbles into my hair.

I squeeze him a little tighter, letting all of the tension

in my body melt away, "I really thought you hated being touched, but I love this affectionate side of you."

His body instantly stiffens.

I look up to see confusion in his eyes, "Why would you think that?"

"I told you I see you Auggie. You used to act like my touch burned you at the first few shows. It's okay though. I get it. I'm not really affectionate with people either unless I am comfortable with them."

He relaxes slightly, giving me that crooked grin I love so much, "Does that mean you are comfortable with me?"

"Getting there," I shrug in his arms.

"Me too," he whispers in my hair.

Pulling out of his embrace, I grab his hand and tug him upstairs.

I sit back down next to Khaos, who doesn't move an inch, and tap the seat next to me.

Khaos scoots over and rests his head on Auggie's leg. August softly pets his head and continues to run his hand in a soothing motion down his back.

I'm transfixed for a moment watching that sexy tattooed hand run through my dog's soft golden fur.

He catches me watching and smirks, and I just smile softly at him from under my lashes.

"That coffee is yours," I point to the one on the coaster in front of him on the coffee table to break the tension.

"If I wanted to order this for myself on a day you weren't here, what would I order? Because it's always so good, and your lips always taste like vanilla, but this isn't quite vanilla," August takes a sip and smiles.

"It's a salted caramel iced latte with almond milk. My

favorite. I'm glad you like it," I smile back.

"These are just BLT's and some *Flamin' Hot Cheetos.* I'm lazy on Sundays. I hope that's okay," I point in front of him.

"It's perfect. Thank you, Sunshine," he responds in that velvety voice.

"*S*o where do we start?" I ask pointing to his notepad and guitar.

"Well, I started writing some lyrics last night. I wanted to see what you thought. You can add to them. I sort of see us singing it in verses separately, kind of like the song *Broken* by Seether and Amy Lee, and then the chorus we will harmonize together. You sound a little bit like her, so I feel like we can really make this work. If we can get it finished this week, I'd really love to perform it with you on Saturday. The guys are onboard. They were also shocked that I asked," August chuckles with more excitement than I've ever seen from him.

"Okay," I agree.

"Just, okay?" He scrutinizes me.

"You are the musician, August. I am honored that you think I'm good enough to sing with you! I love singing, but I have no idea how to create music. But if you want me to sing with you, I'm happy to try," I gush.

"Are you sure you're okay today? You aren't as feisty as

you typically are," he asks cautiously.

"I told you. I didn't sleep well. I had a nightmare. I'll be fine. Just still a little shaken up, but your company helps. Music helps. So, let's do this," I explain.

August squeezes my hand, "I have nightmares too sometimes, so I understand how they can tip you off your axis a little bit. That's kind of what happened that night before that show I was off, when that guy asked for a refund. So, I'm here if you want to talk about it, or if you don't."

"What are yours about?" I ask, still refusing to meet his eyes.

He's silent for what feels like minutes.

Clearing his throat, August barely croaks out, "What are yours about?"

"I..." I start to say, but my voice cracks.

"It's okay. You don't have to tell me," He placates me, squeezing my hand.

Squeezing his hand even tighter to ground me.

I croak out, just above a whisper, "I... um... was assaulted by an ex-boyfriend and his friend when I was 16. My nightmares are about that night... What I can remember of it..."

I feel him tense next to me.

"My mom killed herself in front of me when I was 17. My nightmares are about that night..." he croaks.

Finally meeting his eyes, his look as broken as my heart feels, but there's no pity or disgust. Just two shattered souls, seeing and accepting the broken pieces.

Wrapping his arms around me, August pulls me closer to him into a hug. Leaning his forehead against mine.

His eyes are closed, so I close mine, and just sink into the feeling of him.

Letting his leathery tobacco smell, the heat of his skin, and his comforting touch settle my racing mind.

After we sit like this, just breathing each other in for what feels like the sweetest eternity, August breaks the silence, and softly asks, "Are you ready to make some music, Sunshine?"

Nodding, I open my eyes and gently smile back at him. If only he knew just how him being here with me, sharing his darkness with me, his gift with me, calms the storm going on inside me.

We spend all afternoon scribbling down lyrics while August strums on his guitar. Humming some of the sound together to see where we want it to go. It's truly special watching him in this moment. He's so serious and in the zone. The way that the music just pours out of him. The range of his vocals and the way he tries to weave mine in with his. He's mesmerizing.

Every time I sing a line or harmonize with August, he gives me that gorgeous smile of his.

I love listening to him sing, but I also really love singing with him. It makes my heart flutter in my chest and is such a rush.

Writing down the last part of the chorus, my stomach growls loudly.

He chuckles, "Getting hungry, Sunshine?"

"Starving! Do you like tacos? I think I want to order tacos. With chips and salsa. I'm a slut for a good taco," I grin at him.

August bursts out laughing.

My chest tightens and warms at the sound. This man.

This beautiful man. He rarely smiles, but when he does it is brilliant.

"Tacos sounds great. Whatever you're having is fine," he concurs.

"Why do you always do that?" I ask.

"Do what?"

"You just give me control. You let me choose your food. The latte I make you. Your tea. What if my choice isn't good?"

"You haven't disappointed me yet. If you like it, I'm sure I will."

Ugh my heart! My stupid, stupid heart. Why is that so sweet?

*T*he tacos arrive and we devour them. I don't think either of us realized how late it had gotten and how hungry we both were. We don't even say a word as we shovel food into our mouths.

I'm leaning back against the couch, eyes closed, stretching out.

Khaos licks my cheek, and I let out a giggle.

I give him a kiss on his nose, and he woofs at me.

When I open my eyes, August is staring at me, burning a hole straight through my heart.

"What?" I whisper.

He blinks like he's snapping out of a trance, "It's getting late. I better head out. I know you have work in the morning."

"Or you could stay," I invite and try to give him my smolder eyes.

"Sutton, you said you wanted to go slow. I'm trying really fucking hard to respect that. You were right, I do hate being touched. I always have. But when it comes to you, I always want your hands on me, and I always want to touch you. I want to feel your warm body against me. Those incredibly soft lips against mine. Your pulse under my hand when it's wrapped around your throat. I crave your touch. I have never craved anyone's touch before now. Listening to you sing takes my breath away," he rasps.

"I..." I start to whisper.

August puts his finger against my lips, "Shh, you don't have to say anything. I understand why you're torn. I see the way Beck looks at you. How comfortable you are with him. But I see you, and when you see me, the world stops for me. You make me feel like the only person in the room. You are this radiant sunbeam blasting color into my life. No one has ever looked at me like you have! They see the tall, dark storm cloud walking the streets. The kid with no future, slumming it, trying to make a living with his guitar and his voice. They judge me without even knowing me. They think I'm a joke. I was cold to you the first day we met, because I don't let people in, especially women. You could've been cold back to me. Sure, you were feisty, but you still showed me respect. Showed me kindness. That's more than most strangers. I can't offer you much, but every second I spend with you, you breathe life back into my life. I want to prove to you that you aren't just an option for me. You are the most precious gift!"

I kiss his fingertips, as a tear rolls down my cheek.

He immediately swipes it with his thumb and puts it in his mouth.

"If we make a promise to only kiss and hold each other, will you stay. Unless you don't want to? Then I respect that too," I beg.

"I'll stay. But we have one more verse left, and the song is finished. Think you have a couple more hours in you to finish it?" he grins.

I nod and grin back.

It's one in the morning when we finally finish the song. We haven't given it a name yet, but the lyrics are beautiful and tortured and the sound is haunting. It's perfect! It's us!

"I think this is our best song yet! Will you sing it with me on Saturday?" he asks with so much hope in his eyes.

"As long as you don't sing it as your first song, I will sing it," I smile.

August leans over and pulls my face to his, kissing me, "Deal, thank you, I can't wait."

We each take a quick shower. Grabbing my toothbrush, I hand him one from under the sink.

"Um... is this someone else's?" he questions giving me side eye.

I burst out laughing, "No Auggie, it's a new toothbrush. I keep spares under the sink."

He hesitates, but then I add toothpaste to the brush and push it toward him.

He stares at me and slowly brings the brush to his mouth as I grin like a *Cheshire* cat at him.

Then he finally brushes his teeth and winks at me in the mirror.

Sticking my tongue out at him, I leave the bathroom,

yelling down the hall, "Actually I just cleaned the toilet with that one this morning!"

I hear the sound of the toothbrush hitting the sink, before he's chasing me to my room, tackling me onto the bed, and then starts tickling me until I'm out of breath.

A few minutes later, we snuggle up close, with Khaos snuggled in between our feet.

Yawning, I turn on my side.

August pulls me into his chest. "Thank you for today," I whisper at him and kiss his chest.

"Thank you," he whispers back, kissing my forehead, nose, and lips softly, "Goodnight, Sunshine."

"Why do you call me that?" I ask.

"My mom, used to sing that song to me. 'You Are My Sunshine.' It's the one good memory that I have of her, and you remind me of the sun. You always give everyone your undivided attention. You light up every room you walk into. You are my sunshine," August's voice caresses me.

I kiss his jaw and his lips one more time, "Thank you. Goodnight, Auggie."

He kisses the top of my head.

The sound of his heartbeat against my ear lulls me into a dreamless sleep.

34

Sutton

Just under my ear, I feel soft lips and warm breath that wakes me from the most peaceful sleep I've had in what feels like forever.

Not quite ready to open my eyes yet, I wiggle a little deeper into his warmth.

His grip on my hip squeezes and halts my movements, "You're killing me, Sunshine," August groans in my ear, sending goosebumps all over my skin.

Rolling over to face him, so I can kiss him, but my goofball dog has his nose pressed right between our heads. We both look up at him passed out, snoring softly. I giggle and August lets out a warm chuckle.

My eyes immediately connect with his. I'm not sure I've seen them this up close in the daylight. They always seemed black as coal to me, but up close they are the darkest midnight blue.

I reach up and trace my fingertips gently across his cheek, over his lips, to his jaw; my eyes following the same trail. August holds perfectly still, not even taking a breath, just watching me. He's so fuckin beautiful it physically hurts to look at him all those dark, sharp edges.

My fingertips reach his lips again and he gently nibbles the tips and smiles softly at me.

"I think I..." I start to say, but immediately stop myself. Instead, I tilt my chin up and kiss him.

August hesitates for just a second before he melts into my kiss.

For someone with an aversion to touch, August can kiss. This kiss isn't frantic and desperate like our previous ones, but somehow, it's better. We're taking our time exploring each other's mouths. It's like a slow dance under a starlit sky with fireflies buzzing around us. I feel his kiss everywhere, lighting me up from the inside. Completely obliterating every kiss before August's kiss.

Time completely stands still; and then wet sloppy kisses are raining down on both of our faces and August lets out the deepest belly laugh, and it's a shot straight to my heart. I can't stop staring at him as he laughs so gleefully, letting my dog just give him all the kisses.

I think I'm falling in love with this beautiful man.

*Q*uinn and I make it just in time before the self-defense class starts.

"You two are always late," Asher scolds at us.

"Sorry, sorry, we were so busy today, we barely made it

here at all," I apologize.

Asher just shakes his head.

Beck pops his head out from the back office and asks if he can talk to us really quick before class starts.

He pulls me into a hug and kisses my forehead. "Hey, so there's this new girl that showed up for class," he starts to say.

Quinn and I both go to look out, "Don't look; she'll know I'm talking about her, she's already skittish," he gripes.

We snap back around, and Beck continues, "So she has black hair, but she's just in a really baggy sweat outfit and asked to keep her hood on. Anyways, she showed up a couple weeks ago to find out about the class and seems kind of like a cornered animal. We wanted to try to figure out if something was going on with her, to see if we can help her, but it seems like she's more spooked by men than women, just from the short interaction today. So, could you ladies maybe try to gently approach her? See if she's safe? If she needs anything? Maybe one of you try to team up with her today, instead of each other, just to see what you can find out?"

"Yeah, of course," Quinn and I say at the same time.

"All right ladies, I am Asher, and this is Beck. Who's ready to learn how to fight off an attacker?" Asher stands in front of the room asking everyone.

"We are going to have you ladies team up. Choose a partner. You will take turns being the victim and the attacker. This will be a very controlled setting. You are completely safe. Asher and I will demonstrate everything to you on each other. If you have any questions, don't hesitate to ask. We will walk around the room and make sure everyone learns the moves properly," Beck instructs.

"First and foremost, you must remember the three A's: Awareness, Assessment, and Action. Always try to be aware of your situation, look around you and see what you, or your attacker could use as a weapon, and then finally we will teach you some techniques today for you to use in the event that you need to take action," Beck explains as we get set up next to our partners.

I decide to partner up with the new girl. I love Quinn, but sometimes she can come on a little bit strong, and I don't want her to scare off the new girl just yet.

"Hi, I'm Sutton, wanna be my partner?" I ask softly.

She eyes me tentatively, and then glances around the room, "It's a really great class. I've taken it several times. The guys are both really professional. I've never felt threatened here. It's safe," I add.

The new girl looks at me again, maybe noticing a kindred spirit. She tucks her head and tips it into a nod that I almost missed, "I'm...I'm Sloan," she whispers.

"It's nice to meet you, Sloan," I smile softly at her.

"All right ladies, our first move, I bet you guessed it, is going for the groin," Beck says, and I look up and lock eyes with him.

He winks at me and continues, "So whoever wants to be the attacker first, you are going to come at your partner like you're going to grab them from the front, like this," he demonstrates, as he goes to grab Asher.

Asher immediately makes eye contact with Beck. He stands tall and still, appearing calm on the outside, but as soon as Beck gets his hands on Asher's shoulders, Asher grips Beck's shoulders and goes to knee him as hard as he can in the groin.

Beck pretends to fall back and releases his grip, and Asher looks back and takes off running, yelling for help.

"As soon as you strike and break your opponent's grip, you want to take off and try to get to help or go to a safe place as fast as you can. You don't stay and keep fighting and put yourself at further risk. You break out of the hold, and you run," Asher explains.

"Now it's your turn," Beck says to the class.

"Do you want to be the attacker or the victim first?" I ask Sloan.

"Um... I'm not sure," Sloan says so softly, I almost miss it, "I guess maybe the victim, since you said you've taken the class in the past. I need to learn how to defend myself."

I hold her eyes for just a second and nod, "Okay."

I get in the stance, like I'm going to attack her.

"I'm going to pretend to come after you now, okay?" I warn her, so I don't catch Sloan off guard.

"Okay. I'm ready," Sloan prompts.

I pretend attack her quickly, and Sloan freezes and closes her eyes. Stopping dead in my tracks, I give her space until she realizes I never touched her, and she opens her eyes.

"Let's try that again, but let's keep your eyes open, k?" I say softly, smiling gently at her.

"I won't run at you. I'm just going to put my hands on

your shoulders like I'm grabbing you, and I want you to act like you're going to strike me as hard as you can in the groin with your knee."

Sloan nods at me, and I grab both of her shoulders.

She tenses at first, but then she pulls her knee back and slams it forward as hard as she can. I jump back to avoid actually getting kneed, but I'm proud of her.

"Now what are you going to do? I'm in agony for a few seconds, and I lost focus on attacking you," I play act.

"I run away and try to yell for help or find a safe place to hide until help can come," Sloan says matter of fact.

"Yes!" I respond and clap my hands together.

Sloan grins back at me.

The next hour of our class goes a lot better. Sloan isn't as hesitant with learning the techniques. Remembering all of the moves and breaking out of holds well.

My praise of her techniques seems to help her crawl out of her shell a bit more. Opening up about recently moving here by herself. Needing an escape. Sloan didn't seem to want to discuss that any further, so I didn't pry.

I told her about my café, and she said she'd love to stop in some time.

When the class ends, I give Sloan my cell phone number and tell her if she needs anything at all, anytime, not to hesitate to call me or stop into the café.

I also encouraged her to attend a few more classes, really trying to iterate how safe the gym was and how good the guys were at teaching the class, as well as other classes in the gym. Sloan seemed more open about reaching out, than she had in the beginning of class, so I took that as a win.

"**S**o, what do you think?" Beck asked me, pulling me aside at the end of class.

"I think Sloan may be running from an abusive situation or partner. She didn't say that in so many words, but with how timid and soft spoken she is, her fear of men, being untrusting, wanting to learn to fight back, recently moving here and needing an escape, which would be my guess," I surmise.

"She definitely seems like she's hiding, or trying to blend in," Beck guesses.

"That's what I was thinking too. I gave her my number and encouraged her to come back for more classes, so hopefully she sticks around and feels comfortable enough to reach out," I shrug.

"That heart of yours!" Beck says pulling me into a sweaty hug, "Thanks, Sut."

"Women need to protect other women. It's our duty as women," I say.

"Damn, right," Quinn says, throwing her arms around my shoulders from behind me.

"Oooh! Bear hugs," Asher chimes in, squeezing into our giant hug behind Quinn.

Quinn and I both giggle.

I catch a pair of violet eyes across the room and smile softly at her.

Sloan's small hand reaches out from her hoody sleeve,

and she gives me the smallest wave before turning and heading out the gym door.

35

August

Our *From Troy* sign was already placed outside when we got to WaggingWithWords. Sutton's Instagram had a sick action photo of Knox on the guitar promoting us tonight too.

Sutton told me yesterday we're the only ones performing tonight. We're setting up our equipment on the stage. I'm never anxious for a show, but I am tonight.

This new song is completely different from our norm. It's vulnerable. Raw.

Sutton promised she'd perform it with me, but I haven't seen her yet.

Usually she's down here by now.

If it goes well, I'm planning to ask her to sing it with us at The Wicked Tour.

The chime on the door goes off, and I look up hoping to see Sutton, but in walks Quinn with Beck and another really fit guy.

"Hey, have you seen Sutton?" I ask Quinn, trying to

avoid eye contact with the other two.

"Umm...no. I left at lunchtime today. Sutton said that she had everything covered," she frowns.

"I can go see if she's upstairs," Beck smirks.

Quinn shoots him a glare, "I will go check to see if she's up there. Ash," she looks at the fit guy next to Beck, "Knox," she looks at Knox behind me; "Please make sure these two don't kill each other."

"Yes ma'am!" Knox winks at her.

Asher glares at Knox. *Interesting.*

Quinn rolls her eyes and takes off up the stairs to Sutton's apartment.

*A*fter what feels like an eternity later, but really is only twenty minutes, Quinn makes her way down the stairs and grimaces, and I swear I see her lips say, "Lord give me strength!"

The room is deathly silent as Sutton walks slowly, tentatively, down the stairs to the café, looking like a fuckin magnificent dark fallen angel, sucking all of the air completely from my lungs.

I think my heart stops. Or at least skipped several beats.

Wearing a tight black, mesh high necked top tucked into a black skirt that hits mid-thigh with a black buckled thigh cuff and knee-high black leather platform boots; violet locks curled down her back to just above her perfect ass, coal eyeliner rimming those vibrant green eyes and a deep violet lip that matches her hair, Sutton finally looks up and stops dead in her tracks.

You could hear a pin drop.

Everyone's eyes are on her.

"You might actually knock'em dead tonight, girl!" Knox lets out a low whistle and breaks the awkward silence.

"What's he talking about Sut," Beck barely chokes out, eyes devouring every inch of her.

"We're singing together tonight. As long as you still want to Angel?" I smile greedily at Sutton. Begging her with my eyes to say, "Yes."

"Angel tonight, is it? What happened to Sunshine?" Sutton winks at me.

"Definitely knockin'em all dead tonight!" Knox shakes his head grinning.

"Quit hitting on my bestie, Knoxie," Quinn chirps up.

"Really, Blondie?" Knox groans.

"Are you really singing tonight, Sut?" Asher asks.

Asher is the only one not outwardly ogling her, but still smiling at her appreciatively.

"Just one song, but yeah, I really am," Sutton smiles softly at me. It is the sweetest smile! I feel like I hit the jackpot.

"Well, let's get this show on the road! The line is wrapping around the block. Ash came for extra back up. We're expecting a full house," Quinn yells.

"Sut, you're singing? With him?" I hear Beck ask her.

She glances over at me, and then looks back to Beck, "Yeah, Beck, I am. We wrote a song, and we're singing it and just seeing how it goes. I hope you can support me,"

Sutton shrugs and walks to the door with Quinn to start letting people in.

This girl is so fiercely loyal. I'm not used to people saying they'll do something for me or with me and sticking to it. But every time she shows up for me, it makes me fall for her even more.

I can't wait to show the world what she's made of!

We flicker the lights on the stage to let everyone know we're about to start the show. The guys are doing all the sound checks on stage.

I look around in complete awe!

Never in a million years did I expect to ever fill a venue, and because of Sutton, every weekend we've completely maxed out seats at the café. She told me she felt bad because they had to turn people away tonight.

I expected Sutton to be at least a little bit nervous tonight, but unless she's wearing a phenomenal mask, she doesn't appear nervous at all. Vibrating with energy is more like it and more beautiful than words.

As promised, we didn't start the show with the song that she and I wrote together. We played a mix of our softer metal and heavier metal songs for about a half an hour before I decided to call her up on stage. In hopes of maybe having her stay up here with me after our song, if she wants to do so.

"How's everyone doing tonight? We are *From Troy* and it's an honor to have so many of you supporting us and coming out for our shows! We're going to try something a little different tonight," I announce into the microphone.

"So, you see, there's this girl," I start to say, and people start whistling, "She and I sort of started off on the wrong foot, but it turns out she has become my biggest supporter. My muse. A few months ago, I heard her singing karaoke at a bar downtown and was blown away by her voice. A week or so ago we harmonized a few cover songs together which led to us dabbling in writing a song together. I asked her if she'd be willing to come up here and sing it with me tonight," I croon into the microphone.

People start cheering and looking around the room.

"You all actually may know her," I grin. "Sutton," we shine our blue light down on her in the crowd. "Get your gorgeous ass up here and show this crowd what you're made of."

"That's our girl!" I hear Quinn yell from the side of the stage.

People are cheering and wolf whistling, as Sutton sashays her way up to the stage.

Grabbing the microphone from my hand, "So poetic, as always," Sutton says. "Thank you all for showing up for these guys tonight. They're pretty amazing, aren't they?"

The crowd, "Whoops" and cheers and screams so loud.

Sutton smiles so brightly, "And guess what? You want to see them live in the wild? Want to be able to bring more friends, since I'm pretty sure not another human being would fit in this place?" she pauses for just a second, "They are performing at The Wicked Tour next month! So, make sure you purchase a ticket, and you show up and scream your faces off for them! These guys deserve to make it.

The more fans they have that show up for them there, the better their chance of getting picked up by a label. So, buy your tickets y'all!"

Everyone cheers so loudly; it feels like the room is vibrating. Sutton did that. She makes my soul vibrate on an entirely different frequency.

"Anyways," I snag the microphone back and wink at her.

"Anyways," she croons, leaning over into the microphone.

The crowd starts laughing and wolf whistling.

"This is our song that we wrote together. It's currently untitled, but we hope you love it!" I set the microphone in the stand and grab my guitar from Knox.

Knox hops off the stage and wraps his arms around Quinn's shoulders, who's standing in the front row to watch her best friend. She leans back into his embrace and beams up at Sutton. I notice Asher is glaring at the back of Knox's head, and Beck is glaring up at the stage, but thankfully Sutton is completely oblivious.

This is so surreal.

The lights go off and then the soft blue hue of the spotlight is directly on the two of us.

Our eyes meet and I lose myself in August. It feels like it is just the two of us in this room.

I nod my head to let him know I'm ready, and he starts to strum his guitar.

The haunting melody wraps itself around me and cocoons us in our own space and time.

I open my mouth to sing, *"They wanted me to break, they wanted me afraid. I couldn't show the pain, but it had me in a chokehold. Was already broken, living in the silence. I wouldn't give them the satisfaction, wanted to run from all the violence,"* keeping my eyes closed.

Each strum of the guitar from August's fingers plucks on a different string in my heart, and then he joins in and croons his soft, tender gravelly voice into the microphone with my haunting sound; *"And then it happens, one day you're in this place, when just your embrace, is a balm to my soul, and your kiss lights a fire, and I finally feel whole,"* we harmonize together.

August so tenderly sings, *"Solitude always felt the safest, life had taken all that I ever had, love wasn't meant for me, not for a moment, not even the briefest; but that didn't mean I craved to be alone, going utterly mad."*

We finish the song, harmonizing the chorus together, August continuing to strum the hypnotic tune on his guitar, our voices completely in sync and so desperate and tender, *"I won't give them the satisfaction. I finally feel whole, no longer alone. No longer in a chokehold. You're the balm to my soul."*

Feeling the softest touch on my cheek, my eyes flutter open.

August's staring at me, eyes hooded and filled with, it can't be, love? Could it? He wipes the tear stains off my face and sucks on his thumb.

I'm a second away from kissing him, when the crowd goes absolutely insane, and I blink, then blink again.

I completely forgot we were on stage!

August pulls me into a side embrace and whispers in my ear, "You were..." he clears his throat, "You were otherworldly, Sunshine! I am in awe of you!"

I look up into his midnight eyes and smile at him, "Thank you. I am in awe of you, August!"

"One more song! One more song! One more song!" The crowd is madly cheering.

I shake my head and laugh, waving at them.

I'm about to hop off the stage when August wraps his arm around my waist, "You wanna sing one more with me?"

"We only wrote the one song," I dispute, looking back and forth between his eyes.

"You don't know the words to our other songs?" he asks me with a smirk.

"Of course, I do, but I can't scream, and with the one song, I might cry if I try to sing it. You always make me cry when you sing it," I frown.

"You just sang so fuckin beautifully through your own tears, Sunshine! I think you can do it, but no pressure," I squeeze her to me and kiss her forehead.

"Okay. Fine. One more, but that's it," she caves while grabbing the microphone.

"Ya'll fine with Sutton singing one of our songs with me?" August asks the crowd.

The sound is deafening as people whoop and holler, cheering me on.

We finish the rest of the set, with me singing the rest of their songs with *From Troy*.

August and I are perfectly in sync.

The crowd is going absolutely wild.

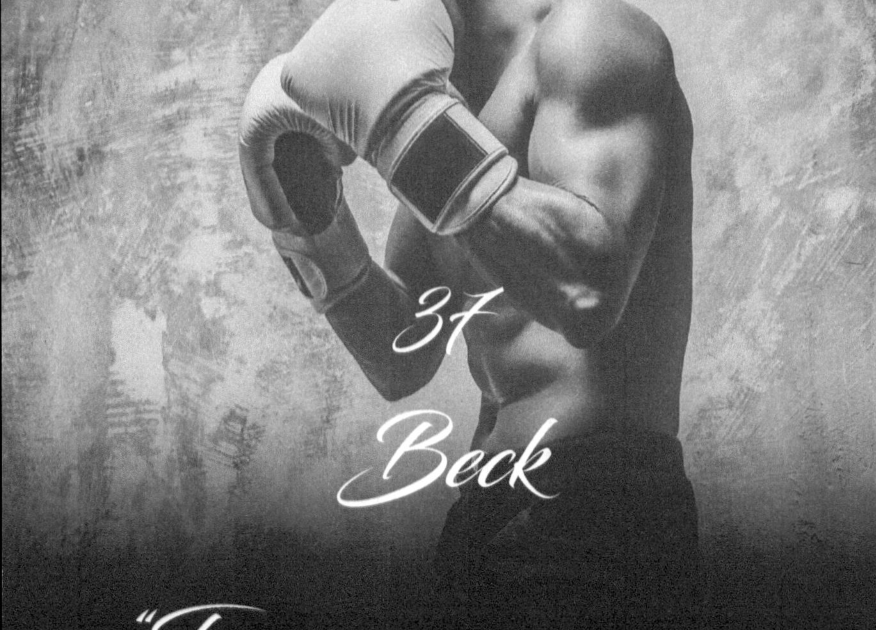

37

Beck

"Fuck!" I shout, as I make my way through my apartment door.

Running my hands through my hair, I think about how Sut looked so fuckin beautiful and that voice, that fuckin voice!

I had no idea she could sing like that!

Bracing myself against the counter, I feel like I've been punched in the gut.

To know that the girl I've been in love with could sing like that.

I've heard her humming and occasionally she'll sing softly to herself, but never that. Never like what I saw tonight. She was made for the stage!

Mayhem pushes his nose against my leg.

Bending down, I give his head a scratch and confess what I feared.

"I've lost her, buddy, I just know it! I can see it in her eyes. I'm too fuckin late!"

Fuck!

38

August

It has been a month of Saturdays singing on stage with Sutton.

And it has been nothing short of exhilarating!

That girl has a set of pipes and whether we just sing our song, or Sutton sings with me on a couple of *From Troy's* songs, she's absolutely incredible!

I've spent more Sunday mornings waking up next to her and Khaos than I have in my own bed but then every Monday morning I've woken up alone in my apartment just wishing to have her back in my arms.

I can't remember a time I ever felt like this. I'm not even sure I can put into words the way that she makes me feel. I don't remember a time where I ever felt whole before, but with her I feel what I think is pretty damn close.

If I'm the moon, Sutton's the whole fuckin starry night sky.

There's just something about Sutton.

The way that she sees me, instead of through me, like

so many other people do. Always listening and quietly observing, never judging anyone. It's like she knows what it feels like to be invisible, so she makes sure that she sees everyone. Or at least that she makes them each feel seen. I've never met anyone like her. A literal ray of sunshine, in my dark, gloomy world.

Our Instagram has slowly grown; honestly all thanks to Sutton and Quinn. They know how to run social media, and they've done everything in their power to get our name out there.

So I'm hoping we have a good turnout for Wicked Tour.

*T*he day is finally here.

I am still mind blown that we are performing at *Wicked Tour*.

This has been my dream since I was a teenager, but it always felt so out of reach.

I can't believe we're here!

We're early in the day, on one of the smaller stages, but fuck, we made it here! This is our chance to prove to the world what we've got.

The guys and I are vibrating with energy. It's just coming off us in waves. We're that amped up! The air is buzzing around us.

I never got up the courage to ask Sutton to sing our song with me, so I think she thinks we are just skipping that song.

Little does she know; I might call her up from the audience.

There's a fairly good chance that I will. She might murder me though.

The stage manager and stage crew come back to let us know that it's our turn to set up.

"You ready, boys?" I yell.

"Fuck yeah! Let's do this!" Knox whoops.

Beau and Ty just grin at me and nod.

We head out to the stage with the crew and start getting everything set up.

Sound checks and microphones are perfect.

Our light equipment is thankfully working right too.

Taking it all in. I glance around the stage.

A whole ass stage for us!

Sitting in a wide-open field.

I look up and see our lights shining down on the drum set. Two microphones are set up at the front of the stage. The boys have their guitars slung around them. They're perfectly tuned.

Then I look out into the field and see a crowd even bigger than the crowd normally at WaggingWithWords. It's more than double.

My jaw drops and I glance over at the guys who are all wearing shit-eating grins on their faces. Their faces are lit up with joy and exhilaration.

Knox walks over to me, throwing an arm around my shoulders. *I don't flinch.*

"Our girls did that," Knox points out to the crowd.

"Our girls?" I tilt my head at him, smirking.

"Yeah, Auggie, our girls," he gently punches my arm.

I smile softly to myself.

Then I hear my name being yelled, and I look out toward the crowd.

I look up to see Sutton at the barricade, waving at me and giving me a thumbs up.

Smiling at her, giving her the smallest wave, and a wink.

I walk up to the microphone.

With Knox to the left of me on bass, Ty to the right of me on guitar, and Beau behind us ready to go on the drums.

Our girls. I like the sound of that.

I smile again and raise my hand to the crowd.

39

Sutton

Thank goodness Quinn and I got VIP passes for this festival! The general admission line had to be a mile long. There is no way in hell I was going to miss the boys performance!

And I'm pretty sure Quinn didn't want to miss Knox either. Those two definitely have something going on, even though she tries to deny it.

We tried to get in as early as we could.

They were the second band going today, so we had a little bit of time before we made it over for their set.

I am so excited for them! I could combust on the spot.

There are so many other incredible bands August and I listen to sharing this same space today.

I can't even imagine how they're feeling. How August is feeling especially.

This is all their dreams, but this is it for August.

I'm hoping with all of the posts I made on social media and the sign I put on the café door that they will get the kind of crowd that they deserve.

Quinn and I make our way up to the stage.

There are already quite a few people here for the first band.

This group sounds pretty good, but nowhere near as good as *From Troy*.

We stand off to the side closer to the stage while these guys finish up their set.

Once they're done and some of the people start to clear out, Quinn and I move closer to the barricade.

But not before telling some of the people who are leaving that they should absolutely stay and listen to the next band, because they're amazing!

The stage crew comes out and starts helping tear down the first set and then Knox, Beau and Ty are out setting up their equipment and tuning their instruments.

I haven't spotted August yet, but the butterflies in my stomach are fluttering like mad. The happiness I feel for this man getting to live out one of his dreams before my eyes makes me want to burst!

A few minutes pass as I chat with Quinn, and then I feel a pull in my chest.

Looking up at the stage, my heart skips a beat because there he is.

August doesn't see me yet, but I see him.

I watch as every emotion crosses his beautiful face as he takes in everything in front of him. Excitement, awe, surprise, and then blinding joy when our eyes meet.

August is a fuckin star!

Absolutely heart stoppingly gorgeous too!

He steals my breath, radiating his dark aura.

Dressed head to toe in his signature black tee and distressed jeans, long hair wavy down his back, all black combat boots with the laces loose, chunky metal rings on his fingers, utter perfection.

My cheeks hurt from smiling so wide at him!

My heart stops again when he winks at me!

August makes his way to the microphone, my *Lucifer*.

He raises his hand to the crowd, and they go absolutely wild.

It is deafening.

Quinn and I immediately turn our heads around and take in the sight in front of us. This crowd is two, if not three, times the size of the crowd at the café.

The crowd is roaring! Clapping and hollering.

My heart soars for August.

A deep voice in the microphone immediately gets my attention and I turn back around to face the man who has completely stolen my heart in just a couple of months.

Starting off with a bang, he starts out with one of their heavier songs, screaming, growling, and singing into the microphone.

"We are *From Troy*!" he yells into the microphone.

The crowd starts screaming, and August immediately goes into another one of their heavier metal songs.

He works every angle of the stage, twisting and contorting his body. Pouring everything into his performance.

Ty and Knox are perfectly in sync, even throwing in a few little dances with their guitars. Circling them around their bodies, jumping in the air.

Almost karate kicking each other at one point.

"Now this is the part of the song where I want you to part down the middle," August requests in the microphone, while the guys continue to strum the tune of the song.

He makes hand motions to get everyone to part like a sea in the field, "Give me the biggest wall of death you mother fuckers got!" August yells in the microphone.

Everyone does as he says, making space, pushing each other back until the crowd is split in two perfect halves.

The crowd jumps up and down, getting amped up.

The guys pick up the instrumentals right where August left off, when he started trying to get people to mosh.

August immediately starts singing in the microphone again.

Then he lets out the deepest, growliest scream from the depths of hell, "*NOW!*" and everyone rushes to the middle of the pit they parted.

They start pushing and shoving each other.

Bouncing off one another like ping pong balls.

Doing these little dances in the pit. Throwing their arms out in front of them like they're punching the air, as they scream the lyrics with August.

When he finishes the song, August yells "Fuck yeah, that's what I'm talkin about," into the microphone.

I look up at him, our eyes connecting for a second as we smirk at each other.

"Now, some of you may have heard this song before now, if you came to our girls' café. And if you have, then you know that I need a certain girl up here with me to actually make this song sound good," he chuckles into the microphone and looks straight at me.

My eyes go wide, and I immediately start shaking my

head no at him.

"Did you know he was going to call you up there?" Quinn asks, eyes as big as saucers.

"Nope. I'm gonna kill him!" I growl, but making sure I say it slow enough that he should be able to read my lips.

August must be able to because he smirks at me.

"I don't think our girl wants to get up here. So, I'm going to need a little help from you all," he croons into the microphone.

"If you would all chant her name, Sutton, to get her to come up here and sing our song with me."

"Sutton! Sutton! Sutton," the crowd starts chanting.

I send August my best death glare.

In seconds August and Knox are scooping me up over the barricade and pulling me up onto the stage.

The crowd goes wild!

I wave at them with one hand, and then rip the microphone from August's hands.

"I am going to murder him after this, so I hope you all enjoyed his very last show," I grin like a lunatic at him and growl into the microphone.

Running my finger across my throat to show him he's dead after this.

"Oooh, babe, you should growl more often," August quips into the microphone.

Everyone starts laughing and clapping.

Quinn whistles and yells my name.

August pulls me against him and kisses the side of my forehead. Like it's the most natural thing in the world. Like he does it every day.

I swoon just a little bit.

The guys sit on the edge of the stage, as August takes Ty's guitar.

"I know it's still daytime, but I'd like to do something special for this one. Can you all take out your cell phones and turn your flashlight on," August asks the crowd.

I watch as every single person in the crowd takes their phones out and raises them in the air. Their arms sway from side to side, following the motion of Knox, Beau, and Ty who are holding their phones in the air.

Smiling at August, I nod at him like I have every Saturday since we started singing together.

He instantly starts strumming the guitar to the song that I couldn't forget if I tried.

Our song.

I start to sing softly into the microphone. Closing my eyes like I always do. Just feeling the song. Letting the strum of the guitar strings and the melody put me into a trance of just August and me.

August joins me at the chorus.

Our voices create this tender, haunting sound.

We couldn't be more in sync. Every time I sing this with August, we sing it better than the last time.

And every time, my heart breaks wide open, goosebumps run down my arms, and he steals my breath.

And every time, I fall just a little bit harder for this man.

I hear a boom of thunder in the distance. The smell of rain permeates the air.

But I don't open my eyes.

The electricity buzzes throughout the air while I sing with this man, or maybe from the impending storm.

Regardless, it holds me hostage.

The sound of August's velvety voice wraps around me like a cloak.

I could get lost in him, in us, forever.

"*I don't want to be alone, unless I'm alone with you,*" we harmonize at the end of the song and then I feel a drop of water hit my face, and then another.

I open my eyes and realize it's started to rain.

As I look up at the sky, raindrops mix in with my tears as they hit my face and the static finally clears from my ears.

All I hear is the crowd cheering so loud, it's deafening.

My eyes make it back to the crowd. It's even bigger now than it was when I was down on the ground.

This is such a heady rush being on such a huge stage!

I always forget I'm in front of a crowd when I'm singing with August.

It's as if the world completely disappears. And it's just us.

I look back toward August, as rain continues to pour from the sky. His smile is so bright, it warms every inch of my skin.

Instead of rushing off the stage, we just stand there, enraptured by one another, as the rain pours down around us.

The feral look in August's eyes as he stares at me right now sets my core ablaze.

I go to walk off of the stage when August catches me by the throat and slams his mouth on mine. Setting fireworks off inside of me! Stars exploding behind my eyes!

I don't even hesitate. Melting into this kiss and nipping

his lip with my teeth.

Growling, he pulls me tighter to him, burying his hands in my hair and deepening the kiss.

Rain continues to pour down over us, as lightning cracks in the near distance.

Time has completely stood still, and it's just us and the rain and the rapid thump of my pulse, where August's thumb is gently squeezing my neck.

The crowd wolf whistling, mixed in with a loud boom of thunder and an extremely close crackling of lightning, breaks us out of our haze.

"Anyone else want to play Russian roulette with this storm a little longer?" August growls into the microphone, not missing a beat, and never letting me out of his grip.

"Hell yes!" the crowd roars.

"Well how about one more song before they kick us out of here?" August yells into the microphone.

I go to leave him to hop off the stage, but he keeps me pinned tight to his side.

"You guys cool with me letting my girl sing this next one with me too?" August asks the crowd, grinning wide.

They all whoop and holler.

Quinn screams, "Hell yeah!"

Shaking my head, I lean into him whispering, "Your girl hmm?"

Pulling me back to look into his eyes, August verifies "My girl."

Giving me that devilish grin.

The guys set up, and we both share the microphone, singing the song that took my breath away the first time that I heard it in my café.

A sense of peace washes over me as we sing together. Like being with August makes everything feel safe for me. Like together, we could take on anything.

Once we finish the last line, August gently wipes the lone tear streaming down my cheek. Sucking it from his thumb, he leans down and presses a chaste kiss to my lips, making the crowd roar.

"We are *From Troy*. You all are fuckin amazing! Thanks so much for coming out today and standing in this storm for us," August says in the microphone.

The crowd is yelling and clapping so loud for them.

"And let's not forget our incredible girl, Sutton," he adds, when they die down.

Clasping my hand with his, August holds our joined hands in the air.

The crowd continues to cheer.

With a smile so big on my face, I give them a wave.

We all run off the stage to finally get out of the rain, even though we're all already drenched.

"You guys were amazing! That was amazing! Thank you for letting me be a part of it!" I beam at them.

"Let's get you dry before you get sick," August wraps his arm around me and pulls me toward the back of the stage.

He pulls a dry tee shirt from his bag and hands it to me.

I pull my top off and unhook my bra from inside the shirt, sliding it out.

"Aren't you going to change too?" I ask.

"I only had the one shirt, and you're more important," August kisses the side of my head and my nose.

I'm pretty sure I swoon on the spot, "Thank you," I whisper.

"Hey, I wanted to talk to you," I start to say.

"What's wrong? Is everything okay?" August asks, nervous, looking between both of my eyes.

"Everything's great. I just...I'm going to tell Beck, that..." I start to say again.

"That was a hell of a show!" a man in a dark suit walks in, interrupting us.

I don't fail to notice that August immediately stands in front of me to block me from the man, just in case he's a threat.

"Thank you. Who are you?" August inquires, on edge.

"The name's Rod. Rod Goodman," he reaches a hand out to August.

August just stares at it, then at the guy again.

The guy pulls his hand away and puts it back in his pocket.

I smirk behind August. Remembering when he once did the same thing to me. But things are so much different now.

I put my hand in his back pocket for silent support.

"I'll keep it short. You guys are incredible performers. You put on a hell of a show! Didn't stop even in a storm. Drew a hell of a crowd for your first time performing here! I'm from Thriller Records. We'd like to talk to you about joining our record label and possibly going on tour with a couple of our bands as an opener. If that's something you'd be interested in doing. I think you have a bright future, kid," Rod offers.

I am frozen in my spot. I can feel the tension radiating off August in waves.

"Can I go grab the other band members for him, so you

can have a discussion with all of them?" I ask from behind August's back, offering him support since he seems to be speechless.

"I'm actually in a hurry. Here's my card. All of my information is on there. Talk to the rest of the band. I'll give you 72 hours to get back to me. If not, then I'll take that as a no and move on. I hope you consider it. I think you guys have what it takes. Oh, I also need to add that you must also be on the record for your two songs," Rod says looking directly at me.

"Two songs? We only have one song together. The first one we sang," I squeak out so fast.

"Ah, but the second song you sang was incredible with your vocals together. Even if you didn't create that together, it should be recorded with both of you," Rod goes on.

"But," I go to say.

Finally snapping out of it, August takes the card from Rod. "I'm fine with that, but that's ultimately her choice. I'll have to talk to the rest of the guys about all of this as well. Thanks again. We will be in touch."

"Good. Remember you have 72 hours," Rod says walking away.

Turning toward August, I reach for his hand again, giving him a look of confusion.

He's so quiet. So tense. This is literally his dream come true. So why isn't he acting like the happiest man alive?

Feeling the heaviness between us, I realize I'm going to have to put our conversation on hold. This is so much bigger than us.

40

August

"He's right you know," I say softly, still facing away from Sutton.

It's been so quiet you could hear a pin drop since Rod Fuckin Goodman walked out of here.

"Who's right? About what?" Sutton asks, confusion lacing her soft voice.

I can still feel her small hand in my back pocket, grounding me.

"Rod," I bite out his name. "The song sounds better with you singing with me. Most of our softer metal songs do," I almost whisper.

"You don't mean that. You guys are incredible without me. You don't need me!" Sutton exclaims exasperated.

"But what if we do? You heard what he said. There's no label without you," I bite out.

"That's not what he said, and you know it," Sutton retorts defensively.

"That's literally what he said! You" I whip around

facing her and point at her. "You have to be on our song, plus the other one we just sang."

"That doesn't mean there's no label without me. Maybe I can just record those songs with you, then you guys can record the rest of your songs as you've written them," Sutton says infuriated.

"That's probably not how that works. What about performing the songs? You think he'll just let us skip those? On a tour? Huh, Sutton?" I growl.

"Don't you dare get fuckin loud with me, August" she growls back, getting up in my face.

"Why the fuck are you even mad at me? You" she shoves her finger in my chest. "You are the reason we wrote a song together. You," she shoves her finger in my chest again, "Are the one who said my voice needed to be heard. I didn't ask for any of this! This was something fun for me to share with you. With the guy I was falling for. This was never my dream. This was yours! And you just had to go and keep calling me up on stage," Sutton thunders.

"I love singing, but I did this because it made you happy," she adds, tears streaming down her cheeks.

"Gods, August, do you know the things I'd do, the lengths I'd go just to see you happy? Because you rarely smile August, but when you do, it's fuckin beautiful. Your smile makes me feel like I can breathe again. It's illuminating! I'd do anything to see that smile on your face," Sutton says almost broken.

With a flash of fire in her eyes, "But this," motioning around her, "This is not my fault. So don't you dare take your fear and anger out on me! And don't you dare speak to me like this, again!"

Sucking in a shaky breath, Sutton goes to turn.

"Sutton, listen, wait. I'm..." I say reaching for her hand.

Putting her hand over my mouth, she gets in my face again. "No. You listen, August! Go talk to the guys. See what they want to do. This is your dream and their dream. I won't stand here and let you take your frustration out on me. This is a big decision for you. I'm going to head home. Why don't you take some time and decide what it is you want? Then when you're ready to come and talk to me without acting like an asshole, we can talk. None of this pointing fingers."

I go to put my hand on her cheek, and she pulls away, "Sutton. Please."

She shakes her head, turns, and walks away.

Leaving me standing here feeling like we're ending before we even had a chance to begin.

I bow my head down and I'm about to berate myself for hurting Sutton on one of the best days of my life.

"And August," she says so softly, I almost don't hear her.

I look up and meet her eyes, "Yeah, Sunshine?" I barely croak out over the lump in my throat. Fuck why does this feel like goodbye?

"Congrats! On today. You put on a killer show and your crowd was epic. I'm really happy for you! You guys deserve it," chin high, one lone tear runs down her cheek. Sutton smiles softly at me and then turns and walks out the door.

"It was only epic because of you," I admit, under my breath.

11

August

"So good news and bad news guys," I say as we pack up the van to head back to Ty's place.

"Hit us with the good stuff," Knox chooses.

I pull the business card out of my pocket that's been burning a hole in there since Sutton walked away from me earlier.

"Rod from Thriller Records wants a record deal with us and wants to put us on a tour. We have 72 hours to call and tell him yes or no," I grit out.

Why the fuck am I so angry? Sutton's right. I have wanted this for so long. This has been my dream, but I'm not even sure if it's everyone else's dream. I know it certainly isn't hers, but Rod said no deal without her. I'm not sure if there's a loophole for that stipulation, and I highly doubt she'd be willing to tour with us and give up her café.

"No shit! That's amazing! That's the break we've been waiting for," Knox yells, smacking me on the shoulder.

"Wait, what's the bad news? Why aren't you happier about this?" Ty asks, looking around confused, "And where's Sutton?"

"I'm not sure that it's necessarily bad, but it isn't ideal, and I'm not sure how you guys will feel about it," I start to say.

"Spit it out, man," Beau says. Always being the one who wants people to get directly to the point.

"Rod said no deal unless Sutton is on the record for our two songs. So, I assume that would mean he wants her on tour too, and she isn't going to give up her café, so I'm not sure this is even going to be possible," I grumble.

"Did you ask her? Is that why she's not here celebrating with you?" Ty asks, frowning.

"By two songs, do you mean the one you two wrote? Is the second song the one that she sang with *From Troy* tonight? The one you've been having Sutton come up and sing with you? Because it sounds fuckin incredible with you both on it! I think Sutton's been the missing link to our sound," Knox chimes in.

"Yeah," I grind out. "Those two. And no, I didn't ask her. I may have, accidentally, yelled at her, because I was frustrated when Rod said it was no deal without Sutton."

"What the fuck! Why would you yell at her? And how do you know she wouldn't be willing to split her time on a tour with us and keep her café too? A record wouldn't take much time to record, so that doesn't seem like an issue," Ty says. Always the voice of reason.

"We haven't even had a conversation about our relationship yet. I still don't know if it's me or Beck, or neither of us. Fuck. Sutton said she wanted to talk before Rod interrupted us. I completely forgot. She said she wanted to talk to me about Beck. If she's choosing him, there's no way in hell she'd be on board with this record label deal. Ha, there's no way he'd let her go on tour with us!" I run my hands through the ends of my hair and tug. Fuck!

"So why don't you have that conversation with Sutton. If she chooses you, maybe she'll be willing to do this for you," Knox encourages swinging his arm around my shoulders.

"We love making music with you Aug, but when it's Sut and you, man, there aren't even words for the magic you two create onstage. The crowd multiplied while you two were singing to each other, even as it poured down rain. Neither of you had a clue because it's just the two of you when you sing together. It was such a sight to see," Knox says grinning.

"Plus, if you get her to say yes, maybe Blondie will come to a few extra shows if she misses her bestie," Knox jokes, tugging me closer with a chuckle.

"Oh yes, just to see her "Bestie," not her "Knoxie," I shove him and laugh.

"Anyways, you two are such children. All in favor of having Sutton on the record, hands up," Ty grins raising his hand first.

"Fuck. I guess you guys better hope that it's me and not bouncer boy she's choosing," I grumble.

42

Sutton

"**S**ooooo what happened with you and August after the most magical thing I've ever seen happened to my best friend!" Quinn squeals rushing from the kitchen.

Popping my head up from the display case, Quinn stops dead in her tracks.

"Oh honey, why aren't you beaming like the sunshine you are? Why do you look all dark and gloomy."

Finally walking up to me, she throws her arm over my shoulder, pulling me into a side hug.

Pulling away from her, I start to set up the espresso machine and rearrange pastries in the display case. Organizing pastry after pastry. Anger bubbles up inside me, suffocating me. Standing, I slam the display case door closed and make my way to the cabinet.

"Rod fucking happened. That's what!" I all but growl out.

Pulling out cups, I make my way back to the machine to make our lattes.

"Whoa! Who the fuck is Rod?" Quinn asks, leaning against the counter beside me.

"The manager or something from Thriller Records, who offered the guys a record deal," I start to say, turning to face her.

"OMG! WHAT?" Quinn squeals, hopping up and down.

Stopping abruptly, "Wait, why aren't you happier, and why didn't Knox tell me? What the hell happened, Sut?" Quinn's basically yelling in my ear now.

Pulling her in front of me.

"If you'd let me finish," I grit out.

"Rod showed up, handed August a card, said he had 72 hours to talk to the guys to see if they'd be on board for a record label and a tour, but only...ONLY, if I was on the record with them."

"Oh, fuck!" Quinn lets out a sigh.

"Yeah. Oh fuck," I grumble, handing her a latte.

Taking it from me, "What are you gonna do?" Quinn asks.

"You ask that like it's not the craziest thing in the world!" I let out a laugh.

"What do you mean, what am I going to do? Hello?" I say waving my hands around the café.

"We literally run a café together, Q," motioning around the café again.

"This has always been my dream! I can't go on tour. I can't be on a record singing with August. That's his dream, not mine!" I dispute the idea, slumping back against the counter.

"But what if you did do both?" Q suggests, shrugging her shoulders.

"Pardon? In what universe can I do both?" I gawk at her.

"Hear me out. We co-own the café, Sut. Your loft is a two bedroom. You sublet the extra room to someone else, and I can still keep an eye on it. I can run the cafe while you're on tour. We hire an extra set of hands to help out while you're gone. That way when you are back from the tour, you can still be as involved with the café as you want to be, but you can also go out there and show the world what you're made of. And Sut, you can finally get the guy! The one you deserve. And who deserves you. Plus, you love to sing. August and you sound amazing together. You deserve the world!" Q persuades me, hugging me to her.

"That actually," I blow out a breath. "That actually could really work! If you really would be okay with that."

"I just want you to be happy, Sut. We've had this dream of running this café since college, and it's running beautifully, but that was almost seven years ago. We can have more than one dream. We're human. We're always evolving. We're always searching for more," Quinn says smiling at me.

"I think you're right," I smile softly back at her. "Fuck, what am I going to tell Beck?"

Just then the doorbell chimes and in walks Beck.

43

Sutton

"Tell Beck what?" he almost growls.

Quinn's eyes go wide, and she squeezes my hand twice. "Just tell him the truth," she whispers in my ear and walks back into the kitchen.

"Can we sit?" I ask and go over and lock the door to the café and put up a sign that says, "Be back in 15 minutes."

"Sure," Beck hesitates but takes a seat toward the back of the cafe away from the windows.

Sitting across from him, I start to ring my hands together. I look down at them and then back up at him and try to take a few deep breaths before I can make eye contact with him.

"It's him. Isn't it? Just spit it out, Sutton," Beck's tone is sharp and almost makes me flinch.

"I… I never expected… it was all-wways y-you…" I start to stutter.

"Until it wasn't," Beck says with anguish laced in his words.

"I thought I loved you. For so long Beck. I felt so safe with you, but you always felt so out of reach. Not once did I ever think you'd reciprocate my feelings, and I never wanted to ruin the friendship we had. And that weekend in Vegas, it was perfect! It was everything I ever imagined it could be with you, better even..." I start to whisper.

"But then you met August. What's so special about him, Sutton?" Beck can't even meet my eyes, just shakes his head, "I don't understand."

"I'm not even sure, Beck. It just feels different. It feels more. I love you, but I'm not in love with you," I whimper.

"But I'm in love with you, Sutton. How can you know you aren't in love with me? You haven't even given us a real chance," Beck agonizes.

"It's been years, Beck. There have been plenty of chances. I do love you and I do care about you, but we are just on different paths in life. I'm sorry!" I squeeze his hand, tears running down my face.

"He got offered a chance at a label the other day, if I agree to sign on with them, and I'm going to do it," I further explain, not meeting Beck's eyes now.

"What? You're just going to throw your life away for some stranger?" Beck laments, standing abruptly, making the chair flip back and clatter to the ground.

Quinn comes running out of the kitchen, on guard.

"He isn't a stranger, Beck. I'm not throwing my life away. I'm adding to my life! Trying something new. Going on an adventure. This will always be my home and the place I come back to. Quinn will just take over running things while I'm gone," I stand tall, shoulders back, meeting his eyes, letting him know this is what I want.

"So, I guess this is goodbye then," Beck growls and strides toward the door.

"WHAT???" I almost squeak out.

"I can't watch you throw your life away for a lowlife, Sut. I won't stand around and watch that happen. So, this is goodbye!" Beck unlocks the door and walks out of the café without looking back.

"He'll come back. Beck can't stay mad at you forever. Let him nurse that heart that you broke of his. Let him see how good this can be for you!" Quinn murmurs in my hair, hugging me close to her as tears stream down my face.

44

August

When I first picked up a guitar over a decade ago, I only dreamed I would make it big one day. I had been walking home from middle school, when I saw a guitar sticking out from an overflowing dumpster. I didn't know a thing about playing, but I picked it up, took it home and cleaned it up.

The next day at school, I brought it with me and asked my music teacher, Mr. Eddie, if he knew anything about repairing them. A few new strings and a tune up later, it was good as new.

A few days a week after school, Mr. Eddie gave me lessons. Teaching me everything he knew, from how to hold the guitar, to the proper finger position, to establishing the difference between chords and notes.

He let me pull up YouTube videos on the computer in his class to teach myself how to play different covers of songs, since we didn't have a computer at home.

Playing became muscle memory.

Every night, when my mom worked late into the night and I was alone in our apartment, I would sit in front of the only window we had. Staring up at the moon, which provided the softest light, singing softly and strumming guitar strings, playing song after song to fight off loneliness. Just me, my guitar, and the moon. Getting lost in the music and the chords. Trying to drown out the racing thoughts that plagued me, wondering if my mom was even going to come home for me.

Before I knew it, I was playing even better than Mr. Eddie.

Not a year later I met Ty and found out he played as well.

What I didn't realize was I'd find a family I never knew existed in the guys.

We worked hard creating song after song, playing any chance we could, but there was always something missing. No matter what we tweaked or changed, it just never hit the mark, until Sutton.

Everything is better with Sutton. Our sound. Our lyrics. She makes it better just by being her. By feeling everything so deeply and just being in the moment. Turning our already good songs into something special.

45

August

$\mathcal{W}$aiting for the café to close, I stand outside. I need to talk to Sutton, but I'm trying to build up the courage to walk through that front door. Since we have to let Rod know by tomorrow what our decision is.

The guys are happy to have Sutton on board in whatever way that looks like for her. I wanted to be able to come sit and talk to her. About well, everything. About us. About the label. About the tour. I'm hoping with everything in me that when she brought up his name the other day that it wasn't her walking away from me.

Finally building up the courage, I knock on the glass door.

Sutton looks up from wiping down the counters, and I'm met with a blank stare. Making her way over, she opens the front door.

"Hey," she says with her head down.

"Hey. Can I come in?" I ask.

Sutton pushes the door open wider so that I can walk

in.

Once I'm in, I turn towards her, gently lifting her face to me, rubbing my thumb on her cheek, "I'm sorry for yelling at you. I had no right. That had nothing to do with you."

I never break eye contact with her. I kiss her nose and give her a chaste kiss on her lips. Let her know how sorry I am. I breathe into the kiss and then pull her to me and wrap my arms around her.

Sutton sighs into me and pulls me tighter to her, so I tighten my arms around her even more. "You wanna talk about it?" I whisper into her ear.

"Okay," she whispers and nods, "But upstairs, please."

Sutton shuts the lights off and throws the washcloth on the kitchen counter.

I follow her up the stairs to her apartment. Khaos greets us both at the door, and I crouch down to pet his head.

46

August

$\mathcal{M}$aking our way into Sutton's apartment.

I grab Sutton's hand, pulling her to face me. "How about I run a bath for you?"

Holding my hand, she looks at me through her lashes.

"Will you join me?"

Stepping back, I run my hands through my hair.

"Um...I don't know, Sut. Is that a good idea?"

Nodding her head, her entire body looks like it deflates with disappointment. She turns to head to her room.

"Wait. I'll join you, Sunshine," I change my mind, stumbling after her.

Turning to face me, Sutton has a soft smile on her lips.

"But listen, we really do need to talk, Sunshine. So, no distractions, okay?" I say brushing a piece of her hair behind her ear.

I make my way into her bathroom, setting out two towels for us. Turning on the water, testing to make sure it's not too hot, I let the tub fill up. Throwing a lavender bath bomb into the water and watching as it becomes a milky violet hue. Lighting two candles that smell like vanilla and placing them on the sink.

The room is dimly lit, filled with steam with the softest hint of lavender and vanilla in the air; when she steps into the bathroom in a robe, with her hair up in a messy bun on top of her head.

And I swear my heart stops.

Sutton stands completely still, looking over every inch of my naked body. Tracing every tattoo with those jade eyes.

"August," she whispers, licking her lips. Fire burning in her eyes.

"Sunshine," I croak back.

I sink into the hot water first so that she can climb in front of me.

My eyes never leave hers, as Sutton gives me a devilish little grin and shimmies out of her robe.

I suck in my breath at the sight of her.

Completely bare in front of me. Even in the dim light of the bathroom, Sutton's lit up by the candles and is so fuckin radiant! My eyes take in every single inch of her gorgeous body from the tips of her lavender toe nails to the floral tattoos painted all over her curvy thighs, up her ribs, and under her breasts, the soft smile spread out on those soft pink lips and those stunning jade green eyes staring directly into mine.

I hold her hand as she lowers into the warm water, facing me, never breaking eye contact.

"August. I.." she whispers, causing me to blink out of my haze.

"Sunshine, you are, Gods, you are breathtaking!" I sigh out, gently brushing a piece of hair behind her ear.

"August...I. This is...this is the sweetest thing anyone's ever done for me," she murmurs and looks around the bathroom. "August. I wanted to tell you after the show on Saturday I think I'm falling for you, and I want to try this. Whatever this is between us."

"I want to try this too, Sunshine. I don't think I'm falling for you. I've already fallen. I want to be with you. Only you! I'm sorry for the way I treated you the other night, because you don't deserve that," I declare, gently running my fingers up and down her ribs.

Goosebumps pepper her skin with every brush of my fingertips.

"I also talked to the guys, and we are leaving it up to you. No pressure. If you don't want to do this, we will turn Rod down. We'll keep trying and maybe another label will come around."

"I'm in. For everything. With you, August," Sutton announces with the sweetest smile on her face, biting her lip.

"Sunshine," I moan as Sutton adjusts over my lap, my dick already hard and nudging her thigh.

"August," she whispers before crashing her mouth down on mine.

Sutton runs her hands through my hair, scraping her fingernails against my scalp at the base of my neck. I melt into the kiss, sucking her tongue into my mouth. Gods, she tastes like fuckin vanilla and honey! I can't get enough of her. I grab a fistful of her hair at the base and tug her head back, biting and licking my way down her neck to her breasts.

"August, I need..." she whimpers, digging her nails into

my back.

"I got you, Sunshine," I croak as I suck a nipple into my mouth and with my other hand that's not in her hair, start rubbing tiny circles around her clit.

She starts to grind against my hand, letting out tiny moans and whimpers.

"August," she breathes out. "I'm close."

I pull my hand away from her, and she groans.

"I want to be inside you when you cum, Sunshine. Need to feel you squeeze my cock," I grind out.

"Please!" she whimpers, wrapping her hand around my cock, stroking me from base to tip.

Sutton raises up and aligns herself but before she sits down on me, she stops herself, "Um, is it okay, if, we don't use anything? I want to feel all of you. I'm on the pill," she whispers and looks down.

I grab her chin and make her meet my eyes, "Yes." I grind out and thrust up into her.

We both let out a moan at the same time.

"Sunshine, you're squeezing me so tight. You feel so fuckin good! So warm and wet for me."

As Sutton starts to ride me, I drag my hand to the front of her throat and bring her mouth to mine. I lick her lips and she opens them up for me, letting me dive inside her mouth with my tongue. I suck her tongue into my mouth and then kiss her again. I begin to feel her clenching around me, so I pull away to watch her face as I put more pressure around her throat, taking her breath away.

Eyes never leaving me, Sutton doesn't even try to gasp for air. Dipping my other hand into the water, I rub circles around her clit, as I continue to put just enough pressure around her throat so that she can't take any air in.

Thrusting up into her tight pussy. I watch as her eyes start to roll back and then she clenches so hard around my cock as she cums so beautifully.

"That's my good girl!" I groan, as Sutton's orgasm sets mine off, causing mine to come barreling out of me. I release the pressure around her throat and pull her toward me to crush our lips back together.

I devour her as we come down from our orgasms together, feeling her little spasms every so often around my cock, making me twitch inside her. She feels incredible, warm, and soft.

I give Sutton one last deep kiss and pull away to kiss her nose and forehead. She leans forward and lays her head on my chest, just under my chin. I rub small circles up and down her back, matching the pace she's rubbing on mine.

Every inch of us, connected.

Skin to skin. Breath to breath. Soul to soul.

I've never known a peace like this one. But there is nowhere I'd rather be than in this beautiful woman's arms.

47

Sutton

Who would've known the dark, broody man in my bed would be such a romantic?

I guess I shouldn't be surprised with the lyrics he writes, but he has no idea how much I needed that. Needed this. This as in, he's still wrapped around me; the best cocoon I never want to escape from.

August quiets the chaos in my head. Completely shuts it off. For someone so dark and gloomy, his company is so peaceful and all-consuming in the best way.

"Are you still awake?" I whisper.

"Barely. You're so cozy," he nuzzles in closer to me.

"Who would've thought you'd be such a cuddler, Mister I Don't Shake Hands," I chuckle.

"Only with you," August whispers and kisses the side of my head.

I turn in his arms to face him, "So, are we going to tell Rod yes?" I ask him.

"If you want us to say yes, we will say yes," he says softly

"I think we should definitely read all of the fine print, but if Rod's not a scam artist, I think we go for it. I talked to Quinn about it and she thinks I can make it work. I can keep this place and sublet the spare room. She'll run the café and hire someone to help out while we're on tour," I tell him.

"So, I was thinking. You can totally tell me I'm crazy or no, but I thought maybe while we are home from tour, you could just stay here. I just thought it would make the most sense for you to let your apartment go and stay with me. Since we will already be essentially living together on the tour bus anyway. I know it's crazy and probably way too soon, but something about this, you and me, feels like home."

August stares back at me with no emotion in his eyes.

I crumble, burying my face in his chest. "Oh, Gods, never mind! I'm sorry! It's too soon, isn't it?

"Shh. Stop. Sunshine, I'd be happy to stay here with you. I want that. I just want to make sure it's something you really want. I have to let my landlord know in a month if I'm renewing my lease or not. We don't have any details yet about the contract. So, I don't want you to feel like we have to rush this." August says lifting my chin toward him and pressing his soft lips to mine to settle my racing heart.

"I want that. Want you. To stay here. No matter when we go or not," I stutter.

"Okay, we can talk about it more tomorrow. We can all go tomorrow to talk to Rod," August says rolling his eyes at the thought of having to see Rod again.

I start loudly giggling.

"What is so funny?" August asks, starting to tickle me, making me laugh even harder.

"You...rolling your eyes," I wheeze. "I have never

seen you roll your eyes. It's so out of character for you!" I continue to laugh hysterically.

"Hmm...how about we make you, roll those eyes into the back of your head again, Sunshine?" he growls and nips at my neck with his teeth. "Like you did in the tub for me."

*T*he next morning we walk into Thriller Records as a group. Shoulders back, chins up, August leading the pack of us. He wastes no time looking around and heads straight for the receptionist.

"We're here to see Rod," August says affirmatively to the woman behind the desk.

"Is he expecting you?" she inquires while typing away on her computer.

"Yes. We are *From Troy*. I'm August. I emailed Rod last night, and he said for us to meet him here at 10 a.m." August replies, clearly annoyed already.

I cover my mouth with a chuckle.

August pulls me to him and wraps his arms around me and puts his chin on my head, "Something funny, Sunshine?"

"Just you, Auggie, just you. Always so growly," I chuckle again.

The guys try to fight back laughs and August death glares them.

"Mr. Goodman will be with you in a moment, if you'd like to take a seat over there," the woman points to a seating area away from her desk.

*T*en minutes pass, then Rod finally comes out, "Gentlemen and the lady," he invites, waving a hand toward his office.

August growls under his breath and grabs my hand, keeping me tucked close to him. I love how protective he is of me. Ty, Knox, and Beau are directly behind us as we all walk through the door.

"Sorry! I only have the two chairs," Rod states.

August sits down in one of the chairs and pulls me onto his lap. Knox hops into the other one, and Ty and Beau stand behind us, hands braced on the backs of the chairs.

"Here's the deal. You get one chance. You fuck up, you're done. We record the songs you performed at Wicked Tour. You played, what eight? Do you have one or two more you didn't perform to make an entire album?" Rod asks, straight to the point.

"We have about fifteen written," August shoots back at him.

"Okay, great. I'm going to need to hear the others that you didn't perform and choose which ones belong on your album. We'll aim for ten on your first album. Maybe save the others for another day if they're good enough," Rod rambles on.

August tenses under me but then just nods his head.

"Any more songs with her on them, or just the two?" Rod asks, pointing at me.

"Just the two, but if we need more, I'm sure we could come up with something. We have a few slower ones that she hasn't sung with me, but she could possibly be added," August says, looking at me with a question in his eyes, asking if that's okay.

I nod my head at him, letting him know I support him.

August looks at the guys, and they all nod their heads too.

"Great, so we start recording say next week once all of the paperwork is signed. You use the studio here. You can continue to promote yourselves on social media, like it seems you've already been doing, and fairly well actually. We will also start promoting you on our page," Rod continues to talk.

We all nod in unison.

"Last is the tour. *Motion In Black* is going on tour here in about 6 weeks; we can have you as an opener for them, and then we will start pushing your album about a week before that to start getting your name out there. Think you can make that work?" Rod asks.

I feel like a deer in headlights staring at this man. That's a lot! In six weeks! Fuck!

August's fingertips making circles on my knee snaps me out of my own head.

Ty speaks up first, "I think I can give work a six-week notice. That shouldn't be an issue."

"Shouldn't be an issue for me either," Beau says.

"Works for me!" Knox says.

"Sunshine," August stares at me, smiling softly. Eyes pleading with me.

"How long will the tour be?" I ask quietly.

"About eight weeks. You will have your own tour bus. The five of you. We provide this service," Rod states.

"If things go well on this tour, and if your album does well, you could be looking at your own headline tour maybe next year. That is a big maybe. But you certainly have potential if you bring the same energy and same crowds as you did at Wicked Tour. That was impressive, as a new band," Rod continues.

"Okay," I whisper.

"What was that?" Rod asks.

"Sutton said yes!" The guys all yell and whoop.

August ever stoic, "Are you sure, Sunshine? Really sure?"

"Can Khaos come on the tour bus?" I question.

"Who's Khaos?" Rod asks.

"It's her service dog. It's a deal breaker if he can't come," August says on edge.

"Oh, yeah. That's fine. I'll just make sure whichever driver you're assigned is fine with dogs." Rod responds, shrugging his shoulders.

"How long is this contract for?" August asks.

"Like I said, you get one chance. You fuck up, you're cut. We expect at least two albums and two tours for this contract. This first album and tour count as your firsts. After this, everything in the future will be negotiated depending on how you are performing and how many shows you are selling out, etc." Rod explains.

August looks at each of us and we each give him the subtlest nods.

"Where do we sign?" August asks Rod.

48

August

"Hey, do you think Ty can drop me off by the nursing home? I know she won't understand but I want to share..." Sutton starts to whisper to me.

"Of course, Sunshine. You don't have to explain it to me," I squeeze her hand and kiss her forehead.

"Hey, Ty, can you pull over at the next block? Sunshine and I want to walk the rest of the way back to her place," I ask, gripping the back of his seat.

"Yeah, you guys sure? It's hot as hell out," Ty comments.

"Yep, we're sure," I smile at her.

"Thank you," she mouths to me.

I know Sutton isn't comfortable letting people see this side of her or her interaction with her grandmother. I've been grateful since the first time she took me with her and allowed me in to see this small piece of her that she keeps close to her heart.

Ty pulls over not even a block from our destination without even knowing; so, we won't have to walk too far

I help Sutton out of the car, taking her hand in mine.

"Bye guys. See you all soon. And I promise you won't regret letting me join in on the tour," she says ducking back into the car, smiling at the guys.

"We know we won't," Ty says smiling back at her.

"Have you heard those pipes? Plus, maybe you can talk Blondie into coming to a few shows," Knox says wiggling his eyebrows at Sutton.

I just chuckle at their interaction.

Beau just gives Sutton a small grin and nods his head. Ever the silent one.

After the guys drive off we walk hand in hand to the nursing home doors.

"Ms. Sutton, you're here early today," Charlie, the security guard, greets her.

"We have good news! I want to share it," Sutton beams at him.

"Are yinz getting married?" Charlie asks, eyeing me up and down, then looking at our clasped hands.

Sutton giggles. "Not that kind of news, Charlie. We got offered a record deal. We start recording next week!"

"That's incredible! Congrats to both of you! I know they have loved you two around here. You're going to do great things!" Charlie encourages us.

We talk with Charlie for a few more minutes then make it over to the sitting room. Sutton spots her grandmother sitting in a chair watching a movie. I notice Sutton take a deep breath and blow it out softly, preparing herself for this interaction.

I give her hand a little squeeze for silent support, because I know this takes a little piece of her every time she visits, but her heart is so big, she does it anyways.

"Hi Ms. Margaret!" Sutton says softly, trying not to startle the older woman as we approach her.

She turns her head, looks at Sutton, and shocks both of us speechless, "Oh my sweet girl, what are you doing here?" Sutton's grandmother asks while trying to get up from her chair and then pulling Sutton into her arms.

I release her hand so that she can hug her grandmother.

My chest squeezes watching as Sutton's eyes light up with pure joy. Wrapping her arms around her grandma, she finally lets the tears fall.

"Gram, I'd like you to meet someone special to me," Sutton says pulling away from her, reaching for my hand.

Realizing that I'm standing here, she looks at me with curiosity, like she's seen me before now, but can't quite put her finger on it.

"This is August, my boyfriend," Sutton says looking up at me with those gorgeous jade green eyes and a smile that lights up the entire damn room.

"August is an amazing musician!"

"A musician? How exciting!" Her grandmother smiles softly at me, brightness in her eyes.

Walking up to her, I take her hands in mine. Her hands are so frail, but her strong grip is comforting.

"Ms. Margaret, it's so nice to meet you. I just want to say that without your granddaughter, I wouldn't be the musician I am today. She's been singing with me at her café. Because of her, she's made my dreams come true. I just want to say thank you, for raising such a special woman!"

Looking up at Sutton, I see her cheeks tinted a beautiful shade of pink.

"Well, come on, let's sit. I want you to tell me all about this band of yours!" Her grandmother invites us to the table that she had been sitting at.

Sitting across from Sutton, I wrap my leg around hers under the table. I can see the tears she's blinking back. Trying to soak in this lucid moment with her grandmother, since they are few and far between. Today is already so special, but this makes it one we'll never forget.

"Okay. Start at the beginning. Tell me everything!" Ms. Margaret requests, giving us her full attention.

Sutton and I both, tell her how we met, when I heard her sing for the first time, how we wrote a song together, and that we were just offered a record deal today.

"We start recording next week and start touring in six weeks. How exciting is that?" Sutton smiles ear to ear while telling her grandma everything.

The look on her grandma's face makes my heart squeeze even more. She's so proud of Sutton. The way she beams at her while she's talking, you can tell she's so proud of the woman she's become.

"You always had such a beautiful voice, my sweet girl. I'm so glad you're letting the world hear it. Your parents would be so proud!" her grandma says squeezing Sutton's hands in hers and then kissing her on the cheek.

"And thank you for seeing her and letting her be heard. I wish I could see the two of you sing together! You make a beautiful couple," Sutton's grandmother says squeezing my hand and smiling at me.

Sutton can't take her eyes off her grandma. Hanging on to her every word.

A few minutes pass as we sit in the glow and love pouring from Sutton's grandma and then it's gone in a blink. Almost like a light switch flipped off.

Her grandma looks at me and then at Sutton, squinting her eyes and then turning her head, not making eye contact with either of us. "Who...who are you?" Her grandma asks.

I watch Sutton immediately tense and then deflate, shoulders immediately curling in on themselves. She goes to answer her grandmother, but she's fighting back tears.

Extending my hand to her grandma, "Hello Ms. Margaret, we just stopped by to say hello. We were just getting ready to head home. Would you like us to walk you back to your room?" I ask her softly.

"Um, no thank you," her grandmother responds looking anywhere but at us.

I take that as our cue to leave. I squeeze her grandmother's shoulder and tell her goodbye, then take Sutton by the hand.

She stands up and squeezes her grandmother's shoulder too, and I notice her softly kiss the side of her head and whisper "I love you!" to her.

Her grandma sits still as a statue. As soon as we start to walk away, I pull Sutton to my side.

My chest hasn't ached like this since I lost my mom.

*S*utton's been so quiet since we left. She silently clung to my hand, like it's a lifeline, during the entire walk back to her apartment.

She stops a block away and pulls me into an alleyway.

"How do you..." she starts so quietly I almost can't hear her. Clearing the lump from her throat, "How do you always know what I need? Without even asking?"

Sutton lets out the saddest laugh that I've ever heard and just shakes her head.

"What do you mean, Sunshine?" I ask, tilting her chin up so she meets my eyes.

"You just always know. For someone who won't even shake someone's hand because physical touch burns you, you always keep me anchored to you when I need it most. You know when I need a hot bath to scrub away the day; when I just need held; when I need someone else to find the words because I'm too busy falling apart. How do you know all this when we barely know each other?" she says almost in disbelief, tears running down her cheeks wrapping her arms around herself.

"Don't do that," I say, unwrapping her arms from around herself and pulling her into me.

"Don't try and start a fight and say we don't know each other, because you're hurting right now and don't know what else to do," I comfort her while kissing her hair, holding her tight to me.

"I'm not starting..." she starts to sob in my chest, digging her fingers into my shirt.

"You are, and I get it, but you don't have to do this alone anymore. I've spent most of my life pushing everyone away too, Sunshine. So, I know that's what you're doing," I say rubbing slow circles on her back.

"I know what it's like to allow people to see the real you, to be vulnerable," I add, giving her a tight squeeze.

"Letting people in is scary. It's giving them the

opportunity to use you, to tear you down, to make you feel like you and your dreams are less than. It's giving them the opportunity to hurt you..."

Taking my hands, I run my fingers softly through Sutton's hair, never breaking our embrace.

"When..."

Clearing the lump in my throat.

Giving me an encouraging hug, I take a deep breath.

"When my mom killed herself," I whisper and I feel Sutton immediately tense and go to take a step back from my hold.

"Please, let me hold you while I tell you this," I ask softly.

I feel Sutton nod her head and rest back against my chest, holding me a little tighter to her.

"She did it in front of me one night. Took her own life in front of me. When the one person who is supposed to love you more than anyone else in this world chooses to end their life, instead of staying here for you, it makes it incredibly hard to ever get close to people. My mom struggled in this life for years. She never meant to bring me into this world. I forgive her for leaving me, but I still have nightmares since that night. My grandmother let me live on her couch to keep me out of the foster system, but she passed a couple weeks before my eighteenth birthday. I still struggle with accepting human affection and kindness. I've never known affection. I barely remember the few times my mom showed me love when she was sober. My grandmother was never affectionate. So, it's foreign to me, but with you it's so easy," I stare out at the street over her head, her fingertips pressing into my skin keeping me grounded in the present.

"I've never been able to get close to anyone. Ty's

probably the closest, most consistent, person I've had in my life," I shrug.

I tilt Sutton's chin up so that I can look in her eyes, "But for some reason, since you Sutton, it's like my soul always seeks yours out. It knows when you're in the room; I can feel you before I see you. When I'm with you, my soul just knows what you need; being with you is like breathing. Singing with you, it feels like we're in our own universe. I've always loved to make music, but with you it's so much more. Being with you, spending time with you, I see the cracks in your heart, and I just want to merge them with mine. It's like your soul fills the piece of mine that's always been missing. I've never felt more whole than when I'm with you," I lean back and put my forehead against hers. Just breathing her in. "I'm in love with you, Sunshine. With everything about you. You are everything to me! So that's how I know."

Sutton tilts her head up and when her lips are just a breath away from mine affirms, "Thank you for sharing that with me. I know that couldn't have been easy. Thank you, for being everything I didn't know I needed. Because of you, I know that light can hide in the darkest of places. I love you, August!" and then she kisses me with every ounce of emotion she felt today. I feel her excitement, her sadness, her love for me, every ounce of it pouring into this kiss.

Color explodes behind my eyes. This kiss feels like it's just us against the world. Like our souls found the very thing they needed.

I love this woman with everything inside me! My life will no longer be dull with her in it. No longer walking through this world alone. Everything always so black and white. So empty. Soulless. Numb. The world has taken pieces of me. Taken pieces of her. But together we'll mend.

Together we'll rewrite our own stories. Together we have hope for a brighter future.

49

Sutton

We have spent the last several weeks recording our album and it's been some of the most fun I've ever had in my life. The guys have been great to play with.

I've been able to still help out at the cafe but have slowly given Quinn the reigns to run the show. That's been hard for me, but not as hard as I had expected.

We even hired Sloan from the gym to help out during the weeks while I'm gone.

Sloan stopped by one morning for a coffee, asking for recommendations for safe neighborhoods to look for a job and a place to rent to live, and it just so happened we had both, plus she was familiar with us. So, she accepted and has been training with us and really coming out of her shell. She's a really sweet girl when you get to know her.

I feel like between Quinn, Sloan and Krysta I'm leaving the cafe in good hands.

Sloan moved in upstairs in my spare bedroom just a few days ago.

August's lease ends while we're on the road, so he moved the little bit that he owns into my room and officially moved in this week too.

The stars seem to be aligning and everything's falling into place; except I haven't seen Beck or heard from him since our conversation a few weeks ago. Sloan's mentioned that she's seen him at the gym every time she's gone for a class. And she goes to a lot of them.

Quinn said he's stopped in twice while we've been at the recording studio and has been in and out. Barely even making small talk.

I understand why Beck's upset. He has every right to be. I essentially pulled the rug out from under his feet. I always hoped things would be different between us; maybe in a different life; but things changed. My dreams are changing every day. But I still wish I was leaving on better terms with him.

We are having one final show this weekend, as a sort of goodbye but see you soon for all of our fans and our friends. One last hoorah, if you will.

And then we pack up and hit the road on Monday for our tour. It's so surreal! I never could've imagined my life looking like this.

50

August

The tour bus pulls up in front of Ty's house first thing Monday morning. It's a sleek black bus. We immediately start loading up our equipment.

Patrick, our driver, gives us a tour once we're finished packing up. He has a small door that closes him off from the rest of the bus, but there's a window built into it, giving everyone a little privacy if it's needed.

There's a small kitchenette, with a fridge, microwave, sink and countertop with a couple cabinets. A small lounge area sits just behind the kitchen, with a seating area and a TV that drops down from the ceiling. Followed by an area with six bunk-like beds; where Patrick says we can choose where we each sleep, and states that one of those is his as well. There are two smaller closets just after the bunk beds, where Patrick states we can store our clothes.

Next, there is a small bathroom with a toilet, small sink, and a shower. I have to bend down to fit inside of it, but I can't complain.

At the very back of the bus is a smaller bedroom with a

queen size bed, a sunroof in the ceiling and a small closet.

"This is where Sutton, Khaos and I will stay," I claim as Khaos jumps up on the bed and makes himself comfortable.

We all start laughing. I put Sutton's and mine duffel bags in the closet in this room.

Knox lets out a whoop and taps the side of the wall.

"First stop, Scranton, Pennsylvania," Patrick announces.

"Scranton, Pennsylvania," I say, and pull Sutton to me and kiss her head.

"You gonna come tell us bye?" Quinn yells from the front of the bus.

Knox charges at Quinn and picks her up and spins her.

"Put me down you big oaf," she grumbles at him, while smacking his back.

"I'll miss you, Blondie," I hear Knox whisper to her and kiss her cheek.

Quinn blushes and kisses his cheek back, then pushes him away.

Sutton pulls Quinn into the tightest hug, "I love you! Thank you for doing this for me. If something happens and you need me to come back, just call me."

"The café is in good hands. Go be a rockstar. I love you, Sut!" Quinn says squeezing Sutton tighter.

Ty is off to the side with Rachel. I overhear them saying their *I love you's* and *see you soon's*. I know Ty's going to miss her because she's his best friend. It's always been something I admire about him, that he can keep his relationship so strong with her.

I look around and feel like the luckiest man in the world. We are finally getting the chance to make something of ourselves. And I get to do it with my best friends and best girl at my side. Just as I turn to search for my girl, I see her walking up to me. She wraps her arms around my waist, and I bend down to kiss her.

Patrick pulls the door shut, hops in the driver's seat, and starts to drive away.

We all kneel on the seats in the lounge waving to everyone as the bus pulls out.

*A*fter we all get situated and choose our sleeping arrangements, we sit in the lounge and try to write a song. Ty, Knox, and I have our guitars out, strumming a beat. Beau just sits with his eyes closed and listens to what we're creating, every so often giving advice.

Sutton is curled up on my side, humming a tune, while Khaos snuggles up against her.

I couldn't have dreamed up a more perfect picture.

*F*our and a half hours flies by in a flash when you aren't the one driving. I could get used to this.

We arrive in Scranton within a few hours before sound check.

Patrick parks the bus right next to *Motion In Black's* bus.

This is so surreal. I can't believe we actually get to meet them.

We head into the venue with all of our equipment.

Since we go on first, we set up our equipment now and run through sound check.

Our sound is perfect, and the lights are working exactly as we want them. The stage crew is extremely helpful making sure everything is placed exactly where we want it to be.

I stop dead in my tracks when I walk into the back lounge and see Rhys Motion.

This. Is. Actually happening! Trying not to fanboy. Is fanboying a thing?

"Hey, I'm August. This is Sutton, Knox, Ty, and Beau. Thank you so much for allowing us to tag along on your tour," I say as we walk into the lounge to meet the guys, trying to keep my cool.

"Hey. You are *From Troy*, right?" Rhys says. "We've heard good things about you guys!"

"Yes. Thank you. We're stoked to open for you guys!" Knox responds grinning from ear to ear.

We sit and talk with them like we've been friends for years. They never make us feel like we don't belong. This is seriously one of the coolest moments in my life!

Sutton is so animated talking to them. Telling them that she loves my screams. However, Rhys's *"Bleghs"* are hands down the best, and I won't argue that.

Telling them how much she loves their makeup for every show and how she's been listening to them for years. Sutton especially loves their pyrotechnics during their shows.

We never really talked about what our look as a group was going to be, and we definitely can't afford pyrotechnics yet. Maybe someday. But I can't take my eyes off Sutton. I love watching how her face lights up as she talks to them. Treating them like she does everyone she meets, with her full undivided attention. Like they're human. And I think I love that the most about her.

"Ten minutes before you guys go on!" the stage crew manager yells out to us.

"Where is Sutton?" I ask anyone who's listening, looking everywhere for her.

"I'm right here, Auggie. Relax," Sutton yells out to me.

I turn in the direction that I hear her voice and stop dead in my tracks.

"My Gods!" I exhale, swallowing hard.

My feet have a mind of their own, and I'm in front of her and pulling her to me by the throat and slamming my mouth down on hers.

Sutton whimpers and kisses me back with just as much heat and then pulls back, "You're gonna mess up my lipstick," she giggles.

"Fuck your lipstick!" I growl and pull her mouth back to me.

Sutton nips my lip, licks it, and pulls away again. "They said 10 minutes. It's probably like seven now. I don't have time to touch it up."

"Gods, you're beautiful! How are you even mine?" awed, I press my forehead to hers.

"Thank you. So are you. Because you are also mine. Now let's go!" Sutton whispers and kisses me softly.

*T*he lights go out on the stage and the crowd starts cheering.

A light follows Beau as he makes his way over to his drums, sits down, and lifts his sticks together above his head.

The crowd cheers louder!

Ty walks out to the left side of the stage, guitar strapped around his shoulder, spotlight on him next.

Knox then walks out to the right side of the stage with his bass strapped around his shoulder, and another spotlight shines on him.

"I love you!" I say letting go of Sutton's hand and running up to the platform and jumping on it in the center of the stage, as a light shines down on me.

The boys and I bow our heads.

Beau hits the cymbals, Knox and Ty strum their guitars, and all our strobe lights come on; smoke shooting up from the stage.

The sound of the crowd is deafening.

I bring the microphone close to my mouth and growl so deep, bending backwards, projecting my voice from deep within my chest.

Our lights go out again as the guys continue to play for a few more seconds, and then all our strobe lights come back on, and I start singing our first song of the night.

The energy in the room is electrifying. This is insane! This has to be the largest crowd we've ever played for. I know they're probably here for *Motion In Black*, but this crowd is wild!

I can't help but amp them up even more. I've always loved a good mosh pit!

"Open the fuckin pit!" I growl into the microphone and these fuckers deliver.

They make a giant circle in the middle of the crowd. Everyone is bouncing up and down, getting ready.

"Now!" I growl and continue singing and screaming our next song; as the crowd pushes and shoves each other, running circles around each other in the middle of the pit.

We perform two more of our heavier songs before I call Sutton out.

"We're going to slow it down a bit. Give you guys a breather," I chuckle into the microphone.

"If any of you follow us, you know that we have a couple songs with a very special girl," I croon into the microphone.

The crowd starts cheering and chanting.

"Oh, Sutton," I growl into the microphone.

Her fine ass struts out onto the stage; dressed head to toe in black, matching me perfectly; black leather combat boots, black skintight leather pants, black leather jacket, with her long violet locks curled down her back.

"I haven't killed him yet. But no promises!" Sutton winks at the crowd.

There are a few wolf whistles from the crowd as she turns and smirks at me.

Then Sutton gives me her signature nod and we end the night singing our hearts out together. Pouring every ounce of emotion we have into every lyric, every vocal.

It's haunting and tender, and we couldn't be more in sync if we tried.

"Thank you all so much! You were incredible! We'll be at our merch booth for a while afterwards, if anyone wants to stop by and say hi," I gratefully inform this crowd.

51

Sutton

Two hours earlier.

"That might have been your best performance yet!" *Rhys Motion tells us as we're running off stage, adrenaline coursing through our veins.*

"Did you hear that, Sunshine? Our best performance yet!" August lifts me up, spinning me in a circle while planting the sloppiest kiss on my lips.

"Ah, that was incredible!" I sigh, snuggling up to August in our bed.

Khaos is curled up perfectly between our legs.

"It really was," he says softly, kissing the top of my head.

"I'm tired, but also so wired. I'm not sure if I can fall asleep yet," I start leaving tender kisses on his chest.

"It's also weird trying to sleep while we're moving. At least I feel like we're moving," August says face buried in my hair.

I giggle, "No, I definitely feel us moving. I imagine Patrick does most of his driving at night and sleeps during the day."

"Yeah, he did mention he was going to get a jump on the next destination. I think it might be Michigan," August says running his fingers through my hair.

"Gods, that feels good!" I moan from the sensation of his fingers running through my hair and grazing my scalp.

"Think you can be a good girl and be quiet?" he teases in my ear.

"Mmhmm..." I moan quietly.

August gently pulls his tee shirt from over my head, leaving me in just cotton panties.

Slowly kissing his way down my neck, nipping my skin as he goes; leaving the perfect mix of the tiniest bit of pain with pleasure as he licks and kisses. Sucking my nipple into his mouth and nipping it lightly, causing me to moan. I turn my face into the pillow to muffle the sound.

He leaves soft kisses down my belly, on my pelvis, and then nips and licks my inner thighs; purposely avoiding right where I need him. Where I ache for him.

"Auggie. Please," I whimper, running my fingers through his hair, trying to drag him where I need his face most.

"Patience, Sunshine!" he nips my thigh again and then so slowly pulls my panties down my legs, tossing them to the floor.

August slowly kisses his way up my inner thigh, then leaves the softest kiss on my clit. I beg, "Please!"

"Since you asked so nicely," he growls and then swipes his tongue right up my slit, sucking my clit into his mouth and lightly grazes his teeth over it.

I dig my hands in his hair, tugging lightly and then harder, getting completely lost in the feel of his warm mouth on me.

August continues to devour me, like I'm the best thing he's ever tasted. I don't realize how hard I'm pulling his hair until his groan in my pussy sets off my orgasm. My entire body tingles and my legs are shaking.

August doesn't let up until he's rung every ounce of my orgasm out of me.

Slowly climbing back up the bed, leaving light kisses up my body, until he's smashing his mouth down on mine. I can taste myself on his lips and it just makes me crave him more.

"Please. I need you," I cry out.

Without breaking our kiss, August slides into me to the hilt with one deep thrust. We both let out a soft moan.

I wrap my legs around his waist and tilt my pelvis up to take him deeper. One of my hands is still wrapped in his hair. His is perfectly placed over my throat where it belongs, as he continues to devour my mouth and every sigh and whimper that he fucks out of me. I'm not sure where either of us begins or ends, but all I know is that this is exactly where I belong.

52

Sutton

A whole month has gone by since we've been on tour. It's been a whirlwind. A different city almost every night. Living on a bus that's always in motion. I'm still not sure this is even my life. It's the best kind of chaos though. Almost every show has been sold out.

During our time on tour, we've written a few more songs as a group, and I've gotten to be included on all of them.

We're excited to get back into the studio when we get back and start album number two.

August and I haven't really left Pittsburgh much in our lifetimes, so every chance we get to in a new city, if we have a little bit of time, we try to sightsee or try new food or anything else, just to actually be present and experience what that city has to offer.

We're in Nashville, and this has to be one of the coolest cities we've stopped in.

Lucky for us we are here for two days, so we get an

entire day to explore.

We stopped at Milk & Honey for breakfast and the second-best iced coffee I've ever had, because obviously no one's is better than mine.

The Country Music Hall of Fame was so cool to see different outfits worn onstage over the years, the albums that are plastered on the walls, and different awards won by different musicians.

The variety of bars on Broadway were fun to pop in and out of; listening to different bands play, learning how to line dance, and even singing an Amy Lee and Seether song on karaoke together. Tootsie's was also just as fun as everyone told us it was!

Our performance in Nashville as a group had to have been our best performance to date. The atmosphere of being in the city of music was beyond amazing!

I miss Quinn and the café, but she tells me things are going great and Sloan has really been coming out of her shell.

Knox loved jumping on Facetime calls anytime Quinn and I talked.

I miss Beck. He's still been radio silent. I'm guessing he's still taking time to figure out his feelings. I just hope that we can work things out when we get back. Not having him in my life is not something I want to consider.

But I'm still not sorry that everything turned out the way it did. August and I have grown even closer and have time to figure out what exactly we want out of this relationship. We've had time to just get to know each other. And I've also had time to get to know the other guys in the band too.

Surprisingly, none of them ever brought girls back on the bus. It had never crossed my mind that the band members would have groupies, since August and I were together, but girls still tried.

August was quick to let people know that we were together. Ty often headed back to the bus to call his girlfriend after our shows. Knox really seemed to be into Quinn and unless he met people during the day while August and I were out exploring, I never saw him with anyone either.

Beau always kind of kept to himself unless we were working on new music.

Patrick had even commented on how shocked he was at how tame we all were, especially being so new to the industry.

It also turned out, Patrick really loved Khaos being on tour with us, because he kept him company anytime we were performing or out somewhere that we couldn't take him with us.

"Wow! That. Was. Just. Ah. Amazing!" I squeal dropping back onto our bed.

"It really was. That crowd was just awesome! They were even singing along with some of our songs. And that little boy, screaming our lyrics. The coolest thing!" August enthuses, his eyes the brightest I'd ever seen.

"I'm going to take a quick shower. Want to join me?" August offers, reaching his hand out to me.

"Yeah, I'll be right there," I smile up at him.

I grab a tee shirt out of his stack of clothes to sleep in and a towel and head to the bathroom, when I see my phone light up in the corner.

Picking it up from the floor, I notice that I have four missed calls from the nursing home. My heart immediately sinks. Dread courses through my veins.

Sitting on the edge of the bed, I hit play on the first voicemail that I have, "Hi, Sutton, this is Briar Nursing Home. Please return our call as soon as you get this."

I hit play on the next one, "Sutton, you are the only emergency contact we have for Ms. Margaret. Please call us as soon as you get this message. Thank you."

With a sinking feeling in my stomach, I hit the call back button.

"Hello, Briar Nursing Home, how may I direct your call?" the operator says on the phone.

"Hi, this is Sutton Raven. I had a few missed calls about my grandmother, Ms. Margaret..." I start to say, fingers trembling.

"Yes, one minute," she replies.

"Hi, Sutton. It's Nurse Susie. I hate to do this over the phone, but I know you're out of town. Your grandmother," the nurse pauses briefly. "Your grandmother passed away this evening. We went to get her to take her to dinner and she was gone. It seems like she passed peacefully in her sleep during a nap. I'm so sorry, Sutton!" the nurse says softly.

Frozen in place. All I hear is my heartbeat pounding in my ears. My vision blurs from the tears filling my eyes.

"Sutton..." the nurse continues softly.

"I'm... Thank you..." I try to hold back a sob, "Is that

all?"

"I'm so sorry, Sutton. I hate doing this to you. You will need to notify a funeral home and decide on burial or cremation. They will come and move her to the funeral home," the nurse gently instructs.

"Um, okay..." I croak out. "Do you have any suggestions? For which funeral home? I'm not familiar..." I sob through my tears.

"Yes, Sutton. We have one that we recommend often. If you want, I can call them and have them take care of things until you can get here. You will still have to decide on burial or..." she says, and I cut her off.

"I will try to get a flight back to Pittsburgh hopefully in the next 24 hours. Please just let me know the funeral home information. Thank you, Susie," I tell her and hang up.

53

Sutton

August walks in ten minutes later.

"Sunshine...?" August asks cautiously.

I don't even realize I'm laying curled up in a ball on the floor. I can't see through my blurred vision, but I hear August's voice and feel Khaos' warm body pressed up against me.

"Sunshine...what happened? Talk to me..." he says lifting me up off the floor and sitting us on the edge of the bed. Softly rocking me. Kissing my hair. Rubbing soothing circles against my back.

"Gram's gone!" I barely croak out.

"Oh, Sunshine!" August holds me closer to him, "I'm so..."

"She's gone. And I wasn't there. Because I'm here. With you. I shouldn't be here with you. I should have been there with her. She died. Alone. Because I'm here!" I choke out and sob, pushing August away from me.

"Sutton, I'm so sorry you lost Gram. I know this has got

to be wrecking you. But she would've wanted you to take this adventure. Not sit and wait for her to pass," August tries to hold me tighter to him, as I fall apart.

"How would you know?" I sound so defeated.

"She was so happy for you. For us. When we told her the news. She wanted you to live your dreams, Sunshine! I truly believe that Gram was lucid that day, so that when this time happened, you would be able to rest knowing she was so proud of you!" August whispers, running his fingers through my hair as I continue sobbing against his chest.

"I have to leave. I have to go bury her. Gram wanted to be buried. She had a plot already. With my pap," I sniffle.

"I'll go with you. You don't have to do this alone," August kisses my forehead, both cheeks and nose.

"You can't. You have the tour. You can't ruin your chance! You get just one chance," I plead with August.

"Sunshine. There is no band without you. There is no tour without you. They will have to understand. Bands have to miss a show or two every once in a while, for a number of reasons. You are more important than this tour to me," August tells me, making sure that I can see in his eyes just how much he means that.

August lifts me up and tucks me under the comforter of our bed. Khaos curls up right next to me.

"Keep an eye on your mama. I'll be right back," August pets his head and kisses my forehead before walking out the door.

I head out into the lounge where the guys and Patrick are sitting playing some video game.

"Sutton's grandmother just passed away. She just got a phone call. We're going to have to head back to Pittsburgh for a couple days. I know this may be an issue, but I'm not letting her do this alone. I will go talk to the *Motion In Black* guys to make them aware," I inform the guys.

"I'm not sure if you can drive us back, or if you can at least drop us at the airport so that we can fly back," I say to Patrick.

"Unfortunately, the tour bus itself has to stay on the tour route, but I can take you guys to the airport," Patrick replies.

I nod at him and then head out the door to go call Rod, plus let *Motion In Black* know what has happened.

*S*urprisingly, Rod was more understanding than expected and gave us "Three days of bereavement." Over those three days we only had had one show scheduled, so we wouldn't miss too much.

Sutton has barely eaten. Barely slept.

Quinn and I have made the funeral arrangements based off her grandmother's wishes.

A lawyer contacted Sutton, when we landed back in Pittsburgh this morning, to inform her that her grandmother had a will that stipulated everything that she wanted for her funeral outlined in it. Everything financially was also covered.

That was the first time Sutton showed any emotion, other than being numb since we returned. Something like relief crossed over her face before she succumbed to the void again.

A short viewing, followed by a small service, and then the burial was all that Sutton's grandmother wanted. Sutton was her only family.

Quinn and I each sat on one side of Sutton at the cemetery with Khaos lying guard at Sutton's feet, as she stared blankly at her grandmother's casket as they lowered it into the ground.

We sat quietly side by side for what felt like an eternity but may have only been minutes, before Sutton stands up and walks over to an arrangement of purple roses and plucks out two of them.

Standing next to the grave, Khaos walks up and sits next to Sutton, leaning his body against her legs, reassuring her that she isn't alone, as Sutton stares down into the hole.

I watch as a lone tear streams down Sutton's face and

she mouths, "Please don't forget, that I'll love you forever! It feels like I've missed you endlessly, but this is just the beginning of a lifetime of missing you. Thank you for being my everything!"

Dropping two roses onto the casket. Sutton walks back towards us. I notice a small tinge of blood on her thumb from the thorns. She never even flinches.

Then I hear a soft gasp.

Looking up and following her gaze, I see what startled Sutton. Out of the corner of my eye, I see her take off running.

There Beck stands, looking like the damn hero, holding my girl. In his arms. While she grieves for her grandmother.

His eyes never leave mine, as she hugs him tighter.

Quinn finally senses that I am tense and turns around, "I'm shocked Beck showed. But I'm glad he did!" she exclaims.

"I'm so sorry! I thought he knew. I told him I was coming here this morning before I locked up," Sloan whispers to me, grimacing, eyes bouncing back and forth between Quinn and me.

"It's okay. You didn't know that Beck would come. And Sutton would probably be more hurt if he wasn't here," I try to say calmly, keeping the edge and hurt out of my voice toward both Sloan and Beck.

Quinn squeezes my hand, "She loves you, August! Be patient with her."

"She just lost one of the most important people to her!" Quinn whispers.

"What if she doesn't come back?" my voice cracks.

"August, Sut always goes inside herself. When her parents died, she disappeared for a while. After her assault she internalized it. But she'll come back. Sut always comes back when she's ready," Quinn reassures me.

Please come back to me, Sunshine!

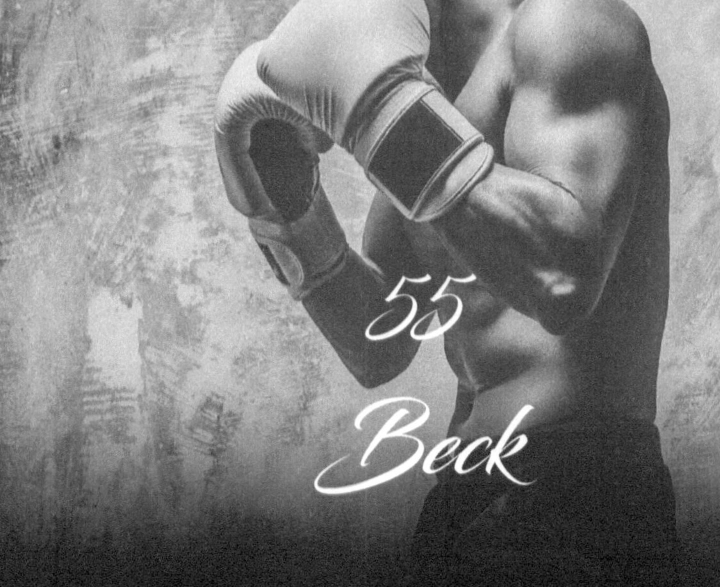

55
Beck

The second Sloan told me she was locking up to come to the funeral, I knew that instead of the gym I needed to come here this morning.

I watched Sutton from a distance from the back of the cemetery, just staring off into space. Completely disconnected from herself and her surroundings. I've never seen her so distraught before now. Not even when I first met her all those years ago, when she always stood in the shadows at parties.

She looked so sad. So, broken.

I'll protect her, like I always do. Hold her up, so that she can fall apart in my arms. Because she's my best fucking friend! Once the woman of my dreams. But I got my head on straight now...Thanks to Sloan.

Storming out of the café, I headed straight to the gym after Sut told me that she was going on tour with August.

"What did that bag ever do to you?" Sloan asks as she walks into the gym.

Great! I thought I would be alone today. Looks like my

luck isn't starting today. Now I must figure out how to get my mind right with her in the room. Not likely.

"Don't worry about it," I grunt out between jabs.

"Well, I'm a good listener, if you want to talk. Otherwise, I'll be over here working on some defense techniques." Sloan offers as she begins stretching.

"You wouldn't understand."

"You'd be surprised what I understand. I know a broken heart when I see it. And you, good sir, are the victim of someone ripping yours out."

"What?" I turn to tell her to mind her own damn business but then see the look in her eyes. Demons of her past alive in them. And I don't know what comes over me but when I look into those violet orbs, I'm drawn in. The need to truly know Sloan overwhelms me.

"Let's talk then, Little Dove."

And we talked. For hours. Sloan confided in me that she had an abusive ex-husband. She moved to Pittsburgh to start over and was terrified to do it.

Sloan has spent many days at the gym with me, helping me work through my heartbreak. We've developed a sort of friendship. I teach her self-defense. She gives me lessons on love.

Our talk helped me understand that I had to start looking at my relationship with Sutton from a different perspective. I have always loved Sutton and I will always protect her, but I can see what she means now about our paths being different.

When I first met her, she was timid and untrusting, kind of how Sloan is. I'm a fixer. A protector. Sutton seemed broken when I met her, and I wanted to be a safe space for her.

Being friends allowed Sutton to heal her past wounds, allowed me to shield her. And that may have blurred the lines for us. This dynamic of I love you. I feel so comfortable and safe with you. But love isn't always enough for a relationship. Somewhere along the lines, things changed.

Sutton bloomed into this incredible woman; built herself back up from the ground up and flourished. She doesn't need anyone to save her anymore. She saved herself.

So, while I'm not sure yet if August is right for my girl, I'm going to trust her heart, because Sutton always seems to find the goodness in everyone, and I'm going to be here for her while she navigates this new path that she's chosen for herself. Because Quinn's right. Sutton deserves happiness more than anyone we know.

"It's okay. I'm here. I got you, Sutton," I whisper in her hair, squeezing her tighter to me as she silently sobs in my arms, shoulders shaking.

I never got to meet her grandmother, but I know she raised Sutton into the incredible woman she is today, so she had to be just as special as my girl.

Looking over her head, I notice August sitting, whispering with Quinn and Sloan, every so often looking back at us with what looks like sadness in his eyes.

"Come on, let's get you out of here," I comfort Sutton, kissing the top of her head and trying to turn her toward my car.

"I'm..." she croaks out.

Sutton glances back toward the hole in the ground, shoulders slumping forward, and then turns back and walks toward the parked cars.

"Watch your head," I warn, as I help her get inside the passenger seat of my car.

"What are you doing?" Quinn asks so softly from behind me, glancing first at Sutton, staring straight ahead, and then back at me.

"I'm going to take her home and tuck her into bed with Khaos and Mayhem, and keep an eye on her," I tell Quinn quietly.

"Okay. I'm going to go pick up some takeout and then we will all be over soon," Quinn says looking at me and then back to Sutton.

"August has to get back to tour, doesn't he? He isn't going to stick around to take care of her," I almost growl at Quinn.

"That's not right, and you know it! August loves her! He has begged her to allow him to stay and allow him to be here for her, but she doesn't want *From Troy* to lose their big chance," Quinn says defensively, getting into my face.

"Don't make me out to be the villain, Quinn. I'm just taking care of our girl," I explain firmly.

"We can all take care of our girl," Quinn replies, pointing at Sutton, who is still staring off into space while sitting in the front seat of my car.

Ignoring the argument between Quinn and me.

August walks up to the door and leans in, "Sunshine, come home with me. What are you doing?"

"August, I love you, but I can't right now. Please just go finish the tour. Let the guys know I'm so sorry. I just...I can't right now," Sutton hiccups on a sob.

"Sunshine, I love you. Forget the tour," August whispers.

"No, August! Go follow your dreams! They were always your dreams anyway," Sutton sobs out.

"Sunshine..." August agonizes.

Sutton turns her head and stares out the window with a faraway look in her eyes.

"Please...don't push me away..." August's voice cracks.

August leans in and kisses the side of her head, "I love you, Angel. Please don't give up on us!"

Sutton only sobs harder.

My heart breaks at how tormented she looks.

August turns to face me, "You better not lay a finger on her, Beck. Sutton and I are not over," he demands.

"I'm going to keep her safe, like I always do. In whatever way Sutton needs. I'm not going to let her grieve by herself," I declare.

"Sutton will never be by herself again," August vows.

"Do. Not. Take advantage of my best friend. So, help me Gods, Beckett! Sutton loves him! She loves him so much that she will let him go, so that he can make his dreams come true," Quinn growls at me before walking away.

August, Quinn, and Sloan get in the car parked behind me and follow me out of the cemetery.

There is no way in hell that I'm allowing Sutton to grieve alone!

56

Sutton

I can't think about my grandmother, or about August, without it ripping my heart out.

Four weeks have gone by. Four long agonizing weeks. My body aches for him.

The tour has to be over by now.

I briefly remember Quinn telling me that Rod gave me an extension to grieve after August explained the circumstances to him and allowed *From Troy* to continue the tour without me.

August hasn't been home.

Home. I don't even know if this is August's home anymore.

All I know is this never-ending void deep inside me.

Have you ever held your breath and sunk to the bottom of the deep end of a swimming pool?

Everything around you is moving slowly. It's muffled. It's dark. It's like you're still, but also in constant motion.

That's what this loss feels like. Hollow. Empty. Like a black hole of nothing.

Strong arms scoop me up off the floor and put me in bed, pulling the covers up to my chin.

"August?" I try to croak out.

I've barely spoken in weeks. My voice is cracked, frail from all the crying and lack of use.

Soft lips touch my forehead, "Why do you keep laying on the floor, Sut?" Beck's voice breaks through my haze.

"Because you can't fall any further when you're already on the ground," I whisper, as another tear falls down my face. *I'm so tired of crying.*

"Oh, Sutton," Beck says, curling around me, brushing my hair from my face.

I roll to face him but try to keep some space between us.

"Beck, what are you doing here?" I ask softly. "I appreciate you being here, taking care of Khaos..."

"I'm here for you, Sutton. I will always be here for you. August had to go back on tour. None of us wanted you to be here alone. *From Troy* are still touring. Quinn said the tour got extended because they were selling out every venue," Beck informs me nonchalantly.

The sides of my mouth lift in the slightest smile at the sound of that news.

"Let me take care of you. You won't eat. You barely sleep. You just stare off into space. Every time I come back from the gym; you're lying on the floor with the dogs. You need to get some fresh air. Go back to work, or at least come with me to Vegas next weekend for my fight," Beck continues to say, but I just zone out.

"Sut, did you hear me?" Beck asks.

"Yeah...let me just," I say pushing up from the bed to head toward the shower.

"Yeah? You'll come to Vegas next week?" Beck asks.

"No...I'll try to go back to work..." I whisper and shut the bathroom door.

Starting the shower, I climb inside and sit on the floor of the tub and just let the water pour down over me.

Vegas with Beck seems like so long ago. He's been here every day for the last month. Never letting me out of his sight. Doing his best to try to take care of me.

Should I go to Vegas with him?

Is that what I want? Someone to take care of me? That sounds nice.

The sting of the water beating down on my skin makes me groan. The warm spray feels so good and makes me feel the slightest bit alive again.

The water is freezing by the time Beck knocks and walks into the bathroom. All of the steam leaves the room when he opens the door. He immediately shuts the water off, wraps me in a towel and scoops me out of the shower.

"What are you doing?" I ask as he carries me back into the bedroom.

"You were in there forever, Sutton," Beck mutters.

"Beck. I'm fine. I'm going to get dressed and go check on things downstairs," I whisper, not making eye contact with him.

He tilts my chin up to him, "Sutton, please. Let me take care of you."

"Can you find my phone for me please?" I ask, looking around the room for it.

He sighs, "It's on your nightstand..."

I scroll through pictures of us until my vision blurs, but I just can't find the nerve to call August back.

There are 23 missed calls from August. Three voicemails. The last one was a week ago. I haven't had the courage to listen to them. I've let every call go to voicemail.

August needs to focus on the tour. Not on me wallowing in my depression.

I miss the sound of his voice desperately, but I'm afraid if I hear it, I'll break down all over again.

A couple of texts from Knox, Ty, and Beau, just checking in.

All left unanswered. Unread.

Slumping down to the ground, I notice the number of Instagram notifications. It's staggering! I've kept off of social media these last four weeks too.

Deciding to click on those first, I'm taken immediately to *From Troy*'s page.

My jaw drops and tears, I didn't even know I still had left to cry, fill my eyes when I see they have 450 thousand followers.

Their tour with *Motion In Black* had been extended.

They even posted that they got a headline tour that starts next week in Vegas.

They did it!

From Troy did it, even faster than Rod thought.

And without me.

My hand lifts to my mouth to cover the sob that comes out.

I sob for the little girl who lost her parents at an early age.

I sob for the teenager who lost a piece of her soul

because of two heartless boys.

I sob for the loss of my grandmother, the beautiful woman that raised me.

I sob for August, who deserves every single wonderful thing that comes to him after everything he's been through. I sob for the man who worked tirelessly on his album and his sound. Putting in so many hours, taking every opportunity he could get his hands on to play his music, living in less than stellar conditions to try to live out his dream.

I sob for the loss of a soul deep love.

I sob for the friendship I ruined with Beck.

I sob for myself for the loss of a dream that I didn't even know that I wanted until now.

Sitting on the floor of my living room. Staring at the phone in my hand.

Khaos laying in my lap, grounding me, "Thank you sweet boy," I murmur into his fur.

And then I push off the bottom of the swimming pool and kick for dear life until I break the surface and take the first deep breath of air that I've taken in a month.

57

Sutton

It feels good to be back at work. Meeting with bands to set up performances for the next few weekends.

The café has been busy, which has been great for keeping my mind off everything.

Even though I occasionally catch myself longingly looking at the stage. What I wouldn't give to hear that rasp of August's voice again and how it calms my soul; it's been five long weeks.

Having Sloan around, and getting to know her better, has been nice too. And not coming home to a completely empty apartment has been even better. She's a hell of a roommate and an even better cook. Between Quinn and her, I don't think I'll ever go hungry.

We've had a couple girls' nights in this week, which I needed more than I realized. Quinn is always my fiercest protector. And Sloan is really a great sounding board. No wonder Beck and her have gotten so close!

Beck has stopped by to check in daily, but has been

training hard this week, so he hasn't stayed over, since he has a big fight in Vegas on Saturday.

Which I decided to travel with him to just to get out of town.

$\mathcal{S}$itting on my grandmother's fresh grave the night before I leave for Vegas, I finally got up the nerve to listen to August's voicemails. Needing to feel Gram's presence around me, I hit play.

"Sutton, please know I didn't want to leave you. This is as much my dream as I think it's become yours, and I don't want to do this without you; but I don't think we'll be able to do it at all if I don't go back on the tour. Just know every night that I sing on that stage, I'll be waiting for you to come back and sing with me. I love you!"

"Hi Sunshine! I miss you! Rhys let me sing on stage with him tonight and it was fuckin insane! I still feel like I'm on cloud nine! I wish you could've been there. I love you!"

Tears start to stream down my face.

Gods, I wish I could've been there to see that! He was probably spectacular.

A soft breeze blows through my hair, *"Hi grandma!"* I whisper softly.

"Sunshine. We did it! Rod called. We're getting a headline tour! I wanted to come home to you in the worst way, but we immediately have to go to Vegas when we finish here. I'm

so sorry, Sutton! I wish you were here. This isn't the same without you. Come back to me, Angel! I'm still waiting for you. I love you, even in the darkness, especially in it," August's voice fades on a choked, pained sound.

That was two weeks ago. He hasn't called since.

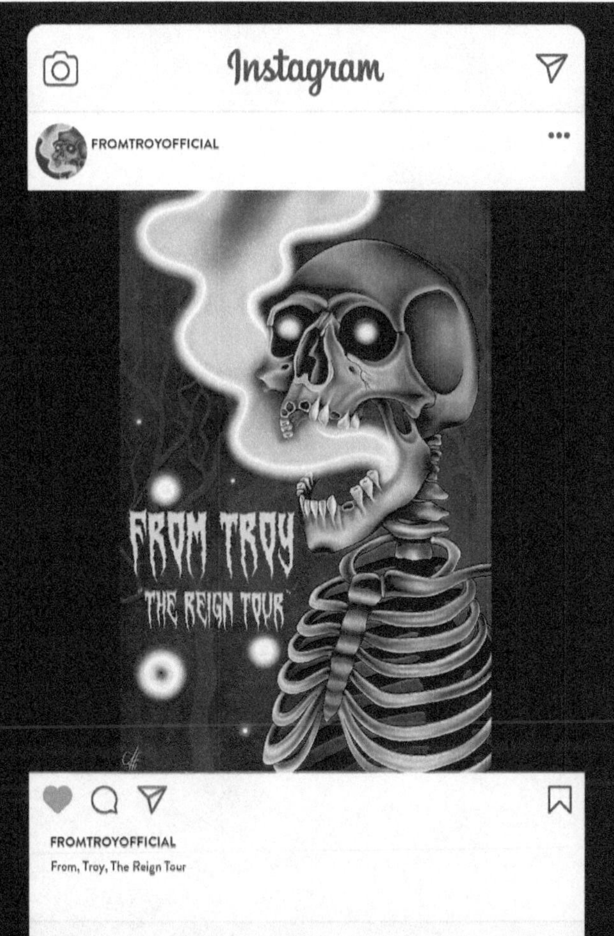
Instagram
FROMTROYOFFICIAL
FROM TROY
THE REIGN TOUR
FROMTROYOFFICIAL
From, Troy, The Reign Tour

58

Sutton

$\mathcal{L}$anding in Vegas today feels different than it did all those months ago.

Leaving Pittsburgh with just my purse and a bleeding heart.

No reservation with a place to stay.

Just blind hope.

Two different pieces of my heart are in this city tonight, and I have to decide which to follow.

Beck arrived yesterday. He let me know what time his fight started tonight and that there was a ticket waiting for me.

Instagram informed me of what venue *From Troy* was performing at tonight.

The show is sold out, but there are a few people reselling their tickets for an obnoxious amount of money.

Calling for an Uber, I step outside of the airport and wait.

"*P*lease someone just send me a sign!" I yell out to the universe.

I slam my hands against the seat of the Uber.

"Sorry," I whisper, making eye contact with the driver.

My heart is split in two. I love them both, but each so differently.

The devotion and love Beck has shown me in the weeks after losing my grandmother, proving over and over that he is my rock. Always stable and strong. Carrying the weight of my burdens. My protector. My safe haven. Warming me from the inside out with just a kiss. So many memories with him, days to reminisce.

So many days I was silently angry with Beck for not seeing that he meant more to me when things were never clearer in my head.

Then my mind wanders to August's tattooed hands covered in thick metal rings, a broken man cloaked in darkness, who creates music to drown out the demons in his head. Lyrics that grip my heart and only allows it to beat for him. August's the moon luring me into the dark unknown, setting my soul on fire, and causing stars to burst behind my eyes every time that he kisses me.

I gasp, and stare at the screen in the car, listening to the lyrics to the song that August wrote for me, with me. *"I look at you and see everything in that beautiful mind, the vein in your neck pulses and the heat in your stare is all I see until I'm blinded."*

"Can you turn the volume up please?" I ask the driver, wildly.

He thankfully blasts it and I let it drown out every thought in my head.

August actually did it!

From Troy made it. Really made it!

I knew they would go viral, but this is the first time I've heard our song out for the world to hear. Tears streaming down my face, is this my sign, to choose him?

The song ends and the radio broadcaster announces, "That was *Chokehold* by *From Troy*, and now speaking of chokeholds, onto the big fight tonight between Beckett Scott and Kenzo King."

Really universe?

I let out the biggest sigh, "Can you turn the radio off please?"

The car goes silent. We keep driving, the tears keep coming, I can't breathe, this poor driver probably thinks I'm insane.

I need a minute to just take this in.

August is selling out venues with his band *From Troy*.

Beckett has held and earned his title as a heavyweight champion.

They are both here. In this city. Right now.

I am so proud of them.

I am so in love with him.

I take one more deep breath, a calmness settles over me, and then it's his face I see so clearly.

I tell the driver to turn around up here and let my heart lead the way.

When he pulls over to drop me off. I'm diving out of the car before he's even at a complete stop, apologizing profusely, throwing an extra couple twenties at him for my behavior.

I start walking to the building where my future lies, if he'll still have me.

I wipe the tears away.

Deep breath, shoulders back, and head up.

I made this choice.

One will always have a piece of my heart but I can only be in love with one of them.

I keep walking and finally get to the entrance.

I open the door and walk through.

"Bag," the security guard says, and scans my bag; "Clear."

"Ticket," the woman says at the next door.

She scans my ticket and waves me through.

Making my way through the crowd.

I manage to find my spot. I hope he'll be able to notice me.

Taking a deep breath, I finally lift my head up and our eyes meet.

His are blazing. Holding mine in a chokehold. The air between us feels electric.

With a devilish smirk, staring right at me, he mouths, "*Mine!*"

"*Yours!*" I breathe with a teary smile.

59

August

"*Yours!*" I read her lips say.

Am I dreaming?

I feel my soul immediately return to my body. Sensing the presence of its other half.

Finishing the song, we were playing, I nod at the guys so they can see that Sutton's here too.

Knox smiles so brightly, and even Beau has a small smile on his face. Ty just nods at me with a knowing look in his eyes.

"If you all have been following us from the beginning, you would know there is a very special woman that we've brought on stage with us at previous shows," I croon into the microphone.

The crowd goes wild!

"Unfortunately, she had to take a break from the band for personal matters. But it looks like she's here tonight," I smile so big, and have them put the spotlight on Sutton in the crowd.

"Let's give a warm welcome to Sutton. Can you all help crowd surf her ass up to this stage!" I whoop into the microphone.

I hear her squeal from up here, but the crowd wastes no time getting Sutton up to the barrier, as security grabs her and helps her up onto the stage.

The sound of her musical giggle cracks the remaining ice surrounding my heart.

"You mean it? You're mine?" I ask desperately the second that she's in front of me.

Looking between her eyes, making sure there's no doubt hiding there.

"Yes, Auggie. I'm yours. I've always been yours," she smiles softly at me.

"And I'm yours, Sunshine. My love for you is as infinite as the stars in the galaxy!" I exclaim as I grab her by the throat, pulling her to me and crashing my mouth down on hers.

Sutton melts into the kiss and wraps her arms around my neck.

Wolf whistling and cat calling breaks us out of our haze.

Sutton covers her face, blushing.

"Ready, Sunshine?" I ask never taking my eyes off my beautiful girl.

She gives me her little signature nod.

We are instantly in sync, harmonizing perfectly like we never missed a beat, song after song.

Snapping out of our trance, Knox, Beau, and Ty are on either side of us bowing, as the crowd goes absolutely wild!

"You did it!" Sutton beams at us.

"We did it!" I smile down at her.

"I love you, August! I want all of this, with you," Sutton exclaims, eyes as bright as the stars in the night sky, not a doubt in her mind.

"I love you! I wouldn't want this dream to come true with anyone else," I declare before kissing her like we're the only two people in this room.

60
Beck

*T*here's a knock on my hotel door. Opening it, expecting to see Ash, but it's Sutton. Her arms are wrapped around herself like she's holding herself together.

"Sut, baby, what happened?" I ask, going to pull her into a hug.

Except she backs away, shaking her head.

"Can I come in?" she barely croaks out.

"Yeah, of course," I open the door wider for her to walk through.

She starts pacing my room, chewing on her fingernails.

When she realizes what she's doing, she stuffs her hands in the pocket of her sweatshirt.

"Sut. Talk to me," I step in front of her, gripping her chin, halting her movements.

"Beck, I love you," she starts to say, tears running down her face.

"I love you too, baby," I smile at her, going to pull her into my arms.

She shakes out of my hold, "Wait, Beck, let me finish, please."

"I love you, and I appreciate everything you've done for me since I lost my grandmother, but I'm not in love with you," Sutton's voice cracks. "I'm so sorry, Beck! I never meant for this to happen. For years, it was you. Years of this thing that never was, but always is. That will never be, but I always had wished it was. But we lost each other waiting for the other to show they cared more. My heart belonged to you. My rock. My safe harbor. My protector. My shield. The sunshine on my darkest days. You've brought so much light into my life when I was drowning in my own darkness. Having your full attention is like basking in the warmest glow. Loving you felt safe. You were always my one constant, your friendship unwavering. It was easier to love you from a distance because I didn't have to risk losing you. Now, I've realized that's not the kind of love I need. I need someone who sees me, someone whose demons play well with mine. Ours aren't the same. It would be so easy to fall into you, and let you take care of me, but I don't need a protector. I learned I can protect myself. I need to face my demons, not hide from them. I love you. I hope one day you can forgive me. You deserve someone who is going to love you so fully. Someone who needs your strength and stability, and that warm, kind heart. It's just not me," Sutton says voice breaking, tears streaming down her face.

I watch her face contort into agony. Knowing that this has to kill her, because the thought of hurting anyone guts her.

"I love you too, Sutton. I did a lot of thinking while you were away on tour. And I think you're right. You have been such a light in my life for years. I think I clung to you, for your light, like you clung to me for safety and security, but I don't think we're meant for each other in that way. You deserve to be so happy. I see the way August looks at you and I understand now how he complements you. You're the sun and he's your moon. The moon loves the sun enough to let them shine so brightly. You should never be hidden in the shadow of the sun. So, I get it. I hope that we can still be friends. Obviously, that will look different moving forward, but I'm willing to try, because I do love you." I say as warmly as I can.

Sutton swallows hard. Holding my eyes for a beat, making sure I'm being honest with her, as her tears keep coming.

"You mean it?" Sutton barely asks above a whisper.

"I mean it," I say pulling her into a hug.

Nodding, she wraps her arms around my waist. And I rest my head on top of hers, just breathing her in. Not quite ready to fully let her go.

After a few minutes I break the silence, whispering in her hair. "I have to leave and get ready for my match. Go to August's show. He misses you!"

The second that Sutton leaves I slide to the floor and bury my head in my hands.

My heart annihilated.

I just let it break.

Crying for the first time since my dad walked out on my mom and me.

What feels like an eternity, but is only an hour later, I get back up and head out the door for my match against Kenzo King.

"*L*adies and Gentlemen, this is the main event of the evening," I barely hear the announcer say over the roaring of the crowd.

The room sounds muffled, almost like I'm under water.

I've had tunnel vision since Sutton walked out of my hotel room.

My chest shouldn't ache like this. I know now that we aren't meant for each other. We may have been what we needed at one time, when we first met, but we aren't those same people anymore. Sutton deserves the absolute best, and I wish that was me.

It's going to take me some time to truly process losing the chance of a future with her by my side. But I'll do it for her to at least keep her in my life in whatever way that looks like now.

The referee comes to the center and explains the rules. He confirms that we understand. I think I nod.

I walk back to my respective corner.

I don't even want to be here.

This is one of the biggest fights of my life.

I've been preparing for this all year.

I make my way back to the center of the ring barely noticing Kenzo King snarling at me.

We touch gloves.

"Let's go!" the referee yells.

I start to bounce on my feet and before you know it, stars explode behind my eyes and the arena goes dark.

61

August

After the show in Vegas, Sutton and I flew home to pick up Khaos and hopped right back on a plane to head to Salt Lake City for the next show.

Thankfully, one of the things Beck did do for Sutton while she was grieving her grandmother was get Khaos registered as an emotional support dog. It's made it so much easier to travel with him.

We have spent three months living on a tour bus, visiting city after city. Performing almost every night. I couldn't have asked for a better partner to be on this adventure!

We've spent the days exploring each city. Trying new foods. Writing songs. Taste testing every coffee shop we find to see if there are any out there better than WaggingWithWords. Khaos has loved the attention and daily pup cups, too.

We sang karaoke together on Broadway in Nashville on one of our off nights, which turned into us singing for almost an hour, cover song after cover song.

Sutton's beautiful all the time, but when she sings, her beauty radiates to a whole other planet.

*I*t's the final night of our tour, playing at the famous Red Rocks.

After tonight we head back home to our little apartment above WaggingWithWords.

We've loved every second of this wild ride, but we're excited to get back into the recording studio. Sutton's excited to get back to the café for a few months.

This entire tour has been nothing but a dream! I've had to have Sutton pinch me several times just to remind me that it was real.

*"H*ow the hell ya'll doing tonight, Denver?" I yell into the microphone, after singing and growling our four heaviest songs.

The crowd immediately goes wild.

"We are *From Troy*! We want to thank you all for coming out and selling out this tour. It has been an unbelievable experience. We wouldn't be here without you all!" I say, smiling at them in wonder.

Once the clapping and hollering die down, I sit on the ledge of the stage.

"So, I have a favor to ask you all. Sutton's backstage, with noise cancelling headphones on. I want to ask her to marry me on stage tonight, are you guys cool with that?" I ask with a devilish grin.

It feels like an earthquake surrounds us from the people stomping and clapping.

"When she gets out here, I'm going to have Ty start strumming our song Chokehold. When he starts, I want you all to start singing. You know the lyrics, right?"

"HELL YEAH!" the crowd screams.

*F*ive minutes later Sutton comes out on stage and waves at the crowd.

My dark angel, stunning, in a black lace bodysuit, black leather mini skirt, and her black platform boots.

"Hi, Sunshine," I pull her to me, placing a chaste kiss on her lips.

"Hi, Auggie," she smirks at me, cheeks flushed pink.

I sling my guitar over my shoulder and pull up a chair for her to sit on by her microphone.

Once she's seated, I nod subtly to Ty and he starts

strumming the chords to our song, Chokehold.

The crowd starts singing the lyrics, waving their cellphones over their heads with their flashlights on.

Sutton looks all around, eyes sparkling, as the lights reach her eyes.

"What is..." she starts to say but gasps when she sees me down on one knee.

"Sutton. Sunshine. You joke that I lured you in like the moon, but you are my entire universe. You are my beginning and my end. Instead of swallowing my soul, you became my brightest fuckin star. I am a better man because of you. I love you, wildly, madly! Will you marry me?" I ask desperately, as all of our fans serenade us under a beautiful full moon.

"Yes, August. Yes, I'll marry you! I love you so much!" Sutton answers joyfully, pulling me up from the ground, gripping my face and kissing me fiercely.

Sliding a black solitaire diamond ring, with a crescent moon and star kissing the sides of it around the band, on her left ring finger.

The crowd wolf whistles, as they continue to sing, flashlights swaying in the night sky like little fireflies.

Grabbing my guitar, I start the song over. My eyes never leaving hers, as I sing with the love of my life, the woman who has had me in a chokehold since the very first night we met.

"I finally feel whole, no longer alone. No longer in a chokehold. You're the balm to my soul."

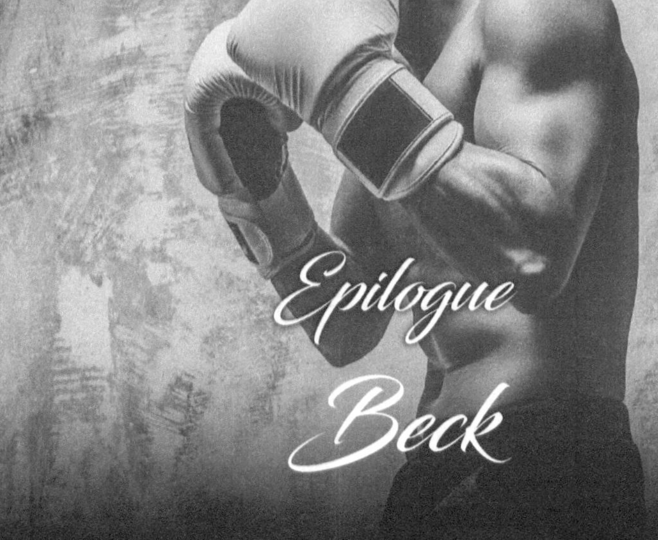

Epilogue

Beck

*B*eep...Beep...Beep...

Gods, my head feels like it's been put through a meat grinder!

Beep..Beep..

Why does it smell like Clorox?

Why is it so dark?

What is that groaning sound?

What is fucking beeping?

"Beck..." a soft female voice.

"Sut?" I think I croak. *Maybe I just think it.*

"Hey, Beck...It's okay...Try to open your eyes," she whispers.

It doesn't sound like Sutton. But that voice is so soft. So soothing.

"Beck...Try to open your eyes. It's me, Sloan," she says softly.

"Beck, man. Open your eyes," Ash says more firmly.

"Maybe he isn't ready yet," Sloan says softly.

Sloan? Why is Sloan here?

Acknowledgements

Where to start.

My first thank you goes to my brother, Tyler. I appreciate all of your encouragement and support throughout this process. My hype man. Always encouraging me to keep doing what makes me happy. For making my gorgeous website, exactly as I dreamed. And for letting me use your high school bands name, for my story, because it was so fitting. We're going to have our own band someday, LOL.

My family and dearest friends, thank you for putting up with my crazy mood swings, hysterics, incessant questions about your opinions on things and overall, just insanely overwhelming amount of support and encouragement in this. I couldn't have forged forward without you. To Todd especially for proofreading a hundred different versions of this manuscript, over and over.

To Abby, my soul sister, for helping me come up with my bad ass pen name and for always being a soundboard for my crazy ideas.

Krysta, my bestie, my alpha and beta reader, you are the absolute freaking best. I don't know how you put up with me as a friend. I'm just so grateful you were placed in my life and have become such a ride or die. My life is better with you in it. Thank you so much for helping me on this writing journey. @mamas.secret.book.nook

To my editor Brittni, thank you for working so hard to make this flow smoothly and dealing with my chaos and impulsivity. You the real MVP. @running_bookworm

To my Aunt Cindy, who became my line editor, you are a Godsend! I am so incredibly appreciative; for all of your guidance through these edits and helping with the flow of the story.

To Idalis, you are an angel. Thank you so much for proofreading the heck out of this and being so supportive. I'm so grateful that we met at BB and have so many adventures this year! @idallyvreads

To Cleo, thank you so much for the beautiful designs and formatting and coaching me along the way. @devotedpages_designs

To Sarah, my cover designer, thank you for knowing exactly what this book needed to be brought to life! This is so beautiful! I cannot wait to see what you create for book two. @enchantingromancedesigns

To Kay Riley, thank you so much for answering all of my questions, being a sound board, and guiding me through this process. I couldn't have done it without you. @kayrileyauthor

To Ali, one of my besties, my tattoo artist, thank you for this gorgeous tour poster. It's perfect! @alikattattoos

To my ARC readers, I owe you the world. Your support and excitement mean so damn much to me.

To my Bookstagram and Booktok friends, you all are the greatest support and community. You have had me in tears with your outpouring of love and support. I wouldn't be here without you. Some of you have become some of the greatest IRL friends, and some of you have been the realest friends, even through a screen, and I hope to meet you in real life someday. I love you all to pieces.

To my Readers, I love you. I love you. I love you. Thank you so much for taking a chance on me and this book.

You are all magic. I love you. Thank you so much for supporting and encouraging the chaos, that is my brain. I will be forever grateful for this little story, that bloomed into a beautiful dream. The fictional world is a wee bit less stressful than medicine. XXXXX

About the Author

Chokehold takes place in Pittsburgh where Britt grew up and went to college. She now resides in the beautiful mountains of West Virginia. Whether she's reading books, listening to books, or writing books, her head is always buried in one; rain or shine; but her favorite is on rainy days, cozied up under a soft blanket with a few dogs nestled in around her.

When she's not writing or reading, she loves to attend concerts with her best friends, travel to different restaurants or coffee shops in different states, or is singing and dancing around the house. She also has the deepest love for the ocean.

If she isn't dancing like a fool, she's meditating with crystals and tarot cards. Or she's blogging about the other amazing indie author books she reads. (@ waggingwithwords)

To stay up to date on all things Britt, make sure to follow her on her socials and feel free to shoot her an email or a DM.

Links to everything on her website:

https://brittreignauthor.com

https://www.instagram.com/brittreignauthor

https://www.tiktok.com/@brittreignauthor

https://www.goodreads.com/brittreignauthor

https://www.facebook.com/britt.reign.23

The Foster Farm (is also very near and dear to my heart.) It's a rescue in Pittsburgh, PA that my sweet Leo and Hazel came from. With Emily's permission, I happily used their name for the book. If you'd like to donate to them. Please see the link below. It is also linked at the bottom of my author page. They help so many lovely animals every year and are mainly a donation based rescue.

https://thefosterfarm.org/how-to-help